"What are you saying?" Gabriel asked them. "Are you saying you'll pick up your guns and fight them?"

"Yes!" A forest of ancient, muzzle-loading shotguns shot up into the air, with here and there a Winchester or an old Henry rifle. "If we have to!" In front of Madelaine, Moïse Ouellette was thumping the butt of his rifle on the back of a pew and bellowing. Beside him, Gabriel's sister Isabelle was shouting just as loud, and Isabelle was old enough to know what it meant to kiss her husband good-bye and watch him ride toward the sound of gunfire.

Gabriel's eyes found Madelaine out in her corner. They held on her for a moment and then returned to her relatives and neighbors, who had yelled themselves out for the moment. He said softly: "I know every one of you like you were my children, and I'm asking you: How many of you are there? How many of you are saying that you've willing to stand up and fight if it comes to it?"

They all roared that they would stand up to whatever the government chose to throw at them. He didn't wait for the sound to die down but let loose the bass bull-roarer voice over them: "If that's what you want, if that's what you've decided—that the only choice left is to march—then I'll march in front of you like I always done."

⸎

LORD OF
THE PLAINS

Alfred Silver

BALLANTINE BOOKS • NEW YORK

Copyright © 1990 by Alfred Silver
Maps copyright © 1990 by Anita Karl and James Kemp

All rights reserved under International and Pan-American Copyright Conventions. Published in the United States of America by Ballantine Books, a division of Random House, Inc., New York, and simultaneously in Canada by Random House of Canada Limited, Toronto.

Library of Congress Catalog Card Number: 89-90926

ISBN 0-345-37700-1

Manufactured in the United States of America

First Trade Edition: April 1990
First Mass Market Edition: August 1992

This book is for two dear friends who died too young—
John Hirsch and Paula Schappert.
Both, in their own ways, still help to remind me that
"That's good enough" usually isn't.

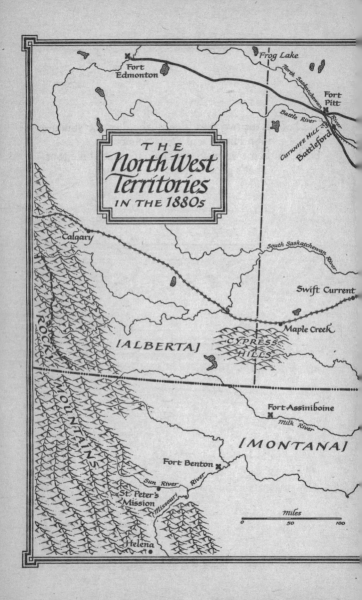

THE
*North West
Territories*
IN THE 1880s

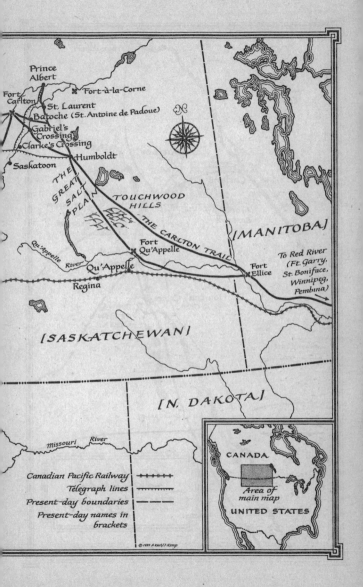

Prince
Albert

Fort
Carlton

✶ Fort-à-la-Corne

St. Laurent
Batoche (St. Antoine de Padoue)

Gabriel's
Crossing

Clarke's Crossing

✶ Humboldt

Saskatoon

THE GREAT SALT PLAIN

TOUCHWOOD
HILLS

[MANITOBA]

THE CARLTON TRAIL

Fort
Qu'Appelle

Qu'Appelle
River

Qu'Appelle

Fort
Ellice

To Red River
(Ft. Garry,
St. Boniface,
Winnipeg,
Pembina)

Regina

[SASKATCHEWAN]

[N. DAKOTA]

Missouri   River

Canadian Pacific Railway
Telegraph lines
Present-day boundaries
Present-day names in
brackets

© 1984 A.Karl/J.Kemp

CANADA

Area of
main map

UNITED STATES

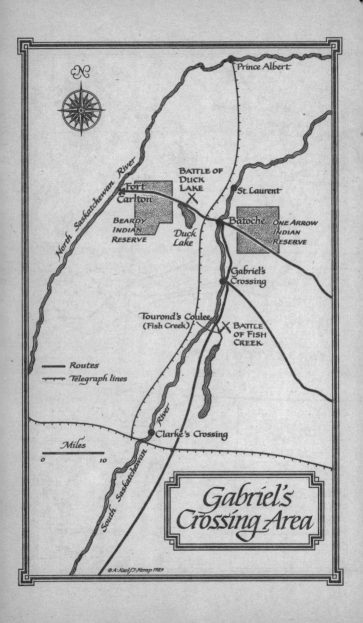

N

Prince Albert

North Saskatchewan River

BATTLE OF
DUCK LAKE

St. Laurent

Fort
Carlton

Batoche

BEARDY
INDIAN
RESERVE

ONE ARROW
INDIAN
RESERVE

Duck Lake

Gabriel's
Crossing

Tourond's Coulee
(Fish Creek)

BATTLE
OF FISH
CREEK

—— Routes
—•—•— Telegraph lines

River

Clarke's Crossing

Miles

0   10

South Saskatchewan River

Gabriel's
Crossing Area

© A. Karl/J. Kemp 1989

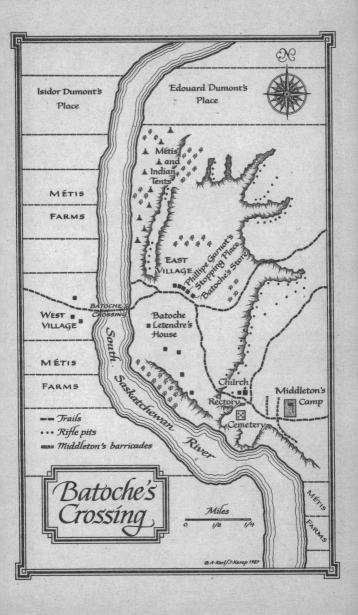

Isidor Dumont's Place

Edouard Dumont's Place

MÉTIS

FARMS

Métis and Indian Tents

EAST VILLAGE

Phillipe Garnot's Stopping Place

Batoche's Store

BATOCHE'S CROSSING

WEST VILLAGE

Batoche Letendre's House

MÉTIS

FARMS

South Saskatchewan River

Church

Rectory

Middleton's Camp

Cemetery

- - Trails
••• Rifle pits
⊷⊷⊷ Middleton's barricades

Batoche's Crossing

Miles

0   1/8   1/4

MÉTIS FARMS

© A·Karl/J·Kemp 1989

A Note to the Reader

The story that follows was built from historical accounts and firsthand reminiscences. While there is a great deal of fiction between these covers, it was only applied to color in the sketch that has come down to us, and I've done my damnedest to keep my crayon inside the lines.

Since the people in this story spoke a stew of different languages, a decision was made to render all their conversations into the colloquial English of that time and place—except in cases where someone is trying to struggle by in a language they wouldn't speak at home. I apologize in advance to those readers who prefer their French characters' dialogue peppered with "by the Blue" and their Irish with "begorra and bejabers."

PART ONE

One might travel the plains from one end to the other . . . and never hear an unkind word said of Dumont.

SIR SAM STEELE

Like the American peasantry, these people are all politicians, but of a peculiar creed, favouring a barbarous state of society and self-will; for they cordially detest all the laws and restraints of civilized life, believing all men were born to be free. . . . They cherish freedom as they cherish life.

ALEXANDER ROSS,
"THE HALF-BREEDS IN THEIR GLORY,"
from The Red River Settlement, Its Rise,
Progress and Present State

CHAPTER 1

Where the northwesterly meanderings of the Carlton Trail came to the woods along the South Saskatchewan, a hand-painted signpost proclaimed in French and English and Cree syllabics: "GABRIEL'S CROSSING. One Scow—the Best on the River. By 25 Miles the shortest route to Fort Carlton." In the spring of 1884 the sign was looking a little weather-worn, in need of a touch-up if prospective customers were going to be positive which fort it referred to.

Kitty saw it first. She had jumped down off the wagon a couple of miles earlier to walk some blood back into her legs and had opened up a good lead in front of the plodding oxen. She turned and waved her left arm over her head, pointing at the signpost with her right. Her mother waved back. Her brothers and sisters crowded forward to peer over their mother's shoulders or the much broader ones of their mahogany-faced guide.

Kitty hitched her skirts and scampered ahead, leaping over mud patches and scratching her shins in clumps of thistles and wild roses. The trail split on either side of the signpost, forking due north and west. She was hoping they'd take the west fork so she could add Gabriel to what her father so humorously referred to as her "collection." On the prairies that stretched from the Rocky Mountains almost to the shore of Hudson's Bay, there were a lot of men whose Christian name was Gabriel. But if you didn't add a surname, you were understood to be speaking of Gabriel Dumont.

As the wagon jounced past the signpost onto the west fork, Kitty grabbed the tailgate and scrambled back on board. She sat swaying with the jolts of the wagonbed, toying with the doubled string of brass beads around her neck and watching the country amble by. The scooped sides of the knolls bordering the trail were creamy white with carpets of phlox and vetch, dotted with

3

violent yellow bursts of golden bean. Stands of gooseberry and balsam-scented poplar were unfurling their new leaves. The South Saskatchewan country had more of a roll to it and was less dusty dry than the country around the Qu'Appelle Valley where she'd lived all fourteen of her years. Although she'd spent parts of those years in the Red River country, she didn't count the terms served in the Red River Ladies' Academy as living.

The wagon ground to a halt, and Kitty stood up to see why. Beyond the nodding ox horns, the trail disappeared into a cleft in the prairie. Jerome Henry, the black-bearded guide, said: "Got to set the brake hard here and crawl down slow—she's a long drop to the river. If we was traveling in a good old Red River cart, now, this'd be easy as drinking eggs."

Kitty jumped back down over the tailgate as Jerome clucked the oxen into motion. If the wagon was going to crawl, she might just as well take the opportunity to get a vista of the South Saskatchewan. Her mother called after her: "Kitty!"

"I'll catch you up at the bottom, Mother." She walked out along the meadow as the wagon disappeared down into it, brake lever smoking. A long pistol shot ahead of her there was a false horizon where the prairie dropped away toward the river. She was halfway there when she stopped dead. A patch of tall grass and sweet clover on the rim was moving in a direction contrary to the wind. Within it there was a long, low, fur-edged shadow. It was too low to the ground for a bear or a buffalo, and the buffalo had been all killed off anyway. It could be a large wolf; wolves came in such a variety of colors and sizes that anything was possible. But a wolf should have heard her or seen her by now. This thing just kept circling back and forth with erratic, stiff, jerky movements and wheezy, snuffling sounds.

As a "Girl of the Golden West," Kitty liked to think she knew every species of creature that roamed the plains and the wooded parklands, but this one had her buffaloed. She knew that she should back away and let it go about its business. She heard in her mind's ear the jolly old family axiom: "Curiosity killed the Kitty." She swallowed a couple of times, took a deep breath, and stalked forward with the tall grass hissing against her skirt. She hadn't gone three steps when the creature suddenly froze, hunkering down low to the ground. She froze as well. It sat back on its haunches, as though sniffing the air, and the pelt of its head fell off.

Kitty laughed at herself and called out: "*Waciye, Kimoso*, Hello, Grandfather!"

The gray-braided scarecrow cocked his hawk nose in her direction, clutching the buffalo robe tighter around his shoulders and blinking in the sunlight. It seemed to Kitty there was something unnatural in the way the rheumy black eyes focused on her. He rasped at her in Cree: "My remembering ain't what it was, granddaughter, but it seems to me I don't know you."

"I don't think so. My name is Kitty McLean. My father is Mister McLean of the Hudson's Bay Company."

The old man wrinkled his already corrugated forehead, sucked on his remaining teeth, then grunted and nodded decisively. "Fort Qu'Appelle. And then up north at Lac La Biche the last couple winters. They call him Straight Tongue."

"Just so, Grandfather." A wandering Cree War Chief had given him the name, and he was very proud of it. "He's been reposted to Fort Pitt. We're going to join him."

"Fort Pitt?"

"Yes."

The old man's eyes hooded, and he shook his head ominously while a kind of wary growl passed through his throat. Before she could ask him what was wrong with Fort Pitt, the cloud passed and he announced brightly: "Ahsiweyin!" slapping one parchment hand against his hollow chest. The dialect was a bit unfamiliar, but Kitty thought his name might mean "Falling Sand."

"I didn't mean to disturb you, Grandfather—I just saw something moving through the grass and didn't know what. . ."

"No, no—I was just doing some hunting." He peered down at the ground in front of him. Again, there was something peculiar about the way he directed his gaze. Kitty looked down at the spot he appeared to be looking at. Among the whorled grass stalks there was a black mouth about the size of a mouse burrow. "Guess I lost him now."

From the birch thicket behind Ahsiweyin came a sound of crackling and rustling and soft thuds. Two sprung-ribbed Indian ponies broke out onto the meadow. Each carried two Cree young men who looked even more scrofulous and emaciated—if possible—than their horses. As far back as Kitty could remember, the wild horsemen of the plains had been part of the landscape of her life. But she'd never seen warriors reduced to riding tandem or wearing raggedy scraps of clothing utterly devoid of beadwork or any other kind of ornament.

The front rider on each horse cocked his leg over the matted mane and slid down to the ground. One of them cocked back the hammer on a rusted old muzzle-loader; the other stood lazily swinging a hand axe. The back riders on both horses slid forward to take hold of the halters.

Kitty raised her hand and said: "*Waciye*." None of them responded, although their eyes were all on her. There was no trace in their eyes of the unsettling flame that she'd encountered at times in mean-drunk trappers or buffalo hunters on a tear. These eyes were listless and slack and reflected nothing.

The one with the old trade musket took a few bow-legged steps toward her, pointed the muzzle at the loops of brass around her neck, and said over his shoulder: "That's a few sides of beef right there."

Kitty's hand flew up and clapped itself across the gorget bone under her throat. "Chief Sitting Bull gave this to me! He said, 'So that the Great Mystery might smile on the best white friend I ever had.' " When she'd toddled back down off Sitting Bull's knee, the necklace had tickled her toes and rattled on the floor.

The Cree with the musket didn't appear to hear her, just kept gazing at the brass beads. She added feebly: "It cost him six horses."

From the ground, Ahsiweyin said: "They belong to her."

"They took the country that belonged to us, old man. A string of beads to keep us from starving don't seem like much to pay." One hand came up off the musket and took hold of the necklace, brushing against one embarrassingly budding breast. Kitty clutched the beads tighter against her throat. It was doubtful, if she yelled for help, that Jerome Henry would hear her over the rattle of the wagon or be able to stop safely on the slope if he did. "Give them to me," said the young man.

"No."

The musket swiveled up to present its muzzle to her nose. She could smell the black powder down the barrel. There was a thumping noise off to her left, and all five Crees looked in that direction. The one gripping her necklace let go, lowered the musket, and stepped back. A gray pony with a nose halter lurched up over the crest of the ridge. On its bare back sat a big, broad-boned woman who appeared to be constructed of coal and metal: black dress, copper skin, silver-tinged black waves of hair, and sunlit flares of gold and silver at breast and wrists and ears.

The woman clucked the pony to a halt and swept her black eyes over the tableau of Crees and Kitty, settling on Ahsiweyin. In a voice a few tones below an alto, she said: "*Waciye*, Ahsiweyin."

The old man squinted fiercely in the general direction of the horsewoman and said: "Who's that?" Kitty realized why she'd found something peculiar about the way he cocked his head and focused his gaze—he was next to blind.

"Have you worn out your memory as well, Grandfather? It's me—Madelaine. What are you doing on this side of the river?"

"Hunting. Or trying to. I guess they"—waving one smoked-leather hook of a hand to take in the young men—"was afraid my hunting luck's gone so bad I'm more likely to get ate than get something to eat."

The young man with the hand axe murmured, "Oh, there's hunting luck and hunting luck," significantly sliding his dull eyes back and forth from Kitty's necklace to Madelaine's jewelry. There was no particular bite of cruelty or malice in his voice, just the matter-of-fact drawl of a young man with no hope and nothing to lose. Madelaine swiveled her head in his direction. There was no discernible trace of apprehension in her expression, but Kitty couldn't imagine how she proposed to deal with four armed warriors.

Ahsiweyin chirped: "So, how's your man Gabriel?"

The menace was yanked out of the young men like a conjurer's tablecloth. Kitty wasn't dead sure how the trick had been done, but the suffocating hand that had closed over her mouth and nose when the Indian ponies came out of the bush was now gone.

Madelaine turned back to Ahsiweyin and said: "Same as always—Gabriel don't change. You come on home with me, Grandfather—we'll give you something better to eat than last year's saw grass." She leaned out from the horse, stretching her right arm down toward him. He raised his arm toward his blurred perception of her movement. She wrapped her hand around the withered forearm and swung herself back upright, lofting the old man like a bag of bird bones onto the withers of her horse.

The four young Crees and their horses melted back into the woods. Madelaine watched them go, then for the first time turned her attention directly on Kitty. As the hammered-copper head revolved toward her, Kitty registered impressions of a broad chin, heavy jaw, and high cheekbones, and then the glittering black eyes pinned her to the landscape like a butterfly on a card. "What the hell are you doing wandering around up here alone?"

"I . . . we . . . we came to cross on the ferry."

"Well, you'll have to go down to the river, it don't dock here." She twitched her horse's halter, slapped some slack into Ahsiweyin's arms wrapped happily around her waist, and disappeared over the brink of the plateau. Kitty walked to the edge and looked down. She was standing on a clay cliff about a hundred feet high. Halfway between her toes and the steel-gray glint of the river, a white cloud of pelicans wheeled and soared. To her right, a more gradual slope led down to a shelf of land and a cluster of wooden buildings, some of them plastered with white clay. A couple of squares of plowed land showed black among the spring green.

The winding of the road brought the wagon into view below her. She scampered down the slope, clambered up over the tailgate, and worked her way forward through her brothers and sisters to her mother and Jerome Henry, who was easing back off the brake as the road leveled out. "Jerome, do you know a woman named Madelaine?"

"I known a few women named Madelaine."

"This one is middle-aged, a big métis woman who lives around here. I think she's Gabriel's wife. There's something almost . . . queenly about her."

As soon as the last phrase had left her mouth, she found herself blushing at her childishly romantic choice of adjectives. But Jerome just nodded and said: "In this country that's just about exactly what she is."

Jerome reined the oxen to a halt in the farmyard Kitty had seen from above. The farms of white settlers had always seemed to Kitty to be sadder and grimmer than the homes of the métis, whose approach to farming was as much a mixture of white and Indian as their blood. The métis had come to accept the fact that raising a few crops and cows and chickens was a good way to fill the gaps between the proceeds of hunting and fishing and carting freight across the plains. But they held on to the belief that farming should never interfere with horse races and all-night dances and painting the family buckboard red or green with contrasting curlicues. The Dumont farm was no exception, just on a grander scale than most. The barn was bigger, with more sheds around it—icehouse and smokehouse and woodshed and others whose purpose Kitty couldn't guess. The herd of glossy horses quartering the paddock was twice what she'd seen on any other family farm, with more woolly foals prancing to keep up.

The house itself was two houses, almost identical, story-and-a-half plastered log buildings joined by a roofed passage. What prevented them from being identical twins was the bright blue paint job covering half the face of one, as though the painter had just got a good start in when he'd been called away.

The most remarkable aspect of the place, though, was a black-haired young woman, a few years older than Kitty's eldest sister, who was washing a mass of laundry and hanging it out to dry on ropes strung to the barn. What was remarkable was the way she was doing the washing—dropping the clothes into a squat, galvanized-steel washing machine run by a foot treadle. Although Kitty's personal experience at clothes washing was minimal—Hudson's Bay Company traders and their families had their laundry done by fort servants—she was well aware that most women in the North West whacked river rocks with wet rags and dreamed of nothing higher than a scrub board and tub.

Madame Dumont appeared in the doorway of the half-blue-faced house and beckoned. Jerome Henry and all the McLeans except the sleeping babies climbed down and headed that way, scattering chickens and dodging the black and yellow dogs tearing around the yard. Kitty paused inside the doorway, blinking her eyes to adjust from the bright sunlight. The first floor was one open room, walled with shelves of tinned food and blankets and bolts of print cotton and pigs of lead and cartons of cartridges and jars of beads and buttons and biscuits and rock candy. A row of barrels gave off an herbal odor of brewing beer. In the middle of the room, covering half the floor space, stood a monumental billiard table with legs like carved oak trees. Kitty's mother gawked at it and said to Mrs. Dumont: "How ever did you . . . I won't even ask how you managed to get it shipped here, but how ever did you get it through the door?"

"We didn't. We just laid down the floor, put the billiard table on it, and built the walls and roof around it."

Kitty attended to the business of keeping her younger brothers and sisters from pulling down the candy shelves. It wasn't so much a duty as a perfect opportunity to mask what she really was intent on doing—which was to get an unobtrusive look at

Madame Madelaine. As much as she loathed to admit it, there
were some grounds for her father's teasing about her "collection" of celebrated men. Madame Dumont presented Kitty with
the novel notion that there were celebrated women as well.

Looking her over without being looked back at, Kitty gauged
that Madelaine Dumont was what was termed a handsome
woman—too heavy-boned and solid to be called pretty. No one
this side of an anemic poet would have called her fat, but everything about her had a breadth and weight to it—hips and shoulders and breasts and mouth. Kitty herself was a sturdy girl, but
she had never imagined carrying it off with that sort of gypsy
élan. Although Madelaine had to be a good ten years older than
Kitty's mother, and weighed a good thirty pounds more, there
was a lithe, wild-horse limberness to her movements as she
stooped under a plank nailed across one corner of the room like
a countertop, negotiating her broad beam past Ahsiweyin, who
was squatting in the shadows spooning something meaty out of
a tin cup and smacking his gums.

She stood up on the inside of the counter plank and said to
Kitty's mother: "We had this deal, you see—Gabriel and me.
He got his billiard table and I got that clothes-washing machine
outside. Of course once Gabriel had a billiard table, old 'Batoche' Letendre up at Batoche's Crossing had to get one, too,
but his wife didn't get no washing machine. Then 'Batoche'
built a big new house and painted it green, so Gabriel had to go
out and get some blue paint. . . ." She trailed off with a shrug,
opened a tin box that rattled, and plucked out a flat, stubby
pencil. She tapped the pencil against a printed broadsheet tacked
up beside the counter. "The rates are all set standard since the
government decided we have to have a license to run the ferry."

Kitty's mother moved forward, opening her reticule. Kitty
drifted along in her wake. The broadsheet listed a series of rates,
from "50¢ for every double vehicle, loaded or unloaded, including two horses, or two other animals, and driver," to "5¢
for every sheep, hog, calf, or colt." Madame Dumont toted up
the fare, writing the figures upside-down on the plank so the
addition would be right-side-up to the customers. The sunlight
seeping through the thick-paned window gleamed dully on her
silver-and-ivory rosary where the beads showed between the
thick waves of hair.

When the fare had been paid, she said: "The boat's just starting back from the west shore." Kitty's mother went back out to

the wagon to see to the babies. "So, Jerome, you still got your hair on, I see."

"Hell, there ain't been any danger of losing it for years. Even Big Bear's taken a treaty and settled down."

They spoke in Michif, the métis patois of French and Cree amalgamated with a few other ingredients. It made it easier for Kitty to eavesdrop, assuming that they'd assume she didn't know the language. "Don't be too sure, Jerome. Hungry people can get dangerous. Ain't that right, Miss McLean?"

Kitty didn't know whether to reply or pretend she didn't understand. Instead of leaving her pinned and wriggling, Madame Dumont said: "I know it's hard not to blame those four up on the hill for acting like they did, but the Cree ain't like that naturally. The fact is, the Chiefs all made sure the treaties promised that if they settled on reserves, the government would feed them in times of famine. What they didn't figure was that the government'd decide what was a famine."

"I understand. At Fort Qu'Appelle we never had to lock our doors until the white settlers came."

The broad brown mouth broadened further into a smile.

Kitty's mother called from the doorway: "Madame Dumont, your daughter's calling for you."

The twinkle in the black eyes hardened into a glint, and Madame Dumont called back in a flat voice: "She's not my daughter." Then she stooped out from behind the counter, brushing past Ahsiweyin, and headed for the door. She stuck her head back in the doorway to announce: "Ferry's here."

When Kitty came back out into the sunlight, she could see that the boat wasn't there yet, but it would be by the time the family got loaded back onto the wagon and the oxen had towed it down to the landing stage. While everyone else piled on, she walked ahead to the river. The floating dock rocked gently to the slapping of the waves under her feet. The ferry scow, essentially a raft with a fence around it, was still about twenty yards out. It was held more or less in line against the current by a wrist-thick cable anchored to a home-built crane device for raising it to clear the way for passing steamboats.

Two brown-skinned men, one tall and one extremely tall, stood on the deck working two twelve-foot sweeps. As the ferry hove in toward the landing stage, the smaller of the two big men let go his oar and moved to the bow. The other rower shifted his stance to the middle of the deck and shifted one hand off his oar to the pommel of the other. He started rowing harder, propelling the boat along like the pumping heart of an oversize water beetle. The man in the bow flapped his arm over his shoulder and shouted in Michif: "Too much, Isidor—back water!"

Isidor obediently stopped rowing, but he didn't back water. Instead, he leaned down on both oar hafts to raise the blades out of the river, braced his feet, and looked back over his shoulder with a wolfish grin splitting his copious gray beard. His partner just had time for one more frantic "Isidor!" before the blunt prow of the scow rammed the dock with a concussion that almost threw Kitty into the South Saskatchewan. The ferry boat stopped moving, but the man in the bow didn't. He flew out over the rail, whirling his arms like a hummingbird, and landed chest down on the landing stage with an unhummingbirdlike thunk. Isidor shipped his oars and came forward innocently to moor the lines.

The man on the dock heaved himself back up on his feet, inhaling through his teeth and exhaling French words Kitty wasn't supposed to know. Although Kitty wasn't all that sure of gauging ages, he looked to her to be much younger than Madame Dumont. He had an oval face with a trimmed mustache and forget-me-not blue eyes that were quite startling in that setting of red-oak skin and ebony hair.

Kitty's mother called to him from the wagon seat: "We've paid the fare to your wife, Gabriel."

"What did you call me?"

"Well, this is Gabriel's Crossing, and you called your friend another name, so . . ."

"Madame, I am and have been many things in my life, but not one of them is Gabriel Dumont. Me, I'm Michel Dumas. This here little gray-haired child is Gabriel's big brother, Isidor, but that's as close as you're going to get today. Gabriel had to go up north to Lindsay for—"

"Business!" Isidor interjected. "He had to go to Lindsay for some business to do with his freight contracts." Up close, Gabriel's big brother put Kitty in mind of a grizzly bear in a calico shirt.

Jerome Henry said: "Part of one of his cart trains was these people's furniture—consigned to W. J. McLean, Fort Pitt."

"Was yours the musical machine, the pumping organ?"

"Yes!" Kitty's mother cut in. "What's happened to it?"

"Nothing," Isidor assured her. "It went on past here all in

one piece. I just was wondering—I play a little on the fiddle, and I thought maybe since you got that pumping organ you maybe got some sheet music, too."

"They were all packed into one of the crates that went on ahead."

"Oh. Well, maybe sometime if I'm passing by Fort Pitt, you wouldn't mind if I was to stop by and copy some of them?"

"Of course."

The oxen grew suddenly skittish when their forehooves thumped onto the floating dock. Isidor took hold of their leads and guided them onto the bobbing deck of the scow. Kitty followed the wagon on board. As the lines were cast off and the oars unshipped, the blue-eyed Mr. Dumas announced: "The more of us that rows, the faster across we goes." He pointed toward the bow, which had been the stern coming across, where another pair of sweeps was propped against the rail. Jerome climbed down to tackle the portside one. Kitty immediately ran forward and wrestled with the starboard oar.

Isidor laughed and said to his partner in Michif: "That little yellow-haired one, she's just like Madelaine, eh?" Kitty tried to pretend she didn't understand, but she could feel the betraying blush.

Back on the shore, Madelaine stood in the doorway of the half-blue-faced house, watching the passengers dutifully doing half the work their fares had paid for. Ahsiweyin huffed up from behind and propped himself against the doorway beside her. He said: "I would've thought Straight Tongue McLean would know better than to bring his family out here now."

"Why shouldn't he?"

He wafted one bird-claw hand up onto her shoulder, clucked his tongue at her, and rasped: "Maybe you can be a real good liar about a lot of things, but don't try pretending you're stupid. It ain't just the young men saying it anymore, it's the old men and even some of the women."

"Saying what?"

"'Better to die fighting than die starving.'"

"The McLeans ain't the government."

"No, but they're white and so's the government. And they're here and the government ain't."

"You're the one playing stupid. There might be a little bit of snarling like your four young men up on the ridge, but there ain't going to be any real trouble."

"Tell that to Gabriel." Ahsiweyin's hand had gradually drifted off her shoulder and down her back. It now began to work its way over the curve of her hip. She swung her arm out and pushed him back against the doorpost—not too hard, his old bones were brittle. She headed around the corner of the house to give Annie a rest from the washing. Ahsiweyin called after her: "Is there any more of that good rabbit stew?"

"Help yourself."

"I just tried."

CHAPTER 2

When Madelaine had been as young as Kitty, she was out on the plains with the buffalo hunt, as she had been every summer of her life. She'd been born on the hunt, on a buffalo hide spread out under a cartbed, and her first howls at the indignity of being hauled out into the air had mingled with the choir of prairie wolves singing to the moon. But the hunt had changed even in her short span of memory. The great Red River hunt that used to parade across the plains in a train of thousands of carts and hundreds of families of hunters had split into two very unequal halves. Madelaine wasn't exactly sure of the cause, but it had something to do with politics and bad blood between Mister Grant and the métis of Red River. The result was that Madelaine was now part of a cart train rolling southwest into Sioux country with only sixty-four men with rifles. When the split had come, it was inevitable that Madelaine's father would side with Mister Grant's White Horse Plains hunt, along with the Dumonts and Falcons and the other unredeemed métis clans that the priests in St. Boniface referred to as *les sauvages*.

Their little splinter group kept up the standard practices that Mister Grant had laid down for the Red River hunt, beginning with the election of the Captain in Chief and the affirmation of the eight commandments the hunt was ruled by. In Madelaine's lifetime, any hunt that Mister Grant didn't take part in had been captained by her father, Jean Baptiste Wilkie. Mister Grant had come out of retirement to lead the three hunts since the great rift, on the chance that the little caravan of the White Horse Plains hunt would prove too great a temptation to the Sioux. Nothing had ensued beyond the usual run of horse-raiding skirmishes, so Mister Grant had stayed back at Grantown this year with the people who were too old to take part in the hunt. Madelaine's father wasn't too old yet to take his horse's reins in his teeth and gallop in among stampeding buffalo, but he said he'd grown too old to stand for Captain.

They wound their way southwest across a shifting, rolling ocean of spring-green grasses sprinkled with wildflowers, with the ungreased wooden axles of two hundred carts shrieking a chorale of what her father called the "Ban Shee." The line of carts was barely a speck on the face of the prairie. If that speck kept on traveling in a straight line all summer long, fording the rivers and climbing over the occasional low ridge of hills, the only change it would see was that the horizon rolling up in front of it had grown a little sandier and drier. Somewhere across the eastern horizon, the much larger caravan of the Red River hunt was grinding along on a parallel course. Every few days, scouts would ride back and forth to keep each caravan informed as to whether the other had come across any sign of the herd yet, or the Sioux.

Madelaine kept occupied with helping her mother load and unload the cart and stretching the remnants of their winter stores of flour and dried meat to feed the whole family. The first days, and sometimes weeks, of the summer hunt were always lean times, until they found the herd.

They crossed a stream where the herd had settled for a while the year before. Women and children fanned out from the line of carts to gather dried plates of buffalo dung for their campfires. Madelaine had just about filled her sack when she heard a horse approaching. She looked up and saw one of the Dumont boys on a spotted pony. The Dumonts' habitual stomping grounds was to the northwest of her father's, so she only saw them during the summer hunts. Since last year it had become obvious that this one—Gabriel—wasn't going to grow into a giant like his father and uncles; his little brother was already taller than he was. Nor were Gabriel's lumpy features likely to elongate themselves into the statuesque, fine carvings that usually signified a Dumont.

He reined his pony in beside her and pointed south with his handed-down flintlock relic of a rifle. He said: "You're getting left behind."

She followed his point. The remuda of saddle horses following the carts had already left her behind. The other buffalo-chip gatherers had kept working their way along parallel with the caravan while she had struck straight out onto the prairie. She said: "The day I can't catch up with a line of lumbering oxen . . ."

"If the Sioux don't get you first."

"No one's seen any Sioux."

"They ain't seen any big war parties. That don't mean there ain't a few of their young men sneaking along hoping to luck on to a straggler." It was quite a ridiculously authoritative pronouncement from a thirteen-year-old boy. He extended his arm toward her and said: "Hop on. I'll give you a ride back."

She had an urge to slap his hand away but decided she'd look even more foolish by refusing a ride when it was obvious she couldn't fit much more into her sack anyway. She took hold of his forearm and jumped as he lifted. He was a lot stronger than she would have guessed, but damned if she was going to say so.

They'd just broke camp the next morning when one of the scouts came galloping back to say they'd sighted the herd. The men ran to saddle their buffalo runners while the women hauled out their whetstones and knives. The Dumonts' carts were just in front of the Wilkies', so Madelaine overheard when Gabriel came jogging forward leading a saddled buffalo runner to where his father and uncles and older brother were taking a last check of their guns. His father said: "What do you think you're doing?"

"It's about time I learned how to run buffalo."

His father laughed and shook his head. "Next year."

"Isidor started when he was—"

"I *said*: 'Next year.' "

Gabriel tore off the saddlepad, threw it on the ground, and kicked it out onto the prairie. His father and the other hunters mounted up and galloped ahead. The women and children followed along in the carts.

As the sun reached its height, Madelaine heard distant thunder with a barely discernible popping noise among the rumbling; they were running the herd. A few miles farther on, the waving grasses gave way to a trampled matt of green, dotted here and there with black hummocks. Madelaine and the rest of the children jumped down and went running from buffalo to buffalo. A few were still flailing their legs spasmodically, rolling their big brown eyes and lowing, but most of them were dead.

Beside one of them, Madelaine spotted a deerhide glove embroidered with the wild-rose pattern that her mother favored. She turned and waved her arm over her head, shouting: "Over here!" Her mother turned the cart out of the line. The oxen yoked to the other three Wilkie carts followed along behind.

Her mother climbed down, unsheathed two long knives, and handed one to Madelaine. Madelaine's younger brothers and sisters were running ahead to find the other buffalo their father had shot. Madelaine and her mother went to work slicing the buffalo open and stripping off the hide, then proceeded with the butchering. Madelaine had had only half as much practice as other girls her age, so she worked twice as hard. Since she had been old enough to be of any use when the autumn hunt rolled out, she'd been left behind at the convent school in St. Boniface to keep on polishing her education. No amount of wailing to her parents had ever stayed the sentence.

She scraped the blood off the hide and pegged it out to dry while her mother threw the offal to the dogs and started slicing the meat into thin strips. They hung the meat on a willow-wand rack to let the sun and the dry air do its work. No matter how often Madelaine licked the blood off her hands, it was impossible to keep it from caking her dress and the hair at her temples. The younger boys ran around chasing off the dogs. The not-quite-men who were old enough to have guns but too young to hunt patrolled the borders of the killing ground for wolves and coyotes, trying to look like they were doing something important.

The men came draggling back, slumped in their saddles. A few of them were riding two to a horse. The man perched behind Madelaine's father was holding his side and coughing blood. The sight brought home to Madelaine—and to all the others, she suspected—how much they missed Mister Grant, with his chestful of medicines and powders and bandages. Madelaine missed Mister Grant for another reason. His courtly and commanding manner and weathered Byronic features were a perfect, harmless compass point for a girl just beginning to be a woman.

The work went on into the night, banking up fires under the

meat racks. Crews of men and boys had foraged off to the nearest islands of poplars or scrub oak and come back with cartloads
of firewood to supplement the buffalo chips. Madelaine slept for
a few hours and then was shaken awake to take her turn tending
the fire. All across the black slate of the prairie there were other
fires like hers, dwindling to pinpricks in the distance, a handful
of warm, orange stars flickering back at the vast field of ice-blue
ones overhead.

By morning the strips of meat were getting leathery. Leaving
the sun to finish off the baking, the women built new fires while
the men wrestled the big iron kettles out of the carts and rigged
up the tripods. Madelaine got put in charge of their kettle,
scooping in the mounds of fat stripped off the carcasses and
stirring it with a wooden paddle. When it was bubbling away
nicely she went to help her mother with the meat. The crisp
strips were loaded into a wooden trough and pounded with mal-
lets into flakes. It was hard work, but it wasn't wearisome. There
was singing and old jokes and gossip. The men cutting the hides
in half and sewing the sides together to make bags puffed their
pipes and drank tea and traded stories of yesterday's run and
hunts in the past.

Madelaine had settled into a kind of dreamlike haze. She
gradually became aware that the sounds of human activity had
died down to the point where she could hear a meadowlark
trilling somewhere out on the plains. People were putting down
their tools and moving somberly toward the circle of carts that
made up the camp.

The gored hunter that her father had brought back yesterday
was beyond missing Mister Grant's medicine chest. Father La-
flèche prayed over another knife-lettered cross stuck on the
plains, and the men piled up stones to keep the wolves from
digging up the grave. Gabriel Dumont's father informed the
widow that she and her children were part of the Dumont clan
for the duration of the hunt and would take their share in the
proceeds like any other Dumonts.

They went back to work with a respectful muteness that dissipated over the course of the day. Madelaine was appalled at
first when someone struck up an old voyageur song and other
voices joined in. But she told herself not to be so harsh-minded—
these weren't convent sisters who could afford to center their
lives around mourning and praying. It could just as easily have
been any of the other hunters who'd misguessed which way a

bull was going to swerve. Their souls looking down would have expected that the laughter and the singing and the work would go on.

The pounded flakes of meat were packed into the buffalo-hide bags, each bag about the height of Madelaine's hips. When a bag was a little more than half-full, it was carried over to the kettle for the dangerous business of pouring in sizzling tallow and stirring the gumbo together. Once the fat had congealed the top would be sewn up, and there was one more sack of pemmican—the almost indestructible rations that fueled the Hudson's Bay Company's boat brigades and kept many a lonely trader from starving to death in the lean winter days. Summer pemmican wasn't as good as the kind made on the autumn hunt, when the prairies were rife with ripe berries to mix in with it, but the best sauce—hunger—was rarely in short supply.

As the western sky blazed into a sheet of red-and-purple flame, the loaded carts plodded back to expand the circle of the camp. Madelaine threw herself down on the buffalo-robe bed she shared with her sisters, sure that the next thing she'd know was her mother shaking her awake next week. After a sleepless hour, though, she surprised herself. She was far less interested in oblivion than in the smells of roasting buffalo tongue and buffalo hump and in the sound of fiddles trying to tune themselves to a concertina. She crawled back out into a firelit festival. She stuffed herself with juicy, hot handfuls of all the tenderest and tastiest parts of buffalo until she was too bloated to walk, and then began to dance. She jigged around the bonfire with a string of partners including the two oldest Dumont boys—tall, handsome Isidor and squat, lumpy Gabriel. Gabriel surprised her. There were flares of light in his black eyes that made her quite forget his ungainly structure.

A hand came down on her shoulder, and her father said: "Time for bed."

She looked around at the other girls younger than she, including her own sisters, still uninhibitedly bouncing away. "But Papa . . ."

"I *said*: Time for bed."

The hunt took up its dogged pursuit again, like the wolves that killed and ate their fill and then went back to padding patiently along in the wake of the herd. The buffalo grass grew yellow and powdery as the sun sucked out the spring juice. Water grew more scarce. In mid-July the hunt reached Le Grand

Coteau—the sudden upthrust that separated the northern rivers from the Missouri. It was a series of rising terraces and ridges, resolving on the south side to the tortured convolutions of the Missouri Breaks.

Madelaine climbed down to walk up the slope beside their lead ox and encourage him as best she could while her father laid the whip on from behind. Before they reached the crest of the ridge she knew that something was wrong. She heard shouting from above and the angry bellowing of oxen.

They came up onto the first terrace of the *coteau*. The line of carts ahead of the Wilkies' was hooking into an arc to start a circle, the drivers whipping their oxen or draft horses into a ponderous trot. Her father followed suit without asking questions. Madelaine ran along beside. The usual camp circle was a rather loose affair, but this time her father butted his lead cart up tightly against the last of the Dumont carts, which were formed up wheel to wheel with the animals facing the inside of the emerging circle.

When the carts were all in place, the Captain in Chief—a nephew of Mister Grant's—stood up on top of the load in one of his carts and announced, "One of our scouts spotted a big camp of Sioux off that way," pointing at the next ridge to the south. "I want five men to go and get a better look with this," producing his uncle's remarkable brass spyglass. The Captain of Ten whose turn it was in the daily rotation of responsibility stepped forward as he should, took the spyglass, and rode off with half his squad.

There was nothing the rest of them could do but wait. The cart animals were left standing in their traces, complaining bitterly at the spectacle of the buffalo runners and saddle horses gamboling freely inside the circle. Madelaine's mother told her to get a fire going and started rattling out her cooking pots. With the younger children holidaying around them, they went to work, kneeling on opposite sides of the fire, Madelaine's mother building buffalo stew with her pouches of sage and wild parsnips and other fruits of the plains spread out beside her while Madelaine kneaded flour and water into a skillet to make bannock. Madelaine's father took his saddle and bridle out of the cart and went to cut his saddle horse out of the herd.

The family was just settling down to eat when a crackle of gunfire came from the other side of the ridge. The whole camp ran to the south side of the circle, squeezing against each other to get a look out over the cart rails. Two horsemen broke over the crest of the ridge and came galloping down, trailing plumes of dust. A fan of other horsemen came charging after them, firing from the saddle. Even at that distance, Madelaine could see the bright colors and trailing feathers—the Sioux were already painted up and decked out for war.

There was a crash of a gunshot next to her ear. She looked over and saw Gabriel Dumont with his cut-down old flintlock pointed in the air. A few of the other boys followed his example. Her father held his fire, but she saw him turn his head toward Gabriel Dumont and nod approvingly.

The Sioux pulled up short. A cart was wheeled aside quickly, and the two horsemen they were chasing galloped in through the gap—two of the five who'd gone to scout out the Sioux camp. They reined in in front of the Captain in Chief. One of them said breathlessly: "We rode in to say hello, and they grabbed us—said we was going to be their guests, but it was pretty plain they meant prisoners. We saw a chance and made a break, but the other three couldn't get away. Saved this, though." And he handed the brass telescope back to the Captain in Chief.

"Thanks. My uncle would kill me. . . . How many are there?"

"Maybe two thousand warriors. Yanktons, Sisitons, Hunkpapas, you name it. They didn't all come together to celebrate St. Jean Baptiste Day."

Madelaine's eyes moved away from the scouts toward the stalled pursuit party of Sioux. They were walking their horses toward the circle of carts. She said: "Papa!"

"What? Ah! Captain . . ."

The Captain in Chief, Madelaine's father, the Dumonts, and several other men swung up onto their horses and trotted out through the gap. Madelaine watched the parley, but it was impossible to guess what was being said. After a few moments the Sioux rode away and the métis came back. The Captain in Chief climbed back up onto his cart podium, and the camp assembled in front of him. He said: "The Sioux say they've only come together because they're all trying to find the buffalo herd and had no luck. They say they're in a bad way and hope for help from their half-breed cousins. They say they'll come back tomorrow with only a few warriors, bring the three scouts to set free, and hope we'll give them a few presents in return, then they'll leave us alone. Anyone want to make a bet on that?"

No one did. "All right. I say we spend the night getting ready to fight. When they come back tomorrow we ride out and meet them halfway instead of letting them come in to parley. It may mean we're condemning the prisoners to death, but better that than let the Sioux get in here and kill us all. You all know as well as I do we've only got sixty-four guns. . . ."

"Seventy-seven!" The shout came in a tinny, half-formed voice. Madelaine turned to seek it out like everyone else did. Squat, peach-fuzzed Gabriel Dumont brandished his old gun in the air: "I counted me and twelve others that maybe ain't grown enough to run buffalo, but we got guns."

The defenses were arranged along the lines that Mister Grant had laid down before Madelaine was born. The draft animals were unyoked and left to pasture themselves inside the circle. In a normal night's camp, the carts were left propped forward on their harness poles, with the butt ends pointing at the sky. Now they were angled backward, with the poles pointing up and the cartbeds building a wall. Tent poles and the frame poles for meat-drying racks were jammed between the spokes of the wheels to lock them into a chain that couldn't be pulled apart. Sacks of pemmican, spare saddles, and cooking pots were piled up to fill the gaps between one cartbed and the next. When all that was done, the women and children went to work digging trenches under the carts while the men went out onto the prairie. Each man—or boy—picked his spot and dug an individual rifle pit, making a circle about a hundred yards outside the circle of carts. The perimeter of rifle pits were where the fighting would take place, not the cart barricade. If the Sioux got in close enough to lob arrows and musket balls into the herd of oxen and horses inside the carts, it wouldn't matter if their pitiful seventy-seven rifles managed to hold off the attack; they would all be easy pickings on the long march back north.

The sun went down and the work went on by the light of a bonfire in the cart circle and the big yellow moon rising over Le Grand Coteau. Madelaine was dully hacking at the ground with her father's axe, each second backstroke whacking up against the ceiling of the cartbed and jarring her hands to remind her. Her mother said: "Stop! Father Laflêche has something to say to us." Madelaine sloped the axe down and climbed out of her hole. In the middle of the circle was an empty cart that had been wheeled out of the line before the rest were locked into place. Father Laflêche was standing in the cart, looking from one hand to the other. In one hand was his pocket watch, the other held a book that wasn't a Bible.

The men drifted back in from their excavations. Father Laflêche's congregation was a dazed mass of buffalo hunters, women and children, horses and oxen, all packed together. He looked up at the moon, now changed from gold to silver, then back down at his watch, and said: "My children, there may be a miracle tomorrow or there may not, but you will see a miracle tonight. Look at the moon."

Madelaine looked up. It was a lovely fat, summer moon, big and bright in the clear prairie air, but no different from the thousands of other summer moons she'd seen. But then a small black arc appeared on its rim, as though some monster of the skies had taken a bite out of it. More and more of it began to be eaten away. Madelaine had learned about lunar eclipses in school, and her father had told her of seeing several, but it was still eerie. Some of the grown people around her, who knew more about Satan and Machie Manitou than astronomy, began to murmur and cross themselves. One of Madelaine's little sisters began to cry. Madelaine picked her up and jogged her on the crook of her elbow and explained about the shadow of the earth passing between the sun and the moon. She didn't think the explanation got through, but the fact that there was an explanation had a calming effect.

By that time, the moon was almost gone. The white light on the faces around her dimmed and then went out. Where the moon had been there was only a black hole among the stars. Madelaine suspected that she wasn't the only one wondering whether that was what was going to happen to the White Horse Plains hunt tomorrow. Then a thin sliver of light appeared, growing quickly to a crescent. The hush around her was broken by appreciative oohs and ahs and laughter, as though it had been a conjuring trick put on by Father Laflêche for their benefit.

They all went back to work. When the trench under the Wilkie cart was dug, Madelaine and her mother lined it with buffalo robes and ladled in the sleeping children, then climbed in themselves. Madelaine didn't sleep. She heard the men coming back and going to work hobbling the stock inside the cart circle so they couldn't stampede when the shooting started. Madelaine climbed out to help. She was stooping down to hobble her father's saddle horse when he called to her: "No. Leave him saddled and just loop his reins around the cart shaft."

When the sky turned gray, the men went back out to their rifle pits before there was enough light for the Sioux to see them going—all except her father and the Captain in Chief and a dozen others who stayed inside the cart circle. Father Laflêche called the camp to assemble around his cart pulpit once again. He addressed them as hopefully as possible, reminding them of the two gallopers that the Captain in Chief had sent to inform the massed rifles of the Red River hunt and pointing out that God would naturally be supportive of Christians fighting for their lives against a horde of pagans—provided that they shot straight and didn't panic. Then he led them in a prayer that was cut off abruptly by a woman's voice shouting: "There they are!"

Over the main ridge of Le Grand Coteau came more mounted warriors than Madelaine had ever seen in one place in her life. Her father and the others jumped onto their horses and rode out to meet them. The Sioux stopped and fanned out in a line a mile wide. When the métis party were a couple of hundred yards away, a horseman broke from the Sioux line and galloped toward them—one of the three scouts the Sioux had taken yesterday. From Madelaine's vantage point on top of one of the tilted carts, it appeared that he was gesticulating wildly. Her father and the others reined in to confer with him, then walked their horses forward toward the Sioux. A war-bonneted Chief came out to meet them. From the way he was flourishing his feathered spear—its steel point glinting in the sun—he wasn't addressing them as brothers.

The métis horsemen suddenly wheeled their horses and charged back at a gallop toward the carts. At the same time, two dark-coated riders broke from the Sioux line—the other two scouts. The Sioux wavered for an instant and then came on, whooping and firing guns and bows from the saddle. It was a race for the gate where a cart had been wheeled out of the circle to let Madelaine's father and the others go out and come back in. If the Sioux could stay close enough on their heels, the people inside the circle would either have to let the Sioux in or lock out their own fathers and brothers and sons.

A gap opened up between the two escaping scouts. The one with the slower horse turned to fire a shot over his shoulder. He must have had his gun loaded with buckshot because three Sioux went down. But in the next instant the scout was jerked up off his saddle, riddled with bullets and arrows.

The prairie between the fleeing parley party and the oncoming Sioux suddenly erupted. Clumps of sage and twitch grass sent off puffs of smoke as the men in the rifle pits on that side crashed off a volley. When the smoke cleared there were lots of empty Sioux saddles. Madelaine wondered how many of them signified a shot Sioux and how many meant a warrior who had slid down to slink forward through the grass.

The rest of the Sioux pulled back out of range. Madelaine's father and the others galloped through the gate, and the cart was wheeled back and locked into place. Madelaine jumped off her cart to scuttle back into the trench where she belonged. She passed by the escaped scout. His withered old mother was weeping on his neck and saying: "If you're too tired-out to fight, my son, go have a little nap and give me your gun so I can take a shot at those bastards out there."

Madelaine slid down into the fur-lined cocoon, swerving in midslide to keep from coming down on her baby brother. She announced: "Papa came back safe," and then helped her mother soothe the little ones. When they'd been calmed and grown accustomed to the sound of sporadic gunfire and howls, she took her skinning knife and cut a gap out of the sod where the rim of the cartbed met the lip of the trench. She poked the long blade out and managed to saw off just enough grass stalks to be able to see out.

There were no more volleys from the rifle pits. Every now and then some innocuous lump on the ground would give off a firecracker pop and a painted body would snap up out of the grass in front of it and fall back down. Sometimes a single horseman or a group of them would charge in firing from under their horses' necks and then sheer off laughing or fall screaming as their punctured horses came down on top of them. Some of the Sioux lay unseen chanting their death songs, some flopped up and down in the grass roaring in pain. Several warriors were prancing their horses back and forth just out of range, brandishing some red things and shouting. Madelaine was too far away to make out details, but she was sure that the red things were pieces of the dead scout.

She grew accustomed to the occasional woody thunk and shudder from the roof of the trench as a spent arrow or musket ball hit the slanted wall of cartbeds. A quavery but determined tenor began to sing a hymn. The voices of women and children joined in from the necklace of trenches. Madelaine shifted over to the other side of the trench and peered out. Through the shifting forest of hobbled animal legs, and the dust their hooves were raising, she caught a glimpse of Father Laflêche standing in his cart wearing his white surplice with the starburst on the chest. He was leading a hymn about gentle Jesus, but next to his hand was a hatchet with its head stuck into the top of the railpost—like a splitting axe waiting in the chopping block until the time came to put it to use.

A bellow of pain broke out of the lowing and whinnying of panicked livestock, and the ground shook as an ox went down right next to the trench. The legs kept flailing, slamming its hooves against the cartbed. Madelaine's younger brothers and sisters screamed as splinters rained down on them. Along with the hoof hammering came a sound of creaking and groaning as the poles locking the wheels to those of the next carts began to give way. Madelaine's mother was busy with the children. Madelaine snatched up her knife, leaned out, and slashed the blade across the ox's neck. Moist heat splashed across her arm. The ox kicked a few more times and stopped.

The light began to turn red. The shooting and the screaming grew more intermittent. It didn't seem possible that an entire summer day had gone by without the Sioux breaking through, but the red light dimmed to purple and there was no more gunfire. Madelaine crawled out. The animals had quietened down and were directing their attention to the few remaining tufts of grass they hadn't trampled. The men began to come back from the rifle pits. Their families tightened their jaw muscles and waited grimly to see which ones didn't come back. Gabriel Dumont's father had taken an arrow in his thigh, but his was the only blood the Sioux had drawn—other than the butchered scout, one hobbled buffalo runner, and the ox that Madelaine had finished off.

The Dumonts broke open an illicit keg of rum to share around. Madelaine's ox was carved up and distributed. When it was sizzling over several dozen fires, the camp was called to assemble once more. First Father Laflêche led them in thanking God for the miracle of life for one more day. Then the Captain in Chief said: "The question is, should we wait to meet them here again tomorrow, or move out at first light toward the rescue party coming from the Red River hunt? I've talked it over with the Captains, and we figure the best thing is not to wait. We're going to move out at sunrise in four lines, so be ready."

An hour before sunrise Madelaine was shaken awake and put

to work groggily hitching up the carts. She'd been on hunts in the past when they'd taken the precaution of moving in four lines, but never when she'd been old enough to be expected to take an active part. The men were split into four sections of riders, leading, following, and flanking the carts, but out of sight of them. The women, and the men too old or young to take their place in the flying columns, drove the carts along in four parallel files. If there was trouble, the two outside files pincered inward while the front and rear halves of the two inside files peeled off forward or back to turn into a circle. Madelaine's mother drove the lead Wilkie cart, and Madelaine was put in charge of the second.

The eastern sky was still red when the White Horse Plains hunt headed back down Le Grand Coteau, cutting across the grain of the slope so the loaded carts wouldn't overrun the oxen and cart ponies. They had barely traveled an hour across the prairies, in the direction they hoped to find the Red River hunt, when two scouts in silhouette galloped past each other across the top of a distant butte. The Captain in Chief shouted the order to transform the cart files into a fort. Madelaine panicked, trying to envision the entire maneuver and gauge what part she was supposed to play in it. Then she took herself by the nape of the neck and told herself to just prod her ox along to keep its nose in the tailgate of her mother's cart. The men came galloping in from all four directions, leaping off their horses and snatching spades out of the carts. By the time the cart circle was locked together and the animals hobbled inside, the men were dug in and waiting. The Sioux came at them for the rest of the morning and through the afternoon. The black breasts of a bank of thunderheads loomed up over Le Grand Coteau and sailed forward, spitting lightning. The gunshots stopped. Madelaine poked her head up over the rim of the cart. A Sioux Chief was riding forward with his palm held up. The men in the rifle pits warned him to stop. He reined in his horse and demanded to be allowed to pass into the cart circle. They warned him off. He boomed out with stiff dignity: "Very well. I only came to tell you we have had enough. From this day forward we will never fight the Wagonmen again." He wheeled his horse and trotted back, raising his spear over his head. At the signal, the entire Sioux nation came in a breakneck wave. Madelaine ducked her head to the point where the cart rim cut off the bottom half of her field of vision. The Sioux whirled around and around the circle, firing from the saddle, then spun off and disappeared into the south like a summer dust storm that hits and moves on.

Something hit Madelaine on the cheekbone and spattered up into her eye. She dropped her head and flung her hand up to her eye. A bucketful of fat raindrops came down on the back of her head as the storm broke. When she looked up again, the men from the rifle pits were running back, throwing their guns in the air and laughing. Another rolling thunder was coming in from the north—seven hundred métis buffalo hunters and their Saulteaux cousins from the Red River hunt.

When the White Horse Plains hunt caught up with the buffalo herd again, Gabriel Dumont was standing with his arms clasped, stoically watching his uncles and cousins and older brother saddling up their buffalo runners. His father came forward, hobbling on an improvised cane, with his other hand holding the lead of a buffalo runner. He stopped in front of Gabriel and said gruffly: "What the hell's wrong with you that your crippled old wreck of a father has to saddle your horse for you?"

"You said—"

"What I said was, boys don't hunt buffalo." Gabriel blinked at his father twice, then snatched the halter from his hand and leaped up on the horse. "Wait!" Gabriel hauled the horse to a halt in midrear. "That old shit-tube of a gun you got might be good enough for Sioux, but . . ." Gabriel's father's rifle spiraled up toward him. He snatched it out of the air. Madelaine stood watching Gabriel Dumont gallop off to catch up with the other hunters.

CHAPTER 3

Madelaine lit the lamp over the billiard table and the one on the end of the counter plank so she could amuse herself with toting up the freight accounts while Michel Dumas and Isidor attended to the serious business of improving their bank shots. The click and murmur of the billiard game and

Annie's humming as she worked her way through the mending basket were a soothing undercurrent to the hard-edged numbers of cartloads and miles and ox skinner's wages versus invoiced charges. Ahsiweyin rolled himself in a blanket under the billiard table and wove soft snorings into the fabric of sounds.

The game of billiards as played at Gabriel's Crossing was about as forgiving as a knife fight in a locked room. For one thing, it was French or carom billiards, played on a table with no pockets, with two cue balls and an object ball, and every shot had to hit three cushions before the red ball. For another, it was played by men who'd been potting squirrels through the eye since they were twelve years old.

A raucous shrieking came out of the night, the squealing of the ungreased wooden axle of a Red River cart. Isidor looked up from his game and said: "Little late for passengers." Madelaine went to the door. The dogs set up a racket and started rocketing around the yard as the cart rolled across the border of their domain. Madelaine shushed them, and they came over to stand guard on the house. In the moonlight, she could see that the cart was piled high with baggage and there were children perched on top of the heap. A cow was following along on a lead tied to the back rail, mingling its indignant lowing with the wheels' squeals and the crying of a baby.

The cart stopped in front of her, and the driver climbed down. It was Michel Desjarlais, from the parish of St. Louis de Langevin north of Batoche's Crossing. "Hello, Aunt Madelaine. I know it's late, but do you think Uncle Gabriel could row us across? We still got a long way to get to my brother's place tonight." Although the Desjarlaises, like all métis, could be proven to be related to the Dumonts and Wilkies if one cared to trace the strands of blood and marriage far enough along the web, that wasn't why he called her "Aunt." "Aunt Madelaine" and "Uncle Gabriel" were standard usage along the South Saskatchewan.

"Gabriel ain't here, but Isidor can take you across. What's happened to your brother?"

"Nothing. We're going to live on his place. They took our place away from us."

" 'They'?"

"The Prince Albert Land Company."

"What? I don't understand. How could . . ." A sudden upsurge in the baby's squalling drowned her out. The light from the doorway fell on Michel's wife trying to quiet their baby and on the droopy-eyed children sitting up on their heap of possessions. When the howls had died down to a plaintive mewing, Madelaine said: ''Forget taking the ferry tonight. You'll stay here and Gabriel'll take you across in the morning. We got plenty of room upstairs.''

Isidor and Michel Dumas helped Michel Desjarlais get the cart unhitched and the horse and cow settled in for the night while Madelaine and Annie and Madame Desjarlais put together bedding and a bite of cold supper—just enough so the children could put something in their stomachs before they dropped off. The loft above the billiard room and store had been arranged for putting up family and hired hands and stranded travelers.

When Madame Desjarlais had herded the children upstairs, Madelaine dipped tin cups in the current barrel of beer and said to Michel Desjarlais: ''Now—what's this about they took your place away from you?''

''Just that. The government in Ottawa sold a big piece of land to the Prince Albert Land Company, and our place was part of it.''

''They can't do that without your say-so.''

''They could and they did.''

''Dammit, your father was living on that place before there was a Dominion of Canada.''

''That don't mean nothing. Anything that happened before Canada bought this country from the Hudson's Bay Company don't mean nothing. The man told me that the government's mapped out the whole North West in mile squares, running north from the medicine line. If somebody's place happens to be in one of the squares the government's sold to some land company or gave to the railroad, that's that. I got no legal title, and the Prince Albert Land Company does. So the man told me if I don't clear off, the Police'll come and clear me off.''

''They wouldn't do that.''

''Oh, not to *you*. As soon as the land office got a title claim with Gabriel's name on it, it was all stamped and sealed and that was that, wasn't it? Me, they been stalling for eight years.''

Over Michel Desjarlais's slumping shoulders, Michel Dumas and Isidor stood leaning on their cues, pretending to pay attention to the game. Michel Dumas's family had been among those who'd elected to try and stick it out at Red River when it started filling up with white swindlers backed by the government. Madelaine could remember Michel Dumas saying: "Back home these days, a breed's lower than a dog. I took my dog into a saloon—they threw me out and let him stay."

Madelaine tried like hell to think of something she could say to Michel Desjarlais. He yawned and rubbed his face with both hands and said: "I never seen such a long day. That's all there is to it. Except the one thing I still got to figure out once we're settled in at my brother's is what to do about my mother and father."

"Your mother and father?"

"They're buried back there. I don't like the thought of some stranger digging a basement through their graves. Well, I'm just about wore out and Uncle Gabriel ain't home yet. . . ."

"Go up to bed. You'll see him in the morning."

She went back to her accounts and turned up the lamp—either her handwriting had grown smaller or her eyes weaker. She had just closed the freight ledger and cracked the one for the store when three gunshots sounded across the river. She looked up at Isidor. "Le Petit?"

He said: "Sounds like it," racked his cue, and headed for the door with Michel Dumas falling in behind. "Le Petit" was what Gabriel named every rifle he'd ever owned, back to the stubby little Hudson's Bay Company trade gun he'd been given when he was ten. The old Dumont family story went that they'd been camped out on the prairie one summer night when little Gabriel mistook the sound of a distant buffalo herd for the hooves of a Sioux war party and demanded that someone loan him a rifle so he could help in the fighting. His father had shushed the rest of the camp's laughter and had solemnly rummaged out the sawn-off relic of a flintlock, announcing that Gabriel was obviously enough of a man now to have a rifle of his own. Thirty-six years later, Gabriel's rifle was a gleaming brass-bound Winchester carbine that could take the head off a duck at a hundred yards—at least in his hands. But it was still "Le Petit."

While one part of Madelaine's brain carried on toting up papers of pins and kegs of nails, the other part counted off the time it would take for Isidor and Michel Dumas to unlimber the scow and row it across the river and back, for Gabriel to lead his horse up from the shore, strip off its saddle, and slap it into the corral, to pause halfway across the yard to ruffle the dogs' ears . . . There was a rumble of low-pitched voices approaching the door, then the old man was home.

Madelaine affected to spare only a glance from her account books as he obliged her by taking off his silly made-for-all-weathers black felt hat with the upturned brim and scaling it toward an empty shelf. The head underneath wasn't what anyone was likely to call pretty—a high, battered forehead receding to a thick mane of tangled black hair that, like his beard, was stippled with frost; high, heavy cheekbones; broken nose; a straight hedge of eyebrows; eyes that were long and narrow, as though permanently slitted against the prairie glare of summer sun and winter snowfields, with irisless black centers that were like looking down the barrel of a gun. But after a quarter century of waking up with that head on the pillow beside hers, Madelaine's knees still insisted on going soft and caroming off each other.

Annie ran to the doorway and kissed her "Uncle Gabriel" hello. She'd always been an affectionate child, but Madelaine suspected at least part of the reason for that particular kiss was to make Michel Dumas wonder what it felt like. Gabriel rumbled at his brother: "Who's winning?"

"Tied at twenty."

"Good. I'll play the winner."

Michel Dumas said: "Maybe better you should play the loser."

"Big talk for a man that still owes me twenty dollars from the last time."

Gabriel came over to the counter and dipped his cup in the beer barrel. Madelaine licked her pencil and said: "Managed to find your way home in the dark?"

"The horse knows the way. Whose cart is that outside?"

Madelaine didn't want to get into it until she'd got his news, but one question led to another and pretty soon she'd told him all about what had happened to Michel Desjarlais. His reaction was even worse than she'd feared. He didn't throw his cup across the room or shout and pound the counter with his fist. With each question, his voice got lower and colder, and the black flares of his eyes settled into a steady gleam staring straight ahead. He said: "I ain't rowing the Desjarlaises across tomorrow morning. I'm taking them back to their home."

"What are you going to do? Start a fight with the Police?"

"You think that'd be worse than letting them steal our homes? Today it's the Prince Albert Land Company, tomorrow it's some other colonization company or the railroad, all with their pieces of paper from Ottawa.''

"Well, that's why you're going to Ottawa. . . .''

"I don't figure I'll be going to Ottawa.''

"I thought that's what the meeting down at Lindsay was for? To put together a delegation.''

"It was. But once everybody started yelling it got obvious—at least to me—that it'd just be a waste of money. The government could ignore us face to face just as easy as they ignore our petitions. What we need is somebody that knows how to make the government listen. So what we're going to do instead is send a delegation down to Montana to see if we can get some help from a man that's done that in the past.''

"Who's that?''

"Louis Riel.''

Isidor said: "The white settlers'll never stand for it. Most of them come from Ontario where they hang up Riel's picture somewhere between Herod and Judas Iscariot.''

"It was one of them that suggested it.''

Michel Dumas said: "Riel's crazy.''

Madelaine said: "He got the government to give the people at Red River their rights. That ain't crazy.''

"They locked him up in an asylum.''

"You never been sick and got better?''

Isidor lumbered over to the beer barrel to refill his cup and said to Gabriel: "What do you figure Riel'd do that we can't?''

"For one thing, if we can talk him into it, he can write us up a petition to send to Ottawa.''

"We been sending them goddamned petitions for fifteen years! The only thing that's changed is things keep getting worse.''

"Those were petitions written up by buffalo hunters and farmers or maybe a parish priest that don't know anything more about the government than we do. If somebody like Riel writes up a petition that they don't pay no attention to—well, then at least we know for sure that no petition is going to do it.''

Isidor grunted, shrugged, and leaned down to take the shot he'd been studying since Gabriel started his reply. Madelaine looked back down at her columns of figures. She heard the padded tap of the cue against the cue ball, the hum of ivory rolling across felted slate, three soft thunks, and then a double click as Isidor chortled: "Twenty-five!'' Michel Dumas racked up his cue disgustedly. Gabriel sprang toward the cue rack, but Isidor shook his head and said: "Best I head home before Judith figures I'm going to be gone all night and starts getting ideas. Want to row me across, Michel?"

Michel Dumas flashed his cornflower eyes in Annie's direction but caught against Madelaine's on the way. He looked up at the ceiling, scratched the stubble on his cleft chin, and allowed as how he might as well ride along with Isidor. Gabriel reached for his hat: "I'll row you both across. Standard rate."

"Hah! Like the standard wage you're going to pay us for running your goddamned ferry all goddamned day long while you were goddamned gallivanting around the . . ." As the bickering baritones and basses faded into the night, Annie packed up her mending and headed through the passageway to the twin house and her bed upstairs. Madelaine finished up with the store ledger and opened the bank book to be sure the numbers balanced with the dollars. There was also the tin box under the loose plank under the pool table, but Ahsiweyin was snoring on top of it.

Gabriel came back in, blew out the lamp above the billiard table, looked underneath at the source of the snuffling sounds, and said: "Might as well let him lie. I'll take him across tomorrow."

She closed up the bank book, put away her pencil, and said: "Better do it first thing, before you take the Desjarlaises back north and get yourself shot or locked up." He puttered his lips dismissively and reached down his cue. "You think the Police are going to disobey their orders just because of you?"

Lining up a practice trick shot, he growled over his shoulder: "They have before."

"Not when it was black and white like this. If the law says the Desjarlais farm belongs to the Prince Albert Land Company, the Police have to enforce it whether they want to or not."

"The *law*? The law gets made by the government out east to help out their rich friends that got them elected. Because we in the west don't get to vote, they figure they can do anything they want with us. Well, maybe it's time we showed them different."

"By getting yourself thrown in jail?"

"You think it's going to stop at the Desjarlaises' place? They're going to take the whole parish of St. Louis de Langevin, and then who's next? Isidor's place? Michel Dumas's? Our place?"

"You know they can't take our place."

"So you think we should just bar the door and build up the fire while our brothers and sisters and cousins freeze to death in the snow."

"I think you shouldn't blow it all apart over one family's troubles just when everybody's agreed to wait and see if Riel can help us."

He didn't argue or give in, just grunted and went back to studying the angles on his billiard table. She decided if she pushed it further, he'd just feel obligated to get stubborn. She waited for him to take his shot, then said: "So is that why you decided not to go to Ottawa—for the same reason Isidor figured it was time he headed home?"

"Huh?"

"Afraid if you left the old woman alone too long, she'd start getting ideas? Or have you stopped worrying since I got too old?"

He said: "You'll never get too old," vaulted over the counter, and pinned her against the wall.

Long after they both should have been asleep he whispered out of the dark: "You still awake?"

"No."

"This notion about bringing Riel up here to help . . . A long time ago, the Dumonts made a treaty with the Sioux: 'You don't mess with us and we won't mess with you. . . .' But there was this Sioux that had a grudge against me, and when I came out of the council lodge he jumped me from behind and cracked me across the head with his gun and put the muzzle to my head and pulled the trigger."

Madelaine had heard the story before, but she figured he was using it to tell her something.

"Well, he'd let his powder get damp or got a dud cap, so you didn't get the chance to get yourself a worthwhile husband. The Sioux Chiefs were so ashamed that one of their own should try such a thing under a white flag, they took him and beat him till he couldn't walk—maybe he still can't. You see, the Sioux had honor. This here John A. Macdonald and his government in Ottawa—I don't know how to deal with men like that."

Madelaine was well aware that Gabriel had been dealing very effectively with men like that all his adult life. But she didn't say so since it usually entailed things like planting himself on Michel Desjarlais's porch with Le Petit across his knees.

The next day was bright and warm, almost enough to convince her it was safe to start putting in the garden. After breakfast, Gabriel rowed the Desjarlaises and Ahsiweyin across the river. She threw the slops to the pig and piglets and sat down on the bank with her back against a sun-warmed rock to smoke her pipe and itemize the arrangements that would have to be made before Gabriel went away. It was a matter of course that he'd be asked to lead the delegation to speak to Riel, and that he would go.

Out on the river, the Desjarlaises' cow was bawling and causing trouble. The ferry was too far across for Madelaine to see exactly what the problem was, but it appeared that she was backing into Gabriel and interfering with his rowing. He shipped his oar and twisted her tail to convince her to move forward. Suddenly he flew straight up into the air, jackknifing—as though he'd been yanked by a string fixed to the small of his back. He came down on the rail with his center of gravity on the wrong side and plummeted headfirst into the river.

Madelaine stood up, staring at the spot in the water where he'd disappeared. He came up a little farther downstream, waving his arm at the yelling Desjarlaises and yelling back at them. Madelaine couldn't hear his words, but she assumed he was telling them that he could swim, which most prairie people couldn't. When he was a boy there was nothing Gabriel could resist learning, as long as it had nothing to do with books and schools. The Desjarlaises went back to rowing for the western shore, and Gabriel struck out swimming, but he didn't appear to be angling toward the shore, just heading straight downstream. She watched him worriedly, and the impression didn't change—he wasn't fighting the current at all but racing it to Hudson's Bay. Then she figured out why and sat back down and relit her pipe. He was chasing his hat.

By the time she'd made up a list in her mind of men who didn't have too many responsibilities on their own places and could hire on for a month or two while Gabriel was gone, he was rowing the ferry back across with his feet planted wide on the deck and his ridiculous little black hat planted firmly on his head.

He squelched up beside her, sat down on the rock next to hers, wrung out his tobacco pouch, and set it in the sun to dry. She handed him hers, and he packed his pipe. She struck a match. He blew it out with a superior air and dug out his waterproof tin match case. Once he had his pipe lit—the smoke from the bowl mingling with the steam rising off his clothes—she said: "Break anything?"

He shook his head and replied in a squeaky soprano voice: "No, she hit me low." Madelaine hit him even lower. He winced and wrung out his hat and set it down beside his tobacco pouch. In his natural bass rumble he said: "Phillipe Garnot's offer to buy the ferry's still open."

She laughed, then saw that he was serious. Phillipe Garnot was their downstream neighbor—a five-foot-tall immigrant from Quebec who seemed set on making himself a big man. Not satisfied with a piece of land that, like theirs, was twice the width of all the other strip farms up and down the river, he'd built a log cabin inn down at Batoche's Crossing that brought him in a lot of money, and he was continually angling to buy Gabriel out of the ferry business. She said: "You've turned him down ten times before. Just because you went and twisted the tail on the wrong cow don't mean—"

"That ain't why. He doubled his offer."

"Naturally—the money we're making off the ferry has tripled. And it's going to keep on doing that every year as more and more people come into the country."

He didn't reply, but she could see that he had something more to say, only it was going to take him a while to work up to it. She watched the river. A chunk of ice bobbed by, furred with green moss where it had peeled away a bit of riverbank. From the plateau behind her, a killdeer and a meadowlark informed each other in some detail that they'd staked out their nests and weren't moving. An otter ducked its head and front paws up out of the main channel and studied the strange, smoke-puffing creatures on the shore while the current carried him past.

Gabriel finally dragged the pipe stem out of his teeth and said softly: "Maybe."

"'Maybe?' I sit here for half an hour letting you work out what you got to say, and you say 'maybe'? Maybe what? Maybe you won't get hooved in the gut no more? Maybe Phillipe Garnot might up his offer next week? Maybe the traffic along the road ain't going to get any higher? Maybe Gabriel's going to blow his horn tomorrow?"

He didn't yell back, just shot one homicidal glance at her and then sat staring at the river with his boulder jaw grinding down his back teeth and his hands fisting and unfisting. Of its own volition, her spine fused itself rigid and went cold.

He said: "Maybe . . . if things keep on building like they have been, we'd be fools to let go of the ferry. But if other things keep building like they have been, we might be a lot gladder of some gold cash money in the box."

"You think there's going to be trouble, old man?"

"There's always trouble—just a question of what kind. And maybe . . . maybe a man just gets tired of rowing his boat back and forth in the same river."

"That ain't what you said last night."

"Well . . . there's rowing and rowing."

She looked out over the river and sucked on her dead pipe. Maybe if she'd given him children, she wouldn't be so scared that he'd always be the one to stand up whenever somebody had to. Or maybe he'd have felt even more obligated. She said: "My father told me once that there's this tribe who's got this custom—whenever a Chief dies or gets too old, everyone comes around to the family of the one chosen for the new Chief and gives them funeral gifts and sings mourning songs, and the family paints themselves with ashes. Because his life don't belong to him or his family no more."

"I don't see what the hell that's got to do with getting a good price for the ferry."

She didn't quite pick up a rock and add a new bend in his nose, but it took some doing.

CHAPTER 4

The delegation for Montana convened in the yard at Gabriel's Crossing. While the others made last-minute adjustments to harness rings and load distribution, Gabriel stood leaning on his paddock fence trying to decide which saddle horse to cut out before opening the gate to the pasture. This one had good wind, that one had a steady temperament . . . He even

considered the blasphemy of taking one of his buffalo runners.
Conventional wisdom had it that you ruined a buffalo runner by
using it for anything but running buffalo. But since there were
no more buffalo left to run . . .

In the end, as always, his eyes kept sliding back to Starface—
a white-stockinged bay with a head too big for his body and a
droopy forelock curtaining the blaze between his eyes. There
were a few horses along the South Saskatchewan that could beat
him in a short sprint, but after the first few miles they would all
be gasping for breath watching Starface lope away.

When he came out of the corral leading Starface, Madelaine
said: "I don't know why you waste time with that charade, you
always end up picking that one anyway."

"Not always." He fixed the lead to the back of the wagon,
which Starface made clear was an affront to his dignity. "Well,
I guess we'd best get moving." He kissed Annie good-bye and
turned to Madelaine.

She said: "Don't forget your way home, old man."

"Don't you forget I'll be coming home. And don't let those
pretty young men Phillipe Garnot hired to row the ferry forget
it, either." He put his arms around her, squashed her big breasts
against his chest, and brushed his mustache down against the
rim of her upper lip so he could get his naked mouth on hers.
He let her go, climbed up onto the wagon seat, and shook out
the reins. As the trail wound up the slope and into the woods,
he looked back, and she waved her arm over her head. Then the
trees hid her from view, and he turned his attention to the road
ahead.

His little convoy consisted of the one-horse wagon, two two-
horse buggies, and the string of saddle horses following behind.
There were four men in the delegation—himself, Michel Dumas, Moïse Ouellette, who was married to Gabriel's sister Isabelle, and a delegate from the predominantly English-speaking
half-breeds up around Prince Albert. Two young men from Batoche's Crossing had decided this would be the perfect opportunity to visit relatives in Montana, and Gabriel figured that six
rifles would be enough to smooth out any little wrinkles that
might come up along the way.

Rumor had it that the Mounted Police patrols had been instructed to keep an eye on them. They weren't doing anything
they could be arrested for, but Gabriel took it as a logical prin-
ciple that if someone thought he should keep an eye on you, you

probably had good reason not to let him. So he planned on following a roundabout route, arcing southwest to the Cypress Hills, keeping off the main trails and watching the horizon.

Although he certainly hadn't said so to Madelaine, a certain part of him was glad that the trip had been foisted on him. For all his life, this was the time of year when all métis left their winter homes along the rivers and lakes and struck out across the plains. For twenty of those springs, he'd ridden out at the head of five hundred hunters with their wives and families and thousands of carts in the hunt that had melded itself back together after the death of Mister Grant. Gabriel was the last in a long line of succession that stretched back through previous Captains of the buffalo hunt all the way to a young Mister Grant and the founding of the métis nation. It wouldn't be spring without the rumble of wooden wheels and the pulse beat of hooves and in front of him the whole, vast, blossoming body of the prairie spread out under the sky.

Seventeen days and seven hundred miles later, they rolled into St. Peter's mission on the Sun River. They'd seen a few Police patrols along the way, and a few American cavalry patrols, but none had seen them. The Blackfoot in the Cypress Hills had been delighted to show their cousins how to slip across the border without the formality of an interview. Most prairie métis were Cree, but the woman Gabriel's grandfather had decided to abandon civilization for had been Sarcee—one of the four tribes of the Blackfoot Confederacy. That didn't cut much ice with the Gros Ventres, whose territory lay just south of the border. A dozen warriors barred the delegation's path and launched into the opening gambits of that old intimidation game—"That sure is a fine-looking horse; wished I had a horse like that. . . ."— until it sunk into them that they weren't facing tenderfoot white settlers or prospectors but wagonmen who knew how that game ended. Gabriel couldn't blame them for trying, and had been pleasantly surprised that the current crop of Gros Ventres young men had been well-enough educated to recognize a porcupine before sticking their noses in for a close sniff.

Now Gabriel reined the wagon to a halt in front of St. Peter's mission church and climbed down stiffly, slapping dust off his hat. It was Sunday. The choral responses of the mass seeped out through the walls of the church, with its rough-planked spire standing dully against the white spires of the mountains beyond. Gabriel beckoned to a little brown boy throwing a stick for a black-and-yellow dog. "We're looking for your schoolteacher—Monsieur Louis Riel."

The boy pointed at the church, said: "I'll get him," and bounded up the steps, shooing the dog back from following him through the door.

A curious fluttery feeling started up in Gabriel's stomach. He thought at first they'd gone on a bit too long since stopping for lunch, then he surprised himself with the realization that he was nervous about meeting Riel. Although they'd both been boys in the little community of St. Boniface, they'd hardly known each other in those days. For one thing, Riel was seven years younger. For another, Riel had been a child of the church and the parish school while the Dumonts were charter members of *les sauvages*. When Riel came back to St. Boniface from his years of seminary school in Quebec, the Dumonts had long since relocated to the South Saskatchewan. The only communication Gabriel had had with Riel since childhood had been fourteen years ago, when Riel was enmeshed in the Red River Rebellion. Gabriel had ridden two hundred miles to make an offer to furnish five hundred *sauvages* from the west to deal with the British soldiers, and Riel had politely declined.

The boy came out of the church and paused in the doorway to peer back at the darkness within, pointing out at the delegation standing around the wagon. A chestnut-bearded man in a blue cloth coat stepped out into the light. Gabriel started across the road toward the church steps. As he got closer he could see that Riel's coat was shiny at the buttonholes and elbows, as were the knees of the trousers. Within the thick, curlicued chestnut frame of hair and beard, two haunted gray eyes studied him warily. Riel came down the steps to meet him. He was somewhat taller and broader than Gabriel. Gabriel stuck out his hand. Riel shook it and held it awkwardly, saying in a soft, resonant voice: "You seem to be a man from far away. I do not know you, but you seem to know me."

"I do, and I think you ought to know me as well. Don't you remember the name Gabriel Dumont?"

"Of course!" The wary veil melted off the gray eyes. Riel clasped Gabriel's right hand between both of his. "Of course I do—I remember it very well. I am very happy to see you again. But . . ." He snuck a guilty glance back at the church. "You must excuse me; I must hear the rest of the mass." He let go of Gabriel's hand. "If you would wait for me at my home, my wife would be delighted to give you a cup of tea. Straight down this road, on the left-hand side next to the schoolhouse. . . ." He stepped backward, fluttering his hand back over his shoulder. "Excuse me, but . . ." Then he turned quickly and went back up the steps and into the church.

Moïse Ouellette spat a tobacco plug and muttered: "Hell of a welcome after seven hundred miles."

Gabriel said: "So he's a religious man," and climbed back up on the wagon.

The schoolhouse turned out to be a surprisingly substantial complex with a cross over the front door and Blackfoot children peering out of grill-covered dormitory windows. Next door was a slant-roofed log cabin with a lean-to extension grafted onto one side. The door was opened by a young man with a mouth and cheeks as pursed in as if he were sucking on a spoonful of alum. Gabriel began to explain to him in French that Monsieur Riel had sent them here to wait for him, but the man cut him off with: "Talk white."

Moïse Ouellette growled: "Talk polite."

A melodious female voice called from the interior: "Is that someone to see us?" A velvet-eyed, lithe-waisted métis girl of about Annie's age blossomed behind the alum-faced man. She introduced herself as Madame Riel, saving Gabriel the faux pas of saying they'd come to wait for her father.

Madame Riel beckoned them graciously inside. She introduced the young man as the schoolmaster they shared the house with as he put on his hat and rattled the door shut behind him. She sat the delegation down and excused herself to stoke up the fire in the hearth and fuss with the teakettle. Gabriel could see now that she was a few years older than Annie, but not many.

After seventeen days of being enclosed by nothing smaller than the horizon, Gabriel perched gingerly on the edge of the chair with his elbows against his sides and his hat on his knee, surveying his surroundings. The room he was in appeared to serve as parlor, kitchen, dining room, and study. There was a well-polished crucifix on one wall, a shelf of books over a washstand, the table the delegation was seated around and the four wooden chairs they occupied, a shelf of cooking pots and plates beside the hearth, and that was the entire inventory. A jury-rigged stepladder led up to a sleeping loft. Behind the stepladder was a blanket-curtained doorway leading, presumably, to the added-on side room.

From the expression on Moïse Ouellette's face, he was thinking the same thing Gabriel was. The man who called this home for himself and his family was the same man who had forced the Canadian government to create the Province of Manitoba and grant rights to the people who lived there, who had been formally thanked by the lieutenant governor of the whole North West Territories for saving the country from a Fenian invasion, who'd twice been elected to the Parliament of Canada.

Michel Dumas, as always, appeared to be aware of nothing but his obligation to be charming to his hostess. When Madame Riel brought the kettle to the table, they all stood up uncomfortably to offer her their chairs. But it was of course Michel who smoothed away her objections by flashing his blue eyes and begging her to please give him an excuse to stand since he'd been sitting on a wooden wagon seat for seventeen days.

Since they'd come through the door, a muffled, constant murmur of children's voices had been emanating from beyond the curtained doorway. As Madame Riel was pouring out good, thick, black métis tea into tin cups, the sound came to an end. The curtain was pushed aside, and two solemn-eyed, knee-high children emerged. When the smaller of the two saw there were strangers in the house, she stopped in her tracks and clasped her brother's hand. He said: "We did our prayers, *Maman*. May we go out to play now?"

"Good boy, Jean, yes—but first you should meet these men who made a pilgrimage from all the way up in the north country to see your father. This is our son, Jean, and our little daughter, Marie Angelique."

Gabriel got up out of his chair and crouched down to bring his head to a level with theirs. He shook Jean's hand and said: "I am pleased to meet you, Monsieur Jean Riel. My name is Gabriel Dumont." When he let go of Jean's hand and turned to Marie Angelique, she hid both her hands behind her back and turtled her head down between her shoulders. Gabriel laughed and stood back up and introduced the rest of the delegation. Their mother nodded that the formalities were over, and they ran outside.

Madame Riel said apologetically: "By rights we three should have been at the afternoon mass with Louis, but they're too young to sit still for long. So the whole family goes together to morning mass and then Louis goes back alone in the afternoon. When Louis was Jean's age he would go with his mother to hear mass three times on Sundays, and to confession every day, but . . ." She shrugged her pretty shoulders in benign acceptance of the fact that it would be cruel to expect any ordinary child to conduct himself like the infant Louis Riel.

It became apparent that she was less comfortable in French than in Michif or Cree, so Gabriel shifted the language of the conversation. Michel Dumas ascertained that her maiden name was Marguerite Monet. Gabriel said: "Not old Bonnehumeur?" She blushingly acknowledged that her father was Bonnehumeur Monet and that she'd inherited a version of his nickname, being known when she was younger as Bellehumeur. Both versions could be very roughly translated as "good-humored." Although Madame Riel was pleasant enough, the only trace in her of what Gabriel would have called *bellehumeur* had been when the children had been in the room with her. After that brief sun flare, she had scuttled back under her bushel.

Once the general pleasantries had proceeded through Madame Riel ascertaining who they were, where they'd come from, when they'd started their journey, and what method of transportation they'd employed, it dawned on Gabriel that her next question was going to be "Why?" It put him in a bit of a quandary. He wasn't sure just how secretive they ought to be. As it turned out, he needn't have worried. Madame Riel just kept smiling benignly and batting her immense, lustrous eyes and asking how the weather'd been up their way.

Joyous squeals erupted outside, and Madame Riel became La Bellehumeur again as her husband came in with a child in the crook of each arm. Once Riel had been sat down with a cup of tea in front of him—Moïse borrowing Michel Dumas's excuse to give up his chair—Gabriel tentatively introduced why they'd come to see him. Gabriel was well aware that all marriages weren't like his and Madelaine's, especially those between forty-year-old men and women as young as Marguerite Bellehumeur.

But when Riel didn't show any qualms about involving his wife, Gabriel plunged into the meat of it, handing over some letters from old friends or enemies of Riel's from Red River who were asking him to come help them on the South Saskatchewan, and from representatives of the immigrant settlers who only knew him by reputation but still thought he was their best hope.

As he read through the letters and listened to Gabriel, Riel's spine grew longer and his shoulders lowered themselves from around his ears. He sprang up out of his chair and paced away from the table and then back again, furling the fingers of his right hand through his chestnut beard. At last he stopped in front of Gabriel and looked down. He shook his head and said: "As much as I might wish to, Monsieur Dumont, there is little I can do from this side of the line."

"Then come back north with us. Schools get shut down over the summer, don't they? We could wait till you've finished your teaching, bring you back up north with us, and have you back down here again by the time school starts up in the fall."

Riel's head snapped back, bringing his eyes over Gabriel's head again. He stared fixedly through the log wall and then said in a misty voice: "God wants you to know you have chosen the right way—for there are four of you and you have come on the fourth of June. You wish to have a fifth man to return with you. Obviously I must not answer you today."

CHAPTER 5

Madelaine was milking Evangeline when she thought she heard a shout from a long way away, somewhere beyond the borders of Evangeline's stall. She dismissed it and sank back below the surface of the cloistered world made up of her own humming mingling with Evangeline's lowing, the warm teats squeezing between her fingers, the hiss of milk squirting into the bucket, the soft-furred flank against her temple, the rich, moist smells of composting bedding and new milk.

The shout came again, sharper and closer: "*Maman*!" Madelaine leaned back to see around Evangeline's twitching tail. Annie was standing in the doorway of the barn, looking over her shoulder anxiously. "The Police are coming."

Madelaine moved the bucket so that Evangeline wouldn't kick it over and went to have a look. There was only one horseman coming down the trail, but Madelaine could see how Annie would have got the notion there'd be a whole troop following behind. He wasn't a patrol-rumpled constable but a crisp vision done in altar-painting colors—gleaming brass buttons and gold frogging, blazing scarlet tunic and a hat like a snow-capped mountain peak. Both horse and rider were on the tall side and immense through the chest and shoulders.

Annie said: "What should we tell him?"

"Tell him? We'll tell him he'll have to go down to the dock and pay his fare to the new owner of the ferry. Why else would he be coming by here?"

"What if he asks about Uncle Gabriel and Michel and them?"

"Then we'll tell him the truth—they're not here. You just stand here next to me and keep your mouth to yourself and give him something prettier to look at than saggy old cowhide."

The horse pranced up to them, and the rider dismounted in a flare of burnished leather and white gauntlets. He ducked the pipe-clayed pith helmet off his head and settled it into the crook of his arm, clanked his spurs together, and jerked his head up and down the full inch his bull neck would allow. "Compliments of the day to you, Madame Dumont, Mademoiselle Annie."

"*Bonjour*, Superintendent." She never knew whether to call him "Superintendent" or "Major." The North West Mounted Police couldn't seem to make up their minds from one day to the next whether they were a police force or an army. "I'm afraid you got all the way down off your horse for nothing. Phillipe Garnot's who you got to pay to cross on the ferry now, and he's down at the dock."

"I'd heard a rumor that you'd sold, but I didn't believe it. I would've thought the ferry was a gold mine, what with more people coming into the country every day."

"Gold mines get sold off all the time, when the price is right."

The superintendent nodded contemplatively and knuckled his tremendous mustache. Despite the uniform and the parade ground manners, Madelaine didn't lump him in with the machinery of the faceless government in Ottawa. Lief Newry Fitzroy "Paddy" Crozier had come to the North West ten years ago with the first contingent of Mounted Police, and she considered him almost as much of a native as she and Gabriel. Almost. He said idly: "Gabriel about? I was hoping to have a bit of a jar and a jaw about this and that."

"He ain't here. I hope this was just a stop along your way and you didn't ride all the way over here for nothing."

"The opportunity to pass the time of day with you, Madame

Dumont, is hardly nothing. But I did have to pass this way regardless. The Force is negotiating with the Hudson's Bay Company to lease Fort Carlton. The commissioner decided it's high time we had a permanent presence somewhere between Prince Albert and Saskatoon."

It seemed a remarkable coincidence that the government should move the Police into the area just after the people who lived there had sent for Riel to help stop the government from pushing their heads under. She said: "Seems funny the Company'd want to sell off Carlton. I'd've thought it was a gold mine."

Crozier's round little eyes narrowed. He raised one gauntleted hand to his mouth and gave out a surprisingly delicate little cough. "Well, drat, I have to head north as soon as I've done my business at Carlton, and I was counting on having a few words with Gabriel—especially since it looks like we're going to be neighbors come the fall. Perhaps I might wait around for him, if you didn't mind? . . . When do you expect him back?"

"When he gets here—you know Gabriel. But you might as well come in and wet your throat, if you don't mind having no one else to pass the time with but me."

"Madame Dumont, had I but known that might be in the cards, I would have posted scouts on that ridge to heliograph me whenever your husband saddled his horse." He hitched his charger by the water trough and loosened the saddle girth. Madelaine told Annie to finish up the milking and led Crozier into the house.

She ducked behind the counter and dug out two tin cups. "You're in luck, Superintendent, the last batch of beer's just come ripe."

"Well, actually, I was . . . um—not to be ungracious, but I was anticipating the taste of something stronger."

"Why, Superintendent! You know we only got a permit for one little keg of rum and one of brandy—for personal use."

"I am certainly aware of that, Madame Dumont—just as I'm aware that both of them are always miraculously full. It's a comforting kind of miracle for a man who wasn't bred to live on loaves and fishes alone."

She poured him a tot from the rum keg and another for herself. He raised his cup, said: "God bless all in this house," and tossed it back. He slapped the hollow cup back on the counter, gratefully sighing out the fumes, and said: "So, Gabriel been gone long?'' She shrugged and shifted his cup under the keg tap. He marched over to the billiard table, took hold of a corner of the sheet of canvas covering the felt, and gave it a shake. A cloud of dust rose up. He let go the canvas and looked pointedly from the dust cloud to her to the smudges on the fingers of his gauntlets.

She said: "I don't remember hearing about this new law where people have to ask permission from the Police to go out hunting for a few weeks."

"I know where he's gone, and I know who he's gone to see."

"Well, you could've said so right off and saved us both a lot of circling around."

"But would you then have asked me in for a jar?" She laughed. He came back to the counter, took a healthy quaff from his recharged cup, then tugged off his gauntlets and wrestled open the neck button on his tunic. "Oh, for the days when the service uniform was 'anything and a slouch hat.' The truth of it is, Madelaine, I'm worried—matter of fact I'm *damned* worried—that Gabriel might be taking a step we're all going to regret. I know as well as anybody that a lot of things out here need remedying, and soon. But bringing Riel into it isn't the way to go about it."

"What is?"

"Well, if I knew that . . ."

"Then let him try. Maybe he knows a way to get your bosses in Ottawa to listen."

"If they haven't listened to me and every other senior officer in the Force and the whole North West Council, they're hardly likely to listen to Riel."

"Well, they better listen to *somebody* damned soon!" She was surprised at her own vehemence. Apparently, so was Crozier. He looked down at the floor, then picked up his cup and drained it off and set it back down again without meeting her eyes. She poured another little tot into the cup.

"Ah, bless you for a generous woman. It has to turn itself around eventually, Madelaine, if we all keep on hammering away at the government. But this Riel has a reputation for stirring people up—I know, I know, they're stirred up already. But if Gabriel brings Riel into the country . . ."

"Maybe you should remember the last time."

"The last time?"

"The last time you Police decided you knew better than Gabriel—when you first came out here and found him running his own government and laws. Seems to me all you got out of trying to arrest him then was your bottom spanked by the Queen.''

"Well, it wasn't *my* bottom, just the bottoms of some of my bosses in Ottawa and a few tin-plate magistrates. And it wasn't the Queen, it was the colonial secretary. But nonetheless . . .'' He shrugged his monumental shoulders, then his voice grew softer and lost the bantering tone. "But things have changed since then, just as they've changed since 1870. When Gabriel was enforcing his own laws here, there were no other laws—he disbanded his government when we came out here. When Riel declared his provisional government at Red River, the country wasn't yet legally part of the Dominion of Canada. If either one of them were to do the same thing today . . .'' The little round blue eyes in the immense squared head looked straight into hers. "It would be treason.''

"It seems to me, Superintendent, that these are things you want to say to Gabriel, not me.''

There was a blue twinkling, and his voice shifted back into the lilting "Paddy'' brogue. "Somehow I don't doubt that it comes to much the same thing.'' The twinkle hardened into a gleam, and the mountainous shoulders thrust forward across the counter. "What you have to understand, what you have to make him understand, is that this isn't an aberration that can be solved with a snap of the fingers. There are millions of other people around the world trying to untangle the same knot. The simple fact is that the North West has become a colony. I know you don't know what that means, but—''

"I have heard the word before, Superintendent.''

"I'm sure you have, but you haven't had the 'opportunity' to learn what it means. You and Gabriel and all the others who were born here are the only people in the Empire who grew up in a place that never was a colony. So far as I've been able to make out, the Hudson's Bay Company left you all to do as you pleased so long as you didn't interfere with the orderly commerce of the fur trade. Well, like it or not, fifteen years ago you became a colony of the Dominion of Canada, and you can't change that. There are other colonies all around the globe that are finding ways to slowly work themselves free without . . .'' He trailed off significantly.

"Without what, Superintendent?''

"You are a charming hostess, Madame Dumont, and you

perform the role of bartender admirably''—nudging his empty cup across the counter at her—''but don't play the fool with me.''

Outside, the superintendent's horse was still standing patiently hitched to the fence, enduring the spectacle of Gabriel's herd frolicking in the pasture on the other side. The superintendent tightened the cinch strap, clapped his pith helmet back on, and maneuvered the chin strap under his dimpled chin. ''Thank you for the lubrication, Madame Dumont. It may be some time before I'm back in the neighborhood again. Poundmaker's hosting a thirst dance for Big Bear and some other Chiefs, and the Indian agent demanded that I take a patrol up there to keep an eye on things.''

''Do you think that's a good idea these days?''

''The thirst dance or the patrol?''

''Both.''

''Ours not to reason why . . .'' He heaved his beef-fed bulk onto the saddle. ''Ours but to keep a lid clamped on things without letting the pressure build up too high. And that 'ours,' Madame Dumont, means every old hand with enough wit to read a steam gauge: me, Poundmaker, Gabriel . . .'' The blue eyes settled directly onto hers, then he twitched the reins and nudged his horse with his spurs.

Madelaine stood watching the big bay gelding prance down to Phillipe Garnot's ferry. Annie came out of the dairy shed, where they kept Evangeline's accoutrements and made their cheese and butter, and said: ''You were in there with him a long time.''

Madelaine started to shrug and then wheeled around to face her. Annie shrank in on herself. Madelaine reminded herself yet again that some bizarre accident of inherited bone structure made her appear frightening to some people. She said: ''Some men like to talk when they're afraid. What do you say we play a little billiards before supper?''

CHAPTER 6

WWW Gabriel had built a fire and boiled a pot of tea by the time the other three delegates rolled out of their blankets. They'd found a shady spot by a creek outside of St. Peter's mission, a pleasant change from some of their dry camps out on the plains. While the other three were sipping their first cups of the day and sluicing the sleep off their faces with creek water, Gabriel hauled his saddle out of the wagon and threw it on Starface. The delegate from Prince Albert said: "Going hunting?"

"Don't you remember—Monsieur Riel asked us to go with him to confession and take communion before he gives us his answer."

"I ain't forgot. He don't need my help praying." He tossed a slice of bacon fat into the skillet.

Gabriel said: "It ain't a bad idea to remind God once in a while you're still alive."

"Remind him for me."

Michel Dumas picked up his saddle, snorting over his shoulder: "Protestants—they figure once they got their baby hairs washed that's all there is to it." But Moïse Ouellette, who was certainly no Protestant, had also settled in beside the fire and was kneading flour and water to make bannock.

Riel was waiting on the church steps. The three of them went in and shared the morning service with the widowed grandmothers and a smattering of recently converted Blackfoot. When they got back to the schoolmaster's house, the other two were sitting at the table sharing another pot of black tea with Madame Riel. Gabriel waited until Riel was settled at the head of the table with a cup of tea in front of him and then said: "Now, Monsieur Riel, what is your answer?"

Riel rose to his feet and swept his eyes around the delegation. "Fifteen years ago I gave my heart to my nation, and I am ready

51

to give it again. But fifteen years ago I did not have a wife and two young children. As much as I feel called to come with you, I cannot leave them here alone. If you can arrange to take all of us, I will go back with you.''

Gabriel said: ''There's spare room on the wagon''—leaning down to pinch Jean's button nose—''even enough to squeeze in this big bull. And we got plenty of money left to buy a cart or another wagon.''

''I do have other obligations. The school year won't end until the tenth of June. . . .''

Gabriel turned to the other three. ''We can wait around here a few more days, eh?'' Moïse Ouellette looked like it wouldn't take much straining for him to think of better things to do, but he didn't argue.

Gabriel looked back to Riel. The gray eyes had taken on a diffuse glow, like moonlight through a mist, and a flush was extending down into his beard. ''I have more to say, but it would be better that I put it in writing. If you would excuse me, for a quarter hour at most. . . .''

The delegation trooped outside. They stood leaning on their horses and puffing on their pipes, Moïse and the delegate from Prince Albert exchanging sideways glances through the smoke. At last Riel emerged and handed Gabriel a couple of sheets of foolscap folded together. The bell above the schoolhouse door began to clang. Riel excused himself and started herding his pupils in out of the summer sun.

Back at the camp, Gabriel handed the papers over to Michel Dumas, who'd wasted several winters of his childhood in a mission school when he could have been learning the ways of buffalo and blizzards. Michel sat down by the fire with a cup of tea at his knee, cleared his throat, and cracked open the papers. '' 'Gentlemen, your visit honors and pleases me, and the letters you bring assure me that I would be welcomed by those who have sent you as though I were returning to my own family. . . .'''

Riel's written words went on to talk of the injustices that had to be resolved, including the fact that the Canadian government still owed him title to several pieces of land in Manitoba ''despite the fact that I have chosen to become an American citizen.'' He concluded with: ''In your interest therefore and in mine as well, I accept your friendly invitation, and I will go and spend a little time among you. Perhaps by presenting petitions to the government we will be able to gain at least something. But my intention is to return here in the coming autumn.''

When Michel had finished reading there was silence for a moment, except for the scratching of beards and the drumming of a woodpecker. Then Moïse Ouellette said: ''Well, I don't much care personally for all his praying and prophesyzing, but there's no denying he did a better job of writing that up in ten minutes than we did on that last petition we spent two months chewing our tongues over.''

''Funny thing, though,'' Michel said. ''Just about everything he wrote down here are things he already said to us face to face. Why'd he figure he had to write us a letter?''

Gabriel shrugged it off. He was hardly in a position to gauge why someone who could read and write would decide to do so.

Although Gabriel had told the truth when he'd said they had enough money to buy a cart or a broken-down old wagon, it seemed a shame to throw it away when he had a week ahead of him with nothing to do with his hands. There were plenty of American métis in the area—métis who'd been just as confused as their Indian cousins when they'd learned that the drawing of the Medicine Line meant that they were American métis as opposed to Canadian métis, as the Blackfoot Confederacy was now cut into two different Blackfeet. Gabriel went around from farm to farm looking over their woodlots and bought a wagonload of seasoned oak and maple. For five days the woodpeckers around the campsite were drowned out by chopping and sawing and hammering, and on the sixth day the Riel family's entire worldly possessions were loaded onto a serviceable Red River cart. It wasn't a benchmark in the art of cart making, and the wheel sections had to settle for being bound together with cowhide since there were no more bull buffalo hides to slice into *shagganappi*, but it would hold together for seven hundred miles. If it didn't, Gabriel had a good axe and plenty of wood for spare parts. The wood he didn't use up was worth hauling all the way back home, where the only deciduous trees were birch and poplar.

When they reached Fort Benton they stopped for the day to rest the horses and restock their supplies of flour and tea and salt pork. Pemmican, the traveling rations on the plains since the dawn of time, was as much a thing of the past as *shagganappi*. While the others were taking care of the provisioning, Gabriel took Michel Dumas along to translate for him and went hunting through a few other stores. It would have been a shameful waste to go to all the trouble of slipping back and forth across the border undetected without loading at least a few illicit articles on the wagon.

The first stop was Fort Benton Farm Implements & Dry Goods—If We Ain't Got It You Don't Want It. Gabriel said to Michel: "Tell the man I want a drive cog for a McCormick reaping machine."

"You ain't got a reaping machine."

"You think I don't know that? What the hell would I want a reaping machine for? The old Scotchman downriver can only cook up so much barley in a given year. Tell the man I want a—"

"Well, then what the hell would you want a drive cog for, if you ain't got the machine to—"

"You know that young fellow from Quebec that started a farm up past Isidor's? Well, he brought a Massey reaping machine out with him, and then made the mistake of trying to move it from shed to shed in the middle of February, and the drive cog snapped like glass. The problem is, Massey parts cost more'n anyone can afford, about twice as much as the ones down here. But the men that run the Massey company are friends of the men that run the government in Ottawa, so the government put a fat tariff on any farm machines crossing the border."

Michel brightened considerably. "So we'd be cheating the government!"

"More like keeping the government from cheating us."

Michel started to tell the man behind the counter what they wanted, then broke off in the middle and turned back to Gabriel. "What good's a McCormick cog going to do someone with a broken Massey machine?"

"'Cause they're the same goddamned machines. The Massey company just bought up the rights to make them in Canada. By the time you get around to translating I could go out and learn English."

"All right, all right, I'm telling him. . . ."

When they came back out onto the boardwalk, Michel said: "If I have to go to jail for smuggling, I'd rather it was for smuggling something more interesting than a cog for a reaping machine."

"When your children's winter coats are flour sacks and you've borrowed money against your next harvest to feed them through the summer, a cog for a reaping machine gets pretty damned interesting.''

They camped on the outskirts of Fort Benton, and the Riels went into town for mass. In the morning, Riel went back to the church while the rest of them broke camp. He came back almost immediately, flushed and animated. ''Father Eberschweiler has agreed to give us God's blessing on our journey and our mission! I asked him yesterday and he was hesitant, but this morning he agreed. He's waiting for us at the church.''

Marguerite rushed to dig out her best shawl and the children's Sunday coats. Moïse looked at the sky and grumbled: ''We're losing daylight.''

Riel said gently: ''The blessing of God is more precious than sunlight.''

Moïse said: ''You go on and get it for me. By the time you get back we'll be ready to go,'' and went back to the business of getting his recalcitrant team hitched to the buggy.

In the end, only Gabriel walked into town with the Riels, Marguerite carrying Marie Angelique and Louis bouncing Jean's bottom on the crook of his arm. The priest was at the altar, fastening on his surplice over his dusty black cassock. As Gabriel was creaking his knees down at the altar rail, Riel said: ''Father, will you permit me to offer up my own prayer while you are speaking the blessing?''

''I thought you came here to get the blessing of the church, my son—not to bless yourself.''

''I only wish to say a few words to express my humble gratitude for the divine benefice you have granted us to receive.'' The priest looked suspicious, but he nodded and launched into the blessing. As the sprinkling of holy water tickled Gabriel's forehead, he could hear Riel at the rail beside him murmuring fervently through the priest's Latin: ''Dear God, bless me according to the light of your Providence, which is loving and without measure. Bless me with my wife, with our little son, Jean, with our little daughter, Marie Angelique . . . and with Gabriel Dumont.'' It was simple and direct, but Gabriel found himself surprisingly affected. He was touched that Riel should choose to include him in his prayers, but there was something more in the way Riel went about the business of praying. It started Gabriel thinking along a line he'd never considered before.

The priest asked if he could come back to their camp and

hitch a ride to visit an invalid parishioner on a farm a few miles down the road. Gabriel went mechanically through the motions of getting his little caravan back on the road, but his mind was elsewhere. It seemed only a moment passed between snapping the ribbons against the wagon horse's rump to Moïse calling from behind to pull up. Gabriel reined in the horse and looked back. The priest was climbing down off Moïse's buggy. Riel climbed off the wagon seat to say good-bye. The priest came forward, but Gabriel could see that Riel's eyes weren't on the priest at all, they were riveted above the cassocked shoulder.

Gabriel followed the line of Riel's gaze to a little hill crowned by a lightning-blasted tree. Riel took hold of the priest's arm and said: "I see a gallows on that hill, Father, and I am hanging from it."

When they were under way again, Gabriel went back to grappling with the strange new notion he'd caught from Riel at the altar rail. He wasn't too concerned with Riel's vision of the gallows. Visions weren't all that uncommon among the people he'd lived with all his life. Old Ahsiweyin alone had seen death visions at least a dozen times and squatted on a hilltop to sing his death song until he got tired of waiting. Gabriel didn't dispute the existence of visions, he just figured that they didn't always mean what they seemed to mean. They usually only made sense after the thing they were foretelling had happened, so what was the point of getting all agitated about them?

Riel's prayer had introduced him to a new vision of religion. Gabriel had never been a particularly religious or irreligious man. The medicine ways of his grandmother's people and the Christian ways of his grandfather's had both convinced him that the earth and the trees and the wild creatures with four legs or two were all imbued with and influenced by unseen forces beyond his understanding. Since they were beyond his understanding, then by definition the only way he could approach them was to dutifully perform and respect the required rituals and leave it at that. He had long ago accepted the fact that he was one of those born gifted with a power to effect events within the limited world of what he could see, hear, taste, smell, and touch, but anything beyond that was beyond him. The way Louis Riel had spoken to God at the altar rail had made Gabriel consider the possibility that even an ignorant old buffalo hunter could touch what was beyond his perceptions simply by saying what was in his heart.

He went along twitching the reins when necessary and abstractedly clucking out of the side of his mouth in the way one talked to horses. A light rain was coming down—not enough to mire the road, but Gabriel smelled lightning and he'd already decided they'd make an early camp below that ridge of wooded ground a few miles ahead. Marguerite was singing to Marie Angelique and Jean in the back of the wagon, leaving Gabriel and Riel alone on the wagon seat. Gabriel glanced back over his shoulder to make sure no one was listening, coughed to clear his suddenly constricted throat, and said: "You know, uh . . . you know that prayer you said when the priest was blessing us? . . ."

Riel nodded warily.

"Well . . . well, you see, it made me think that maybe I ought to make up a little something of my own to say, to thank God for the blessing. So . . . I been thinking, and I think maybe I thought of something."

"What is it?"

"Well—" He had to clear his throat again. "I thought maybe the kind of thing I oughta say should be something kind of like . . . 'Lord, strengthen my courage and my faith and my honor, that I might profit in my life from this blessing I received in Thy Holy Name.' " Gabriel closed his mouth and squeezed some moisture back into it from behind his back teeth. He could feel his cheeks growing warm under his beard. He resisted the impulse to glance sideways at Riel, keeping his eyes trained instead on the road through the sights of the horse's ears.

There was no sound but the jingle of harness, the clop of hooves, and the coarse grinding of the wheels. Then Riel said: "What a blessing it would be if priests and bishops could learn to pray like my uncle Gabriel."

CHAPTER 7

 Madelaine was helping Annie back the gray pony in between the cart shafts when a whooping came down the trail and the entire Dumont clan broke over the ridge in a procession of painted wagons and beribboned whip stocks and rearing outriders. Grizzled Isidor led the parade with Gabriel's two younger brothers trotting alongside, the three of them empirical proof of the unlikely proposition that Gabriel was the runt of the litter. Behind them came their sisters and brothers-in-law and their families and the numerous descendants of their uncle Jean, who shared the front wagon seat with old Aicawpow himself—both of them pushing eighty and still as straight and tall as a couple of old burl oaks. The second wagon was filled with Gabriel's half-brothers and -sisters and the woman half Aicawpow's age that he'd married after Gabriel's mother died. Aicawpow's Christian name was Isidor, but once his first son had grown big enough to follow him around he'd reverted to the name the Cree had given him: "He Stands."

About the only Dumonts missing, besides Gabriel, were a sister who was married to a trader up around Frog Lake and Gabriel's uncle Gabriel, who'd long since disappeared into the Rocky Mountains after the toll of broken bones and funerals from his drinking bouts rose above even the anarchic standards of the old days on the plains. When Madelaine had been struggling through the first few years of her marriage, Aicawpow used to shake his head and sigh that it was his own most grievous damned fault for naming his second son after his crazy brother.

But Madelaine had known all along that it was that trait of spontaneous explosion that had made her husband the acknowledged War Chief of all *les sauvages* by the time he'd grown his first real beard. The deeper aspects of a Chief had come with time and maturity and with—Madelaine liked to flatter herself—

a wife who had the nerve to rub his nose in the occasions when he didn't live up to himself.

Isidor leaned down out of his saddle to kiss her and Annie as he rode by. They climbed on board the cart and stood watching the parade go by, waving and trading greetings. Gabriel's sister Isabelle Ouellette was at the tail end of the line, driving a wagon crammed with little copies of Moïse. She rolled her eyes at Madelaine, lolled her tongue out, and let out a sigh like a desert-lost moose smelling a lake just over the next sand dune. Madelaine laughed and nodded, then snapped the reins against the gray pony's twitching rump to fall in behind.

The cavalcade of Dumonts rolled south along the east bank of the river. Outriders dropped back to trot along beside a carriage and trade jokes; wagon passengers jumped down to clamber up on the next vehicle in line and exchange gossip. As they passed by other farms, another cart or a wagon would fall into line, loaded down with a family decked out in their brightest sashes and shawls and vests so encrusted with beadwork and embroidery that the deerhide barely showed. It was a bigger holiday than St. Joseph's Day—the delegation bringing Louis Riel from Montana was due to arrive today.

The trail they were traveling along was more like an extended village street. As each cluster of farm buildings dropped behind, another appeared ahead. Madelaine had never been able to understand how the government could fail to understand that strip farms running back from the river meant there was always a neighbor within hailing distance but far enough away that you could keep yourself to yourself when you wanted to. All the government had to do to satisfy the métis along the South Saskatchewan was to survey the plots of land that Gabriel and Father André had roughed out fifteen years ago. But the government liked its maps in neat square-mile sections with the squares divided into smaller squares.

The caravan ground to a halt at Tourond's farm where several hundred of their neighbors were already gathered. Several generations of Tourounds were engaged in basting and turning two spitted oxen. Madelaine and Annie and the rest of the Dumonts climbed down and unloaded their contributions to the feast, the women bearing berry or meat pies and platters of dumplings, the men kegs of hop beer and crocks of homemade wine. Madelaine was in the process of trying to create some order on the haphazard archipelago of trestle tables when she saw Isidor jump onto a wagon seat and peer south with one hand shading his eyes. Madelaine turned to look south.

Above the trees crowded into Tourond's Coulee, a thin feather of dust showed where a horseman was galloping hard up the road from Clarke's Crossing. The dust plume dissipated as the rider reached the wooded ground and went down into the coulee. A moment later, Madelaine heard the sound of hooves coming up the other side, and Michel Dumas burst into the open, waving his hat and whooping. He reared his horse to a halt and basked in the cheering and embracing for as long as he could draw it out, then announced that Monsieur Riel and the rest of his escort were following close on his heels. There was much smoothing of skirts and slicking down of children's cowlicks. It seemed like a long time to Madelaine that they all stood there stiffly facing the place where the trail emerged from Tourond's Coulee. She heard the demonic squeal of a Red River cart. A weary-looking horse dragged a wagon up through the mouth of the road. There were two bearded men on the wagon seat. Madelaine was aware that the second man was the center of focus for every other pair of eyes at Tourond's farm, but to her he was just part of the landscape around Gabriel.

Gabriel reined in the horse, jumped off the wagon, and walked toward her with that awkwardly surefooted, moccasined horseman's gait that, to her, was the natural way a man should walk. He stopped a few feet in front of her, black eye slits flaring in that sledgehammered boulder of a face. "Well, there you are, old woman. Did you miss me?"

"Once or twice. I'm getting sick and tired of chopping my own firewood."

Any further conversation was drowned at birth by a wave of cheers and shouts and crashing *feux de joie* as all the men in the crowd fired their guns into the air. The man Gabriel had left on the wagon seat rose to his feet. Gabriel shifted his feet around to take up a position beside her, one scalding arm settling around her waist.

Madelaine turned her attention to Louis Riel. He was larger than she'd expected—about halfway between Gabriel and his monstrous brothers, but without the Dumonts' kiln-baked tautness. He raised his arm to quell the waves crashing against him and said in a voice that was compellingly soft-edged but overpoweringly resonant: "My friends, it has been . . . so many years. . . ." He stopped and bit his lip and blinked the dampness in the gray eyes to a silver sheen. "To be given such a welcome, after so many years away and alone . . . May the Spirit of God and the Holy Virgin Mary and Saint Joseph bless you, as you have blessed and refreshed me with your kindness. Many of you are old friends from long ago. I hope to learn to know the rest of you as well, in the short time I have to spend among you."

They cheered again. Those with repeating rifles fired off their guns again. He climbed down off the wagon and they mobbed him, except for Gabriel and Madelaine, who went over to the oxen sizzling over the beds of coals and carved off a few blood-bubbling slabs. Madelaine said: "How'd the trip go?"

"*Hmmph*—not bad—*shlrf*—hoo! Hot. *Whoof.* Hot but good. We got stalled up for a few days on the way back when the little ones got sick. Some kind of fever. Wished you was there—I ain't much good at that sort of thing."

"That the only time you missed me?"

"No—there was the time my moccasins wore out and I didn't have no one to chew up moosehide for a new pair. And every morning when I had to make my own goddamned tea. Oh, and it seems all the mares we took along is pregnant." His hands and his eyes took hold of hers. "I've heard some crazy god-damned questions in my time, old woman, but that one beats them all."

A grizzly bear reared up roaring behind him, and Gabriel turned to deal with his big brother and the two rampant black bears behind him. All four Dumont boys bore down on the job of demolishing a cartload of roast ox and tourtières, guzzling beer and guffawing between bites. Then Isidor hauled out his fiddle and turned the Touronds' barnyard into a dance floor. Annie and Michel Dumas jigged themselves giddy. Madelaine kept an eye out to make sure that was all they did. But all of it was just the surface of a flowing stream from which she speared out bright flickers like "Two months hasn't straightened his nose any" and "Sure enough, there he goes leaning his head to the right when someone's telling him a story, just like I remem-bered."

Gabriel let out a satiated sigh, rubbed the beef blood off his beard into his sleeve, and said: "Looks like they got a little breathing space now."

"Who?"

"Who? The Riels. You been dreaming, old woman?"

"For a couple months now."

He took hold of her hand and led her around the dance floor toward the man who a lot of the métis nation regarded as the next thing to a saint. She was just moistening her mouth to say, "*Bonjour*," when someone else loomed up between them—a huge lump of a man with a nose like a frost-killed potato and a right eye set lower than the left. Riel's beneficent expression turned glowering. Although Madelaine hadn't been near Red River in 1870, she'd heard the stories of how Charles Nolin had done his best to undercut Riel and his provisional government.

Nolin made an abortive attempt at extending his hand to Riel, then just stood shambling from one foot to the other. Gabriel stepped in between them and said to Riel: "Nolin's changed his way of thinking since those days. He's been working just as hard as anybody to get our rights out of the government. Matter of fact, there's a couple of times I been hard put to it to keep him from loading up his gun and riding down to Regina to have words with the lieutenant governor."

Riel composed his features and held out his hand. Nolin shook it eagerly and said: "When I moved out here from Red River I built a big house, with more rooms than my family can fill up. . . ."

"That's true," Gabriel put in. "Bigger'n anybody's except old 'Batoche' hisself."

"Me and my family would be honored, Cousin Louis, if you and your family would live in our house with us while you're here."

Riel looked Nolin in the eyes—or "eye," rather—and said: "We would be honored to accept your gracious hospitality, Cousin Charles." Nolin beamed all over, the gargoyle folds over the bridge of his nose disappearing into laugh lines.

When Nolin had moved on, Gabriel stepped back and brought Madelaine forward. "Louis Riel, my wife, Madelaine." Two big, soft hands came out and took hold of hers. There was no question that Riel was what some women would call a handsome man. Seen up close, it seemed to her that the gray eyes held a trace of something hiding behind them, something that resembled a child whipped for an offense he didn't understand.

"Madame Dumont, it is a great pleasure to meet you at last. You must be very proud to have a husband like my uncle Gabriel."

It threw her off. Over the years she'd heard her husband referred to as "Uncle Gabriel" by anyone from scar-faced buffalo hunters to shy-eyed Cree girls. But for some reason the phrase seemed incongruous coming from Riel, and a bit annoying. Before she could begin to wonder why, she was being introduced to Marguerite and their beautiful children.

When the oxen had been gnawed clean and the light had begun to turn amber, the Dumonts and the other clans gathered at Tourond's farm climbed back onto their horses and wagons to retrace their parade route in a more subdued fashion. The sun hadn't touched the horizon yet, but on the northern angle of the South Saskatchewan July sunsets came late in the night. Annie took charge of the cart while Madelaine rode with Gabriel and the Riels in the wagon. The Riels were to spend the night at Gabriel's Crossing before proceeding to Batoche's Crossing and another, larger welcoming celebration. A good portion of the young single folk chose to stay over as well, roistering in tents pitched in the poplar grove behind the barn.

Madelaine got the Riels settled in in the room above the billiard table. She came downstairs to find Gabriel refilling the government-stamped keg with American rum, setting the empty bottles aside for the old Scotchman downriver. She stood leaning her rump against the rim of the billiard table, watching him pouring and chortling and humming "The Star-Spangled Banner," pausing occasionally to lick his fingers. He sloshed the tail end of the last bottle into two cups and came toward her.

After they'd clinked cups and taken the first belly-warming sip, he stepped back to set his cup on a shelf and then lumbered forward with his arms held out, sighing: "It's good to be home." She stepped into his arms, but they swerved around her and he went right past. He jerked the cover off the billiard table, rubbed his hands together, and reached for a cue.

She kicked him in the ass and he turned around and grabbed a double handful of hers, lifting her up despite her squeals that he'd break his back, snuffling his spiky beard into the hollow of her throat. Shushing each other and giggling, they tiptoed out from under the Riels and down the passage to the bed, where both of them were home at last.

She was whistling in the kitchen in the morning, rattling together breakfast while Marguerite Riel drank tea. Marguerite had offered to help, but after all the years it had taken to break in Annie, Madelaine wasn't about to have someone else obstructing her kitchen. Annie had been dispatched to the garden to pull enough new potatoes to flesh out the morning's crop of eggs, the remnants of last fall's sausage making, and the pans of biscuits crisping in the slot under the hearth.

Marguerite clinked down her teacup—part of the delicate delft service that had made its way across an ocean and half a continent packed in barrels of straw—and said: "She's a lovely girl."

"Girl?"

"Annie."

The age difference was three years at most. Madelaine chose to let it pass and carried on pounding flour and water together with leathery strips of gooseberry preserves.

"You must be very proud of her. I only hope Marie Angelique grows up that strong and healthy. And the resemblance is so obvious—well, not to yourself so much as to Uncle Gabriel. Not in her features, of course, but then you'd hardly want that in a girl. Not that Uncle Gabriel isn't a handsome man in his own way . . . But you can see it in the way she moves, and the way she says things sometimes."

Resisting the impulse to lean across the table and relocate Marguerite's pretty jaw, Madelaine said: "Annie isn't our daughter. When she was barely more than a baby, Gabriel found her mother froze to death and brought Annie home to look after until someone else could be found to take her. The only 'else' we could find was the mission orphan school, so . . ."

"I'm sure the holy sisters would have . . . Oh, hello, Annie."

Annie was standing in the doorway with the front of her skirt bunched up to basket the potatoes and to show her smooth legs to the young men folding up their tents behind the barn. She paused for an instant with the sun behind her, obviously aware that the conversation had just come to an abrupt halt, then came in and reached down the delft platter to dump the potatoes on.

Madelaine felt a twinge of guilt seeing Marguerite Riel staring wistfully at the blue-etched example of the Dumonts' wealth. Not that she and Gabriel would seem rich to people from the east, but in the world Madelaine had grown up in, wealth was measured by how much you could afford to give away. Poor Marguerite's wistful stare, though, didn't alter the fact that she had just offhandedly tossed Madelaine back into a habit she'd fought hard to cure herself of: watching Annie surreptitiously for any gesture or expression or feature that could be definitely defined as inherited.

CHAPTER 8

The morning after the welcoming fete at Batoche's Crossing, Gabriel woke up pleasantly surprised to find his wife warming the bed beside him. Not that he'd expected anyone else to be there, but it was going to take more than two nights to take for granted that he wouldn't wake up alone in the middle of the plains. He heaved his aged bones out of bed as quietly as possible, made a pot of tea, and carried a cup outside. He hunkered down in the dawn light with his back against the front wall of his house, manhandling the rusty hinges of his knees into a cross-legged position, and lit his pipe—once the dogs had been persuaded that he didn't need them to lick the sleep out of his eyes.

It felt like someone had finally unbuckled a cinch strap around his chest. Riel could wear it now. Until it had become possible to hand on the privilege, Gabriel hadn't realized how sick and tired he was of leading people. It was flattering when he was young to turn around to take a breather from whatever task he'd taken on and find a hundred men doing their best to imitate him—"Like this, Gabriel?" But somewhere along the line he'd started wishing that other people would just tend their own gardens and leave him to tend his.

Riel would have to be escorted around to the various public meetings—and decidedly unpublic ones—that would have to happen before he could begin the job of cementing all the disparate grievances into one petition. After two months of eating hoof dust, Gabriel figured escorting him was someone else's turn.

That patch of the barn roof definitely needed reshingling. If the clump of saw grass by his knee was anything to go by, it was high time for the first haying. Since he didn't have to row the ferry anymore, there might even be time to finish painting the front of the house.

Madelaine came out the front door with a shawl over her shoulders that didn't stop the backlight of the sun from turning the skirt of her nightdress into misty cheesecloth. Rolling his head back to look made his neck feel as boneless as if there were an empty bottle rolling between his feet. He said: "Sun's been up a long time before you. First sign of old age."

"Not at all. Old people don't hardly sleep at all. I been counting off the days till you got back—there's a skunk that's got in under the henhouse."

"You're as good a shot as most men."

"When it comes to crawling under the chicken coop to shoot skunks in the dark, you want better-than-average shooting. If you just been bragging all these years, I don't mind you sleeping in the smokehouse a couple nights."

"That ain't what you said last night."

"Maybe you was dreaming."

"Maybe it felt like I must be."

"Maybe it did to me, too, old man."

He settled into a summer like any other: fattening up the piglets and pullets for the fall, stringing float lines into the river for whitefish, winning a few dollars on horse races, mending harness and extending the line of split firewood stacked against the wall of the house. In the evenings, one of his brothers or a couple of the neighbors would wander by and they would play billiards and tell each other the news while Madelaine and Annie harassed them from the sidelines. It seemed there had been trouble up at Poundmaker's thirst dance, but Crozier had succeeded in dampening it out. The word on Riel was that he was playing it very smart and soft, alleviating the fears of those white Protestants who'd been told he was a Catholic firebrand. One Orangeman at Prince Albert had tried to turn Riel's audience into a lynch mob, but the Police had ejected him. All in all, the odds seemed good that Gabriel was going to be allowed to carry on with the business of living and let the larger events take care of themselves.

He was working in the woodlot one afternoon with an axe and a saw and a team of workhorses hitched to a drag chain. A woodlot had to be tended like a garden. Good deadfalls had to be dragged out before they started to rot. Trees had to be pruned off if they were interfering with the maturing of others. It was a pleasant change to be working in the dank hush of the woods, with the chickadees twittering between whacks of his axe, but at the moment he wasn't in a pleasant mood. A big birch tree whose time had come had fallen with its head in a tangle of willows, and no matter how many branches he trimmed off it refused to come loose. It was a damned fine tree, too—one more trunk this size and he'd have enough to make a wagonload to haul down to the sawmill at Prince Albert to get turned into planks for the extension to the stables.

He had just thrown down his axe and was trying to wrestle the trunk loose by main force when the back end of the log grew weightless and lifted itself into the air. Gabriel looked back over his shoulder and found a grizzly bear in calico and corduroy holding the other end. With Isidor to help, it broke free in a moment. Gabriel let his end drop and went to fetch the team with the chain jingling behind. It gave him a chance to catch his breath so that Isidor wouldn't hear the gasping in his voice. Isidor said: ''Damned lucky for you I came by.''

''I would've worked it loose sooner or later.''

''Maybe by Christmas.''

''Just passing by?''

''I'm running short of fresh meat, and it seems a waste to kill a half-grown steer, so I figured I'd take a few days in the Touchwood Hills and get some venison. Figured I might as well stop by here on the way. Lucky for you.''

''I just about had it free.''

''You just about had a heart attack.''

By that time, they had the chain secured. Gabriel took hold of the leads and led the team back through the bush with Isidor sauntering along beside. As they broke out into the sunlight, Gabriel said: ''That ain't a bad idea, you know. I'm getting tired of the taste of farm animals.''

''Want me to bring you back a buck?''

''Hah! The day I trust you to do my hunting for me . . . Bet that's what you was hoping for all along—if you could wheedle me into coming with you, you wouldn't have to rely on your feeble excuse for shooting.''

''Yeah, you always hit what you aim for—because that sawn-off little gun of yours ain't worth aiming at anything farther'n ten feet.''

''A carbine in the right hands has got as much range as any overstretched cannon.''

''Which hands are those?''

Madelaine was sitting in front of the house plucking a chicken, dropping the feathers into a sack to save for mattress stuffing. Gabriel said: "Isidor's heading over to the Touchwood Hills to shoot some venison. Why don't we take a few days and go with him?" She looked back over her shoulder at the raggedy border where the blue paint over the whitewash came to an end. "I can get to that when we get back."

"I thought you'd done enough traveling for the summer."

"This ain't 'traveling'—just a hunting trip. And if you came along, I wouldn't miss you."

"We can't leave Annie to look after the whole place on her own."

"Oh, by the way," Isidor put in, "did I mention Michel Dumas's coming along? He's already started out, planning to meet up with me there."

Madelaine said: "I won't do no skinning—I had enough of that in the buffalo hunt days."

"Fair deal. Isidor does all the skinning."

"Bet your ass I will. If you think I'd trust you hacking my bucks to pieces with that feeble excuse for a knife . . ."

Isidor stayed overnight so they could pack together all the comforts of a home out on the plains and load them onto the wagon and so that Madelaine could remember all the things Annie had to be reminded to take care of while they were gone. They set off just after dawn, cutting southeast across the Great Salt Plain, where a tree taller than a man was rare and the ponds were rimmed with a sickly white alkali crust. The sloughs were alive with ducks, but it would be a waste to shoot them at this time of the year when the young ones were only half-grown. It had been a dry summer; more than once they came upon a duck frantically herding her brood into a puddle that had been a good-size pond when she'd arrived in the spring.

Gabriel spotted a few antelope in the distance. They were by far the fastest animals on the plains and used to be the easiest to hunt. In the old days, anyone with a stick and a handkerchief and enough patience could just plant himself in the grass within sight of a herd and wait for them to wander over to investigate. These days, the few antelope left were the ones who'd inherited the most speed and the least curiosity.

On the far side of the Great Salt Plain was the Touchwood Hills, where the subtle folds and waves of the surrounding prairie suddenly thrust up into convoluted crests and ridges sheltering wooded hollows where mule deer and whitetails liked to gather. Michel Dumas was waiting for them at a campsite they'd been using on and off for twenty years—with increasing frequency as the deer along the South Saskatchewan got hunted out.

Madelaine managed to get the tipi erected, after Gabriel'd made the mistake of trying to help her, and by nightfall they were settled in comfortably and he was watching the play of the flamelight on Madelaine's majestic features. It had been too long since he and she had lain down with only a buffalo robe between them and the ground, to watch the herds of stars graze their way across the smokehole at the crown of the tent.

At dawn he left her to go padding down deer trails with Michel Dumas and Isidor. This first hunt was more of a scouting expedition, to get a notion of how many deer were in the area and what their habits were. At dusk they picked their spot and waited. After an hour or so, Gabriel thought he heard something, then was sure he heard something. He strained his eyes into the gathering gloom with the little hairs on the backs of his hands dancing. But Isidor, damn his eyes, fired first and brought down a fine young buck. It wasn't even twitching—taken straight through the heart. Gabriel said: "Lucky shot."

"It would've been if it had come from that short little gun of yours."

They spent three days gorging themselves on fresh venison, staking out hides and scraping them dry, slicing meat into strips and hanging it on willow racks to dry in the sun, tending smudge fires to keep off the flies, bathing in the little river flowing past the campsite, roaming farther afield on their twilight expeditions as the deer in the area got the message. Gabriel would have been quite happy to spend the rest of the summer there, but Annie couldn't be expected to carry the whole place at Gabriel's Crossing on her own, and Isidor had a family to get back to. Michel Dumas had no responsibilities, but he could only go so long without someone to flirt with who was less intimidating than Madelaine.

On the way home, Gabriel found himself reflecting on the ways he'd passed the time since coming back from Montana—the same ways all the other métis families were passing their summers. It was a sweet life that had been won by generations of battling out a place for themselves and learning the ways of a beautiful country that could find a dozen ways to kill you before breakfast. The country was bound to change as more white settlers came in, but they'd adapted to change before. All they were asking from the government was a few pieces of paper that would guarantee they could keep on living where they'd always lived and that their sweet life couldn't be snatched away from them by a stroke of a pen two thousand miles away. It didn't seem like much to ask. He told himself that that was Riel's problem now and went back to thinking about the bits of repair and maintenance he had to get to before harvest time.

He'd only been back two days when Riel came to Gabriel's Crossing in an incandescent lather. Gabriel was playing billiards with little Phillipe Garnot—who had taken an hour away from his farm and his ferry and his inn at Batoche's Crossing to help Gabriel keep his beer from going sour in the barrel. The dogs set up a clamor, and two sets of hoofbeats trotted into the yard, along with a male voice offering up a detailed description of Cree dog feasts—Moïse Ouellette.

Riel burst through the doorway and announced: "Hector Langevin is coming!"

Gabriel looked from Riel to Phillipe Garnot to Moïse hovering behind Riel's shoulder, hoping for some elucidation. He said dubiously: "The Langevin in Ottawa? Some kind of councillor with the government? . . ."

Riel nodded. Madelaine said: "The Minister of Public Works."

Riel said: "That's his official title, but he's much more than that behind the scenes."

"Back home in Quebec," Phillipe Garnot said, "Hector Langevin *is* the Conservative party. If Langevin didn't deliver Quebec, John A. Macdonald wouldn't ever be in power."

"Exactly!" Riel grinned. "And he's coming here! He's on a tour of inspection of the North West Territories, and his itinerary puts him in Batoche sometime next week. That doesn't give me enough time to write the final version of our petition—even if there weren't some groups I've yet to consult—but I can draft a preliminary document outlining the major grievances that have to be remedied, introducing the simple solution of granting the North West Territories provincial status—'until the people of the North West are accorded their democratic rights to a voice in Parliament,' perhaps 'their democratic rights as British citizens . . .' " He trailed off as Madelaine poured out two cups of tea and offered to spice them with a sprinkle of rum. Riel shook his head automatically and accepted the tea. He turned to Gabriel and said: "Don't you see? I can hand it to him face to face, not merely another anonymous document the postman shovels onto his desk. I *know* Hector Langevin, and he knows me."

Gabriel said, "Ah!" and nodded to show he understood. He might not understand much about Ministries of Public Works, but he sure as hell knew the difference between dealing with a Chief as simply a functionary performing his Chief's role and dealing with a man you knew who also happened to be a Chief.

"He was a good friend to me," Riel continued, "when I was in the east. He did all he could to make John A. Macdonald live up to the promises he'd made me."

Gabriel started to say: "Back in the days when . . ." and then hauled back hard.

"Yes." The gray eyes stayed directly on his, although they softened, as did the voice. "Back in the days when I was tumbling through the long descent into the asylum. The truth is the truth, Uncle Gabriel. I know it's difficult to understand for a man like you, who has always looked directly into the face of whatever is coming at him and stood up to it. I find it difficult enough to understand, looking back on myself. . . . But in those years—promised an amnesty but hounded out of the country; running from one charitable friend to another, with Macdonald's agents lurking around every corner; legally elected to a seat among the lawmakers of the dominion but kept out by a lawless mob . . ." His teeth clacked together and his head snapped sideways, rebounding into an apologetic shrug of shoulders and eyebrows and mustache. "Perhaps a stronger man would have . . .

"But!" The gray eyes flared ablaze again, and he slapped the back of his right hand into the palm of his left. "But how is any man to hold on to what is real when the lieutenant governor of the province which that man created shakes him by the hand for saving that province from foreign invasion but will not speak to that man by name, when every newspaper and dispatch thanks 'that man,' although they know full well who 'that man' is but his name can't be spoken or written because he isn't officially allowed to be in the country that he is being thanked for being in and saving for the very government that . . ." The chestnut-furred lips suddenly skinned back to show his back teeth, and the eyes bugged wide, exactly as though his mouth held an invisible bit. He hunched forward with a shudder of terror and looked back over his shoulder, then wrenched himself upright and said composedly: ''But I was cured by the grace of God. Cured . . . It isn't like a broken arm that mends. No matter how much time elapses, there is always the fear that . . . That's why I hesitated when you appeared in Montana. I was afraid that if I thrust myself back into the world of politics and the rights of nations, I would be thrusting myself back into madness. And now''—his face broke into a beatific smile, and he put his hands on Gabriel's shoulders—''Hector Langevin is coming. Despite my fears and yours, God has arranged that I should be here at this time and that all will be resolved in good time for me to return home safely in the fall.''

The next day Gabriel rode around to collect Michel Dumas and a rotation of young men to keep a watch on the roads north from Regina and Fort Qu'Appelle. Hector Langevin was just as likely to choose either stop on the rail line to shunt his private car onto a siding and climb into a carriage for the ride up to Batoche's Crossing. Gabriel wanted plenty of warning for Riel scribbling away in the back room at Nolin's house.

The week passed, and half another. Gabriel was just about to pry the lid off the tin of blue paint when Michel Dumas rode into the yard. Gabriel threw down the paintbrush and grabbed the bridle of Michel's horse. ''You seen him?''

The blue eyes glared out from between the dust-caked eyelids with a surly glint. ''I seen an ox-skinner hauling a load of salt fish up from Qu'Appelle. He told me the Honorable Hector Langevin took one look at what we call 'roads' out here in the territories and decided he'd keep his tour of inspection to the places along the railroad.''

CHAPTER 9

Dressed in her best blue-black silk dress, Madelaine carried the scissors and a kitchen chair outside and called for Gabriel. He came over from hitching up the wagon and sat down obediently while she draped an old sheet over his Sunday suit and went to work on the raggedy edges of his hair and beard. He didn't speak, just sat stiff-shouldered, staring straight ahead. He hadn't said more than a grunt all morning. "Who are you wrestling, old man?"

"Hm?"

"In your head."

"No one. You know they want me to make a speech today. . . ." He trailed off with a shrug, as though that explained it.

"You don't usually worry at those kinds of bones, you just crunch them up and get it over with."

"Maybe this one's different."

"What are you going to say?"

"Maybe some things as should've been said some time ago."

She left him alone with his ponderations and stepped back to get a look at her handiwork. She decided that he looked as civilized as he was ever likely to and called to Annie that it was time to go. The new church at Batoche's Crossing had finally been completed, and the bishop was coming to bless the bell. Annie was all aflutter, and to tell the truth, so was she. They didn't get many bishops passing through.

Gabriel was still ruminating as he clucked the team along, so she turned her attention to watching the countryside roll by. The riffling, silvery poplars were speckled with gold, although it should have been too early for the leaves to start to turn. That brought back a memory of something that had happened in the night. She'd been brought awake for a moment by the distant bugling of geese flying over Gabriel's Crossing. It must have been a dream.

Gabriel said: "Better start stoking up the smokehouse and dusting out the plucking tubs. Few more days and me and Isidor'll take down the shotguns and go visiting the sloughs."

"It's too soon."

"Should be, but it ain't."

The fact that he'd suddenly chosen to mention the geese when they were passing through her mind didn't throw her off at all. She'd long ago given up trying to explain how they could hear each other thinking.

The church of St. Antoine de Padua had been built on a corner of the prairie plateau. Beside the rectory and the cemetery, the earth dropped away in the sheer cliff carved out by the river.

Behind the church was a long slope down to the flats and the little village that had grown up around Batoche's Crossing. The church was gleaming with just-dried whitewash. The walls were built of squared logs trimmed and joined so neatly that they looked like clapboard. The churchyard and surrounding meadow were filled with gaudy-harnessed horses and gaudily painted wagons and even gaudier parishioners. The staid black dresses and Sunday suits only served to set off the embroidered waistcoats, bright shawls, rainbow-woven sashes, and, here and there, a beaded headband or bone necklace. But they all paled when the bishop in full regalia stepped out into the sunlight.

When the bishop had performed the reverently joyous ceremony of blessing the bell, Gabriel and Isidor and every other man who could find hand space on the rope hauled the bell up by a pulley fixed to the mushroom-shaped bell tower high above the church door. The master carpenter, standing balanced on the peak of the roof, maneuvered it into place, fixed the bell pull, and then got the hell out of the way as the first notes pealed out in a voice that must have raised the hackles on the wolves at Duck Lake.

The congregation followed the bishop inside and crowded onto the new carved pews, filling all the standing space along the walls. Since the bishop's traveling companion was the secretary of the North West Council—the figurehead committee appointed from Ottawa to oversee minor matters in the territories—it was both a sacred and a secular occasion. A number of prominent citizens had been asked to speak. The first was Gabriel Dumont.

From her seat in the pew behind the holy sisters from the convent school across the river, who were behind the bishop and secretary and the parish priests, Madelaine watched Gabriel climb up onto the dais. She was quite sure that no one else could tell from his movements that his knees were annoying him again. He turned to face the congregation or, rather, to specifically face the bishop and the other occupants of the front pew. She was close enough to see the little down-and-forward hitch of Gabriel's beard as he unhinged his jaw to turn his head and chest into an open resonating chamber, a trick he'd picked up when he'd first started learning how to give orders to five hundred buffalo hunters at once. She was suddenly alarmed at what he might have taken it in mind to say.

He fixed his eyes on the bishop, and out it came, in that rolling

bass that hummed in the farthest peak of the rafters and vibrated
the solar plexus as much as the eardrums: ''Since the days when
Bishop Provencher first brought missionaries west . . .'' Madelaine automatically crossed herself in the great man's memory.
''Since Mister Grant built the first church west of the Red . . .
since back before even old dogs like me were born . . . the
Church has always stood up with the métis nation.'' The heads
of the priests in front of Madelaine nodded graciously.

''When this country belonged to the Hudson's Bay Company, the Church stood up with us against the Company's mo-
nopoly. When the Sioux tried to rub us out at Le Grand Coteau,
Father Laflêche stood up on a cart in the middle of the circle
and prayed for us—with an axe in his hand in case the Sioux
broke through. When the Canadians bought the country and
tried to trample across the people at Red River, the Church stood
up with Louis Riel and the provisional government. When we
had to make our own government and laws here, before the
Police came, the Church stood up with us and helped us and
advised us.

''But now, when we are trying to stand up against a far-off
government that wants to plow us under the prairie—like we
were weeds they planted to break up the soil—where is the
Church? Everyone else in the North West—the white farmers,
the Protestant half-breeds, our cousins on the reserves—we're
all standing up together, but the Church does nothing and says
nothing. Every meeting we ever hold, we always tell the priests
when and where it's going to be, and ask the priests to come
and listen and advise us. But they never do.

''I think the Church must be misunderstanding what it is
we're trying to do. How can there be anything but misunder-
standings when there's nothing to go on but guesses and silence?
I know some métis are guessing that the only reason the Church
ever stood up with us in the past was to hold back the white
Protestants from Ontario until our homes could be stolen instead
by white Catholics from Quebec. I'm sure they must be guessing
wrong, but it's hard to tell them so when the Church says nothing
to us and hears nothing of what we have to say.

''We all of us grew up with a strong faith in God and His
Church. Anything you might have to say about the troubles we're
in now, we'll listen to you like we always have.''

He jumped down off the dais, padded back up the aisle, and
thumped down onto the pew beside Madelaine. No bolt of light-

ning came through the roof. No priest stood up to thunder con-
demnation. But Madelaine heard the speeches that followed
Gabriel's as a wash of sound that only varied with the exchange
of a baritone for a tenor.

It was a subdued crowd that filed back out into the churchyard—not to the point of being morose or hushed, but the good-
byes weren't nearly as extended as they should have been after
such a joyous occasion. Madelaine walked to the edge of the
ridge and stood alone, with her arms crossed under her breasts,
looking down at the village on the flats. There was a scattering
of houses and gardens dominated by the big, green-and-white
verandaed home of "Batoche" Letendre, and then the little row
of businesses facing the north side of the Carlton Trail for the
last hundred yards before the ferry—two general stores, the
blacksmith's shop, Phillipe Garnot's stopping place, and the shell
of the big false-fronted store that "Batoche" Letendre was
building to catch all westbound traffic before it reached the two
stores down the road. The town turned red as the sun sinking
behind it threw up flares of flame and fountains of blood at the
peak of the sky.

Gabriel came up behind her and said: "Yep, we don't get
many good old barn burners of sunsets anymore. We can watch
it from the wagon on the way home."

"Have things really come to such a pass?"

"What a pass?"

"That you should have to say such things in public to a bishop
and old Father André?"

"Maybe if they don't get up off their cassocks pretty damned
soon, things are gonna come to a lot worse pass."

They had barely got out of their Sunday clothes when Riel
arrived at Gabriel's Crossing. He'd written up two copies of the
current version of his petition, for Gabriel to take over to a
neighboring farm where the bishop and the secretary were stopping overnight. Gabriel saddled up Starface and left Madelaine
and Annie alone with Riel.

She made a pot of tea and carried it into the billiard house.
Any other man along the South Saskatchewan would have taken
the opportunity to pick up a cue and practice his bank shots, but
Riel sat sipping tea and making conversation. As she was filling
up his cup again, he said: "Do you know Charles Nolin well?"

The image of the shambling giant with the potato nose and

misaligned eyes loomed up in Madelaine's mind. "Pretty well,` I suppose. I ain't ever been married to him."

"Would you say he was a . . . trustworthy man?"

"Lots of women'd say there ain't such a thing."

The gray eyes bugged out as though the fireplace had exploded. Then he threw back his head and laughed, slapping his leg and wiping the corners of his eyes. "Madame Dumont—or Madelaine, if I might say . . . I suppose I should have expected as much from the wife of Gabriel Dumont, but you do surprise me. I must remember to tell my wife. Or, then again . . ."

The dogs announced a horse coming into the yard. Michel Dumas appeared in the doorway, dust-caked and smelling of horse sweat, although it appeared that he'd paused at the horse trough to make sure there wasn't so much dirt on his face as to dull the effect of his bright blue eyes. He said: "Gabriel about?"

"He should be back soon. You missed the opening of the church."

"I know. I had something I had to do for Gabriel."

"What was that?"

"Boy, my throat ain't felt so dusty since . . ."

Madelaine tossed him a cup and pointed at the current beer barrel. Even though he'd only been around the South Saskatchewan for four years, Michel had attached himself so thoroughly to Gabriel that he'd become the next thing to family. She wondered sometimes if Gabriel hadn't contributed to stunting Michel's growth. For all Michel's impressive height and breadth, and for all that Gabriel insisted on treating him like an equal, Michel seemed to think that he had a license to continue being a boy as long as Gabriel was there to be a man. He seemed quite content to go on living forever in his ramshackle bachelor cabin on his so-called farm. The only evidence of farming that Madelaine had ever seen on Michel Dumas's place were a few grazing horses and beef cattle and a scythe to mow hay for the winter. Not that she or Gabriel or any other métis was all that interested in approaching farming as a business, but Michel couldn't even be bothered to shove a few potatoes in the ground.

After the first quaff Michel went directly to the rack of cues and then unfurled the tarpaulin, folding it neatly to show Annie how thoughtful he could be. But he showed no inclination to offer up any further information on what the "something" was he'd had to do for Gabriel.

The dogs set up another cacophony, and Moïse Ouellette stuck his head in the door, looking even more dust-caked than Michel. "Gabriel about?"

"Soon. What happened to the cart train?" Moïse had hired on to boss one of Gabriel's cart trains from Fort Carlton to Saskatoon and back. She'd pointed out to Gabriel more than a few times that every cart-train captain they had to hire on was money out of their pockets, but he invariably said he'd done enough traveling for one summer. The fact was that she wasn't all that unhappy he should see it that way, given that they were still pulling in a healthy profit.

Moïse said: "Nothing's happened—they're camped just a day short of here. I figured as long as we were this close I'd ride on ahead and get home to Isabelle late tonight instead of early tomorrow."

Madelaine cracked open the appropriate ledger, but Moïse shook his head, sending out puffs of dust. "No need to sort it out now. I'll take a ride back tomorrow when the carts come in. Just tell Gabriel for me that White Cap smoked his tobacco."

As the door closed behind Moïse, Riel stood up stiffly and said: "White Cap?"

As offhandedly as possible, Madelaine said: "A Sioux Chief south of Saskatoon. He brought his people across the line with Sitting Bull after the Little Bighorn and then decided to stay on when Sitting Bull went back. Gabriel was always friends with him but ain't been through that part of the country for a while, so I guess he figured it was time he sent White Cap an end of tobacco to show he remembers his name." But from the expression on Riel's face, he knew as well as she did that the gesture of sending tobacco to a Chief of the Plains tribes, and him smoking it, meant a good deal more than "Thinking of you."

Madelaine looked back down at the opened ledger, pretending to study the figures to cover her seething. While Riel had been working hard to find a peaceful solution, Gabriel had somehow neglected to mention to him, or to her, that he'd been busily cementing treaties with the Indians. Not peace treaties. Although the tobacco ritual did mean they were swearing not to fight each other, that hardly had to be reaffirmed these days. The other side of the coin was that they were swearing to stand up together if either tribe found themselves in a war.

Hoofbeats thrummed into the yard without the dogs complaining. Madelaine reached down Gabriel's cup like a good wife and set it on the counter, although at the moment she felt like feeding it to him sideways. He came through the door without any noticeable hitch or hesitation in his stride, but she saw the black eyes flicker at Michel Dumas and knew he saw a complication he hadn't expected.

Riel was eager to hear what the bishop and the secretary had said. Gabriel filled his cup from the rum keg and said flatly: "Not much they could say so far. Said they would read your papers, and they asked me a couple questions to make it seem like I was a visitor instead of a messenger."

"How did you answer their questions?"

"With the truth. That we brought you up here for no other reason but to help us with politics, and we ain't looking for trouble with the Police or nobody else—but it'd be a bad idea for the Police to try to take you away for a talk with them. And that when it comes to anything outside of politics, I'm the Chief here."

Madelaine said: "Oh, by the way, Moïse poked his head in on his way home. He wanted me to pass on the message that Chief White Cap smoked your tobacco."

Gabriel hoisted an eyebrow and said: "Did he now?"

Michel said: "So did Poundmaker."

Gabriel sucked his cheeks in between his back teeth and nodded over his cup with hooded eyes. Madelaine said: "How the fuck long has this been going on?"

Michel said: "Well, I'd better be getting on home now."

Riel moved in front of Gabriel and said: "Who else? Big Bear?"

"Um-hm. And Beardy. One Arrow. Little Pine. Some others. And the Blackfoot Confederacy. Well, not them yet. Crowfoot ain't exactly smoked my tobacco yet, but he ain't exactly sent it back, neither. He likes to play it close to his vest, does Crowfoot. But with the Blackfoot, what he says goes, and Poundmaker's his adopted son, so if Poundmaker was to . . ."

"To *what*?" Riel shrieked, burying his fingers in his chestnut mane. "To loose a war of extermination on the plains? Why did you bring me here if you meant to go behind my back this way?"

"You been talking to Big Bear and them yourself."

"Yes! To put their grievances into the petition. Not to . . . not to . . . not to get them to promise they'd unsheath their scalping knives when we did!"

The black eyes bored through Riel without replying, then

swiveled toward Madelaine. Gabriel stalked toward her, and his arm came up. He reached over her shoulder to the wall peg where his French-made .38 revolver hung in its holster. He snatched it down, cartridge belt and all, drew the revolver, threw the harness on the billiard table, and advanced on Riel. She saw Riel shudder and saw him suppress the urge to back away as Gabriel showed him the gun. "You see this?" Riel nodded. Gabriel bounced the pistol in the palm of his hand, spun the cylinder with his thumb, and said: "This ain't like Le Petit. Le Petit can be a hunting gun or a weapon for war, but this here little handgun ain't got no use to it but killing men. I ain't had no cause to use it for more'n ten years now. But I keep it cleaned and oiled, and every now and then I take it down by the river and shoot a few leaves off a tree—to make sure my hand still remembers and the cartridges don't rust in the cylinder. That don't mean I'm planning to kill anybody."

Late in the night, Gabriel said: "I ain't God, Madelaine, I didn't make the world. But I been living in it too damn long to get away with saying, 'Who'da thunk things might turn out this way?' "

She was lying on her stomach with her head turned away from him. She chewed her lip for a moment, then said to the darkness: "You don't really think that, do you?"

"Think what?"

"That it's going to come to a war."

"Did I say that? I been saying all goddamn night that I *don't* think that. Just that if it does, we better be ready to fight back."

"Fight *back*? The Police and the government haven't been riding around shooting people. There isn't going to be any violence unless you start it."

Instead of replying, he leaned up, swung one leg over her, and sat down on her back with his knees gripping her rib cage. "Gabriel, I hate to tell you, but you ain't no child no more. . . . I can't breathe. . . ."

His response was to press his knees in even harder, restricting her lungs to shallow little pants, and to plant his hands on her shoulder blades. "Gabriel . . . please . . . this ain't funny. . . ."

He pushed down harder, sinking her mouth and nose into the goosedown pillow. She tried to reach her hands up to get hold of his hair or beard, but he arced his head back out of reach. Her mouth was filled with the taste of feathers and cotton, working its way back into her throat. She kicked her feet up hard and caught him squarely in the kidneys with both heels. He grunted and rolled off her.

She reared up, gasping in sweet lungfuls of air. Gabriel groaned: "I'm going to be pissing blood for a week."

"Have you lost your mind? I told you to get off me."

"I ain't the one acting crazy. I was just sitting there peaceable, and you had to go and get violent."

CHAPTER 10

The beginning of the school year came and went with schoolmaster Louis Riel still hundreds of miles north in a foreign country. Madelaine didn't see much of him, although he was living only ten miles away, but she thought of him often—spending his days riding about the countryside patiently taking down the grievances of this Chief or that settler, and his nights working his way through a river of lamp oil and ink for their sake. In her prayers at night she never failed to mention that any help given to Riel would be helping a lot of people.

Fortunately, the onset of autumn meant that she had enough to occupy herself with besides worrying. Gabriel sharpened up the scythe and the three of them went out into the fields—Gabriel skimming the scythe through the stalks of wheat and oats and barley, Madelaine and Annie following along bundling them together for threshing. There wasn't that much of it to do this year. An early frost had killed off most of the crops that had been stubborn enough to grow in dust.

The thin harvest from the fields and the garden meant that there was more slaughtering to do. What with Gabriel's horses and Evangeline and the sow and the laying hens and the dogs and themselves, they had enough mouths to feed over the winter without keeping alive animals they only meant to kill in the future. The same applied to all the other farms around them, which made for even more work at Gabriel's Crossing. Gabriel didn't believe in keeping beef cattle since they required so much fencing and there were plenty of neighbors with fat steers to sell in the fall. This fall everybody wanted to sell off as much of their herds as they could, and Gabriel had naturally gone around buying all the butchering stock that no one else could afford to buy. Madelaine had grumbled at him—"What the hell are we going to do with two dozen sides of beef?"—but at bottom she understood. She didn't like to think about the choices that were having to be faced at all those farms that were a lot less prosperous than Gabriel's Crossing.

She clamped the marvelous hand-crank meat grinder onto a trestle table by the smokehouse, and she and Annie went to work turning pig meat into sausages while Gabriel did the killing. No amount of years seemed capable of making her impervious to grinding up animals who'd eaten out of her hand, but until someone came up with a way of staying alive that didn't entail eating other living things, she would have to live with it. At least she knew that the occasional ear-stabbing squeal from the other side of the barn was only a squeal of fear. When Gabriel took on the job of killing something, it was dead before it felt the pain.

Gabriel came out toting the hams off the hog he'd hung yesterday, splashed them into the brine tub, and said: "That's enough for today. We'll get back to it day after tomorrow."

She looked up from twisting a stuffed gut into links and saw that the sun had snuck across the sky while she was immersed in spices and smoke and blood. "What's wrong with tomorrow?"

"We got to go help the Riels pack up and move out."

"Move out? He hasn't finished his petition yet!"

"He's still working on it. They're just moving out of Nolin's and over to Moïse's place. I figure it's better we wait on slaughtering them steers till the winter sets in—if we can get the icehouse laid in good, they'll keep all the way through next summer. . . ."

"You could've given me some warning about tomorrow. Maybe it might have saved me a lot of trouble to wait to start this until the day after instead of having to take this all apart and clean it and then start all over."

"Maybe I made a particular point of telling you all about it last week, and maybe you rolled over and forgot. They say the memory's the first thing to go. All right, if it'll make you feel better, I'll say maybe I forgot to tell you. I know how women are about getting old."

She had just decided that the mirror was trying to tell her these earrings weren't the right ones to go with this necklace after all, when Gabriel bellowed from outside: "We've lost half the morning already!" She tried a couple of shawls, decided the second one would have to do, and strode out the door. He looked down at her from the wagon seat and said: "Who said we was going to church?"

"Do I look like I'm going to church?"

He looked her over again, and his eyelids appeared to grow heavy as his voice dropped to a soft growl. "As a matter of fact, no, it don't look like that's where you're going."

She pushed him back up on the wagon. "You said we're already running late, idiot."

The Riels already had their trunks and bookbags stacked up in front of Charles Nolin's house. Their ex-host was lumbering back and forth, mumbling that they really didn't have to leave if they didn't want to. Marguerite Riel kept suddenly remembering things and running back inside, so Madelaine figured she might take a moment to look in on Madame Nolin—still waxen-faced and haggard, grimacing every time she shifted her position on the bed. The money her husband had spent on doctors over the last few years probably would have built three more big houses.

Madelaine came back outside, ashamed of her complaints against the natural little twinges of middle age, to find the Riels and their possessions all loaded onto the wagon and ready to go. The Riel family had been swollen by an addition. Will Jackson was an eager, green-eyed, highly educated Ontario immigrant who was secretary of the Settlers' Union at Prince Albert. He'd decided he would currently be serving the Settlers' Union best by serving as secretary to Riel in the great work of composing a Petition of Rights.

As the wagon trundled along with Riel on the seat between Madelaine and Gabriel, Riel said: "We're almost ready to begin."

"Begin?"

"Mister Jackson and I are almost ready to begin the final version. I know it must seem like a great deal of dithering to a man like my uncle Gabriel, who always says what he thinks and that's all there is to it. The world would be a better place if more men did the same. But if I were to choose the wrong way to say what I think about métis land rights, the white settlers will think we're trying to deny their own land titles; if I choose the wrong way to describe the inadequacies of the farm instructors on the reserves, it might seem to the Indians as though we're trying to take away even that inadequate assistance. But now, by the grace of God, I believe we're ready. . . .''

When they'd left the Riels at the Ouellettes', where Moïse and Isabelle had offered them another temporary home, Gabriel said: "Did you know Will Jackson's considering converting to the Church?''

"I thought he was already a Christian.''

"Protestant. Riel does have that kind of effect on people.''

"Riel?''

"Well, you got to admit it speaks for a pretty strong effect. Here you got this young man who's the best-educated man between the Red and the Rockies, Orange Ontario family, and after just a little time with Riel he wants to convert.''

"And a little time with Rose.''

"Rose?''

"Rose Ouellette, you remember? Your niece? The Rose we're godparents to? The one with the skin like rose petals, who likes to hike up her skirts and run across the prairie with the front of her bouncing like—''

"I know which Rose you meant. I meant: 'What's Rose got to do with it?' ''

Madelaine looked at the sky and heaved a sigh for the ignorance of mankind.

She was awakened in the morning by a grating, screeching noise, not loud but penetrating and inescapable. She came into the kitchen and found Gabriel sharpening his butchering knives. "I thought you were going to do that outside.''

"So did I, but I don't want to freeze my fingers off. There's ice on the river this morning. You can call me a liar; I would if I hadn't seen it myself.''

She slumped onto a chair and cupped her hands over her eyes. Out of all the years God might have chosen to bring in a winter worse than any in living memory, why did it have to be now when so many people were already desperate?

Gabriel said: "It might just be a freak. Maybe next week we'll be swatting mosquitoes again,'' but he didn't sound convinced. "Even if it does lock in like this, any day now Riel'll have the petition done. The government can't ignore the whole population of the North West speaking in the same voice—not if it's said right. People can dig in and hold on through just about anything if they see a hope of help coming."

She wiped her eyes and made breakfast. By the time they headed out the door with their knives and implements, the sun had come up high enough to dull the milk teeth of the winter, but she could still see patches of mirror glint hugging the far shore. It looked as though they were going to be able to carry right on through to butchering the steers after all.

A buggy came down the trail, but she kept on rubbing pickling salt into slices of fatback and assuring Annie that her tending of the smokehouse fire was perfection itself. Over the course of the summer, Madelaine had managed to accustom herself to the fact that the traffic down to the ferry didn't have anything to do with her. But the buggy turned into the yard. By the driver's black cassock and gray horsetail beard, she recognized Father Fourmond. Automatically she lifted the hem of her apron to wipe the grime off her face, pulling back just in time as the whiff of salt and cloves and pepper stung her eyes.

Father Fourmond reined in his horse and climbed down. Like most of the priests she'd known in her life, he was a craggy foot soldier of the Church Militant and Triumphant—perfectly capable of excusing himself in the middle of confession to take an axe handle to the drunken young men bellowing in the churchyard.

"Good day, Madelaine."

"Good day, Father. You must excuse me, I'm all covered with—"

"Not at all, my child. I only wish more of our parishioners would be so provident about preparing for the winter. I won't keep you but a moment. I brought around a petition that I thought you might be kind enough to sign, and Annie—and perhaps Gabriel would make his mark. . . ."

"A petition?"

"To help support the mission school at St. Laurent."

"Of course. I have a pen and ink inside. . . ."

"Don't trouble yourself, I brought my own. You can sign it right on the table here, and I'll be on my way."

"Gabriel! Father Fourmond is here!"

He came around the corner of the barn with his hands black

with blood, wiping his foot-long favorite knife on his pants leg. Madelaine said: "He's brought around a petition for us to sign."

"What's it say?"

"It is a petition to the government in Ottawa," Father Fourmond said, "in the name of all the people of the North West Territories, demanding that the government provide a subsidy of one thousand dollars a year to the Jesuit school at St. Laurent."

"Are you out of your goddamned mind?" Gabriel roared. Father Fourmond stepped back judiciously as the knife sliced through the air. "Does Riel know about this?"

"I do not need to ask permission of Monsieur Louis Riel to—"

"Who's seen this? How long have you been taking this around?"

"Two days," Father Fourmond said stiffly. "And Father André is circulating a copy in Prince Albert."

Before she could thrust herself between them, Gabriel whirled around, thrust the knife down into one of the table planks, and took off running toward the stables. She chased after him, shouting: "Have *you* lost your goddamned mind?" He vaulted over the fence and charged on into the pasture, bellowing at Starface. Coy Starface couldn't have been more delighted and immediately trotted out of reach. Gabriel ran back to the fence Madelaine was climbing over, snatched up a coiled lariat, and went after Starface again, ignoring her shouts. The horse had cottoned on to the tone of Gabriel's voice. He allowed himself to be roped. Gabriel dragged him back toward the harness room end of the stables. Madelaine planted herself in his path, saw the look in his eyes, and stepped out of the way. He threw the end of the rope at her, bounded into the harness room, and came back out with his saddle and bridle. She snatched the bridle out of his hand and buckled it on over Starface's blocky head, yelling: "What the hell's come over you?"

Gabriel swung up onto the saddle, took the reins from her, and said: "Have you put your name on that piece of paper?"

"Not yet."

"If you do, you might just as well shove a knife in my back. And your own, and everyone else's in the North West." He wheeled his horse and whipped him at the latched gate. They sailed over it and galloped north. He was hatless and coatless, he hadn't even thrust Le Petit into the saddle scabbard.

She went back to Father Fourmond and Annie. "I'm sorry, Father, I don't know what's . . . I can't sign the petition until I've had a chance to talk to Gabriel."

"I understand, my daughter. A woman should be to her husband as the Church is to Christ. But perhaps, Annie, you will be so good as to—"

"No, she will not."

Long after Annie had been fed and put to bed, Madelaine sat up smoking her pipe by the light of the fire in the kitchen hearth. With the crickets and tree frogs frozen silent, she could hear the soft thuds of a weary horse walking into the yard and the happy whimpering of the dogs. Gabriel came through the door with his teeth gritted together to keep them from chattering. He hunkered down on the hearth, and she poured him out a cup of hot rum tea. He thawed out his tongue and said: "I was too late—it's already got around."

"What's got around? Father Fourmond's petition? Where's the harm in that?"

"You still don't get it, do you?"

"That's what I'm telling you! Get what?"

"If we got any chance at all of getting the government to listen to us, it's only if we all speak in one voice—if Riel's Petition of Rights comes from everybody in the North West. But all the different tribes out here are as wary of each other as they are of the government. The white settlers are afraid of what the Indians might do if the government honors its promise to give them ammunition to hunt with, the Indians are afraid that we might want land titles to pieces of their reserves, the Catholics worry about what the Protestants might be hatching up . . . That's one of the reasons we brought Riel up here, and up to now he's been doing a good job of listening to everybody and convincing them that all our separate problems come from the same cause."

He reached into his shirt and pulled out a sheaf of printed paper. "Here. Riel already read it to me, but you can see for yourself if there's any harm in Father Fourmond's little petition."

Angled to the firelight, it turned out to be a copy of the *Prince Albert Times* folded to an editorial: "Now we see that all this wind about 'our common grievances' has been merely a blind for Monsieur Riel to use us to promote his own religious crusade."

CHAPTER 11

By the end of October the river was frozen over and the ground covered in a gritty, compacted layer of windblasted snow. Gabriel sat peering out through one of the few transparent panes on the frost-embroidered window, with the pieces of his rifle and revolver spread out across the kitchen table. It looked like it was going to be, as his father was wont to say, "one of them winters where the wolves are gonna start eating each other." This time it might not be picturesque exaggeration. Gabriel and every other old hunter knew from experience that the rabbits and grouse and deer and all the other game animals went through cycles where they would gradually grow more plentiful over six or seven or eight years and then suddenly would virtually disappear. But this was the first winter in living memory where the low point in all the separate cycles had coincided. Not that it was going to make much difference to the Indians trapped on their reserves. Even if there had been anything to hunt, they had nothing to buy powder and shot with, and the Indian agents were afraid to give them any.

Gabriel considered the odds on using the weather to excuse how he was feeling—he was in a foul and murderous mood, and he knew it. He mashed the cleaning rag in his hand and picked up the extractor bolt cum firing pin for Le Petit, then threw down the cleaning rag and picked up the stubby, sawn-off needle that the hammer drove into the cartridge casings in his revolver. He sat staring at the two pieces of oiled steel. It seemed impossible that these two bitty nubs of metal could ever do any harm to anyone. But just about everyone in the world now accepted as fact that a few pounds of various metals and a few ounces of gunpowder made for very dangerous things. Even Sir John A. Macdonald off in Ottawa must know that, just as he must know that his subjects in the North West Territories knew what to do with them. Over all these years he must have got at least some notion that he wasn't dealing with a bunch of scared grocery clerks whose only recourse was to whine, "It isn't fair," or maybe write an angry letter to an editor.

Gabriel growled at himself to throw the bone away and went back to wiping the excess oil off the parts and screwing them back together. He knew that when he got onto certain lines of thought he just went back and forth like a bear in a cage. That's why he'd decided in the first place that today should be gun-cleaning day, even though he hadn't fired either one of them since the last time he'd cleaned them. It wasn't doing the trick, though. Even polishing up the brass loading gate and butt plate on Le Petit didn't relax his mind. He put Le Petit back on the hooks over the door, reached down his coat, and went through the passage to the billiard room to hang up the revolver. Madelaine was restocking the store shelves. She said: "Got all the rust off?" He growled at her and went outside to chop some wood.

By the time he'd split enough birch and poplar to start thinking about taking his coat off, he realized it wasn't going to work. He sat down on the chopping block and stoked his pipe. The ice on the river wasn't thick enough yet to start sawing out slabs for the icehouse. Maybe he should finish painting the front of the house, but it was too cold to paint in shirt sleeves, and Madelaine would kill him if he got blue paint all over his buffalo coat.

He let his eyes drift around the place. Regardless of whether the government responded to the demands for land titles, this place was his and Madelaine's. Even if the coming of the railroad killed the freight cart business, he and Madelaine would find other ways to get by, just as they had when the buffalo hunt had come to an end. If the Indians did get desperate enough to start raiding farms, there were a lot softer targets than the Dumonts and the rest of the wagonmen along the South Saskatchewan. Whether other people's problems got solved or not was up to Riel, just as it had been up to Riel to calm the anthill Father Fourmond had put his foot in.

Two of the dogs came rolling toward him in a ball of fur and teeth and snarls. He snarled at them and they broke it up. He went back inside, knocking the snow off his moccasins just as Madelaine opened her mouth to yell at him. He said: "I'm going to take a couple sacks of potatoes over to the Duck Lake reserve. Which ones should I take?"

"I'm not sure. How many sacks do we have down in the root cellar, and how many will we need for seed?"

"That's why I'm asking you—I didn't count them."

"Exactly. But did you ask me how many we had before you decided to give two away? The winter's going to be just as long for us as for anybody else."

"We've got plenty, more'n we need."

"We do. But what happens if one of your brothers or your father runs out of food to feed his family come February? Are you going to tell them we already gave away all we had to spare?"

"I'm only talking about two sacks of potatoes. Since when are we so goddamned poor we can't afford two sacks of potatoes? And since when did you start clutching every little penny to your tits while people around you are starving?"

"Since never. But that's the position you put me in when you decide we're going to give something away and leave it up to me to play the miser."

"All right, you're right. Now, can we spare two little sacks of potatoes?"

"The day we can't I'll suck on Le Petit and set you free to find a wife that can do the job. Wait'll I get a lamp lit. . . ."

The root cellar was a dank cavern under half the floor space of the house. To get safely below the winter freezing level of the earth, they'd had to dig it deep enough for Gabriel to almost stand upright. Between the post beams, ranks of bulging burlap bags and shelves of sealer jars marched into the darkness beyond the circle of lamplight. Madelaine kicked at a stuffed sack and said: "The first two in this line. And that sack over there."

"I only said two."

"You hate turnips anyway. Takes me so much trouble to mask the taste it ain't worth trying to feed them to you." She left him alone to tote the load out into the yard, retrieve the lamp, and drop the trapdoor back in place. He didn't see her again until he'd managed to buckle the saddle onto Starface without taking off too many clumps of winter fur and was lashing the root vegetables onto a packhorse. He heard a barking, skating, gutturally cursing noise and turned to look. Madelaine was dragging a side of beef across the snow, kicking at the swarming dogs with one foot while she pushed off with the other.

By the time he'd stopped laughing enough to get back on his feet she was almost up to him. She didn't appear to be amused. He said: "What am I supposed to do with that?"

"Not a godamned thing. I'm coming with you."

"The ice won't hold that much weight yet. Hey, idiot, I didn't mean you. . . . Careful, you'll spoil my face! . . . I meant the weight of a whole side of beef on top of everything else. Why do you think I didn't just hitch up the cutter?"

"Well, if the ice goes and I'm holding on to the lead, that's my lookout, isn't it?"

"If the ice goes and you go with it, I might just as well jump in." He fetched the saw and cut the side in half so he could balance the load. She went and saddled up the gray pony.

The staccato clattering of hooves on ice gave way to the crunch of snow and frozen tufts of yellow grass. By the time they crossed the border of Chief Beardy's reserve, there was rouge dusted on the dove-gray breast of the sky. Gabriel's ears caught a trace of something that didn't fit in. He reined in Starface. Madelaine said: "What's the—"

"Ssh!" It was in the bush off to his right—a wispy voice chanting in Cree: "Great Mystery, I had a lot of good years, and a lot of bouncy wives, and a lot of good fights when I was young and strong . . ."

Gabriel slipped down off Starface, slid Le Petit out of the scabbard, held up the palm of his gloved hand at Madelaine to sign her to stay where she was, and skulked into the bush, leading with the toes of his moccasins so as to knife through the crust of the snow rather than crunch it. Through a stand of wolf willow in front of him he saw a figure sitting on a blanket in the snow. It was hazy, as though seen through a red beaded curtain, but he recognized Ahsiweyin. "Don't you get tired of singing your death song, Grandfather?"

"Is that you, Gabriel?"

"That's right."

"Good to see you one last time."

"What about the 'last time' before this, and the one before that?"

"This time it's for sure. When there ain't enough food to keep the young people alive, it's time for the old ones to go off in the bush and not come back."

"Well, it looks like the Great Mystery's going to have to hear the whole damned thing all over again on another day. Me and Madelaine just brought over a load of food." Ahsiweyin tried to rise, but his legs didn't seem to be working too good. Gabriel said: "Here, Grandfather, hold my rifle," then slid his arms between the blanket and the snow and scooped him up, blanket and all. Carrying him back to the horses wasn't much of a feat of strength, nor was lifting him up onto Starface's saddle.

Madelaine said: "Hello, Grandfather."

"Hello, Madelaine. Seems every time I see you someone's lifting me up on a horse."

Gabriel slid Le Petit into the saddle scabbard and jumped up behind Ahsiweyin. When they were under way again, Ahsiweyin said: "Your man tells me you brought food."

"Just some potatoes and turnips we don't need, and a side of beef."

Ahsiweyin began to make a wheezy, rattling noise that Gabriel finally decided was laughter. "What's funny, Grandfather?"

"I just wish I could still see well enough to see the faces of them young men who say I'm too old to go hunting."

The camp was a raggedy collection of tipis and jury-rigged log shacks with spruce boughs banked up against the walls. It seemed to have decayed since the last time Gabriel was there. There was nothing in the past life of the Plains tribes to prepare them for living in one place for an extended period of time. There were no horses or dogs in sight. As the hooves of Starface and the other two horses thudded onto the trampled-down snow in the middle of the camp, heads began to emerge from tent flaps and doorways, followed by dreamily slow-moving bodies dressed in old blankets and sooty leather and scraps of rabbit fur. Where arms or legs were exposed to the air, they were parchmenty sticks with bulbous knobs of knees or elbows.

Gabriel slid off Starface's rump and lifted down Ahsiweyin, who immediately crumpled down sitting again on his blanket. The old man chortled: "Come see—I had good hunting," and gestured toward the packhorse. Madelaine was already there, untying the lashings on one of the sacks of potatoes. Gabriel took hold of its corners and lowered it to the ground. There was a rustling sound behind him that he would have thought was trembling aspens rattling in the wind if the snow under his feet hadn't told him different. He looked back over his shoulder and saw nothing but eyes and mouths—the eyes black and distended and sheened over with a sickly mirror membrane, the mouths gulping like fishes' or sealed tight to keep the juice from dripping out.

He unsheathed his knife and sliced open the burlap. Potatoes bounced out and rolled across the snow, sending up puffs of dust from Madelaine's garden. There was an instant of hesitation, and then the potatoes were chased and descended upon, snatched up to the mouths, and bit into with closed eyes. But instead of the sound of happy chewing and lip smacking, a wave of curses and cries of pain and childish wailings rolled back at him. A woman in front of him had blood dripping out of her mouth. One of the men started to launch himself toward Gabriel but was held back by another.

Madelaine shouted in Cree: "We can boil them all down to make them soft. Who's got a pot?" And in a moment she and the Cree women were building up fires and filling pots with snow.

Gabriel hunkered down beside one of the frozen slabs of beef and started hacking off slivers. He handed the first one to Ahsiweyin and then started on the children. "It'll be cold—just suck on it to get the juice out and warm it up and then you can chew." It kept them busy until the potatoes and turnips were on the boil. Some of the men chopped bits off the other frozen quarter to throw into the pots and leaned the rib rack by the biggest fire to thaw.

A wagon rolled and squeaked into the camp. Gabriel stood up to look. It was the Duck Lake Indian agent and his interpreter. "Evening, Gabriel. Just passing by?"

"We brought some food."

"Damned good of you. It'll help stretch out this," letting down the tailgate to show a sack of flour and a slab of salt pork. Both were immediately whisked away by the Crees.

Gabriel said: "Damned good of you to come all the way out here just to deliver that."

"It ain't all that much trouble, only once a week."

"A week?" The world turned into a spiraling black-and-red vortex with the Indian agent's face in the eye of it. There was a curious feeling of wafting weightlessness and a bass voice bellowing. "A *week*?" followed by a splintering crash and then a series of thumps accompanied by a very satisfying pumping feeling in Gabriel's arms.

Madelaine had wrapped her arms around him from behind and was shouting: "Gabriel! It ain't his fault!"

Gabriel let his hands go slack. It appeared that he had picked up the Indian agent and hurled him onto the wagonbed and was using the back of his head for a hammer to make sure the planks were all nailed down securely.

The Indian agent sat back up very slowly. There were tears in his eyes. "You think I like this any better than you do? I got orders to cut the rations in half. The goddamned Prime Minister made himself Minister of Indian Affairs as well, and he said we're wasting money on the Indians that should be spent building the railroad. That sack of flour isn't supposed to be a week's rations—it's supposed to be a month's. I don't know what the hell I'm going to do come February when it's all gone."

Gabriel muttered: "I'm sorry."

"So am I. Hell, you didn't shoot me. God knows I've been hard-pressed not to shoot myself every time I come out here."

On the long ride home neither one of them said a word. As they were crawling off their horses by the stable gate, Gabriel said: "I'll take care of unsaddling 'em and feeding 'em and turning 'em out." Madelaine didn't even make a joke about him playing with his horses while she had to work on dinner; she just trudged hump-shouldered toward the window lights across the yard.

She came charging back out, flapping something over her head that the moonlight turned ghostly blue-white. "Gabriel! It's here! Riel came by and left it with Annie. He said he wanted you to be the first to hear it. He's done it!"

"Maybe he has and maybe he hasn't. Maybe we better read it through before we go to celebrating."

CHAPTER 12

Madelaine hung up her coat, filled two cups with beer, and waited, tapping the sheaf of papers on the counter plank. Annie stoked the fire higher. Gabriel finally came in, took off his coat, and carried his cup over to his canvas-shrouded billiard table. He sat cross-legged on top of the table. Madelaine unfolded the papers and began to read the "Petition of Rights for the peoples of the North West." Partway through, she glanced up at Gabriel. He was sitting with his chin in one hand, slowly shaking his head from side to side. She went back to reading.

It was all there. Out of the cacophony of contradictory complaints, Riel had extracted every genuine grievance and set them down in language that was elegantly eloquent but perfectly clear, and he'd managed to do it without kicking any of the trip wires connected to the fears of neighbors with differing complexions and religions and seemingly different sets of problems. More than that, he'd come up with pragmatic solutions, the most fundamental being that the government grant provincial status to the territories, so that the people could elect their own representatives to speak for them in Parliament.

> In conclusion, the people of the North West are currently accorded neither their rights as human beings nor their rights as British subjects. We trust that this fundamental injustice shall be resolved, and we—your humble petitioners—will not cease to pray.

She folded the pages back together and set them down. Gabriel was still sitting shaking his head, with his eyes focused on a point somewhere in midair. She thought she had a notion of what was passing through his mind. All his adult life, he'd been the man expected to sort out other people's messes for them—for the simple reason that he happened to be the best there was at all the things that made the difference between a free life on the plains and a short one. And now along comes this Louis Riel and performs a feat that Gabriel couldn't begin to.

He looked up at her and grinned and said: "I'd say it's about goddamned time we opened that bottle of French brandy."

The day the petition was sent off was also the first day of the novena to cure Charles Nolin's wife.

Madelaine sat down between Gabriel and Annie in a front pew, squeezing in beside the Riels and Will Jackson. The massed prayers managed to drown out most of the stomach growls from the first morning's fasting. Out of the corner of her eye, she watched green-eyed Will Jackson assiduously performing the rituals and wondered how much of it was to show Riel and the priests how well he was learning his lessons and how much was for the benefit of Rose Ouellette in the pew behind. He was certainly a good-looking, bright-eyed, and enthusiastic young man—but Madelaine wondered if he wasn't a bit too enthusiastic, the eyes just a shade too bright.

It struck her that her attitude toward Will Jackson and Rose wasn't all that different from the way she felt about Michel Dumas and Annie. Maybe she was turning into one of those sour old harridans who took an automatic dislike to every young man who was sweet on a young woman. She assured herself that she didn't dislike Michel at all. It was simply the fact that Annie was too young to understand that he'd been born without the gland that secretes responsibility. The days were long gone when a woman who found herself with a child and no man could just attach herself to a wandering hunting clan or put up a lakeshore cabin and live on what she netted and snared.

In front of the altar, Father Fourmond was swinging the censer, filling the church with sweetly acrid smoke, while the prayers were carried on by Father Moulin. Father Moulin beckoned to Charles Nolin, who stood and stooped down to pick up his wife. He shambled forward to the altar, the lump-faced giant with his permanent expression of confusion, cradling his frail wife in his arms. Father Fourmond unsealed the vial of Lourdes water and dribbled it out onto her knees and ankles and elbows while Father Moulin prayed. Madelaine and the rest of the congregation prayed hard along with him for one of their own who needed help.

Like everyone except the clergy and the Nolins and the Riels, Madelaine didn't travel to the church for every day of the novena. She prayed at home on the days when she didn't, certain in the knowledge that a kind of natural rotation would keep the church filled with neighbors picking different days to shovel out their cowsheds or break the ice working its way under their eaves.

The ninth and last day of the novena was Christmas Day. Gabriel decided there was enough snow now to hitch up the cutter and skim down the river in style, joining up with the rainbow procession of painted sleighs and prancing horses in beaded headstalls. The church was crammed to the rafters, with the exception of the empty pew where the Nolin family had been sitting for eight days.

There was a murmur from the back of the church. Madelaine looked back over her shoulder, then stood up along with everyone else as Charles Nolin and his wife came walking down the aisle.

Madelaine pressed her thumb and forefinger against her eyes to squeeze back the tears. Gabriel growled under his breath: "I would've thought you'd be happy for her." She put her elbow into his ribs and kept on crying. Maybe she would try to explain to him later that it didn't just have to do with Marie Anne Nolin and her husband, but with everyone from Ahsiweyin to Superintendent Lief Crozier. Miracles could happen.

PART TWO

Gabriel was always the leader of popular enthusiasm—capable of any hot-blooded heroism within
the hour of danger, but measuring in cold blood up
'til then.

MÉTIS MEMOIRS,
PROVINCIAL ARCHIVES OF MANITOBA

CHAPTER 13

Kitty woke up feeling like Sleeping Beauty. She was certain that when she'd closed her eyes it had been New Year's Eve, but this didn't feel like New Year's Day. The bed was cold. Her sisters had contrived to get themselves up and dressed and out the door without waking her. She screwed up her courage, flung back the quilts, and wallowed up out of the feather mattress. She scrubbed her face in the icy basin on the washstand, dressed quickly, and hurried downstairs into the warmth from the fire in the parlor.

Her father was walled behind his London *Times*, clouds of pipe smoke drifting over the crenellated barricade. She said: "Is it really 1885 now?" He didn't lower his newspaper or take his pipe out of his mouth to reply, just tapped his finger against the general area of the date on the masthead—July 3, 1884. That made it New Year's Day today. His newspaper had come from the top of the crisp-folded stack on a shelf in his office, next to the stacks of the *Illustrated Daily News, The Scotsman, Boys' Own Paper,* and the *Young Ladies' Journal.* They arrived in three-month bundles with the spring mail packet, the summer packet, and the fall and winter packets. Every morning, her father would bring out one edition of each of the dailies and at the beginning of each month or week would release the magazines in their proper order. Her father never tired of telling the rest of the family that they were far more up-to-date than he'd been in his bachelor days, when there had been only two mail packets a year. He'd read of the start of the Crimean War exactly one year to the day the Queen signed the declaration. In the McLean family's criminal code of domestic felonies, setting the house on fire and burning one's brothers and sisters in their beds would have ranked as somewhat less heinous than sneaking a peek ahead in the stacks of periodicals.

Kitty said, a bit petulantly, "It doesn't feel like New Year's," and then realized why. "The Indians! How could I have slept through them?"

"You didn't. They haven't come around yet."

She looked at the clock. It was too late to expect them now. Every New Year's Day she could remember, whether along the Qu'Appelle or at Red River, the local Cree or Assiniboine or Sioux always came around at dawn, firing their guns in the air and shouting, "Happy New Year's!"

Her father muttered: "Maybe the customs around here are different." Although his voice was muffled by the paper and the pipe stem in his mouth, she thought she detected a note of uneasiness. Perhaps it had to do with whatever doings in some far-flung corner of the Empire he was perusing.

She went into the kitchen to scrounge up a slugabed breakfast. The heaping platter of cookies her mother had baked up for the Cree stood untouched on the kitchen table. Kitty felt hurt and offended that the new friends she'd thought they'd made at Fort Pitt should have chosen to ignore them. Big Bear himself had sat at that table several times slurping up large quantities of whatever her mother happened to have on the stove— astoundingly large quantities for such a shriveled little old man, particularly if what was cooking happened to be barley soup. He'd caught her gawking at his prodigious intake, and he'd said: "I'll tell you something, Sunflower—eat as much as you can whenever you can. You never know when you're going to get the chance again." He called her Sunflower because of the color of her hair, which Kitty suspected was her only good feature.

Big Bear was one of the two additions to her "collection" that Kitty had made at Fort Pitt. Although the other was also an Indian Chief, he couldn't have been more unlike the wrinkled gnome that was Big Bear. Chief Poundmaker could have been assembled out of every English schoolchild's imaginings of the Noble Red Man: tall, lean, dignified, and so barbarically handsome as to send any titled lady's fan fluttering. Even his name was Big Medicine. In the not-so-distant days before the Northern Plains tribes had acquired horses, a man who could make a buffalo pound that the herd could be chaneled into and trapped was the savior of his entire tribe.

After her father had been dragged away from his paper for the cracker-pulling ceremony and the obligatory prancing around in paper hats, the family primped themselves up in their best, bundled on their coats, and crunched across the snow to the New Year's levee at the North West Mounted Police detachment.

Halfway across the parade ground, Kitty stopped to look out over the diamond-studded miles of snow surrounding Fort Pitt. Fort Pitt was only a fort by virtue of the fact that all the old fur trade posts had been designated "Fort" Something-or-other. It had only a rudimentary stockade fencing in the guardhouse exercise yard. Other than that, the fort was a smattering of clay-plastered log buildings standing naked on the flats between the North Saskatchewan and the hills to the north.

"Kitty! Hurry along now!"

Kitty turned and looked at the receding parade of her brothers and sisters, her mother beckoning from the front of the line. They suddenly appeared terribly small and fragile, planted here in the midst of the wilds with no walls to protect them. She shook it off—asking herself sarcastically: "Protect them from what?"—and hurried to catch up.

The Police had spent the morning festooning the mess hall with crepe-paper streamers, polishing their boots and buttons and waxing their mustaches into fantastical curlicues. With four constables delegated to band duty, there were only eighteen free for dancing, but they still outnumbered the women of danceable age three to one. After a couple of hours of dancing the quadrille and schottische with fresh relays of red tunics, Kitty found it necessary to catch her breath. She took up a position by the punch bowl, fanning herself with a napkin.

On the other side of the table, her father was in conversation with Inspector Dickens, the prodigiously bearded son of the prodigiously celebrated novelist. Her father was saying: "I suppose it's for the best, Inspector, that whenever a man begins to get the notion he's grown wise in the ways of this country, it has a habit of showing him up. After thirty years in the North West you'd think I would have learned that Indians vary just as much as any other people. But here I was blithely assuming that just because the Indians at all my other postings always came around for a New Year's Morning Shivaree, they would have the same custom here."

"They do. Or at least they have as far back as anyone can remember."

"Oh. Well, then I suppose the reason they didn't come around to our place this morning was because we haven't been here long enough to—"

"No." The inspector shook his head unconcernedly. "They didn't come around at all this year. Probably forgot to change their calendars." He chortled at his own witticism and ladled himself another bowl of punch, the third since Kitty had been standing there.

Her father didn't appear to be amused at the inspector's wit, or offended by it, or even aware any longer that the inspector was standing beside him; he just stared sightlessly ahead, clutching his cup as though someone had just stepped on his grave. His eyes drifted sideways and happened to lock against hers. His head jerked back on the stalk of his neck, and he contorted his features into an imitation of a festive grin that might have taken her in when her entire vocabulary had been "Da-da."

New Year's Day on the South Saskatchewan was celebrated by a banquet for Louis Riel at Charles Nolin's house, sponsored and paid for by Gabriel and Phillipe Garnot. A purse of money had been collected to present to Riel. Madelaine left off dish-clearing to lower herself onto the chair beside Gabriel's and hear what Riel had to say.

The gray eyes were shining, the voice throbbing. "My friends, cousins, my beloved métis nation . . . your generosity and faith in me is one of the blessings of my life. I only hope that my poor efforts on your behalf are some repayment. And it seems that, by the grace of God, it may be so. I am informed by Monsieur Jackson"—indicating the secretary of the Settlers' Union, whose cheeks suddenly blazed pink—"that a telegram has been sent from Ottawa acknowledging receipt of our Petition of Rights. I am certain that the only reason we haven't heard more is the intervention of the holy season. When Parliament reconvenes they will no doubt attend to the matter of the North West Territories as the first item on their agenda. In a week, two at most, we can expect to hear how they propose to deal with our problems. And then"—he winked as the applause died down—"we can get down to some horse trading.

"I should like to propose two toasts. First—the Queen."

They all rose and toasted the Indians' revered Grandmother Across the Water—Riel in water, the rest of them with something more substantial. As Madelaine was settling back down onto her chair, Riel said: "And one more toast, which I'm afraid the fairer sex may not take part in." He smiled at his wife and

Madelaine and the other women around the room. "Gentlemen, I give you"—raising his water glass—"the one blessing in our lives near as precious as the blessing of God—without them, where would we be? The women of the métis nation."

All the men in the room thumped their tables, threw the contents of their cups down their throats, and plumped back down, grinning. All except Gabriel. He sipped his drink and sat down with his arms cocked back over the spindles of his chair, like a fish hawk drying its wings. She said: "We don't seem that much of a blessing to you?"

The black agates slid sideways to spear her eyes, then swiveled away again.

On the way home, skimming along in the cutter between the frozen river and the diamond-spattered black ice of the sky, he said: "Weren't no point in pricking nobody's balloon back there. I'm as willing as anybody to wait to see if Sir John A. Macdonald and his big, rich friends out east might be convinced by fine words to stop making themselves bigger and richer by sucking the blood out of people they figure are little and poor. But I ain't counting no chickens."

"For Christ's sake, Gabriel—give it a chance."

"Ain't that what I said? Pull up that blanket higher—you're gonna freeze your tits off, and I like 'em where they are."

CHAPTER 14

The next time Madelaine Wilkie had met up with Gabriel Dumont after the summer of Le Grand Coteau, she was fourteen years old and he was sixteen. Her father had sold off his buffalo runners and gone into business as a trader. After a less-than-profitable season in the country north of Red River he'd gone west to Fort Ellice, taking his whole family with him. Except Madelaine, who was left to serve out another term in the convent school of St. Boniface. In the spring, when the Hudson's Bay Company's boat brigades fanned out from the great warehouses of Fort Garry, she was set free to go home with the brigade heading west up the Assiniboine River. Traveling as the lone woman among several dozen case-hardened boatmen, she felt perfectly safe. Many of them were her uncles or cousins, and they pampered her like a queen. It didn't hurt that she was working off her passage by helping with the cooking. As one of her uncles remarked: "No one but a damned fool messes with the cook."

Fort Ellice stood in the winding, wooded Assiniboine Valley, near where the mouth of the Qu'Appelle Valley opened into it from the west. On the prairies, a valley rarely signified a place between upthrust hills, but rather a place where a river or a stream had cut a cleft down into the surrounding plain. Madelaine kissed all her family hello on the dock and kissed all the boatmen good-bye. Her education at the convent school was put directly to work, perhaps a bit more assiduously than her father might have wished. His so-called ledgers were a joke. He knew just enough about letters and numbers to get himself into trouble; the equivalent of Sister Agatha launching herself into the horse-trading business with the expertise she'd gleaned from riding in carriages to mass. Her father didn't appear to find the analogy amusing.

Madelaine had had a few weeks to get things into a semblance of order when the Dumonts rode in. They were on their way west from Grantown on Phantom White Horse Plains, to spend the summer hunting along the Saskatchewan. The entire clan crammed into the cabin cum store that her father had built beside Fort Ellice. Although three years had altered Gabriel Dumont as much as her, it didn't take more than a glance to pick him out. He'd added a few feeble inches in height, but he was still barely taller than his sisters, while all the other Dumont males had to be wary of butting their heads against the rafters. He was starting a wispy attempt at growing a beard, which seemed like a wise idea given the lumpy boat stern of his jawline. But if he hadn't grown much vertically, he'd made up for it horizontally. At an age when most boys were stringbeans waiting to fill out, Gabriel's shoulders and chest and coarse-boned skull were spreading out in all four directions. It wasn't the massive statuary of a Mister Grant, though—the effect was more like someone had managed to set up a brandy keg on top of a beer barrel balanced on two sawn-off canoe paddles.

Madelaine held her breath to stifle her giggles and focused

her attention on the ledger opened in front of her. As Gabriel Dumont's mother and aunts and sisters pawed through the bolts of printed cotton, his father lit his pipe and said offhandedly to Madelaine's father: "Sad news about Mister Grant, eh?"

"What's that?"

"Ain't you heard? I thought the moccasin telegraph would've got it here before us. We held up starting out until after the funeral."

Madelaine embarrassed herself by starting to cry. She managed to keep it quiet at least and lowered her head so that her hair fell forward to curtain her face, hoping that everyone would assume she was just concentrating on the ledger in front of her. But she couldn't stop her nose from stuffing up, or the tears from pattering down to smudge her columns of figures, which would never do. She took her handkerchief out of her sleeve and dabbed at her cheeks surreptitiously. A voice beside her said: "I cried when I heard, too." She looked up into the gimlet-black eyes of Gabriel Dumont. His mouth twisted up into a tentative stab at a smile, then he blushed and looked away.

The Dumonts camped by Fort Ellice and then moved on in the morning. The summer passed. It was decided that Madelaine wouldn't be sent back to the convent school this year. Her father said he couldn't spare her since his trading business had actually started to show a profit with her help. Privately Madelaine thought that he'd been making as much of a profit without her, he just hadn't known it without someone to add up the figures for him. But if it was going to save her from another winter in the convent dormitory, she wasn't going to argue.

The living forest on the slopes of the valley turned metallic—bright, brittle flakes of copper and gold and silver—and the Dumonts came back from the west. Instead of carrying on to Grantown, they decided to winter in the neighborhood and threw up a few cabins in the valley of the Qu'Appelle. The winter blew down from the north and locked the fort and the river in snow and ice.

Toward the end of January, Madelaine's father announced that he was sick to death of smoked fish and pemmican, and that he and Madelaine's older brother were going to take a trek down the valley and find a buffalo or two. In the winter the great herds scattered off the plains into small groups hugging the shelter of the wooded country. Madelaine said: "I'm coming, too."

"Don't be ridiculous."

"What's ridiculous? If I'm going to spend the whole winter cooped up here, I might just as well have gone back to St. Boniface. You two need someone to do the cooking and carving for you. Mama has to stay here and take care of the babies. It would be ridiculous if I *didn't* go."

"We don't have enough dogs."

"Borrow a team from the Company men."

In the end Madelaine's father threw his coat on and stumped off exasperated to ask the Hudson's Bay Company trader for the loan of a team of dogs and a *carriole*—the toboggan-based dogsleds that the Indians favored over the runnered sleighs built by the Eskimos up north. They set off in the gray light of dawn in three *carrioles*—one loaded with gear and the other two empty. They took turns riding in the empty *carrioles* while the third Wilkie ran ahead on snowshoes breaking trail. The expectation was that on the return trip they'd all have to run since the empty *carrioles* would be filled up with fresh meat. It was a monochrome, crisp world they skimmed and trotted through—white snow, black skeletons of trees, and gray skies. They saw a few ravens and magpies and white owls and heard a few sporadic bangs that might have been gunshots or trees snapping in the cold, but otherwise their hunting party was the only sign of life on the planet.

They'd brought along enough food for themselves and the dogs to last five days. On the third night, Madelaine was working over the fire as usual, boiling tea and propping up a skillet of bannock dough to face the flames while the frozen pemmican sizzled in the pot. As usual, her brother was scooping out a bowl in the snow with a snowshoe. He would line it with buffalo robes and cover it over with the tent skin. What wasn't usual was that her father wasn't helping, he was squatting by the fire sucking his dead pipe and staring grimly into the flames. There wasn't a better hunter in the country than her father, but there was such a thing as luck. At last he gave out a grunt that signified he'd made up his mind, tongued the mouthpiece of his pipe around to balance it between his side teeth, and said: "We'll keep on going till the food's gone. Even if we don't find buffalo, there's bound to be a deer or *something*. Worse comes to worst, we can eat dog on the way back home."

Madelaine looked over at the happily half-fed pack digging themselves into snowbanks and curling up with their feathery tails around their noses. "'Course it'd have to be our dogs," he went on. "I gave them Company men my word I'd bring their team back whole. But it won't come to that. We're bound to hit sign soon."

They didn't. On the fifth night they fed a last supper to themselves and the dogs and drove on hungry in the morning. As the sun bent to the west her father called a halt. "That's it, we got to turn back. Get a cookfire going—from here on in we only stop when we fall down." He drew his rifle from the scabbard strapped to the side of one of the *carrioles* and stood looking up and down the line of dogs panting in harness.

Madelaine heard, or thought she heard, a tiny tinkling sound. "Papa . . ."

"Hm?"

"Listen. . . ."

"What?"

"Listen! Can you hear. . . ?"

He pulled off his hat and cocked his head to one side. "Madelaine, I don't—"

"Ssh! Listen."

He sighed through his nose and went back to a patronizing impression of a man listening for something. Then he blinked, straightened his head up, and said: "I'll be damned."

Around the bend in the frozen river came two dog *carrioles*, with their tinny little harness balls jingling. Two men in striped Hudson's Bay blanket coats were snowshoeing along with the dogs. One of them was very tall and the other short and squat. The Wilkies' dog teams leaped to the attack. Madelaine leaped onto the drag of the nearest *carriole* to hold them back. Her father managed to catch the second one, but the third *carriole* went bouncing away behind the snarling wolf dogs charging to drive off the invaders. The two new teams sprang forward to meet them. The blanket-coated men jumped between and drove them back with their dog whips. Once the dogs were settled, both parties of human beings advanced toward each other, pulling back their hats and hoods. It was Gabriel Dumont and his very big brother Isidor.

Madelaine's father explained their position. Isidor said: "Get a fire up. Both our *carrioles* are jammed full of meat. We had good luck." Then he laughed and winked sideways. "Well, luck and my little brother."

They stuffed themselves with buffalo tongue and threw the frozen guts to the dogs. Isidor leaned back in the snow belching, squinted up at the sky, and turned to Gabriel. "We still got an hour's light. What do you think?"

Gabriel wrinkled his face up like a winter apple, peered around, sniffed at the air, and shrugged: "Maybe."

Isidor hauled himself back upright and headed over to the two Dumont *carrioles*, calling back: "Get your guns and put on your snowshoes—we got to get upwind from the dogs."

Madelaine crunched along in the trail broken by the four males. Isidor stopped by a clump of spruce trees and whispered back at Gabriel: "What do you think?" Gabriel grunted and nodded his head. Isidor crouched down among the skirts of evergreens and motioned the others to do the same. The only one who stayed standing was Gabriel. He cupped his hands around his silky-furred mouth, cocked his head back, and let out an inhuman, guttural sound halfway between a bellow and a bleat. He listened for a moment, then did it again.

Madelaine strained her ears. There was no other sound but the harsh whistle of the wind curving down off the plains. She said: "What—"

"Ssh!" Isidor hissed at her. The same sound came again, in a wispy, weak version.

It came again, louder this time. There was a crackling of frozen branches, a crisp thud of something heavy crunching through the snow crust, and a loudening bellowing. Madelaine turned to look in that direction just as her father's and her brother's guns exploded in both ears. There was a loud thump, and a big fat buffalo came snow plowing down the hill. She looked again at Gabriel Dumont and heard her father say: "Where in the name of Christ did you learn how to do that? I heard of old Indians that said their grandfathers could, but . . ."

"Don't bother." Isidor laughed. "The old fellow that taught Gabriel taught me at the same time, and I never even been able to get a half-deaf rabbit to come to me."

Madelaine stared at Gabriel Dumont scuffing the rims of his snowshoes together and muttering down at them: "We better go get her carved up and bled before she freezes."

CHAPTER 15

The talk that Madelaine heard around the billiard table in the evening grew steadily more bitter as January passed, and half of February, with no word from the government. Gabriel rode off alone a few times, to Isidor's or Moïse Ouellette's, and when she asked him what they'd talked about, he just passed on some bits of inconsequential gossip.

One eye-searing, bone-freezing morning, she and Gabriel and Annie were on the river breaking a hole through the ice with a three-foot iron spike, a five-pound hammer, and a ten-year-old axe. She was clutching the spike with both hands, idly wondering whether the cold emanating through her moosehide mittens was going to freeze her fingers off before Gabriel missed with the hammer and broke them off. She said: "I don't see why you can't fish through the water hole."

"How would you like it—uh!" Clang. "If I had gone and cut our water hole—uh!" Clang. "In a place where—Uh!" Clang. "Catfish like to congregate?" He dropped the hammer in the snow and stooped down to scoop out the ice chips.

Annie said: "Uncle Gabriel . . ."

He raised his head and followed Annie's eyes toward the downstream bend in the river. He stood up, brushing the snow off his mitts, and nodded: "We got a visitor."

Madelaine pried open her fingers and stood up as well, pushing her numbed knees to unbend. Strain her eyes as she might, there was nothing to be seen but the rippling crust of snow and, here and there along the banks, a few leached-out tufts of buffalo grass and bleached skeletons of trees. Then she began to hear the hoofbeats. A horseman careened around the bend and galloped across the ice toward them.

Madelaine had always heard it said of Louis Riel that although he'd never been able to pry his nose out of a prayer book for long enough to learn the rudiments of hunting and shooting, he

111

could ride like greased Jesus. He was already climbing down off the saddle while his horse was skating to a stop. "Gabriel! We have a reply from the government!"

"What do they say?"

"Macdonald sent a telegram to the North West Council. They forwarded it to Nolin. *Nolin*, for all the saints' sakes—as though my name never appeared on the petition!"

"Well, you got to admit, Louis, you never gave Macdonald much cause to be fond of you. What does it say?"

"It says . . ." He had to stop and swallow, as though choking on something. The gray eyes had gone dead. When he did speak, it was like two scraps of sandpaper scraping across each other. "They are considering . . . appointing a royal commission to look into the matter."

Madelaine looked to Gabriel. His mouth had settled into a straight line. His face had gone utterly placid and expressionless, as though he were asleep with his eyes open. It was the look that meant it was time for her to clear everybody out of the billiard room or to tell the young man sitting at the card table not to be so stupid as to sneak his hand any closer to his knife. Gabriel reached out and took hold of the spike, its point imbedded six inches into the ice. He tensed his arm, the sleeve of his coat vibrated in place for a moment, and then the spike popped free. He expelled his breath and turned to her, with a trace of sentience seeping back into his eyes. He said: "I'm sorry you had to do all that spike choking for nothing. Looks like maybe I ain't going to be doing much fishing."

She said: "Maybe this royal commission can fix things."

"Like the last one? When the commissioner didn't bother coming around here because he hadn't thought to hire a translator? Or the one before, when the commissioner tripped and twisted his ankle so they just forgot the whole thing? Or maybe like the one before that—that gave birth to another pile of papers to gather dust in Ottawa and a bunch of fat salaries for Macdonald's friends?" He looked off at the eastern horizon and muttered: "Old Tomorrow," which was what the Indians called Sir John A. Macdonald. "So long as we keep on being his 'humble petitioners who will not cease to pray,' he's going to keep on throwing us dried-out bones till we got no teeth left."

"You don't know that."

"You want me to wait till they start shoveling our garden over our faces?"

Madelaine waited to reply. She waited through the walk back up to the house, through stoking up the fire and cooking dinner for the four of them, through sitting down to eat and getting up to clean the dishes. Riel was full of plans for declaring a provisional government to force the government to deal with them. In spite of her intentions, she must have let slip some sign of her reaction to that, because at one point the gray eyes fastened on hers and he said soothingly "It isn't as drastic as it sounds. The government itself gave the Icelanders the right to create their own republic on Lake Winnipeg. If new immigrants have that right, surely we who have lived here for generations can do the same." She bit her tongue and waited. Gabriel, said very little, which was a very bad sign.

Isidor arrived and they moved down the passage to the billiard table. Riel looked surprised that Gabriel should choose to reach down a cue at a time like this. He didn't understand that when Gabriel was thinking, playing billiards kept him from scratching his beard off. Riel produced a piece of paper from his coat pocket, saying: "I had a premonition that things might come to this, so I wrote something that I think all the men we hope to rely on the most should be encouraged to sign. 'We, the undersigned, pledge ourselves deliberately and voluntarily to do everything we can to: 1. save our souls by trying day and night to live a holy life everywhere and in all respects; 2. save our country from a wicked government by taking up arms if necessary.' " This was followed by a lot of pious evocations of the names of saints and Holy Mother Church, but they were drowned out by the last phrase echoing over and over in Madelaine's ears.

Isidor paused in lining up his shot to say: "I don't see what difference signing another piece of paper's going to make."

Gabriel growled: "You going to shoot or talk?"

"When are you ever going to learn that some people can do both at the same time?"

Madelaine said: "I think, under the law, anyone who signed that would be committing treason."

Gabriel wheeled around to face her, roaring: "You think I don't know that? Just because I can't read the goddamned piece of paper don't mean I don't understand what it means."

She could feel the warmth of the blush spreading over her cheeks. She held her jaw firm and blinked to keep the tears in her eyes. She was no soft little thing to burst into tears because

Gabriel yelled at her; they'd both been known to yell at each other a lot louder, when they were alone.

Gabriel appeared to be aware of what he'd done. He looked down at the floor and ground the butt of his cue on the toe of his moccasin. Isidor said: "No wonder you don't like the idea of talking and shooting at the same time—odds are you'd shoot yourself in the foot while it's stuck in your mouth."

Gabriel swung his cue at his big brother, who bounced it off his forearm. Wherever her old man had been for the past few hours, he was back now. He conceded the game, racked up his cue, and dipped a cupful of beer. He said: "That oath ain't a bad idea at all. People'll shout all kinds of blood and thunder in a meeting, or around a billiard table and a barrel of beer, but putting your name down on a piece of paper's another thing."

They talked a few minutes longer, then Isidor and Riel put on their coats for the ride back home. Madelaine stirred the fire in the hearth down to coals and went up to bed to wait for Gabriel. When he was lying down beside her, she said: "What are you going to do?"

"Well, I ain't going to load up my gun and ride to Ottawa, if that's what you're worried about. First off we'll have to see if all the bold threats people have been making have just been gas—if that's the way it is, I ain't going to do nothing. If people are willing to stand up, I think maybe declaring a provisional government'll make Ottawa talk to us."

"And if it doesn't?"

"Then maybe we'll take a few hostages. I think Macdonald'd sit up and take notice if we told him we had all the Indian agents around here locked up in a cellar, plus the whole Police detachment at Fort Carlton."

A chill went through her, despite the layers of goosedown quilts and the heat from both their bodies. No one had ever taken on the Police and won. Gabriel chortled low in his throat and said: "Me and my cross-eyed grandmother could take Fort Carlton. The idiot that built it figured it'd never have to stand up against anything but bows and arrows and fur trade muskets. Anyone with a decent rifle could perch himself up in the hills and kill anything that moves inside those stupid little stickwork walls. Crozier's no fool; if he doesn't know it already, we wouldn't have to drop more'n a few of his constables before he figured out they're barricaded inside a trap."

"You can't win a war against the whole damned British Empire!"

"It ain't a war to win. All we got to do is show them it costs less to talk to us than fight us. And if it comes down to that, Macdonald can't afford to stretch it out too long. The American government's just waiting for an excuse to come up here and take the country for themselves—they couldn't ask for much better than a war between the people of the North West and the Canadian government. Riel's got friends south of the line— Fenians and our own people in Montana—who'll help us even if it ain't gone far enough for their government to make it official. Hell, I don't know why we're even talking about that. Just declaring a provisional government'll make Ottawa understand you can only kick a dog so long."

"Do you believe that?"

There was a long silence, except for the growling exhalations through the granite-ridge nose and the rustling of the bedclothes as he sat up, lay back down, rolled over, and sat back up again. When he finally did speak, his voice sounded as if it were forcing its way up through gravel. "I am sorry. Maybe if you'd chose another husband he might have been able to see another way out of this. I keep looking and looking, and I can see all these steps along the line where things'll probably stop there, but if they don't . . ."

"Then some people are going to have to learn the hard way what I could've told them if they'd asked."

"What's that?"

"That they might be foolish enough to think it's sometimes a misfortune to be married to Gabriel Dumont, but it ain't near so much a misfortune as starting a fight with him."

"Well, not near so much a misfortune as starting a fight with his wife."

"You must be tired."

"Not so much."

"That's good."

CHAPTER 16

It wasn't the best time of year to be riding around, but Gabriel didn't have much choice. If he wanted to know what the Chiefs were thinking on the reserves, he'd have to sit down and smoke tobacco with them. If he wanted to sound out the Ouellettes and Dumases and the other old buffalo-hunting clans on this idea of a provisional government, he'd have to ride out to their farms and put it to them face to face. He also wanted to make it known that he wasn't going to be accepting any freight contracts for the coming spring, and he would consider it unfriendly for any of the other freighters to take advantage of the gap. If the people of the South Saskatchewan were going to stand up together against the government, it was no time to be scattered across the plains in cart trains.

Every day he plodded back to Gabriel's Crossing long after dark, with his fingers so numb with cold he'd have to warm them in his armpits before he could unbuckle the cinch strap. Madelaine would sit him down with his feet propped near the fire to thaw out the thongs on his moccasins and hand him a cup of hot rum tea to melt the ice off his mustache.

There was a meeting at Isidor's place one night. All eleven men present signed or made their mark on the oath Riel had written. The names comprised a list of most of the men whose opinions counted along the South Saskatchewan. The notable exceptions were the priests, who had so far refused to say yes or no to Riel's requests for support, and Charles Nolin.

When the ink on the last signature was dry, Gabriel picked up the piece of paper and said to Riel: "It ain't too late to go visiting." On the way out the door he had second thoughts and asked Isidor to come along as well, as insurance against losing his temper.

Madame Nolin answered the door, looking even younger and healthier than she had at the end of her novena. She ushered

116

them into the parlor, where her oversize gargoyle of a husband sat in the halo of a desk lamp, laboriously adding up accounts. He looked up with relief at the prospect of being interrupted. The relief died when he saw who it was. Gabriel handed him the piece of paper. The folds of skin around the misaligned eyes twisted in on each other as he read it through. Gabriel picked up the pen lying beside the ledger, dipped it in the inkwell, and extended it toward him. Nolin didn't reach for it. Isidor, looking more like a grizzly bear than ever in his frost-tipped buffalo coat, drifted over to the side of the desk and stood looming with his arms crossed.

Nolin said with some difficulty: "Don't you think you should think about this, Gabriel?"

"I been thinking about it a long time. We been talking about it a long time. You been saying for years we got to quit begging and stand up on our hind legs. That's what we're doing."

Nolin still didn't reach to take the pen from him. Instead, he sat twisting his sausagelike fingers together and mumbled: "But maybe this royal commission will—"

"You know as well as I do what that royal commission's worth. You were the one that said we oughta've shot the last commissioner, if he'd ever showed up here."

"But what if—"

"Don't give me 'what ifs'!" Gabriel's hand shot across the desk, spattering ink flecks over the tuberous nose. "Are you going to put your name down with the rest of us or not?" Isidor's slab of a hand settled onto Gabriel's shoulder. Gabriel leaned back far enough to take the point of the pen out of the range where Nolin had to cross his eyes to look at it.

Nolin said: "This paper doesn't say what you're planning to do."

"If enough people agree, we're going to declare a provisional government. If Ottawa won't give us any rights as people, we won't give them the right to govern us."

Nolin looked down at the desktop, his lumpy shoulders hunching together. He licked his lips and said rawly: "Miracles can happen. Why don't we hold a novena and ask God to guide us? If He shows us no other way, I'll sign this."

It threw Gabriel off. He peered at Nolin, trying to gauge whether this was a move he'd hatched out with the priests. A novena would mean nine days for the priests to work on softening everyone's resolve, nine days for the Police to send telegrams back and forth to Ottawa. It would also make it a hell of a lot easier for the Police to keep an eye on them if everyone was gathering every day at the church. On the other hand, it would save Starface a lot of trotting through blizzards.

Riel said: "Will you swear, on your hope of salvation, that if the novena shows us no other way, you will sign this oath and stand with us to the end?"

"Yes, certainly, of course!"

On the first Sunday of the novena, Gabriel sat between Madelaine and Annie, watching Father Fourmond take up his position in the pulpit.

The craggy priest didn't look to be in a mood for begging God to bestow the mercy of divine guidance on his flock. He stood there for a moment milking his gray horsetail beard with both hands, then opened his mouth to speak. "The cardinal virtues of all true Christians are humility, patience, and obedience. Deny those and you deny God. The vilest of all sins is the sin of pride and rebellion. The most beautiful of all the archangels became the foul fiend of the pit the instant he raised up his hand against the Throne. No priest of the True Church can ever or will ever"—thumping his hand down on the Bible in front of him to punctuate each item on his list—"Hear confession, give holy communion, or perform the rites of extreme unction, for any man who raises his hand against the lawful government which God has placed over him."

There was a shout from behind Gabriel.

"The Church of Rome is a lie, and the Pope is a heretic!" It was Riel, on his feet with his fist in the air, his voice rolling Father Fourmond's under like sun dance drums over a chorus of crickets. "Priests are not religion—they are meant to be the servants of religion. *You*"—stabbing his arm toward Father Fourmond—"have turned the pulpit of truth into the pulpit of lies and corruption, from the instant that you dared to use the sacred altar to threaten people who only seek to defend their sacred rights." He lowered his arm to his side, turned his back on the altar, and marched for the door.

Will Jackson, the putative convert, was up immediately and scurrying along in his wake. Marguerite, pale-faced, herded the children along in front of her. Gabriel took hold of the back of the pew in front of him and levered himself to his feet. He looked down at Madelaine. She hesitated, then put her big hand in his so he could boost her up. Annie was already on her feet. They joined the shuffling stream flowing down the aisle to the door. There was no sound but the creaking of the floorboards and the whisper of moccasin leather and Father Fourmond's voice pronouncing a hasty benediction.

Riel was standing on the front steps. The crowd emerging from the doorway parted around him and then hesitated in the churchyard, murmuring and scuffing their feet in the snow. Riel looked down at them and then flung his right arm up and back, pointing at the bell spire their hands had raised. "God will not abandon his people. It is the Church who has abandoned God. The Church of the Old World has corrupted herself into the whore of Kings and Prime Ministers. There is to be a new church for the New World, and Bishop Bourget of Montreal shall be her Pope. I have a letter from him blessing my mission." He swung his arm halfway down, to point behind him through the church door. "These priests of the old Church will either stand with us or be dragged down with the reeking corpse of Babylon into their own hell."

CHAPTER 17

Lawrence Clarke was an important man—a justice of the peace, the Hudson's Bay Company's factor at Fort Carlton, an officer in the extremely informal militia unit known as the Prince Albert Volunteers, and extremely well connected with Sir John A. Macdonald's Conservative party. The Cree and métis who made up most of the population of his district couldn't seem to grasp how important a justice of the peace was. They were in the habit of settling their own disputes. This annoyed him.

When Gabriel Dumont and Father André had been running their own government on the South Saskatchewan in the 1870s, it was Lawrence Clarke who'd raised the alarm about Gabriel's attempts to enforce the laws they'd passed to try to stave off the extinction of the buffalo. Lawrence Clarke had called out the Police and alerted the militia and fired off telegrams that had led to newspaper headlines across the country that could have been a blueprint for the current agitation: PROVISIONAL GOVERN-MENT! RIEL RECALLED! 10,000 CREES ON THE WARPATH! When none of it turned out to be true, it was Lawrence Clarke's bottom that took the severest paddling from Her Majesty's icy colonial secretary. This had annoyed Lawrence Clarke and had been festering in his gullet for ten years.

Lawrence Clarke had once been friends with Gabriel Dumont and had awarded him the bulk of the contracts to cart freight in and out of Fort Carlton. In those days there had only been two ferries on the South Saskatchewan—Batoche's Crossing and Clarke's Crossing. When Gabriel's Crossing had opened up be-tween them, it turned out to be more convenient for a number of destinations—and even travelers who didn't find it more con-venient still tended to choose Gabriel's Crossing simply because it was Gabriel's. If that hadn't been annoying enough, Lawrence Clarke was compelled by the Company to keep on awarding contracts to the freighter with the best rates and reputation, who usually turned out to be Gabriel Dumont. Included in all freight charges, of course, was the toll for ferrying each and every cart across the South Saskatchewan—at Gabriel's Crossing.

Consequently, Lawrence Clarke was in a jaunty mood when he passed through Batoche's Crossing on his way home from Ottawa. He'd kindly offered to hand-deliver a list of several hun-dred signatures from prominent citizens of Prince Albert, ex-pressing their support for Riel's Petition of Rights, to his friends in the Conservative party. By the time he'd left Ottawa, the gov-ernment was taking steps to mobilize the militia.

The cutter's runners hissed merrily through the snow. The harness bells jingled. Lawrence Clarke whistled through his teeth. Although the river was still frozen solid, there were a number of men hanging about at the landing stage on the east shore of Batoche's Crossing, as though waiting for the ferry. As the cutter drew parallel with them, Lawrence Clarke slowed the horse to a walk and called out: "Are you still holding your meetings?"

Michel Dumas called back: "More than ever! Almost every day now!"

"Fine. Fine. I hope you enjoy them while you can. When I passed through Fort Qu'Appelle, Commissioner Irvine was mounting up eighty constables to come and reinforce Crozier at Fort Carlton. Once they get there, they're all going to ride over here and arrest Riel and Gabriel.'' He whipped the horse back to a trot and skimmed on across the river, chortling happily and rehearsing in his mind what he was going to tell the reporters from the Prince Albert newspapers: "The petition to Ottawa is going to be answered by bullets. . . ." Perhaps "*with* bullets. . . ." "*In* bullets. . . ?"

Madelaine and Annie were riding north to Batoche's Crossing in the jumper for the second-last day of the novena. A "jumper" was essentially a Red River cart with the wheels knocked off and replaced by runners for the winter. It got its name for its propensity to become airborne when it passed over hummocks of snow. The effect was decidedly unsettling on a stomach that hadn't had any solid food for eight days. Outside of the giddiness, though, Madelaine figured a little shrinkage of her stomach wasn't such a bad idea. After the walkout on the first day, the novena had been carrying on in a kind of unspoken truce— the congregation would continue being devout and docile if the priests gave no more lectures on the sin of pride and rebellion. But so far, no one had been divinely inspired with an alternative to declaring a provisional government.

Gabriel was trotting along beside the jumper on Starface, grumbling: "Jackson, Jackson, what's the difference?"

She said: "From William Henry Jackson to Joseph Honoré Jaxon."

"All right, so he's changing his Christian names."

"He's changing his *whole* name."

"Like I just said: 'Jackson, Jackson, what's the difference?' "

"It's the spelling." Will Jackson had chosen the second-last day of the novena to formalize his conversion from Protestantism to the Church and to adapt his name to fit the tribe he was joining. He couldn't very well usurp the ninth day since it happened to be St. Joseph's Day—the patron saint of the métis nation.

Gabriel slapped his forehead. "Oh! The *spelling*! That's sure gonna mean a whole hell of a lot to a people that mostly can't read or write."

"Well, it means something to him." She saw that he'd stopped listening. He was standing up in his stirrups and peering ahead, squinting against the snow crystals blown on the wind. She looked down the road, raising one mittened hand to shield her eyes while the other kept hold of the gray pony's reins. Through the thin screen of winter-stripped bush, she could see the church and the rectory in the distance. Stick figures were boiling around them in circles, flapping their arms and brandishing guns in the air. One of them jumped onto a horse and came galloping up the trail.

Michel Dumas started shouting as he reared his horse to a halt and fell in beside Gabriel. "The Police are coming! Five hundred of them, to arrest you and Riel."

Gabriel said: "Are they now?"

"Irvine's bringing reinforcements up from Fort Qu'Appelle. Lawrence Clarke saw them getting ready."

Madelaine said: "*Clarke* says?" salting it with as much derision as she could squeeze into two words.

Gabriel said: "Well, there's no question the Police are up to something. Crozier brought over another twenty from Battleford last week." Then he closed his mouth and kept his eyes sighted straight ahead. He might just as well be riding down the road alone. Despite the jouncing of the saddle beneath him, his body had assumed a kind of erect stillness, like the eerie calm in the eye of a storm. Madelaine had seen him go like that many times before, less frequently in the recent, quiet years. She knew that he was still perfectly aware of everything that was going on around him, but he was living out there where his eyes were focused.

As the horses and the jumper pulled into the churchyard, they were surrounded by a shouting mob. Riel came forward, calling to Gabriel: "Have you heard what—"

"I heard." He slid down off Starface, tossed the reins to someone, and accompanied Riel toward the steps of the church. Madelaine handed the jumper's reins to Annie and scaled up and over the cage of cart rails to follow them.

Father Fourmond was standing in front of the door. Riel said: "Something has happened. We need to use the church for a meeting."

"I protest against any use of this church for—"

"Did you hear that?" Riel turned to the crowd behind him, laughing. "He protests! The priest is a Protestant!" Gabriel reached past Father Fourmond and flung open the door.

Madelaine joined the crowd surging inside and found herself

a place in a corner to stand. She was one of the few women there. The church could barely hold all the men, much less their wives and children. Gabriel was leaning on one side of the altar; Riel stood stiffly on the other side. Father Fourmond huffed in and removed the sacraments.

When everyone who could squeeze in had, Gabriel stepped to the front of the dais. He pointed at Riel and said: "Here is a man we brought from seven hundred miles away to help us. Now the Police are going to come and take him away from among us."

Riel said: "We send them petitions, and they send the Police to arrest us—myself and Gabriel Dumont. I have tried to do the best I could to help you, but deep in my heart I am beginning to believe I am doing you more harm than good. The government still hates me for what happened fifteen years ago. So long as my name is linked with yours, they will never listen to you. Therefore, I believe it's best that I gather my family together and return home to Montana. . . ."

He was drowned out by the congregation shouting: "No! The Police won't take you! Don't be afraid of that!"

Gabriel waited them out and then said: "No? Are you saying you won't let them? How do you plan to stop them?"

Michel Dumas hollered: "Any way it takes!" which brought a roar of approval. Annie was standing beside him, looking fierce. Madelaine hugged her arms around herself and pushed back farther into her corner.

"What are you saying?" Gabriel asked them. "Are you saying you'll pick up your guns and fight them?"

"Yes!" A forest of ancient, muzzle-loading shotguns shot up into the air, with here and there a Winchester or an old Henry rifle. "If we have to!" In front of Madelaine, Moïse Ouellette was thumping the butt of his rifle on the back of a pew and bellowing. Beside him, Gabriel's sister Isabelle was shouting just as loud, and Isabelle was old enough to know what it meant to kiss her husband good-bye and watch him ride toward the sound of gunfire.

Gabriel stood stone-faced with his eyes flicking over the roaring assembly. Madelaine knew it wasn't a crowd-quietening trick. When Gabriel wanted a crowd to be quiet, he told it so. She guessed that what he was doing was measuring and counting. There were old men in the crowd who'd fought a hundred battles but could no longer ride out to fight. There were the men of Gabriel's generation, perhaps the last generation of true wagonmen. And there were the young men, who had never had occasion to fire a shot at another man. A song that Isidor had made up passed through her mind: "The old days are dead, and the old men are dying, and the young ones don't know what it means to be free."

Gabriel's eyes found her out in her corner. They held on her for a moment and then returned to her relatives and neighbors, who had yelled themselves out for the moment. He said softly: "I know every one of you like you were my children, and I'm asking you: How many of you are there? How many of you are saying that you're willing to stand up and fight if it comes to it? Raise up your hands."

Not one of them did. They all leaped to their feet, lifting the roof beam with their voices. Riel stood with his hands clasped together and his soul melting out of his eyes. Gabriel looked unmoved, like a rock that the waves of sound broke against. When they were quiet again, he said: "Yes, I see you all got your minds made up—for now. But how many of you would stand with me to the end? Two? Three?"

They all roared that they would stand up to whatever the government chose to throw at them. He didn't wait for the sound to die down this time but let loose the bass bull-roarer voice over them: "If that's what you want, if that's what you've decided— that the only choice left is to march—then I'll march in front of you like I always done."

She'd thought they'd been loud before. Then they spewed out the door so as to be able to fire off *feux de joie* without putting holes in the church roof. There was no one left but her and Gabriel. He stood looking down at the floor, twisting his gnarled fingers around each other. He rubbed the back of his neck, jumped down, and started up the aisle. She moved out of her corner to intersect with his path at the doorway.

She thought at first he didn't see her, but he stopped beside her and one bludgeon of an arm arced up to settle across her shoulders. He still kept staring straight ahead, as though a cable fixed to the bridge of his nose were sprung taut to some living anchor out beyond the church door. He said gruffly: "I could keep on asking them all day, old woman, but that's how it seems to stand."

She said: "I know."

The oak log weighing down her shoulders softened into the

draping arm of her Gabriel. He winked at her and said: "Even if it does come to a war, you oughta know I didn't get to be this old by pure accident."

There was another burst of *feux de joie* from outside. Gabriel muttered: "Gotta put a stop to that. Maybe it's good for their spirits, but cartridges don't grow on trees. Or I guess I should say powder and shot—most of the arms they said they're willing to take up are older'n me."

He took his arm away and rolled out the door. She sat down and wrapped her hands around the rim of the backrest of the pew in front of hers, rolling her forehead from side to side across her knuckles and the curled ledge of wood.

CHAPTER 18

When Gabriel came out of the church, the *feux de joie* had dwindled to a smattering. Riel was standing on the steps. Gabriel stopped beside him but didn't look at him; his eyes were occupied with picking out certain individuals among the crowd. Riel said in his ear: "The first thing we must do is declare a provisional government and elect representatives to the council."

Gabriel shook his head. "Tomorrow. There'll be a lot more people coming in for the last day of the novena. Even more so when they hear what's happened today." Then he carried on with his inventory of the crowd. He was looking for men whose temperament was suited for long, cold rides alone and who could be trusted to think for themselves. As he found them, he called out to them one by one: "Trottier, I hear White Cap's been asking after you. Joseph, I think your wife's cousin up at Poundmaker's ain't seen you for a long time." Each man nodded in acknowledgment, kissed his wife and children adieu, and headed for his horse.

After delegating half a dozen, Gabriel still needed one more messenger, but the suitable candidates in view—Moïse Ouellette, Michel Dumas—were men he wanted to keep within shouting distance. The heads of his three brothers stood out over the back of the crowd: grizzled Isidor, black-bearded Edouard, and "little" Eli, six feet four with grown children of his own but condemned to be the eternal baby brother. Gabriel sent Eli off to Fort à la Corne, and then his mind clicked over to the next thing that had to be done. "Edouard—pick yourself out a half dozen men good with an axe and ride around to the telegraph lines and—"

"No!" It was Riel, and it wasn't a word Gabriel was accustomed to hearing in these kinds of circumstances. "Once Macdonald realizes that we won't be bought off by his stalling promises, he will send a telegram offering to negotiate. If there's no telegraph . . ."

Gabriel didn't like it. Without the telegraph, the Police posts and government agencies would become isolated islands in a sea he ruled. But he had to admit Riel had a point. "All right, Edouard—only on the other side of the river. If Macdonald wants to send us a message, he can send it into Humboldt.

"The rest of you that Edouard don't pick out, put a bit of food in your pockets to get you through the day and saddle your horses. We're going shopping." Edouard would have the sense not to pick out men like Isidor and Moïse to waste on chopping down a few telegraph poles. He turned to Riel. "You got a good horse you can borrow?"

"Yes. Moïse Ouellette has kindly offered me the use of—"

"Good." Gabriel jumped down off the steps and started toward Starface. Halfway there, he remembered and turned around. Madeleine was standing in the doorway of the church. He pursed the corners of his mouth and shook his head to show her that there wasn't going to be any trouble today. She nodded, and he carried on toward his horse.

Isidor and Riel rode on either side of him, with fifty other sets of hoofbeats drumming along behind. It had been a long time since Gabriel had felt the sensation of riding out at the head of a line of armed horsemen. The sun at its height was finally warm enough to draw a sheen of sweat out of the snow. In any normal winter the ice on the river would have started breaking up by now.

Riel said: "Where are we going?"

"Like I said—shopping. All the Indian reserves around here got a general store attached to them, some got two. We can kill

two ducks with one rock. Since we got this provisional government now . . .''

"We haven't declared it formally, or even decided on a form
for the governing council.''

"I told you—we can do that tomorrow. Today we got to move
fast before the word gets around. We can make all the formal
declarations we want, it ain't going to mean nothing unless we
got the strength to back it up. No matter how brave those fellows
behind us are, they can't hold out for long without food and
ammunition. The reserve stores got both. And since the stores
are all government-licensed, the storekeepers are more or less
related to the government. I don't know about how white men
fight wars, but a Chief who'll piss on your campfire on Wednes-
day becomes suddenly respectful come Thursday when he hears
you got a few of his relatives tied to stakes.''

The nearest reserve on this side of the river was One Arrow's.
Gabriel reined in Starface in front of the squat, snow-capped
store and climbed down, flexing his knees to get the blood moving in his legs. The crisp air sharpened the massed harness jingle
and hoof stamp and moccasin thump behind him. He didn't look
back at them or waste words, just snicked Le Petit out of the
saddle scabbard. He grabbed the latch string, jerked open the
door, and then grinned at his good fortune.

The Indian agent and his interpreter happened to be leaning
on the customer's side of the counter, looking back over their
shoulders at the door. The storekeeper was poised in the act of
licking his pencil while scrutinizing the sack of potatoes laid
out on the counter. Gabriel looked at the storekeeper and said:
"Hello, George.''

"Hello, Gabriel. What's doing?''

Gabriel moved forward, peripherally aware that Riel and Isidor and others were crowding in behind him. The store wasn't
nearly big enough to hold them all. "What's doing, George, is
that your government's gone and declared war on us. So we
thought we'd stop by and pick up a few things we're going to
need, and a few hostages,'' turning to the Indian agent and
interpreter.

The Indian agent flared: "Now you wait just a minute!''

"No, I won't. And neither will you. Button up your coats on
the way out.'' The white faces grew a good deal whiter. Michel
Dumas and Moïse Ouellette came around to show them to the
door. Isidor was prowling up and down the store shelves, point-

ing out sacks of flour and barrels of salt pork to the volunteer porters filing in behind him. Gabriel looked back to the storekeeper. " 'Fraid that means you, too, George. And all the guns and ammunition you got in stock."

"You know the Police won't let you get away with this."

"*These*"—Riel gestured at Gabriel and the others—"are the Police now."

"Where have you hid your guns and powder, George?"

"Maybe I'm out of stock."

"Don't give me that shit."

"Maybe I'm not going to tell you."

"Maybe I'm going to cut your heart out and spike it to the door. But that wouldn't help me find them, would it? Tell you what, George, I'll make you a deal. You know I don't want to spend the afternoon taking your store and your sheds apart. If you surrender up all the guns and ammunition you got, we'll let you have your freedom," which as far as Gabriel was concerned meant the freedom to get the hell out of the territory.

Riel led part of the troop back to Batoche's Crossing with the hostages and confiscated goods, including six shotguns, two kegs of powder, and a few boxes of cartridges. Gabriel got back on his horse to head to the next store.

It was after midnight by the time a tuckered-out Starface carried him back into the village of Batoche. His troop had shrunk to ten, escorting two more prisoners and a jumper full of gunpowder and groceries. The others had peeled off in ones and twos as the route back passed by their homes. The last to go had been Isidor, clattering his horse onto the wind-scoured ice of the South Saskatchewan as the rest of them carried on past Edouard's farm. Isidor's place and Edouard's faced each other across the river just downstream of Batoche's Crossing.

The village wasn't asleep yet. As Gabriel and his remaining horsemen trotted past the houses, doors came open, throwing keystones of yellow light across the snow, and questions were called out in low voices so as not to wake the children. There wasn't much floor space in and around Batoche tonight that wasn't covered over with a blanket or a buffalo robe for an uncle or a brother or a cousin bedding down with his rifle.

Where the riverside path intersected with the Carlton Trail, Gabriel turned the remnants of his raiding party east along the row of business buildings facing the north side of the trail. He called a halt in front of the blacksmith's shop, climbed down, and went inside. He struck a match and just about burned his fingers before he spotted an iron bar that would suit his purpose. He heaved himself back up onto the saddle and carried on past little Phillipe Garnot's little log cabin inn, to "Batoche" Letendre's new-built, grandiose, false-fronted general store. He had just shaken his foot out of the right stirrup and was starting to lean his weight down on the left when his eyes registered something strange. He stopped and looked again.

A couple of hundred yards away, across the snow-covered meadow of Batoche's Flats, "Batoche" Letendre's big green-and-white house stood nestled among the trees. There was lamplight shining from the downstairs windows and a moonlit feather of smoke fingering out of one of its twin chimneys. The reason that was strange was the same reason Letendre's new store had yet to open for business, even though it had been completed and stocked on schedule six months ago. Back in the fall, when Riel had been riding around soliciting opinions for his petition and Gabriel had been sending tobacco around to various Chiefs, "Batoche" Letendre had had a sudden inspiration to move his entire household north to Fort à la Corne and spend the winter trading furs.

Gabriel climbed down regardless, detailed a couple of men to fetch the other prisoners from Phillipe Garnot's stopping place—nobody but little Phillipe dignified it with the name of "inn"—and mounted the steps to the front door of Letendre's store. He worked the iron bar down behind the padlock hasp and wrenched the staple screws out of the wood. Inside, the moonlight coming through the extravagant display windows showed him shelves full of stock. He found a rack of candles and lit one. Michel Dumas came in herding the prisoners. Gabriel said: "What's going on over at the Letendre house?"

"Riel took it over as headquarters for the provisional government. Madelaine's over there, too. Riel said he'd leave one of the rooms for you and Madelaine so you wouldn't have to be riding back and forth from your place every day."

Gabriel beckoned to the prisoners and led the way to the stockroom at the back. There was a trapdoor there, leading down to another one of the extravagances that "Batoche" had had built into his store—a stonewalled cellar that underlaid the entire floor space. Gabriel threw back the trap, handed the candle to the first prisoner in line, and said: "Get on down there. We'll get you some blankets and lamps and a bucket of water. Michel, keep an eye on them for a moment.''

''Where are you going?''

''To get a jailer I can trust—unless you want to sit up all night watching them.''

Out behind Phillipe Garnot's stopping place was a stack of firewood, with a pile of deadfalls waiting to be sawed into split-table lengths. Gabriel looked over the deadfalls, trying to gauge length and height by sight, dragged out one about twice as tall as he, and slung it over his shoulder. Back in the store the shelves had been pirated for blankets and lamps and coal oil, and the prisoners had been settled in. Gabriel called down: ''Have a good night's sleep, and don't forget to say your prayers,'' then slammed the trap. He laid one end of the deadfall on the trap-door and stood it up to butt against the ceiling. Michel helped him wedge it into place.

After bedding down Starface in the stables behind Phillipe Garnot's stopping place, he carried Le Petit across the flats to the Letendre house, packed snow squeaking under his mocca-sins. Madelaine was in the kitchen, stirring a pot of sweet-smelling ham-and-pea soup over the hearth fire. He said: ''Scared to use Madame Letendre's stove?''

''I thought you might be hungry when you got back, so I didn't want to waste time tinkering with it. I'll get it fired up tomorrow.''

He laid Le Petit across the table to remind him to take it to bed instead of leaving it out where Riel's children might get their hands on it. ''Riel asleep?''

''No. He set up a table and a lamp up in the attic—said he had to do some writing.'' She set down a big bowl of soup and a loaf of bread in front of him.

''I thought we were still fasting?''

''I'll keep it up through the last day, but there's no reason you should. If the novena was going to show you another way out of this, you wouldn't have spent all afternoon and half the night galloping around through the snow.''

CHAPTER 19

As soon as the sun was up, Madelaine hitched the gray pony to the jumper to drive back to Gabriel's Crossing. She'd sent Annie home on a borrowed horse the night before, to milk Evangeline and feed the other animals. The jumper rode the waves of snow like a canoe on the ocean.

The dogs set up a hungry clamor as the jumper pulled into the yard. Annie came out of the barn balancing an apronfold of eggs. "I've fed the pigs and milked Evangeline, *Maman*, but I only got the two hands." Madelaine climbed down off the jumper and dug out some frozen fish from the back shed for the dogs, then climbed into the loft to fork out some fresh hay for the horses. The cats would forage for themselves. Maurice the rooster would make sure they didn't forage on his hens.

When the animals had all been cared for, Annie gave her a hand bundling together some changes of clothing, half of their remaining winter stores of food, all of the powder and pig lead and boxes of cartridges from the store shelves, and a number of buffalo robes and blankets. Madelaine wrapped up Gabriel's revolver and cartridge belt, along with the foot-long sheath knife he sometimes liked to hang from the opposite hip. On a shelf in the kitchen was his personal store of cartridges—pinfire .38's for the revolver and rim-fire .44's for Le Petit. He'd laid in quite a hoard of them this year. As she was going through her dresser drawers upstairs, she came across her own little .22 revolver with its own box of cartridges. She hadn't fired it in years, although Gabriel took it out once in a while to clean it. You had to be an awfully good shot to kill anyone with a .22, or awfully close in, but you could certainly make them stop and think about coming any farther. She wrapped it up in a bundle of freshly laundered rags that would be good for bandages.

Once they'd loaded it all onto the jumper, there was barely enough room left for Madelaine to stand at the front rail and barely enough time left to get back for high mass and Joseph Honoré Jaxon's christening. The sun had climbed as high as it was going to get—a splotch of white in the gray woolen sky. Annie trudged over to the paddock to fetch the horse she'd borrowed at Batoche's Crossing and hitch him to the back of the jumper. The set of her shoulders and the studied stiffness of her movements told Madelaine that she would dutifully obey the sentence to stay here and take care of the place while Batoche was resplendent with high mass and vibrating with all the other goings-on. Madelaine called after her: "Why don't you saddle up one of our horses and hitch him behind as well? You can ride him back after mass in plenty of time to keep Evangeline from bursting her udders."

Annie charged back toward the house to change out of her hog-slopping clothes. Madelaine stood in the jumper looking over the place. She remembered the main house as a rib cage of beams in a long-past springtime, Gabriel and Isidor perched on its bones nailing shakes over the frame. The half-blue-faced house became only a naked square of floor planking among the summer grass; there was a steamboat docked at the ferry landing, with its crew wrestling a billiard table down the gangway, and Gabriel was jumping up and down on the wharf like a three-year-old on Christmas Morning. Then all the buildings and livestock disappeared, and she was standing beside Gabriel among the chest-high sweet clover and red willow. He was scratching his beard and squinting back and forth between the gulley winding down from the plateau behind him and the coincidental cleft in the clay cliff on the other shore, grumbling: "A ferry? A ferry . . . Don't you think they already got enough goddamned crossing places for one river?"

Annie startled her by materializing beside the jumper and saying: "*Maman*? What's going to become of us and. . . ?" gesturing around to take in their home. She'd managed to get herself changed into her Sunday clothes and to harness the saddle horses to the back of the jumper in the instant since Madelaine gave the invitation.

" 'Become'?"

"With all the talk of a war and the Police and—"

"There ain't going to be no war. Once it's been made clear to the government that we're more scared of their promises than we are of their guns, they'll realize they have to start treating us like human beings. It might take a few weeks and a few more hostages and maybe a bit of standing up to the Police, but it'll all be over in plenty of time to put in the potatoes.''

"Then why are you crying?''

"Oh. Well, when you get to be an old woman you'll understand what a bit of sharp wind and weak eyes and memories can do. Or maybe I just started wondering when he's ever going to finish painting the front of the house. Come on or we'll miss the mass.''

They did anyway, along with the celebration of Joseph Honoré Jaxon's conversion. Madelaine heard later that he'd chosen as his dedicatory verse Matthew 10:34: "Think not that I come to send peace on earth; I am come not to send peace, but a sword.''

The jumper's runners crunched across the deserted churchyard to the rim of the ridge looking down on the village. There were a lot of people standing in the snow in front of "Batoche" Letendre's big green-and-white house and the two men standing on the porch—Riel and Gabriel. There was a gap left open between a black-and-white clutch of priests and nuns and the multihued crowd—as though the clergy had chosen to emphasize their separation from their parishioners' current course of action. Madelaine reined in the gray pony in the gap.

Riel was saying: ". . . shall compose the governing council of the provisional government. These councillors shall be known as Exovedes, which means 'those chosen from the flock,' and the council as a whole shall be the Exovedate.''

Father Fourmond snorted a laugh through his copious nose and said loudly: "The Latin *ovis* means 'sheep.' ''

Madelaine said: "If we were sheep, Father, we wouldn't be doing this,'' then turned to face front again, a bit taken aback at her own effrontery.

Riel stepped back to let Gabriel oversee the election—a process that consisted of Gabriel pointing his finger into the crowd, calling out, "Moïse Ouellette,'' or, "Albert Monkman,'' and the crowd roaring acclamation. Madelaine was more than a little surprised that neither Gabriel nor any other Dumont were among the twelve Exovedes, and even more surprised that Riel wasn't.

"For secretary of the Exovedate,'' Gabriel said, "I nominate Joseph Honoré Jaxon.'' The ex-secretary of the Settler's Union stood twisting his shoulders together and blinking his green eyes to hold the tears in. "As commissioner, I nominate Charles

Nolin.'' Nolin didn't look particularly comfortable with it, but he was now commissioner and that was that.

Gabriel stepped back, and Riel stepped forward. "There is one more position to fill—that of captain general, to advise the Exovedate on all military matters and serve as War Chief to the Army of the Exovedate.''

The entire gathering of métis and Cree and white immigrants started yelling two different names. Some yelled: "Gabriel Dumont!'' and some yelled just: "Gabriel!''

Gabriel proceeded to organize his army along lines that Madelaine's father or any other old captain general of the buffalo hunt would have recognized immediately. All he had to say was: "Captains of Ten,'' and the crowd broke into a businesslike buzz. Some grizzled hunter would say to the man next to him: "I think Moïse Ouellette'd make a good captain for us, don't you? Hey, Moïse, you want to be our captain? Okay, there's me and my three brothers, and Michel here—who else you want in your ten?'' Within ten minutes the crowd had separated itself into platoons, each squad made up of men who knew and trusted each other and could communicate with the shorthand of old friends.

Madelaine wondered if that was just one more thing, and perhaps the worst, that the government in Ottawa failed to understand about its métis subjects. For all their self-willed, almost obsessive individualism, they hadn't spent decades roaming wherever they wished across the territories of the Plains tribes without evolving a very effective system of military organization. It hadn't been used for some years, but it was still there.

One of the Exovedes volunteered his house as military headquarters. Gabriel told the rest of the captains to convene there, and the mass meeting was over. Madelaine said to herself: "Well, that's that.''

Annie said: "That's what?''

Madelaine hadn't intended to say it aloud. She looked into the honey-dewed face of her cuckoo child and said blandly: " 'That's that' for their meeting—now we can get through to the house and unload.'' What she'd meant was: "That's that—he's just committed treason.''

She clucked to the gray pony and guided the jumper through the thinning crowd to the Letendre house. Marguerite Riel came out to help with the unloading. Michel Dumas came forward to show Annie how much he could carry in one armload.

Marguerite had taken possession of Madame Letendre's kitchen, by virtue of having moved into the house a few hours before Madelaine. So Madelaine sat at the kitchen table drinking tea and waiting to be consulted or appointed to a task. Marguerite was busy firing up Madame Letendre's remarkable, ornately tiled, cast-iron-and-porcelain stove—or trying to. Regardless of how fine she feathered her kindling, it would flare up for an instant and then sputter out to a smoldering smudge.

Madelaine's eyes traveled along the blacked tin pipe snaking out of the back of the stove. At the last elbow before it disappeared into the wall, there was a butterfly-shaped black lever. Were she Madame Letendre, Madelaine would have made damn sure to shut all the flues tight before leaving her house for the winter.

The room was growing more and more like the inside of a smokehouse. Marguerite was growing increasingly frustrated, chewing on her bee-stung lower lip, her glazed-apricot complexion flushing as though the stove she was fussing over were red hot. Madelaine sat waiting to be asked for an opinion, but the question never came. She considered waiting demurely until Marguerite's frustration reached the point of tears and then simply setting down her teacup and walking across to the far wall and flicking the lever—serve the doe-eyed little self-important scut right.

But then she considered herself at Marguerite's age—trying desperately to live up to the definition of a grown woman. She liked to think she'd have had the sense to eventually ask for advice. But the entirety of Marguerite's frail pride in herself did seem to be predicated on her ability to take care of all the mundane tasks of living so her husband wouldn't have to worry his majestic head about them.

Madelaine clinked down her teacup and said: "I never for the life of me could figure out how Madame Letendre worked her stove. But it seems to me I remember her saying something once about dampers built into the pipes."

Marguerite stood back and surveyed the stovepipe, prowling along underneath it with her neck cricked back. With a sudden thrill of discovery, she rushed back to the table to snatch a chair to stand on and pulled down the lever. Within a few minutes the firebox was pumping out smokeless heat through the body of the stove and Madelaine was playing the assiduous assistant: "Say, Madame Riel, you know that chunk of stew beef I brought—do you think it would be a good idea if I was to cut it up into cubes and brown it and throw it in the pot here to simmer with a few onions and a bit of dried sage?''

Annie stuck her head in from playing with Marie Angelique and Jean to announce that she was going visiting. Madelaine nodded over her shoulder, which was enough time for Annie to take in the scene and roll her eyes on the way out. A number of people circulated in and out, to drink a cup of tea and exchange news. Edouard Dumont had scooped up another couple of hostages who'd come out of Fort Carlton to see what was wrong with the telegraph line. But the bulk of the "news" consisted of rumors and theories of what Gabriel and Riel were planning to do. Madelaine listened with half an ear and went on building stew. Gabriel would tell her what he was planning to do while he was eating it.

Annie came back from her visiting at a moment when Michel Dumas just happened to be among the tea drinkers. She said she'd best be starting back now if she hoped to get home before Evangeline started suffering. Michel Dumas nonchalantly swung his feet off the table, letting the front legs of his chair crash down, and volunteered to escort her, "since it's beginning to get dark, and what with the Police patrols nosing around . . .''

Madelaine said, just as nonchalantly, "I doubt they got orders to arrest Annie on sight. And Gabriel'd probably rather you stick around here, Michel, since you been in on this from the beginning.''

Annie left on her own. Riel came in, without Gabriel, and poked his head in the kitchen just long enough to say: "What a delicious odor, but I must repair to the study upstairs to write something.''

Marguerite said: "Yes, Louis,'' and followed his departure up the stairs with her velvet eyes. Madelaine spent about half a second wondering whether Gabriel would have preferred a wife who worshiped the ground he walked above, then went back to preparing his dinner.

The stew was steeping on the off side of the firebox when Gabriel came in explosively debating something with Isidor. "It has to be *now*—tomorrow or the next day at the latest. Any day now the river's going to break. Already it's a close bet to ride a horse across the ice. And when it does break there's going to be a week at least when taking a boat across means fighting your way through the ice floes.''

"I ain't arguing with you, Gabriel. You're arguing with yourself." Gabriel opened his mouth to reply. Isidor waved it shut, laughing, and reached up to pluck "Batoche" Letendre's fiddle off the wall. After a bit of rudimentary tuning, Jean and Marie Angelique were mesmerized with the spectacle of the human grizzly bear sawing light-hearted jigs and coaxing lilting métis ballads out of a few ounces of wood, catgut, and horsehair. Then their father came down the stairs folding a piece of paper, and the inhabitants of the Letendre house sat down to dinner while Isidor took himself off across the river to his own home.

As soon as Gabriel had inhaled his first bowlful of stew, he said to Riel: "We got to take Fort Carlton soon, before the ice breaks and before Crozier gets his reinforcements. Not that any number of reinforcements is going to be able to hold that place, but the more they got, the longer it's going to take them to surrender. And the fifty that are there now is enough hostages to make Macdonald sit down and smoke our pipe."

Riel said: "There may be considerably less than fifty."

"No, it's fifty-six exactly. The women that cook their meals are métis, and they oughta know."

"I meant—less the ones you kill."

"I told you time and time again—we ain't going to have to kill more'n a few of them, if any. A few shots in over the walls and Crozier'll realize he's finished."

"Perhaps he does already. He must be given an opportunity to surrender without bloodshed. We must not be the ones to fire the first shot, if we hope to secure the sympathy of the world and heaven. I have written something"—producing the folded piece of paper from the inside pocket of his coat—"to present to Crozier, giving him three days to surrender." He handed the paper to Gabriel. "On the obverse side you'll see the formula that he must use when he accepts our ultimatum—that and no other. 'Because I love my neighbor as myself, for the sake of God, and to prevent bloodshed, I agree to the above conditions of surrender.' "

Gabriel dubiously flicked the paper back and forth, squinting at the calligraphy on both sides, and said: "What's the other side say?"

Riel looked confused for an instant, then smiled apologetically and said: "Of course, how thoughtless of me. . . ." and reached out to take the piece of paper back. Madelaine restrained herself from snatching it out of his hand and reading it to Gabriel, but it took some doing.

In between spoonfuls of stew, Riel surveyed his written words, tapping the appropriate lines with the back of his forefinger. "Essentially, it makes reference to the impossible position in which the Canadian government has placed Major Crozier . . . mmm . . . assures him that we respect him and will not harm his men *if* they surrender . . . and also assures him that if Fort Carlton does not surrender within three days, we shall 'commence a war of extermination upon all those who have shown themselves hostile to our rights.' Marguerite, Jean's dribbling on his new collar."

CHAPTER 20

About a third of the way along the trail from Batoche's Crossing to Fort Carlton stood the village of Duck Lake. There wasn't much to it—a store, the houses of the Indian agency employees, and a few métis cabins. The store was the only one in the neighborhood that the provisional government hadn't stripped yet.

As Crozier's three days ticked away, with the army of the provisional government twiddling its thumbs on the east side of the South Saskatchewan, politely waiting for a reply to their ultimatum, Gabriel grew increasingly anxious to ride across the river and take Duck Lake, and increasingly uncomfortable with waiting around Batoche. He presented his reasons to the Exovedate. "It'll give us a few more hostages. Some of the métis women at Duck Lake are afraid the Police are going to take *them* hostage. They say the Police scouts come riding through there all the time to spy on us."

Charles Nolin said: "What if Crozier's about to surrender? He might change his mind if it looks like we're going to force a war on him."

Gabriel said disgustedly: "Crozier ain't going to surrender, not as long as we stay sitting here. He ain't even bothering to reply to Louis's ultimatum, except for *that*," stabbing his finger at the handbill among Secretary Jaxon's stack of papers. It promised Police protection to anyone who'd joined in the "rebellion" out of fear of the ringleaders. "And why the hell should he? Each day he stalls us, Fort Carlton gets stronger. In case you haven't heard, Lawrence Clarke brought in fifty volunteers from the militia yesterday. If we'd had a few dozen horsemen posted at Duck Lake, we could've met them on the road and chased them all the way back to Prince Albert. And every day that goes by brings the Police reinforcements closer." He shook his head and said what all the individual reasons came down to: "We're giving them too many cards."

The vote split evenly, but Riel broke the tie in Gabriel's favor. Although he had no official position on the Exovedate, no one questioned that Louis Riel would have a vote and a voice in their deliberations—more of a voice than most of the rest of them put together.

Gabriel went up to the room in the Letendre house that had been given over to him and Madelaine. Madelaine was making the bed. As he strapped on his revolver under the cartridge belt for Le Petit, she said: "What's happened?"

"Nothing. I'm going to take a few men over to Duck Lake and take possession of the store. I might stay there overnight."

"You be careful, old man."

"Nothing to worry about." He kissed her and went down the stairs. By the time he'd saddled Starface, Isidor and Edouard had each mounted up their troops of ten soldiers. Twenty-three armed men should be plenty to do the job. It would've been twenty-four, but Riel chose to ride along unarmed. They walked their horses across the groaning ice and kicked into a trot on the other shore.

The Duck Lake store was a palatial affair, faced with a two-storied veranda that could be screened with mosquito netting. Gabriel had spent many a fragrant summer evening on those verandas, playing cards in the open air without the need for a smudge fire. But today the front door was locked, and his old friend the storekeeper was nowhere in evidence. An English half-breed who worked for him ambled over from the woodshed with an axe in his hand. Gabriel asked where the storekeeper was.

"Ain't here. Lit out for Fort Carlton this morning. Warned

the rest of us to do the same. Said you was bound to be coming this way soon.''

Gabriel looked at the locked door and sighed theatrically. ''Well, it's too bad in this weather, but I guess . . .'' He reached for the axe.

''No! I got the keys! Here you go.''

Gabriel tossed the keys to Isidor, who snatched them in mid-air and headed for the store. The woodchopper said: ''You sure you know what you're doing, Gabriel?''

''I don't like it any more'n you do, but it seems that's the way things are going. What do you figure's the best place around here to house prisoners for a few days?''

''Well . . . there's a shack with a stove in it for putting up the hired hands. . . .''

''Sounds good. Edouard—put him in the shed with a guard on the door and round up the Indian agency people. Oh—and Edouard—take his axe away and make sure there ain't no back door.''

It turned out that all the arms and ammunition in the store had either been sold off or hidden away. But there were lots of food supplies, including a shedful of government-stamped provisions consigned to Fort Carlton. It would've been nice to have found more guns, but given the numbers of Police and volunteers already crowded into Fort Carlton, and the fact that Commissioner Irvine's reinforcements wouldn't be hauling along more than traveling rations, intercepting Crozier's provisions was probably a better stroke of luck.

When the place was secured, Gabriel got back up on Starface and rode over to the Duck Lake Cree winter camp. He spent the evening drinking tea with the Chief and old Ahsiweyin, both of whom were annoyed that the Police scouts had been galloping back and forth across the reserve as though they owned the place. Outside the tent, Starface began to make it known that he was annoyed that he hadn't seen a bale of hay since morning. Gabriel took a last puff off the medicine pipe and rode back to the village.

Except for the guard in front of the prisoners' shed, his troop of horsemen appeared to have settled in for the night. Gabriel unsaddled Starface, dragged out a bale of the storekeeper's fodder, cut the twine with his sheath knife, and huffed his weary way across the compound to the light still showing in the windows of the store. As soon as he'd stepped through the door,

Riel was in front of him, saying: "I think there's no need to stay here."

"Huh?"

"The fears of the women here regarding the Police were obviously exaggerated. The Army of the Exovedate should make a policy of staying as close within the boundaries of Batoche as possible."

"Why?"

Before Riel could reply, two horses galloped into the yard. It was two of the scouts Gabriel had posted to the west side of the river. "Gabriel! There's two riders from the fort coming this way along the trail."

Gabriel ran for the stables. Starface had only taken a few tentative nibbles. He had just reached the point of deciding that the hay bale was good when Gabriel slapped the saddle onto his back. He whinnied indignantly, throwing back his oversize head and demonstrating that his teeth were almost as white as the blaze under his forelock. Gabriel clapped the bit in his mouth.

As he swung up into the saddle, he saw that Isidor and Edouard were already buckling the cinches on their own horses. With the already mounted scouts, that made five. Moïse Ouellette was leading a massed charge toward the saddles and bridles lined along the paddock fence. Gabriel called to Moïse and the others: "There's only two of them—don't bother," and kicked Starface into a gallop.

It was a bright moonlit night. Blue shadows danced across the fields of snow on either side of the trail. A full-tilt gallop in the winter was always a chancy proposition. Even the packed-down snow of the Carlton Trail was liable to ball up in a horse's hooves and skate the legs out from under him. But the sheltered dells surrounding Duck Lake meant the odds were good for coming down on a deep-drifted cushion. Gabriel leaned low over Starface's neck and kicked at his ribs with both heels.

He had no doubt whatever that the horsemen his scouts had seen were spies Crozier had sent out to snoop around. Gabriel didn't like being spied on. He did like the idea of two Police scouts added to his stock of hostages. He might have considered the notion of trying to outskulk and surprise them if it hadn't been for the wind in his teeth and the pulse beat of the hooves behind him.

The road wound up over a hill. As he crested the ridge, Gabriel saw two shadows in the hollow below moving along at a trot. They wheeled their horses and set off at a gallop, back the way they'd come. Gabriel whipped the reins back and forth across his horse's shoulders—as though Starface needed encouragement for a race. The snow-muffled drumming of the four horsemen behind him kept pace for a moment or two, then fell behind. The rump of the slower of the two horses ahead began to define itself as something more than an indistinct blot of shadow. Chips of snow thrown up from its back hooves bounced off Gabriel's face.

As Starface's nose surged past the other jockey's knee, Gabriel shifted Starface's reins into his left hand, leaned out, and reached for the other horse's reins. The horseman whipped the trailing ends of his reins across Gabriel's face. Gabriel closed his eyes, felt his gloved right hand butt against a leather strap and a horse's chin, closed his fist, and hauled back hard with both hands. As both horses skittered to a halt, Gabriel opened his eyes again and yelled: "Don't try to get away or I'll kill you!"

"I'm a surveyor!"

"You're a liar." He took a fistful of the "surveyer's" coat and dismounted, dragging the other man off his horse.

Isidor and Edouard were yelling at him. Gabriel looked around and saw why. What with Gabriel and the spy and Starface and the other horse milling around, the road was blocked and the snow on either side looked too deep to ride around. The other spy was getting away.

Before Gabriel could get out of the way, the sound of diminishing hoofbeats was suddenly replaced by a shrill whinny, a loud thump, and a string of curses. Gabriel cleared the road, and the other four charged on.

Looking closer at the man he was holding by the lapels, Gabriel recognized the deputy sheriff of Prince Albert. "Surveyor my ass." He relieved the deputy sheriff of his weapons and set him back on his horse.

Isidor and the others came back escorting a man whose face burned red between the streaks of snow. Isidor was laughing so hard he could hardly get out: "He looked back to see if we was still chasing him and fell off his horse."

The red-faced man grumbled: "Damned horse tripped over its own feet."

"Like hell—you fell off."

By the time they got the prisoners back to Duck Lake, the

sun was coming up. Riel had gone back across the river to Batoche. Gabriel stowed away the deputy sheriff and his partner with the others and unsaddled Starface. The other horses had disposed of the bale of hay, so he dragged out another. He was just cutting the twine when one of his scouts came galloping in. "The Police are coming! They opened the gates and started marching out this way!"

Gabriel wound his hand into Starface's mane, dragged his nose out of the hay, and threw his saddle on again, ignoring the hoof stamping and exasperated whinnies. Isidor shouted from where he was saddling his own horse: "There's not enough of us here. I'll bring help from Batoche." He heaved his massive frame up onto his equally outsize horse and set off at an earth-shaking gallop.

Gabriel shoved Le Petit into the saddle scabbard, appointed one man to guard the prisoners, and rode out at the head of the remainder of his little troop along the road to Fort Carlton. They hadn't gone far when Michel Dumas and gaunt-cheeked, goat-bearded Patrice Fleury came cantering to meet him. Gabriel had made Patrice his captain of scouts. He was also married to Madelaine's younger sister.

Patrice called out: "It ain't a war party like we first thought, only a couple dozen of them riding on sleighs. Looks like they still don't know we're here but figured they'd better come over and pick up their provisions."

Gabriel grunted: "A little late," and slowed his horse to a trot.

Michel and Patrice fell in on either side of him. Michel said: "Tom McKay's riding scout for them," and turned sideways to spit in the snow.

There were two McKay brothers—Tom and Gentleman Joe. Despite the fact that the McKay family stretched as far back in the history of the métis nation as the Dumonts did, the current generation had adopted a policy of being more white than most whites. One of the female McKays was married to Lawrence Clarke, and both Tom and Gentleman Joe had attached themselves like lampreys to the Police.

Not that Gabriel, or any other North West native with any sense, had anything against the North West Mounted Police as a whole, but the Police came in two different varieties. There were the ones like Crozier who did their best to understand the territory they'd come to police and to fit themselves into it. Then there were the one-termers who'd signed on for a few years of handing down Her Majesty's law to the natives of one of Her Majesty's wilder colonies, who saw and knew nothing beyond their closed circle of messmates and duty rosters. It was this second type of Mounted Police that the McKays had melded themselves into, to the point of referring to their own cousins as "those black bastards."

The road wound through the spruce-thicketed hills of Chief Beardy's reserve. The massed drumming of twenty sets of hooves behind him made it impossible for Gabriel to hear the hoofbeats of approaching horses, but he began to hear the jingling of harness bells. The snow on the sides of the trail didn't look to be drifted too deep at this point. He waved his arms to sign his troop to fan out and advance in a broad front, following his own orders by angling Starface off the road and jumping him over the crest of a drift.

Unfortunately, where he came down was probably the one spot in the entire landscape where a depression in the ground had created a bowl of deep snow. Starface sank to his haunches, screaming and plunging helplessly. Gabriel waved at the others to ride on. Edouard came back to take hold of Gabriel's reins and pull. By the time he got extricated, the rest of them were out of sight around a bend. He and Edouard galloped hard to catch up. By the time they did, the parties from Fort Carlton and Duck Lake had already run into each other.

The Police sleighs were clustered together, flanked by an escort of mounted Police and volunteers. Patrice Fleury was yelling at a mustachioed sergeant, who was yelling back at him: "Stand aside, sir! We are officers of the law, going about our duties. If you do not stand aside, I will place you under arrest."

"Maybe you're the one that's going to be under arrest, rabbit face!" Patrice was a good man by and large, but he never could resist the urge to outbark any watchdog he passed by.

Gabriel flipped Le Petit out of the scabbard and slid off the saddle. As he crunched across the snow toward the lead sleigh, the constable holding the reins exhibited his own carbine and bawled: "Keep back, you!" Gabriel kept on walking. "Keep back or I'll shoot!"

Gabriel told him: "Maybe I'll shoot you first." The constable appeared confused by the metaphysics of the situation and by the material problem of holding the reins and manipulating his rifle at the same time. He eventually came to a resolution by

clamping the ribbons under his left armpit and cocking his rifle
with his right hand. But by that time Gabriel was close enough
to swing out and crack him across the side of the head with Le
Petit, knocking him sideways out of the sleigh.

Unfortunately, Gabriel's glove-muffled forefinger was resting
too near the trigger guard, and the jar set off a shot into the air.
Horses spooked and reared; men cursed and rattled their weapons and looked around at each other to see if anyone was hit.
Tom McKay kicked his horse toward Gabriel, brandishing his
rifle and shouting down at him: "You better look out for yourself, Gabriel!"

"Maybe you better," jabbing the muzzle of Le Petit into
McKay's copious midriff. "I'll blow your brains out."

The horse shied in a circle. McKay struggled to rein it in with
Gabriel poking at his back with Le Petit. "You keep on the way
you're going, Gabriel, and somebody's going to put a bullet in
you one of these days."

"Who? You? You won't even stand up for your own people.
The provisions you and your friends came to get, we already
took them. There's not one damn thing you can do about it
except throw up your hands and surrender."

The sergeant shouted a frantic order to get the sleighs turned
around to return to the fort. It took some doing, what with the
narrow road and panicked volunteers and the occasional shot
fired over their heads by Gabriel and Michel Dumas. As the last
sleigh fell into line, they all got back on their horses and rode
back to Duck Lake, except for the scouts detailed to follow the
sleighs at a discreet distance. The ride back was jovial with self-
congratulations and mockery of the Police. All in all, Gabriel
was pleased. He hadn't managed to grab any more prisoners,
but the Police had been sent packing without a fight. The linch-
pin for the authority of the Police was the carefully cultivated
reputation that they couldn't be outfought or faced down. Stories
like Lief Crozier singlehandedly throwing Sitting Bull out of a
fort while his warriors looked on were more powerful additions
to the Police arsenal than batteries of cannons. But now a couple
of dozen métis had stood up in front of an only nominally smaller
number of Police and militia, and it wasn't the métis who'd
turned tail. It was especially good for the younger men to have
witnessed. The older men knew from experience that no one
was invulnerable.

They were trotting back into the compound at Duck Lake

when Isidor and Riel and a dozen others came galloping from the opposite direction. Louis had armed himself with the big silver crucifix from behind the altar. Isidor was surprised and a bit miffed to find them there. He'd raised the alarm in Batoche and immediately started back with those who'd happened to have their horses already saddled, leaving the rest to follow as quickly as they could.

Gabriel told them what had happened, to the great delight of all. "I should've known right off it'd only be a small troop coming for provisions. Crozier's too smart to come marching out today when he'll have a hundred reinforcements tomorrow."

"Damn right you should've," Isidor growled. "Would've saved me two hours' hard galloping."

"Sweating a bit of bulk off won't do you any harm."

"I just been through eight days of fasting, for Christ's sake."

"Yeah, you're fading away."

The next contingent of men from Batoche came pounding in to Duck Lake. Gabriel considered sending someone to tell the rest not to trouble themselves, then decided that he wanted them here in any case. He left Edouard and Michel Dumas to regale them with the story and led Starface around to the stableyard. The second bale of hay had been demolished. Gabriel unsaddled Starface, hauled out another bale, cut the twine with his sheath knife, and reached up to take off the bridle while Starface stood guard over the fodder, whinnying threats at the other members of the provisional government's cavalry.

He had just worked the bit out of Starface's mouth when a lot of yelling and commotion broke out around the front of the store. Michel Dumas came running, gasping for enough breath to shout: "Gabriel!" Isidor and Louis were running on either side of him. "The Police! They're coming out for real this time— the whole garrison and at least one cannon!"

Gabriel shoved the bit back in. Starface didn't fight or fuss, just sighed and looked back over his shoulder with sad, tortured eyes while Gabriel cinched up the saddle. The stableyard was filled with men scrambling for bits of harness and loading their guns. Gabriel swung up into the saddle and shouted to Edouard: "Wait here with Riel for the others and bring them on as fast as you can. We'll meet the Police by the north point of the lake."

He went out the gate with Louis calling after him: "If you surround them, they'll surrender with no bloodshed!" Gabriel waved back over his shoulder to show that he'd heard, but how exactly he was supposed to surround a hundred men with less than thirty was another question.

He did have something along those lines in mind—to arrange things so that Crozier would see he was beaten before a fight got started. Where the road wound past the north shore of Duck Lake, there was a natural horseshoe formed by a low, wooded ridge on one side and a gulley on the other. The open end of the horseshoe pointed toward Fort Carlton, so that the Police would march into an open meadow and find themselves confronted by men hidden in the woods in front of them and on both sides. All Gabriel would have to do was close off the ends of the horseshoe once the Police were inside, and Crozier's whole force would be ducks on a pond. Provided, of course, that the rest of the men from Batoche came up in time to give him enough guns to do it with.

As he galloped back up the road that he seemed to have been galloping back and forth on since the last time he'd slept, his memory was soaring miles ahead, giving him a hawk's view of that piece of ground near the tip of the lake. There was a cabin anchoring one end of the horseshoe—built and abandoned years ago and since kept up by any wandering hunter who liked to have a snowproof place for a base camp. With luck it might not have been used recently, so there'd be no tracks or signs of habitation.

They reached the escarpment that formed the closed end of the horseshoe with still no sign of the Police. Gabriel drew out Le Petit, jumped off Starface, looped the reins around a willow twig, and ran up the slope, followed by the rest of the troop. He got to the top of the ridge and looked out. It was pretty much like he'd remembered it. Within the framing U of bush-covered broken ground, the road passed through a wide, naked meadow of hip-deep snow. He said: "Moïse?"

"Gabriel?"

Gabriel didn't spare a glance off to the side where the voice had come from, just pointed Le Petit toward the snow-capped cabin and said: "Take half a dozen good, steady shots and hide yourselves in there. Don't leave no tracks and stay hid while the Police go by you. And don't let nobody fire a shot unless you hear a shot from here."

"That's done."

Gabriel dismissed Moïse from his mind. The next step was to disperse his pitiful remaining two dozen around the ridge and the gulley as effectively as possible in case the Police arrived before Edouard and Louis. If they did, there weren't going to be a hell of a lot of teeth in the jaws of his trap.

He was in the middle of doing so when a voice like the rattling of autumn leaves murmured into his ear: "Nice, clear day for a fight, grandson."

It was Ahsiweyin with three emaciated young Crees. They were dressed in raggedy blankets and sprung-seamed moccasins and armed with bows and arrows, improvised war clubs, and one antediluvian muzzle-loader, but they had managed to scrape together bits of red and yellow pigment for war paint. Gabriel shook his head and pinched the bridge of his nose and said: "Grandfather—who're you relying on to point out to you who's them and who's us?"

"My eyes are doing much better today. Good clear sun."

"Gabriel." Isidor was pointing toward the far end of the snowfield. Four horsemen trotted into view. Gabriel cursed, turned around, and jumped up on a nearby boulder, balancing himself with one hand grabbing an overhanging branch. He peered back along the road from Duck Lake village, or as much as he could see of it through the tangle of evergreens and naked columns of birch and poplar. There looked to be movement along a distant curve. If it was Edouard and Riel, they were still a long way off.

The Police advance guard came on warily, scanning the bush on both sides of the trail. They passed by the picturesque old snowed-in cabin without a second glance. A few hundred yards behind them, the front rank of the column was just rounding the bend, harness rings and brass hat badges flashing in the sun. Gabriel called to Patrice Fleury: "Mount up a few of your scouts and chase their scouts back. But don't shoot!"

Patrice bounded down the back of the ridge to where they'd left the horses. Gabriel slid off the boulder and rejoined Isidor and Ahsiweyin at the vantage point toward the front of the ridge. The whole of the Police column was in sight now, a few platoons of outriders flanking a line of sleighs varying from one-horse cutters to ponderous three-benchers, all crammed with constables and armed volunteers.

Isidor said: "They're not all going to get past the cabin before Patrice shows himself."

"We got no choice. If they"—pointing at the advance guard—"get much closer, they're going to see everything we're up to."

The four Police scouts were close enough for Gabriel to see that two of them were regular Police and two of them businessmen from Prince Albert—the same faction that had stood up on their chairs and cheered Riel on—when Patrice and four of his scouts charged out of the trees. The Police scouts reined their horses around frantically, one of them waving his arm and shouting: "Enemy ahead," and the chase was on.

The wind gusting from the west carried fragments of Crozier's parade-ground bellow, forming his column into a defensive position. Sleighs were angling off the road and running into each other. Patrice's scouts were steadily gaining on the advance guard galloping full-tilt back to safety. Isidor said: "Five dollars says we catch them before they reach the column."

"No takers." The Police and volunteers might be remarkable horsemen in the eyes of their families back east, but there was simply no comparison with men who had spent half their waking lives in the saddle since the time they were old enough to be boosted onto the back of their father's gentlest pony. Sure enough, Patrice drew even with one of them and leaned out to grab hold of his reins. The Police scout pointed his arm at him, an arm unnaturally extended by the length of a revolver barrel, and Patrice sheered off.

Crozier had lined his sleighs into a barricade. He had sensibly made the maneuver as swift as possible by building his line from the midpoint of the column, calling the sleighs in front back and the ones behind forward. What that meant was that the sleighs that hadn't yet come past the cabin when Patrice rode out had come forward. Crozier's wall of sleighs was right in the middle of Gabriel's horseshoe, with half of Gabriel's hidden soldiers currently licking their thumbs to slick their front sights for a clear aim at the backs of the men huddled behind the sleighs.

Isidor said: "Well, you couldn't have asked much more of Crozier's response to your trap."

"Except maybe enough men to spring it with. You know what to tell Riel and the others when they get here. I think Edouard's the best choice to lead about twenty men around to the point across from the cabin. Tell him to give a loon call when they're in place. I need something for a white flag. . . ."

"What the hell are you talking about?"

"I'm going to go down and jaw with Crozier for a while, stall him up long enough to—"

"Don't be a goddamned idiot! If you walk down there, all Crozier's got to do is arrest you or shoot you, and that's the end of us and the end of their problems."

"We got to keep him where he is until—"

"Damn right we do. That's why I'm going to talk to him."

Ahsiweyin said: "You need a white flag," and shrugged off his soot-black blanket. Underneath it was another blanket that had just discernibly been white in the days of its youth. He peeled it off, disclosing a third blanket. The old rugged Cree shrugged his diminished shoulders and said: "The winters've been getting colder ever since my youngest wife went with the smallpox."

Isidor reached out to take the whitish blanket, but Ahsiweyin pulled it away. "I'll walk out with you and wave my blanket. Maybe my eyes ain't good enough for war no more, but they got this bad from all those nights in smoky council lodges making pipe-long speeches out of 'Not too many rabbits this year, eh?' "

Isidor's face blossomed into laugh lines. "Come on, Grandfather, let's take a stroll."

Gabriel called after them: "If Crozier starts looking too nervous, just get the hell out. If you hear a loon call, say you got to come back to talk to me. As soon as you hear that, you'll know we got them trapped." Isidor waved his rifle back over his shoulder—his other hand was busy holding the old man's elbow to make sure he got to the bottom of the ridge by foot power.

Isidor would know that any loon call at this time of year wouldn't be sounded by a loon. Gabriel hoped that Crozier wouldn't be as certain.

In the small bones at the base of his ears was a soft thrumming, the hundred horsemen galloping behind Edouard and Louis. He looked around and spotted Michel Dumas lining up spare cartridges along a deadfall trunk. "Michel—get back along the road and tell them to slow to a walk. All except the captains—I want them up here to get their orders as fast as they can."

On the white plate of snow below him, rimmed with the tangled wreath of bush cover and quartered with the cruciform of road and Police barricade, the foreshortened silhouettes of his brother and the shriveled old Indian appeared. The white field made Ahsiweyin's flapping blanket appear even grayer than it was. From the midpoint of the Police line, a lone figure marched forward to meet them.

CHAPTER 21

Ahsiweyin sang under his breath as he wheezed along beside Isidor, their moccasins crunching on the hard snow of the road. Isidor couldn't make out all the words, but the repeating chant seemed to go something like

Great Mystery, I had a lot of years
And a lot of bouncy wives
And a lot of good fights when I was young and strong.

"Grandfather—singing your death song ain't real comforting to me."

"It should be. Out of all the times I sung it in the past, I wasn't right once."

"You want I should take a turn waving the blanket for you?"

"My arms ain't that useless yet. Besides, you got your hands full with your rifle. I thought a white flag meant no weapons?"

"How long you had that blanket?"

"Oh, five or six winters, maybe. What does a gray flag mean?"

The man walking out from the line of sleighs was closing the gap quickly, marching at a brisk pace. Isidor said: "Maybe we shouldn't walk so fast, Grandfather, you being such an old man and all."

Ahsiweyin grunted and slowed to a stiff-jointed shuffle. "Is it Crozier coming out?"

"Yeah."

"Ha—I told you my eyes were better today."

"You're a terrible liar. Who the hell else would it be?"

Crozier stomped to a halt a few feet in front of them and stood at ease, his barrel torso looking even broader in his buffalo coat. Ahsiweyin lowered his arms with a grateful sigh and slung the blanket over his shoulders. Crozier said: "Who are you?" gesturing at the escarpment behind them.

"Cree and half-breeds." Ahsiweyin shrugged, sidestepping the invitation to tell Crozier that the army of the provisional government was coming up on him. "What do you want?"

"You're the ones that came out with a white flag—what do *you* want?"

"We want to know what you want here with your Police and guns and cannon."

Crozier blinked at him uncertainly. "Nothing. We only came to see what was wrong."

"Wrong? There's nothing wrong. Who said there was anything wrong?"

Crozier's response was preempted by a horseman galloping out from the line of sleighs. All three turned to look. By the rider's elaborately fringed Wild West garb, by the polished-brass gleam of the cartridge belt slung across his chest, and especially by the long-barreled Sharps buffalo gun, Isidor recognized Gentleman Joe McKay. The glitter of his armory was filled out by a big pearl-handled revolver strapped crossways to his belt. Isidor resisted the impulse to cock his rifle.

Gentleman Joe McKay reared his horse to a halt beside Crozier, pointing toward the woods surrounding the snowfield. "It's a trick! They're trying to sneak around behind us!"

Ahsiweyin stepped forward and took hold of the barrel of the Sharps rifle. "Where are you going with so many guns, grandson?"

McKay yanked the rifle around, whipping the old man up off his feet, but Ahsiweyin kept his grip on the barrel. Isidor started forward. "McKay! That ain't no way to—" The black mouth of the Sharps rifle exploded with smoke and sparks. A railway navvy swung his hammer against a spike set into the hollow of Isidor's breastbone. The bright blue of the sky and the sparkling white snow spun like a whirligig. There was a padded thump as the road slapped him across the back, and a series of sharp-sounding cracks like revolver shots. Ahsiweyin was dancing across the snow with remarkable twirls, new red rosettes blossoming out of his blankets. The last thing Isidor heard was Crozier shouting: "Fire away, boys!"

When Gabriel heard the gunfire he was scuttling hunchbacked along the coulee bordering the woods, showing his captains where to disperse their soldiers, while at the same time trying to pay due attention to one of the younger men who was scurrying along beside him. "Uncle Gabriel—I ain't ever been in a fight where people are shooting at me before. If I get scared and try to hide my head, will you keep at me and make me fight?"

"Anybody that don't duck his head from time to time ain't going to last long. Anyway, with luck there won't be any shooting." Then the deep boom of the Sharps rifle reverberated, followed immediately by the crackle of a handgun skipping all the way around the cylinder. Gabriel bellowed: "Stand up and fire!" and flung himself across the lip of the coulee.

Riel, waving the yard-high silver cross above his head, was yelling: "In the name of God who made you, reply to that!" The winter-stripped bush on all sides was exploding with rifle fire. Gabriel's vision registered an instantaneous frame of the wide white field with two dark shapes lying motionless and of Crozier and Joe McKay scrambling back over the wall of sleighs; then all he saw were the sights of Le Petit and the distant silhouetted barricade. Anything that moved between the black line of scalloped battlements and the bright white behind yanked the sights and his trigger finger like a compass needle.

The trigger was suddenly clicking uselessly. He'd fired off all twelve shots. His right hand dropped to his cartridge belt to poke cartridges out of the loops and insert them in the chamber on its own while his eyes took advantage of the opportunity to take in the larger picture. There were several bodies hanging forward across the sleighs, and Gabriel was certain he'd seen a number of others flung backward onto the snow behind.

There was a clap of thunder and lightning from the Police line, echoed immediately in the woods off to Gabriel's right— the perfection of the echo marred by a shower of tree splinters and a high-pitched scream. All the Plains tribes had a particular horror of the Gun That Shoots Twice—artillery with impact-exploding shrapnel shells.

Gabriel stood up to try and get a shot at the cannon crew, but from the coulee they were walled off by the sleighs. He ran back to where the horses were tethered, jumped on Starface, and galloped up along the ridge, shouting: "Shoot at the gunners!" As soon as he'd reached an angle where he could get a clear shot, he jumped down and slapped his horse away and illustrated his orders by example. He managed to drop one of the gunners, but the rest carried on with their loading drill and lobbed a shell at the men in the coulee. It flew over and exploded in the bush behind, rubbing out a swath of landscape. The only way the cannon would do any damage to the men in the coulee was to lob a shell right into it—with the exception of Riel, who was cantering back and forth waving the cross over his head despite the fact that the ravine wasn't deep enough to shelter a man on horseback. The big silver cross blazed back the sun like a bullet-beckoning beacon.

Le Petit had to be fed again, freeing Gabriel's eyes for another sweep over the battlefield. Although the ridge wasn't much of a ridge, the minimal elevation gave him a better view than the coulee. He could see now that Moïse's sharpshooters in the cabin were playing merry hell with Crozier's troops. Instead of having a sleighwide barricade between themselves and their enemies, the Police found themselves crouching within the bodies of the sleighs for some protection from the crossfire. The only reason the sleighs offered them any protection against rifle fire was that someone—probably Crozier—had thought to armor their sides with a number of old stove tops. Every now and then there was a clear, bell-like clang of a bullet whanging off cast iron.

Their horses couldn't very well crawl in with them, though. Moïse could have easily decimated the sleigh teams picketed behind the barricade, but Gabriel understood how that went against the grain except as a last resort. As it was, there were a substantial number of human bodies stretched out behind the sleighs—some thrashing about and some still—and the screaming of the wounded Police carried over the gunfire.

The cannon crew was frantically manhandling the sled-mounted gun around to point at the cabin. It would be a straight-on shot that Ahsiweyin couldn't have missed. Gabriel emptied his rifle at the gun crew. One of them threw his arms up and fell, but another took his place. Although their movements were discernibly nervous even at this distance, they managed to get the cannon turned around and loaded.

Gabriel pumped more shells into Le Petit. The gun crew began gesticulating at each other and then ran to hide under the sleighs, leaving the loaded cannon still pointing at the cabin. Gabriel perplexedly worked back over his memory of the last few minutes, then began to laugh and called out to the men around him: "They put the shell in before the powder—if they touch it off now, it'll blow them all to hell!"

The news was passed along the line with much joviality, and then they all went back to work, somewhat more methodically now that the cannon had been taken off the scales. Gabriel finished reloading and took a pause to look over the situation.

On his right, the young man who'd been afraid of being afraid was blazing away like a tiger, firing as fast as he could reload. Not that his bullets were likely to be inflicting much damage, though, any more than those of most of the others, since the sleigh fort was at the extreme end of their old muzzle-loaders' range. If you could only afford one hunting gun, there wasn't anything more practical than those virtually indestructible smooth-bores that were just as happy to fire birdshot as buffalo-weight bullets. But they weren't much good against Police rifles.

A rattling of winter-brittle twigs caught Gabriel's attention. He looked back over his shoulder and found his "nephew" Alexis peering out from a stand of wolf willow. Alexis Dumont was only Gabriel's nephew by virtue of the amount of time he spent following Gabriel around—the blood relation was that Alexis was the grandson of Gabriel's uncle Jean. Alexis was also only fourteen years old, but then Gabriel had been thirteen at Le Grand Coteau. Gabriel said in his fiercest growl: "What the hell are you doing here?"

"Well, I thought, Uncle Gabriel, if someone went down I would pick up his gun. I ain't that good a shot yet, but . . ."

"But you can run, can't you?"

Alexis flared indignantly, "I ain't gonna run away!"

"I didn't say 'away.' Look down there. . . ." There were a number of man-length dark lumps lying quite a ways out from the Police barricade, the result of the crossfire driving some of them out of their supposed defense works and of a few lunatic attempts to storm the coulee. For an instant Gabriel's eyes touched on two other bodies crumpled side by side halfway between the base of the ridge and the Police line, but he pulled them away. He couldn't afford to think about that now. "Every one of them dead policemen's got a rifle and cartridges he don't need anymore—a lot better rifle than most of our soldiers have."

Alexis nodded shakily and licked his lips. He was trembling and pallid, but his eyes were shining. He said: "Any métis boy that can't outrun a bullet better give it up and turn white," then started edging forward through the bush.

Gabriel called after him: "Just one at a time! Snatch the cartridge belt off as fast as you can and get the hell back under cover! And only the ones that aren't a far run!''

The gunfire was growing more sporadic. Gabriel stood up to take a look; he never could apply the advice he gave to others to himself.

Gauging the puffs of gunsmoke from the bush behind the cabin, and from the equivalent point on the other side of the road, the number of his soldiers who'd managed to work their way around behind the Police line was almost enough to close off the end of the horseshoe. It wouldn't have taken near that many to close the trap before the shooting started, but now intimidation wasn't enough. If the Police stayed where they were just a little while longer, the only choice left to Crozier would be to surrender or get wiped out.

Gabriel had a sudden certainty that exactly the same thought was passing through Crozier's mind. He ran down the back of the ridge to where he'd left his horse, shouting: "They're going to break! Give them all you got!" He jumped onto Starface and galloped through the whipping branches with two thoughts in his mind. The first was that he had to be at the far end of the clearing when Crozier tried to break out. The second was that the Police retreat had to be stalled as long as possible.

The best way to accomplish both of those was to cut straight across the open snowfield instead of circling through the bush. He could slow down the Police retreat while he was taking the fastest route to seal them in. He gave Starface his head and charged straight down the road at the center of the Police line, firing from the saddle and praying there'd be shallow snow where he meant to leave the road and angle past the end of the barricade. He could feel the tunnels of wind from the bullets whizzing past, but most of the Police had sense enough to keep their heads down.

He nudged Starface with his right knee, and they plunged off the road into the snow. A voice in Gabriel's ear said: "They'll start with the sleighs on the ends first," and he saw over the barricade a constable running forward with a team of horses. Le Petit jumped up to Gabriel's cheek and popped once at full gallop. The policeman curled up like a porcupine.

The bush-fringed shelter of the ravine was just ahead. Gabriel levered another shell into the chamber and twisted around in the saddle to find one more target before plunging into the coulee. A bullet punched into Starface's flank, the impact transmitting itself through his rib cage into Gabriel's legs. Starface screamed and tumbled sideways. Gabriel kicked his moccasins out of the stirrups, but before he could jump free a shellburst cracked 'cross the left side of his skull, driving his head down to bounce against his right shoulder. He hit the ground like a sack of meat. Starface was coming down on top of him but managed to get his back hooves planted at the last second and jumped over him instead, running for the trees with blood pouring down his rump.

Gabriel watched him go, thinking: Poor bastard—shot before he got his breakfast. Then someone blew out the sun.

CHAPTER 22

It seemed the northern lights were dancing under the roof of Gabriel's skull, except he'd never known the northern lights to give off heat. Warm fingers of blood were massaging their way down his forehead. The snow he was lying on was damp, which was a good sign spring was finally on the way.

He tried to pull his hands in underneath his chest to push himself upright, but his right arm refused to move. Out of the echoing cacophony of gunshots and shouts and the thunderstorms raging across his brain, one sound separated itself—the panicked voice of one of his young men yelling: "They've killed Gabriel!"

"No!" Gabriel had meant it to be a roar, but it came out as barely a grunt. He worked his left hand under him, propped his chest up to suck in a full bellow's worth of air, and expelled it all with: "I ain't dead! As long as your head's still on, you ain't dead!" And his was most decidedly still on.

Edouard was running toward him, puffs of snow sprouting up around his moccasins from Police bullets. Gabriel tried to rise to meet him, but his right leg was just as dead as his right arm. Edouard scooped up Le Petit, locked his hand around Gabriel's wrist—fortunately the left one, so Gabriel could help by taking a grip on Edouard's wrist—and dragged him back off the killing ground.

Once Gabriel was safely propped behind a cedar-matted hummock, Edouard knelt to look closer at the wound. Gabriel waved him off. "If it didn't kill me already, it ain't going to. More important you put some heart back into our soldiers before Crozier turns my bad luck into his good."

Edouard nodded and slapped him on the shoulder, laid Le Petit across his knees, and hurried off. Gabriel heard him shouting back in response to someone's question: "He's fine—just took the wind out of him. A little crack across the head ain't going to kill Gabriel."

From behind a nearby deadfall, one of the young men popped up to squeeze off a shot and then dropped down again to ram another load into his aged smooth-bore. Gabriel called to him: "You come here and shoot Le Petit for a while. He has a range of eight hundred yards and never misses."

He didn't wait to be asked twice. He levered Gabriel up onto his knees so he could take off the cartridge belt. Gabriel propped his left arm across the young man's shoulders, blinking against the blood seeping over his eyebrows, while younger hands wrestled with the knotted slack of his cartridge belt. The cold air seemed to be drying the blood quickly but was having no discernible cooling effect on the searing chasm chopped into the top of his head.

The belt buckle finally jingled open, bringing on a strange, loose, cold feeling under his waist. Gabriel looked down. The clever young man had gone and unbuckled the wrong cartridge belt, the one for his revolver, which also happened to be holding up Gabriel's pants.

Between Gabriel's grunting complaints and the young man's purse-lipped puzzling at the problem, they got it sorted out, and Le Petit went back to work while Gabriel settled against the cedar upholstery with his trousers secured. The sound of the gunfire from his soldiers had reassumed the assured rhythm that had faltered when he went down off his horse. The surge of confidence the Police had been given wasn't going to last for long. No doubt about it, despite the fallings-out they'd had over the years, Edouard was a Dumont.

One of the still-active veterans from the buffalo hunt days suddenly leaped up in the air and threw himself back spread-eagle on a pristine patch of snow, as though he'd had a sudden inspiration to make snow angels. Le Petit's temporary owner and several others started to go to him, but Gabriel rasped out: "No—I'll do it. Keep fighting."

Gabriel took a stab at getting up on his feet, but his right leg was still no good. He tried crawling, dragging the dead leg behind him, but his right arm wasn't any better. He flopped onto his left side and plowed his way across the snow by pushing with his left foot while pulling with his left forearm.

The bullet had gone through the upper part of the snow angel's left arm and into the chest. If you had to go, a heart shot was about the best you could ask for. Gabriel raised up his left hand to make the sign of the cross over his dead cousin, but since his left arm was all he had to prop himself up with, as soon as he lifted his left hand off the ground he flopped down on the snow like a landed fish. He tried again, and then a third time, but he couldn't move his hand fast enough to sign the cross in the air within the airborne instant between lifting his hand and hitting the snow. He began to laugh. "I'm sorry, cousin, I'm going to have to owe it to you."

A horse reared up beside him, with a flare of blue-white light on top of it. Louis Riel stepped down and knelt beside him, cradling the silver cross from the altar of St. Antoine de Padua. "The Police are climbing back onto their sleighs. We should order our men to charge them on foot now before they can—"

"No!" Gabriel surprised himself with the resurgence of strength in his voice, but he would have to have been dead not to feel a spring of horror at the notion of transforming the defeated Police into the happy patrons of a 360-degree shooting gallery with all his friends and relatives for targets. "Louis, that would just be pushing our own men into the wolf's mouth."

Edouard was shouting: "Get back to your horses! We can chase along beside them and pot them from cover all the way back to Fort Carlton!"

"No!" This time it was Riel's turn for horror. "There has been enough bloodshed, let them go." Personally, Gabriel thought it was foolish to let them off so easy—Crozier would have been lucky to get half his demoralized force back through that twenty-mile gauntlet and likely would have ended up surrendering. But his head hurt too much to argue.

Edouard came forward leading a limping Starface, stooping to scoop up snow with his free hand and rubbing it where the blood spoiled the glossy winter fur. "The bullet went in and out. He'll have a sore ass for a week or two." They hoisted Gabriel up onto the saddle. But with no life in his right leg he couldn't keep his seat, so they tied him on his horse.

Gabriel said: "Isidor . . . take me to Isidor." Edouard took hold of the reins and led him out onto the white field that just an hour ago had only been marred by the snake shape of the road. Now it was trampled over and dotted with pools of blood and gradually freezing corpses. Most of them were militiamen; the Police had taken their own dead with them. Along with the dead volunteers, Crozier had left behind five sleighs, a dozen precious rifles, several boxes of ammunition, and assorted odds and ends such as Lawrence Clarke's lynx-fur hat, which little Alexis was currently prancing around under to the delight of all and sundry. Unfortunately, Clarke's head hadn't been left inside it, but the hat stood as a measure of just how panic-stricken the Police retreat had been. No one in the North West would ever say again that the red tunics bounced bullets off; they only dyed a darker shade of red.

By the time Edouard had led Starface to the only two bodies on the white field that weren't white, Michel Dumas and Moïse Ouellette had brought up one of the captured sleighs and were gingerly lifting Ahsiweyin aboard. Despite the red flowers blossoming to meet each other on the off-white blanket he was wrapped in, the old bone rack was still alive, breathing out a pink-frothed death song, gazing up more sightlessly than ever into the sky.

Edouard crouched down beside Isidor and shook his head. Gabriel said: "Listen for his heart." Edouard just looked up at him and shook his head again. "I said listen for his heart, dammit!" By the stinging in Gabriel's eyes and the salt taste leaking into the corners of his mouth, the wound on his head must have opened up again.

Edouard stood up and continued shaking his head. Gabriel said: "Give me his rifle." Edouard proffered the rifle toward the only big brother he had left. Gabriel stiffened his spine in preparation for releasing his buttressing left hand off the saddle horn, snatched Isidor's rifle from Edouard, and sniffed at the muzzle. It hadn't been fired.

The procession back to the cluster of log buildings around the Duck Lake store appeared to be triumphal, in the moments when anything managed to penetrate the sphere of numbness surrounding Gabriel and encompassing Edouard and Michel

Dumas walking their horses on either side of his. Outside of the two who'd been shot down under their white flag, the total casualties to the army of the provisional government were three dead and three wounded. The Police and volunteers had been shot to hell.

When the soldiers of the Exovedate got back to the Duck Lake compound, Riel lined them up in two ranks facing Gabriel and bellowed: "Now all of you thank God, who gave you so valorous a leader, and give three cheers: '*Vive Gabriel Dumont*!' "

As the ovations swelled over him, Gabriel screwed his teeth and lips together against voicing the words in his mind: "Cheer quick and get it over with—we're two sore horse's asses, and neither one of us has ate since yesterday." The hot iron wedges in the top of his head had now been driven down past the bridge of his nose, separating his eyes into two separate Gabriels. The one central certainty that bound both together was that it was no longer up to anyone whether there was going to be a war or not. And just as certainly, the question of whether a certain fiddling grizzly bear had died for nothing was entirely up to Gabriel Dumont.

CHAPTER 23

The women and children in the homes along the banks of the South Saskatchewan waited. They could hear the sounds of the guns drifting over from Duck Lake. When the first boom of a cannon broke through the rattling of rifle fire, Marguerite Riel knelt down with her children in "Batoche" Letendre's parlor to pray. Madelaine knelt and prayed with them for a while, but once she'd prayed herself out she went back into the kitchen to keep the catfish soup from boiling over.

When the distant gunfire ended, people began to go from house to house exchanging guesses. Madame Caron said she had just begun to wash her floor when the first shots started and was only half-finished when they stopped.

Finally, Moïse Ouellette ducked into the Letendre house on his way to show his wife there were no holes in him. He said to Marguerite Riel: "Louis asked would I come by and tell you that by the grace of God no bullets came near him," and then turned to Madelaine. "Gabriel had a bullet scrape the top of his head, but when I left he was walking around all right. Isidor . . . well, Isidor's dead."

Madelaine sat down and put her hand over her eyes. Moïse went on awkwardly, "It happened quick. Gentleman Joe McKay shot him and Ahsiweyin when they went out to parley under a white flag. That's how it started. Other than them we didn't lose many, and the Police got kicked to pieces." Madelaine murmured something back, she wasn't sure what, to show that she'd heard him. Moïse hurried off home to tell Isabelle that her husband was safe but her big brother was dead.

Marguerite thought they should kneel and pray again, in thanks for the victory and to beg mercy on Isidor's soul. Madelaine wiped her eyes with the sleeve of her dress, blew her nose, said: "I can pray while I'm traveling," and heaved herself off the chair to go to the stove. She reached down one of Madame Letendre's empty sealer jars and started ladling in soup.

"Traveling? Traveling where?"

"Well, I would go to Isidor's family, but I'm sure Isabelle will, and they've got Aicawpow and all the rest nearby. Gabriel's got nobody around him but a bunch of old buffalo hunters whose idea of a bandage is a dirty rag with a stick knotted into it."

"Monsieur Ouellette said Uncle Gabriel was walking around now. . . ."

"Which means he wasn't right after he got hit."

"Don't you think . . ." Marguerite said timorously. "Don't you think that if they wanted us to go there, they would have said so to Monsieur Ouellette?"

"I didn't say anything about 'us.' You got your children to look after. All I got is one rock-headed old man. Hit a rock with a big enough hammer and it'll crack." She clamped the lid down on the jar of soup and went upstairs to gather together some blankets and some freshly laundered strips of cloth torn off worn-out clothes, along with a shirt and trousers that weren't worn out. Wrapped among the scraps of cloth was her revolver. She looked at it for a moment, then dropped it in the pocket of her skirt. She bundled herself up, loaded her bundles onto the jumper, and hitched up the gray pony.

The roof of the river creaked and groaned under the runners. In a few of the places that got the full day's sun, the snow cover had become a skin of water glistening on the ice. The pony's hooves splashed and skittered through them ominously. There weren't going to be many days left before the ice grew too thin to cross safely. Perhaps it had already, in which case she wasn't going to be much help to Gabriel's wound except as a very large, very cold compress.

The runners jolted over the rim of the opposite shore. She expelled the breath she'd been holding since the first splashing sounds and whipped the pony up the bank. By the time she reached Duck Lake the sun was just about down. A massive bonfire in the compound between the store and the outbuildings was mimicking the blaze across the western sky. A lot of armed men were milling about. Over their murmurings, and over the crackle of the fire, a voice was roaring inarticulately. She only knew of one human chest that could produce that deep and resonant a bellowing.

She reined in the pony but didn't climb down. The jumper gave her a vantage point to spot him from. She didn't have to look for long. At the far side of the crowd a cleared space opened up and surged forward. Bearded métis hard-cases and blanket-clad Cree warriors whorled aside like grass stalks around a dust devil. Gabriel stalked across the compound with his revolver in his hand and a blood-soaked lump of cloth tied to his head. He stopped in front of one of the store sheds and his bull-elk bugling formed itself into words: "Bring out the prisoners!"

Edouard stepped out of the doorway of the shed and said gently, "Now, Gabriel . . ."

"Did you hear me? He was your brother, too! March them out!" Edouard lowered his head, rubbed the back of his neck, looked at the stars, and then went back inside. Gabriel paced back and forth in front of the door, hunching forward and planting his feet awkwardly like a bear walking on its hind legs. Madelaine stood breathing through her teeth, her fingers and toes digging into the bed and railing of the jumper.

Edouard emerged from the shed and beckoned. Five very pale-faced men filed out of the doorway and planted their backs against the wall. Gabriel prowled slowly in front of them, peering nose to nose at each of them in turn, flexing his fingers around his revolver. Except for the crack and hiss of the fire, the compound had become so still that Madelaine could hear the whisper of one of the Indian agents: "What are you going to do, Gabriel?"

"What the hell do you think I'm going to do? I'm going to kill you just like you killed my brother—just wondering which end of the line to start at."

"We never killed anyone. We were locked up in here."

"Your tribe killed him—the side you chose to line up with." But it came out more as a matter of form than an accusation. Faced with the five of them trying to push their spines back through the wall, Gabriel's fury appeared to have given way to a kind of disappointment that they weren't the ones to take it out on. His prowling ferocity burned itself out, and he stood looking down at the ground. They had never been in any danger from him, as long as none of them did or said anything stupid to give him an excuse.

Louis Riel chose that moment to push his way through to the front of the crowd and shout: "In the name of God, Gabriel, think what you are doing! Would you make us savages in the eyes of heaven and the world?"

Gabriel's slumped shoulders straightened up. He turned to face the voice behind him. His features had gone dead calm, except for his eyes. The left one was screwed shut against the pain on that side of his head, and the right was leering with delight.

Madelaine knew exactly what that meant, and she scrambled to get out of the jumper to stop what was coming. Just when Gabriel had resigned himself to the fact that there was no one in the immediate vicinity offering any harm or insult to himself or his family, some kind soul had volunteered.

Unfortunately, the water that had splashed up over the bottom rail of the jumper when she came across the river was now ice. So when she planted her foot on the rail to boost herself over, her moccasin sole skated off and she came down hard on the top rail with the underside of both breasts.

She got her breath back and suppressed the pain and looked to see if she was too late. Riel was still standing in the same spot with all his limbs intact. Gabriel had turned around again to look at the prisoners, some of whom were shivering in their shirt sleeves. He waved them off and growled: "Get back inside before you freeze to death. You people weren't made for this country."

Madelaine took another stab at climbing out of the jumper, a bit more carefully this time, and hauled out the fat bundle of blankets and clothes insulating the jar of catfish soup. She made her way through the crowd, grunting perfunctory replies to the surprised greetings from relatives and neighbors. Gabriel was standing staring at the bonfire with his arms hanging slack, the pistol still in his hand. His head came up as she came into the firelight. He squinted at her as though she weren't his first hallucination of the day. When she didn't disappear, he said: "What are you doing here?"

"Someone told me a bullet bounced off your head."

"They lied. It was a cannonball."

"Is there some place inside where I can sit you down and see to that?"

He started to bring his arm up to point toward the store but stopped the gesture partway and blinked confusedly at the revolver in his hand, apparently surprised to find it there. He put it back in its holster and ushered her across the compound to the storefront, saying: "I took over the storekeeper's room up above." Inside the store, there was a bundle of blood-soaked rags stretched out on the counter chanting a death song. Gabriel murmured: "I thought he would've been gone by now."

Madelaine went to the counter. There was so much caked blood it was hard to guess where the holes were, but there were obviously a number of them. Ahsiweyin broke off his wisp-voiced chanting and said: "Who's there?"

"Madelaine."

"Ah. You take good care of Gabriel, and Gabriel will"—there was a twitching at the corners of his lips that might have been a smile—"will take good care of the ones that took care of me and Isidor." That seemed to take a lot of strength out of him. He muttered something that sounded like "Never thought I'd die under a roof," then went back to his death song, breathing in and out indiscriminately while his lips went on forming the consonants.

There were a number of men's voices coming from a room behind the store. Madelaine poked her head in and saw Michel Dumas and Patrice Fleury sitting with several others around a table. She called Michel and Patrice to come out for a moment and pointed at Ahsiweyin. "He should be out beside the fire where he can look at the stars. Me and Gabriel would take him, but . . ."

Michel waved her off and took hold of two corners of the

blanket under Ahsiweyin. Patrice took the other two, and they carried him outside. Madelaine turned back to Gabriel and followed him up the stairs. She sat him down on the storekeeper's bed, unraveled her bundle to get at the clean rags, and poured a basin full of water from the pitcher on the washstand. On the off chance, she rifled through the drawers under the washstand and came up with a bottle of wood alcohol and a sealed roll of dressing cotton. She said: "This ain't going to be easy on you. Maybe you should have something to drink." He reached for the bottle in her hand, and she slapped his hand away. "Not this, unless you want to go as blind as—" She cut herself off.

He said: "Don't feel too sad for the old man; he don't. I think they got some rum left downstairs. The storekeepers had a personal permit for a keg of rum between them, so they had a keg sitting by their card table and twelve more buried out back."

She went downstairs and filled up the largest cup she could find. Michel Dumas said: "We laid him down by the fire. He said he could see the stars. Patrice stayed out there to make sure nobody steps on him."

While Gabriel worked on the cup of rum, smacking his lips, she peeled off the rag caked onto his head, soaked a clean rag in water, and damp-mopped his hair and beard. Scrubbing the blood off his face and neck finished off half her rags. The shirt she'd made him out of blanket cloth was unsalvageable. Instead of trying to pull it off over his head, she borrowed his knife to slice it open down the front. "Next time you plan on getting shot, don't wear new clothes."

"I promise. From now on, any time someone points a gun at me, I'll say: 'Just wait right here, I got to go home and change into an old shirt or my wife'll kill me.' " He turned the cup upside-down over his mouth and shook out the last drops. She filled it up for him again and then focused her attention on the wound itself. It was a long, puckered furrow matted with hair and patches of clotted blood that the water hadn't dissolved. She shook the alcohol bottle, unscrewed the cap, said: "This is going to hurt you more than it does me," and upended it over his head.

His spine snapped straight and he gasped in half the air in the room, chased with half the cup of rum. The crusted blood broke into flecks and flowed away. Within the furrow, sickly white highlights glistened, but there were no shards or splinters. She peeled the patches of hair onto either side of the new part and then layered it over with gauze that she bound on tight with a strip of jaunty flowered calico.

His spine slowly loosened forward. He smoked a pipe and finished his cup of rum and then sank back onto the bed. The last words he said before he started snoring were: "You enjoyed that, didn't you?"

She peeled off his moccasins and trousers, shrugged off her dress, and crawled in beside him. The storekeeper's bed hadn't been made for two.

She woke up in the middle of the night for no discernible reason. Gabriel was still lying on his back with the back of his neck propped on her arm. She realized that the rhythm of his breathing had changed; he was awake. He said: "It should've been me." It took a moment of fumbling through her sleep fog to understand what he meant.

She stretched the cords in her arms to the straining point in order to clasp her hands around his opposite shoulder. She said: "How could you know?"

"I had a notion. I was going to go out there, but he said if they arrested me or shot me, that'd be the end of us, and I let him go."

"He was right. If he was here, he'd be the first one to tell you you're the only hope we got now."

CHAPTER 24

Gabriel woke up with an axe in his head, which was quite a pleasant change from the hot iron wedges of the day before. The sun had been up for some time, and Madelaine was gone. He put on his clothes, buckled on his revolver and cartridge belt, picked up Le Petit, and went downstairs. Riel, Joseph Honoré Jaxon, Moïse Ouellette, and a few other Exovedes were sitting around the storekeeper's kitchen table. Moïse stood up to offer Gabriel his chair and poured him out a cup of tea. Gabriel said: "I ain't decrepit yet," but sat down nonetheless. "Anybody seen my wife?"

Moïse said: "She's around somewhere."

Riel said: "How is your wound?"

"It's there. I got a hard head."

"We are waiting for the rest of the Exovedate to arrive so that we may convene a meeting here. There has still been no further news of Nolin."

"Nolin?"

"Not since he ran off in the sleigh."

"Sleigh?" This was getting repetitive.

"I told you yesterday, after the battle. Nolin had accompanied the reinforcements from Batoche, but as soon as the shooting started he ran back down to where we'd tethered the horses and galloped away in a sleigh, apparently shouting something about the holy sacrament and the ciborium. It was assumed that he was going to the church to bring the sacraments for the wounded and dying, but he never appeared in Batoche. Someone saw him on the road to Prince Albert."

"Huh. I guess I don't remember the last parts of yesterday so good. Well, if Nolin has run over to the other side, it won't do us much harm. After yesterday it ain't exactly a secret that we're here willing to fight."

"That isn't the issue. He swore an oath, on his hope of salvation. We have his signature." Jaxon immediately riffled a sheet of paper out from the barricade of secretary's materials arranged in front of his place at the table. He handed it to Louis, who brandished it as evidence.

Gabriel recognized it as the oath they'd all signed or made their mark on. He said: "I ain't any happier about Nolin running out than you are, Louis. But you got to remember when he signed it I was leaning over his shoulder, and you were standing in front of him, and Isidor was . . . Isidor was there, too. Nolin was afraid, and no one is the master of fear."

"You are."

"No, Louis. No one."

Suddenly Jaxon sputtered out in a high, tight voice: "It was blasphemous! Nolin committed blasphemy by signing his false oath on his hope of salvation, and by using the name of the holy sacraments to cover his flight, and by . . . and by . . ."

"Honoré," Louis said gently, "I have told you time and time again—the accoutrements of the Church are not God." The *secrétaire* suddenly turned into a fish—mouth popping open and shut and his eyelids skinned back inside the sockets. Then he looked down at his papers and grew calm.

Moïse Ouellette said: "Well . . . now . . . anybody want some more tea?"

The rest of the Exovedate drifted in, pipes were lit, and the meeting was convened. Gabriel wanted to know first off if there'd been any word from Patrice Fleury's scouts watching Fort Carlton. The Police were still locked behind the gates licking their wounds. Louis proposed that a message be sent to Fort Carlton giving Crozier safe conduct to collect the bodies of the volunteers at Duck Lake. Gabriel said: "It ain't right they should be left lying out there for the dogs when maybe they didn't bear us no more ill will than we bore them. We ought to send a crew to pick them up and stack them in the cabin. There's still enough winter left so they'll keep till their friends come out to get them."

Madelaine came in from outside. Gabriel said: "There you are. Where you been?"

"Trying to make some order out of someone's idiot notion of how to feed two hundred men. You ate?"

Gabriel started to shake his head but immediately thought better of it as the serrated lips of the chasm grated together. He followed through with the gesture but slowed it considerably. Madelaine snorted disgustedly, threw a pot on the stove, and poured the contents of a sealer jar into it. The juice-inducing smell of steeping catfish permeated the room.

Some of the Exovedate seemed a bit ruffled at the presence of a non-Exovede during their deliberations. As far as Gabriel was concerned, anyone who objected to the presence of his wife should tell him so or swallow it. Or, if they were feeling monumentally brave, they could tell her.

Michel Dumas came running in. "Patrice sent a rider. Commissioner Irvine and his reinforcements have arrived at Carlton."

Gabriel said: "Boy, I wouldn't want to be in Crozier's boots today. I still can't figure out how he could be so stupid as to march out yesterday, when he only had to wait . . . Well, we would've made dog meat out of them anyway, but his commissioner don't know that. To hell with yesterday—today they're all locked into that trap they call a fort; whether there's a hundred or two hundred of them don't make no goddamn difference. We got to get up into the hills around them now before they got time to think and get the hell out.''

Riel said: ''I don't understand you. A moment ago you were concerned that the bodies of their dead should be preserved from desecration, and now you wish to go out and kill more of them.''

Gabriel turned toward that end of the table, looking for some explanation of just what it was Louis found difficult to understand. Suddenly he found himself peering across an expanse like the Great Salt Plain. He screwed his eyes shut and rubbed his fist against the bridge of his nose and squinted at Louis again. The illusion hadn't changed; the bright gray eyes were still barely discernible on the far horizon.

Gabriel said: ''When I was young, I fought the way a young man does, with no thought of anything except the fighting. Then one day some Crees stole my horse. I went to their camp and found them all painted up for war and dancing around a big fire. I jumped into the circle and said: 'I am Gabriel Dumont. I taken six Cree scalps over the years before we got to be friends. Now I find the Cree are cowards who sneak behind my back to steal my horse.' ''

It became increasingly difficult to moisten his throat. The distant gray eyes had grown soft and kindly, patently humoring a friend whose bump on the head had made him blather. Gabriel bulled on: ''The Cree Chief said: 'We didn't steal your horse. We're going out to fight the Blackfoot in the morning, and our friends are always willing to lend us their horses if we need them to ride out to war.' I told him that if they'd come and asked me as a friend, I would've been glad to let them borrow my horse. But since they snuck behind me to steal him, I would ride out with them in the morning, and if there was any Cree brave enough to be the first to kill one of the enemy, he could keep my horse.

''So we lined up on the prairie the next morning, with the Blackfoot sitting their horses in a line a few hundred yards in front of us. There was a lot of shouting of insults and waving of rifles and everybody working themselves up. Then this young Blackfoot kicked his horse and charged toward us, singing that he would kill any Cree that was stupid enough to fight him. He was something—twirling his rifle over his head, feathers streaming in the sun . . .

''I said to myself: Now's when, and put my heels to my horse. When he saw who was coming out to meet him, he hauled his horse around and lit back at a gallop for his own line. My horse was faster. When he saw I was going to catch him, he turned to fire a shot over his shoulder, but he missed and I didn't. His horse kept on running. I caught the horse just in front of the Blackfoot line and trotted back. When I passed by the spot where I'd dropped him off his horse, I looked down and saw that he was dead.

"This made me very sad"—Gabriel thumped the end of his forefinger against the top of the table a couple of times to focus Louis's attention—"because here was a young man who had never done any harm to me. But it was the only way to make the Cree respect me."

Instead of nodding and saying: "I see," Louis smiled indulgently and said to the rest of the Exovedate: "Now, as to the question of whether or not we should lay siege to Fort Carlton . . ." Gabriel was distracted by Madelaine cracking down a bowl in front of him, splashing hot fish broth on the back of his hand.

The Exovedate decided that the army should remain at Duck Lake while the scouts kept them informed of any developments at Fort Carlton. Joseph Honoré Jaxon, who'd been applying more of his energies to chewing his knuckles than taking minutes, suddenly let out a strangled squawk and dropped the pen as though it were a hot iron. "How can I do this? Those are my own people out there."

Louis said: "We are your people now," which didn't appear to help.

Gabriel said: "Your people promised from the beginning they'd stand up with us against the government. They ain't doing that. But as long as they don't stand up against us they won't be harmed." The *secrétaire* looked from one to the other of them and then flung himself down on his knees with his forehead pressed against the table rim, murmuring fervently in Latin.

Louis stood up and put his hand on Jaxon's head. "Blessed St. Joseph, help our poor brother to see. . . ." The *secrétaire* went limp and slumped to the floor with a thump. Gabriel and Moïse picked him up and laid him on a cot in the corner. They rubbed his arms and legs vigorously to get the blood flowing again. His eyes opened but didn't appear to see them. They left him there to rest and sat back down in their places, looking at each other sideways.

Riel said: "We can't carry on without a secretary. The deliberations of the Exovedate must be recorded."

Gabriel said: "My wife tells me little Phillipe Garnot's pretty good at his reading and writing." So the proprietor of the inn at Batoche's Crossing and the ferry at Gabriel's Crossing became *secrétaire* of the Exovedate.

After a few more matters were discussed, the meeting came to an end. Joseph Honoré Jaxon was sitting up on his own steam but still looking confused. Louis suggested that rest would be the best salve for his mental anguish and deputed a couple of men to escort him back to Batoche. It sounded to Gabriel like a good prescription for the anguish in his own head, so he went upstairs to lie down for an hour or two before dinner.

He was pulled awake by a broad hand shaking his shoulder. Madelaine held a candle in her other hand. He appeared to have slept into the night. There was a lot of noise going on outside. Madelaine said: "The Police are leaving Carlton. The fort's on fire."

He jumped up, reaching for Le Petit, but sat right back down as his head collided against a low-hanging cloud of stars. He said with some difficulty: "How much time have we got?"

"Time?"

"*Time*! Before they get here!"

"They ain't coming here—they're running north for Prince Albert, or that's what the scouts say."

"What? I don't . . . did you say their fort's on fire?" Madelaine nodded. Gabriel looked at the black window. "Did I sleep the night through?"

"No. It's barely midnight."

"It can't be. They'd have to be out of their goddamned minds to . . ." The expression on her face told him it was true. He grabbed his coat and his guns, hit the top of the stairs, and slid down bump-a-bump on the heels of his moccasins while he buckled himself together. On the snow-covered compound, two hundred men were running back and forth saddling horses and loading guns and shouting questions at each other. Gabriel spotted the upside-down triangle of Michel Dumas's back and grabbed his shoulder. The cornflower-blue eyes shot around at him. "Is it true? They're trying to make for Prince Albert in the middle of the night?"

Michel bobbed his head up and down. Gabriel froze for an instant while his memory's eye skimmed over the road from Fort

Carlton to Prince Albert, then he started shouting: "Get on your horses! We can take them in the spruce woods south of Red Deer Hill!"

Louis's chestnut-haloed head appeared in front of him, shaking sadly from side to side. "Uncle Gabriel, we must not. The Police are frightened and demoralized."

"That's exactly why we *must*. If we throw away a chance like this . . ."

"But to slaughter them in the dark, like savages . . . We must be merciful. And perhaps the reason they're abandoning their fort is because they've received orders to leave us alone. Perhaps even now John A. Macdonald is composing a telegram offering to negotiate a peace."

There was a clapper whanging back and forth inside the cracked bell of Gabriel's head. He pressed the palms of both hands against his temples and said wearily: "We could've killed a lot of them."

The next day the Exovedate decided, on Gabriel's suggestion, to move the army back across the river before the ice started to break. There were rumors of a large force of Police coming to attack Batoche from Fort Qu'Appelle. There were rumors that Big Bear and Poundmaker were riding behind their War Chiefs. There were rumors and riders flying all across the plains. The one concrete bit of news came from the scouts posted around Prince Albert. Charles Nolin had reached there in safety, and the Police had promptly clapped him in jail.

The telegram bearing the news of the Duck Lake debacle was all Sir John A. Macdonald needed at the moment. His government and his transcontinental railroad were both about to collapse over embarrassing questions about where the last construction loan had disappeared to. He'd already done all that a reasonable man could do to deal with the agitation in the North West Territories, declaring in the House of Commons that no one in the government had ever laid eyes on this mythical Petition of Rights and that "if we wait the pressing business of this House until Indians and half-breeds are satisfied, we will wait until the millennium." While his right hand had been flourishing oratorically, his left had been signing the order dispatching General Middleton west to mobilize the militia. If bloody Riel and his bloody half-breeds had waited three more bloody weeks, there would have been an army perched on their tipi doorsteps.

PART THREE

The half-breed hunters, with their splendid organisation when on the prairies, their matchless power of providing themselves with all necessary wants for many months together . . . their perfect knowledge of the country and their full appreciation of the enjoyment of a home on the prairie wilds, winter or summer, would render them a very formidable enemy in case of . . . open rebellion against constituted authorities.

If it should ever be considered expedient by Her Majesty to raise a body of irregular cavalry in this country, there exists in the half-breed the most eligible material I have ever seen in any country, and I have seen the Risalus of India and the Arabs.

COLONEL J. F. CROFTON;
CONFIDENTIAL REPORT
RE PALLISER/HIND EXPEDITION

CHAPTER 25

Along the North Saskatchewan the furry purple prairie crocuses began to push up through the snow, the pussy willows began to bud, and Kitty McLean grew increasingly peevish. Except for the occasional sortie to go skating on the river or sleigh riding, the winter had kept them under siege for five months. And now that the spring had finally come, they were forbidden to go out and enjoy it because Gabriel Dumont had fought a battle with the Mounted Police a hundred miles away.

As the days went by and the birds sang louder, with still no news of any further trouble, Kitty went to work on her big sisters, Amelia and Elisabeth, and then all three went to work on their mother. She finally agreed to allow them to go on a picnic, as long as they stayed within sight of the fort. They spent the evening hard-boiling eggs and slicing up the remains of Sunday's roast and wrapping pickle jars in napkins, then manhandled the picnic basket into the pantry and bounced upstairs to try to sleep.

Kitty woke up to the sound of her mother's voice calling her name. She was standing in the bedroom doorway holding a lamp. "Get up and get dressed, girls."

There was no light coming through the window. Kitty murmured: "It's still night. We don't have to start so early if we're not going far."

"You're not going anywhere."

"What? You said we could—"

"Ssh! There's been a massacre at Frog Lake. Big Bear and Wandering Spirit murdered the Indian agent and the missionaries and Lord knows how many others. Get up and get dressed and come downstairs as quick as you can."

As she fumbled into her clothes, Kitty tried unsuccessfully to picture the wizened little old man who'd slurped soup in their kitchen murdering anyone. When she got downstairs there were

177

two constables ferrying sacks of flour in from the storehouse, following her father and one-eyed Stanley Simpson, his slim, young chief clerk. Judging by the lights dancing in the windows, every inhabitant of Fort Pitt was bustling around in the dark with a lamp or a candle.

"Lend a hand here, girls." Her father sloped the flour sack off his shoulder onto a windowsill. "We want to block off all the windows along this wall. Pile on anything that looks thick enough to stop a bullet, but leave the center pane clear for a loophole."

When that was done, they were dispatched outside to hold lamps for the men building barricades out of wagons and barrels. They were extending the line of the little Police stockade to fill in the space between the houses. By the time the sun came up Fort Pitt had been transformed into something resembling a fort.

Kitty's father and Stanley Simpson sat wearily drinking tea while Kitty's mother organized breakfast. Kitty was aware of the fact that there was a Hudson's Bay post at Frog Lake, one of the subposts of her father's district. Stanley said to him: "I think our people should be safe, whatever else may or may not have happened. Even if Big Bear's people grew so agitated that they might have forgotten the difference between the Indian agency and the Company, they wouldn't forget about Pelagie and her brother."

Kitty said: "Pelagie?"

Stanley turned his gaze toward her, which was disconcerting. Not because of the glass eye, which was so perfectly matched with the dark blue of the other that it was almost indiscernible. In fact, the slight incongruity lent a comforting flaw to features that were otherwise surprisingly fine for a man who earned his living wrestling canoes and dog teams through the bush. In his accustomed soft voice, he said: "Pelagie is the wife of our chief trader at Frog Lake. She also happens to be the sister of Gabriel Dumont."

Kitty's father said: "It may well not have been as bad as the rumors have it. It may well turn out that no one was killed at all."

"Oh, I'd bet they killed the Indian agent," Stanley Simpson said, even more softly than usual. "When I first heard who was being appointed Indian agent for Frog Lake, I thought someone was pulling my leg. I suppose some elected fool in the east decided that the best kind of man to deal with the likes of Big Bear and Wandering Spirit was one who'd developed a reputation for brooking no nonsense from the savages. And if they killed him . . . the law can only hang you once.''

Kitty's mother said: "Come to the table.''

After breakfast, Kitty's father assembled all the civilians in the square. In his secondary capacity as justice of the peace, he swore in everyone who could hold a rifle as special constables, including Kitty and her older sisters. They all had to stand watch in turn, with the password exchanged every fifteen minutes. For those not standing watch, there was target practice in the Police stockade. Watching some of the Mounted Police showing off their marksmanship, Kitty hoped that if an attack did come, they'd have the sense to stand back and load for her.

Fort Pitt settled into a siege with no noticeable besiegers. Kitty's father put Stanley Simpson and the rest of his employees to work on the old sprung-seamed flatboat growing moss in front of the store. If the ice broke before Big Bear appeared, the women and children could be sent downstream to Battleford.

Elisabeth's sixteenth birthday gave the whole fort an excuse for a welcome bit of celebrating. It seemed as though every trooper in the detachment had a hank of velvet ribbon or an enameled broach or a lady's-size pair of beaded mittens stowed away in the corner of his footlocker. They had a bit of a dance in the mess hall. For no apparent reason, Kitty suddenly found herself growing quite flushed and confused in the middle of a waltz with Stanley Simpson. The top button of his waistcoat kept going in and out of focus, and his hand on her waist was very warm. She had to excuse herself in midstep and step out into the crisp spring night.

Since the time she was old enough to walk, she'd been a dancing partner for Police officers and her father's clerks and even the occasional resplendent Cree warrior, without ever encountering this kind of debilitating giddiness and weakness in the limbs. Not unless she'd been twirled around for hours, and that was hardly the case. Finally she put it down to the strain they all were under, waiting behind their barricades for Big Bear or Poundmaker or Gabriel Dumont to appear on the horizon. If she was going to put herself into such a state about it, she might just as well go home and take a cup of tea to bed. So she did.

The next afternoon she was standing her regular watch at her regular post, looking out through the sandbagged parlor window at the trail toward Frog Lake. Out of the bush cover along one side of the trail, something black flew up into the air and then flopped back down again. It was about the size of a raven, and its edges were raggedy like a raven's wings, but it didn't flap like a bird. She watched the spot for a moment, but it didn't fly up again.

She asked Amelia to take over her watch for a moment and went outside to find her father. He put down his caulking brush and went to look out over the barricade. "You're quite certain that it wasn't a raven?"

"I can't say for certain, but it didn't seem to be flying. More like something that was thrown up into the air."

"Well, one way to find out. Constable, there's something out there I think we should have a look at." In other circumstances, the constable might have balked at a civilian blithely usurping the authority of the officer commanding, but Inspector Dickens didn't appear to have much authority to usurp. The constable followed Kitty's father over the barricade. She started to follow them, but her father stabbed his forefinger at her and said: "Don't you dare," so she went back to her post and watched them from there.

They went to the spot she'd pointed out and came back carrying a limp scarecrow. She only got a quick glimpse before they passed beyond the loophole's narrow field of vision, but a moment later they came into the house with Stanley Simpson helping them to carry what appeared to be a dead man. They laid him down on the parlor couch, and Kitty's mother began flurrying about heating broth and telling Elisabeth to stir two spoons of sugar in a cup of tea.

Kitty stayed staunchly at her post but spent more time looking over her shoulder than out the loophole. The scarecrow wasn't dead after all. Under the dirt and tattered clothing he appeared to be quite young. Stanley Simpson announced: "I know him. He's the nephew of the Frog Lake Indian agent." The constable went to fetch Inspector Dickens.

Kitty's mother called from the kitchen: "Is he wounded?"

Kitty's father said: "No, just all in. Looks like he walked and crawled all the way from Frog Lake. I'd guess it was all he could do at the end to throw his hat up in the air and pray that one of our sentries had sharp eyes." He winked at Kitty and went on tilting the teacup up to the slack, cracked lips.

By the time Inspector Dickens arrived, the scarecrow had

taken in a bowl of broth and found a rasping remnant of its voice. Inspector Dickens said: "Now then, are you strong enough to tell us what happened?"

"I think so, sir. Just needed a bit of something in my belly."

"Good lad. Are you the only survivor?"

"No. They took the women and children prisoner."

"White women? Oh, God."

"Yes, sir. But all the men are dead . . . except the half-breeds, of course. And one of the Company clerks. The chief trader's wife put one of her dresses on him and led him away with the prisoners. He was shaking so bad it looked like he couldn't stand up—I was watching from the bush. But Pelagie—she's a big, fat woman stronger'n most men—put her arm around his waist and held him up. But other than that, they killed them all—the missionaries, the miller, the agency people, my uncle . . ."

"How did it happen? I imagine they came charging out of the woods with no warning."

"Well, no, sir. They were in and around the agency all the time, and the mission and so on, just like always. But they started to get more, well . . . pushy, I guess you'd call it. Wearing paint on their faces, carrying guns around, talking back to my uncle. We knew something was up, but we didn't know what, and then we started to hear rumors about Duck Lake. It got to the point where Wandering Spirit came into a church service, done up in all his war gear, and went prowling around up and down the pews shaking his war club and laughing. . . . And then my uncle was walking back to the agency store, and Wandering Spirit stepped in front of him. My uncle tried to go around him, but Wandering Spirit stopped him and pointed with his rifle toward the trail to Big Bear's village and said: 'Go to our camp.'

"I guess they'd come up with this plan to take us all hostage. But they didn't know what kind of a man they were dealing with. My uncle said: 'No.'

"That wasn't the answer Wandering Spirit expected. He kind of rubbed his forehead, smearing off some of the paint, and he said: 'You have a hard head. When you say no you mean no, and you don't budge, do you? I am telling you that if you love your life, you will do as I say. Go to our camp.'

"And my uncle said . . ." He had to pause for an intake of breath, overcome by his uncle's bravery. "My uncle said: 'No.'

"And then Wandering Spirit—I was standing just behind them, so I heard every word—Wandering Spirit said: 'I don't know what kind of head you have that this doesn't get through to you. What am I to do with a man like you? I might as well kill you.' And he . . . he brought up his rifle and shot my uncle between the eyes.

"I wasn't armed, so I ran for the bush. I could hear gunshots all around me, and screams, as though that first shot pulled a cork and it all came gushing out. I hid in the woods till dark and then started here."

After a moment, Inspector Dickens said: "Would you be able to ride tomorrow, if it was a chance to strike a blow back at them? We've been crouched behind these barricades long enough. But we can't venture out until we have some notion of Big Bear's movements. If you could take out two troopers as a scouting party to locate Big Bear . . ."

"You can't," said Kitty's father.

"He's a game lad. A bit of nourishment and a good night's sleep . . ."

"That isn't the question. You only have twenty men as it is. Where in God's name do you get the notion that three white men who barely know the country are going to outscout Big Bear's warriors in his own backyard? All you're going to accomplish is three of our men dead and three more horses and guns and ammunition for Big Bear's men."

"Where in God's name do you get the notion that you'd been elevated to the command of my detachment?"

Along with most of the rest of the population of Fort Pitt, Kitty was up and awake to watch the scouting party ride out in the half-light of dawn—two of them in red coats and the third wearing donations from her father's store. They galloped west along the riverbank and disappeared into the bush. The sun climbed to its peak and started to descend with still no sign of them returning. Kitty was standing her regular watch when a rider appeared at the crest of one of the hills to the north of the meadow surrounding Fort Pitt. Two other riders appeared beside the first. Kitty was about to shout: "They're back!" when a fourth appeared beside them, and then another and another until there were two hundred and some silhouetted horsemen lined across the ridge of hills looking down into Fort Pitt. Big Bear had been located.

CHAPTER 26

Gabriel was drawing chalk lines on "Batoche" Letendre's pool table. If chalk was going to hurt the felt, it would have given up the ghost long ago. Letendre's table was the English style, with pockets. Gabriel suspected that Letendre's choice had less to do with his own personal preference than that the American and English Canadian businessmen felt more comfortable with pocket billiards.

Gabriel drew two long, wobbly lines that curved toward each other, ran roughly parallel for a while, and then joined into one wobbly line, making a pattern rather like an oversize tuning fork that had been left sitting on the stove. Partway along one of the arms he added a shorter line running into its side. Louis came in and said: "Madelaine said you had something to show me."

"That I do. Watch." He fished out four red balls netted in a pocket and started spotting them on the appropriate positions along his chalk lines. "This is Fort Pitt. And this one here, where the Battle River flows into the North Saskatchewan, is Battleford. This"—placing the third one near where the two roughly parallel lines forked together—"is Prince Albert. And this here's Fort Edmonton," setting the last one down toward the tail end of the north fork. He reached for a cue and dug out the cue ball. "This is us." The cue ball went into position on the chalk map's equivalent of Batoche's Crossing on the South Saskatchewan.

Gabriel bent forward to sight the cue, then straightened back up and poked his bandage-headband up over the ridge of his left eyebrow. He stooped across the table again, slid the sweet spot of the cue back and forth between his knuckles toward the cue ball, and then straightened back up again without touching it— partly because he remembered something else he should clarify and partly because he wasn't as sure of himself on Letendre's table as his own. Riel stood waiting patiently. "This is going to look like there's some backtracking that ain't necessary, but the reason is"—tapping the tip of the cue by the Prince Albert ball—"a lot of the smaller detachments like Fort Carlton have all brought their men into Prince Albert. They're all barricaded in there even though they ain't being threatened by anything but their own fears and Patrice Fleury's scouts. While it's good that they're staying behind their own walls, it's bad 'cause there's too many of them together for us to take them on our own. Now over at Fort Pitt, Big Bear and Wandering Spirit have got two hundred and fifty warriors laying siege, and Poundmaker's got two hundred in front of Battleford. So if we was to cut across to Battleford and then Fort Pitt . . ."

He lined up the shot with a fair bit of bottom on the cue ball and stroked it. The cue ball hit the Battleford ball, which caromed off the Fort Pitt ball into the side pocket, driving the Fort Pitt ball into the corner pocket. The cue ball vibrated back and forth disconcertingly but finally came to rest near enough to the vicinity of Fort Pitt to pass for the way Gabriel planned it. It really wasn't that much of a trick shot for someone who'd been playing carom billiards for so long, and he was becoming adjusted to the pockets.

"Now"—proceeding to the other end of the table—"with us and Poundmaker and Big Bear all together, we got enough forces to . . ." The Prince Albert ball rocketed into the far corner. Gabriel circled around to the east side of the Great Plains billiard table where the cue ball had come to rest and pointed his cue at Fort Edmonton toward the cushion of the Rockies. "Fort Edmonton's sitting inside the Blackfoot Confederacy. I sent Crowfoot an end of tobacco—he didn't smoke it, and he didn't say he wouldn't. Poundmaker's Crowfoot's adopted son, but Crowfoot'd sit back and watch Poundmaker get thrown off a buffalo jump if it'd mean more power for the Blackfoot. Crowfoot turns with the wind. But once we've taken Fort Pitt and Battleford and Prince Albert, Crowfoot won't have a hope in hell of holding back his young men. They could take Fort Edmonton before breakfast, but if they need any encouragement . . ."

He lined up the long shot and dropped Fort Edmonton in the far corner, leaving the cue ball quivering. "Well, well, look at that—nobody left except us. And if John A. Macdonald wants to throw his other balls on the table, it's still my shot.

"Now in case you ain't noticed, that cue ball's been getting bigger and heavier and stronger with each shot. Not just from

Poundmaker and Big Bear and Crowfoot joining us, but from a lot of the Anglo half-breeds and even some of the white settlers. So far they been waiting like Crowfoot to see which way the wind's blowing. Looks to me like the wind's gone and blown all them redcoats off the table."

Gabriel leaned on his cue. Louis stood with his arms crossed and his lips rolled in on themselves so that his mustache and beard melded into one pelt. He extracted the Prince Albert ball from the pocket and revolved it between the palms of his hands. "There are five hundred people in Prince Albert. You just killed five hundred human souls with your little billiard stick."

"They'd surrender before we killed very many of them. Maybe before we killed any of them, if we show up in enough strength and if the citizens won't stand up with the Police."

"But perhaps they will refuse to surrender."

"Well, if they will, they will. This is a war, Louis—people get killed in wars." His head had started to throb again. "It wasn't me who told Crozier we were going to let loose a war of extermination across the plains."

"That was to frighten him into doing the right thing."

"To frighten him?" The throbbing had become a pulse-beat hammering. He screwed his eyes into slits and brought up his hand to shade them from the lamp hanging over the billiard table. "Louis, in this country you don't use words like that for show."

"What would become of our wives and families in Batoche while our army is chasing across the country meting out unnecessary slaughter? 'Unnecessary' because the government will come to deal with us soon without—"

"They'll deal with us all right—there's a whole goddamned army on its way out here from the east, and the ranchers out west are forming troops of cavalry. If we move quick, we can have the whole North Saskatchewan hostage, and Macdonald won't have no choice but to start talking treaty. But as things stand now, the only talking going on across your precious telegraph line is the Police telling the army what we're up to—or what we're *not* up to."

Louis shook his head. "The silence from Ottawa is entirely the fault of Big Bear and Wandering Spirit. The government was preparing to make terms with us until Frog Lake. How can they make terms with savages? But if we continue to hold ourselves aloof from barbarous acts, Macdonald's ministers will realize that Frog Lake was a terrible accident that was none of our doing.''

He set the Prince Albert ball back on the table, smiled, and put his hands on Gabriel's shoulders. ''My uncle Gabriel is the strongest man in the world, and the wisest when it comes to a battle or a hunt or any other facet of life on the plains. But the less clean and more complex labyrinths of politics and Parliaments aren't your world.

''Now as to your very astute concern about our allies—or rather those who should be our allies but are waiting to see which way the wind blows—you should know that we have other allies. They must not reveal themselves yet, but be assured that they will come in our hour of need. If and when that hour comes, the waverers you speak of will either stand with us or wish they had. . . . I can see that your wound is giving you great pain. You should rest.''

In Madame Letendre's kitchen, Madelaine was ripping out the stitching of the pair of moccasins she'd made for Gabriel last fall, so as to sew the beaded toe pieces onto new soles, while periodically checking the water level around the thighbone rendering itself down on the stove. Marguerite came in from putting her children to bed, poured herself a cup of tea, and sat watching. Just at the point when the aura of performance was starting to make Madelaine's fingers clumsy, Marguerite said: ''Do you know, for the longest time I was afraid of Uncle Gabriel.''

''Hm?''

''Yes, I was. You must have some idea, even after all the years you've spent together, of how your husband can seem to people that don't know him. For the longest time, even though I'd known him for so many months and that whole long journey from Montana . . . Those first few days after Louis declared the Exovedate and we all started living here, I felt about as safe as being in a house with a creature of the wilds—a bear or a wolf or . . . But then Louis told me of how Gabriel was so concerned about the feelings of the families of the dead militiamen left at Duck Lake, and other stories of the same kind, and watching how he is with Jean and Marie Angelique, I began to see that he has a kind heart even though he's uneducated.''

''He's *what*?''

''Well, it is a fact that he can't read or write any better than I can, or speak much English or—''

''Marguerite.'' Madelaine set her sewing aside. ''When I was growing up my father made damn sure I went to the convent school. I can read and write in French and English and Cree syllabics, and I can add up four columns of figures in my head. I read music better than poor Isidor could, and I can quote you the lives of the saints till they're coming out your nose. But after twenty-five years I still get ashamed sometimes at how uneducated I feel next to Gabriel.

"He knows three times as many languages as I do. He can read tracks that I can't even see. Like just about everybody else who grew up on the plains, I never learned to swim, but Gabriel can go back and forth across the South Saskatchewan faster than the ferryboat. I've seen him take one look at a horse and see it ain't worth buying 'cause its wind's gone, or at a smudge on the horizon and know it's Sioux . . ."

She'd meant to say a lot more, but she trailed off in the face of the misty, beatific smile that had locked itself onto Marguerite's picture-perfect features. Madame Riel was genuinely touched by Madame Dumont's loyal touchiness on the subject of her husband's ignorance. Madame Dumont thought it safest to get up and stir the pot on the stove. One of these days, she said to herself.

Gabriel and Louis came into the kitchen for a cup of tea before bed. Gabriel said to her: "You'll be glad to know Louis's been talking me around to believing that there's a lot of men in Ottawa who got some concern for things besides money and power, even if Macdonald don't. They might be able to make him make peace with us. I'm sure they ain't saints, but they got enough thought towards trying to be good Christians they even named their 'Dominion of Canada' out of something in the Bible."

"I told you that fifteen years ago when you were asking what was this new government that was buying us from the Hudson's Bay Company."

"Did you? They say the memory's the first thing to go. . . ."

" 'And God said unto them' "—she quoted the verse from Genesis—" 'Replenish the earth and subdue it, and have dominion over the fish of the sea, and over the fowl of the air, and over every living thing that moveth upon the earth.' "

"Funny," Gabriel grunted. "None of us I know of ever wanted to rule over every other living thing, just to live along with them."

"Then I guess," she said, "that includes us."

"Perhaps it might," Louis said, "if that was the correct reference. Your knowledge of the Holy Scriptures does you credit, Madelaine, but the verse which the Dominion of Canada refers to is from the Seventy-second Psalm, a psalm for King Solomon: 'He shall have dominion also from sea to sea, and from the river unto the ends of the earth.' "

" 'And they that dwell in the wilderness,' " she continued into the next verse, " 'shall bow down before him; and his enemies shall lick the dust.' "

After a moment, Gabriel said: "I think I better take my sore head to bed."

Louis said: "I think it's hardly right to call her a sorehead," then laughed and slapped the table.

CHAPTER 27

Inspector Dickens's squeamishness about civilians elevating themselves into command of his detachment didn't extend to sitting down across a campfire from Big Bear and Wandering Spirit. He seemed quite unperturbed that Kitty's father should be the one to go. It took a day of messengers running back and forth before it was agreed that Straight Tongue McLean would walk out of the fort the next morning, alone and unarmed, to meet the Chiefs at the place where the base of the hills met the end of the meadow, where they would sit down to smoke tobacco and converse about the awkward situation they'd found themselves in.

There was still no sign of the scouting party. Kitty and Amelia stood pressing their heads together at the parlor window loophole to watch their father stride across the last shrinking swaths of snow, swinging his arms in the aged red-and-black-striped Hudson's Bay blanket coat that their mother kept praying would fall apart. He stopped at the far edge of the meadow, a thumb-size red-and-black figure turning from side to side. He turned back toward the fort and waved his handkerchief, the agreed-upon signal of "Not to worry." He walked on up the wooded hillside, disappearing into the delicate green mist of budding leaves.

After peering at the hill a while longer, the three sisters took to spelling each other at the window in between keeping the younger children occupied and helping their mother with the tea things. Their mother sat down at the miraculous pump organ that had been transported across a thousand miles of wilderness to provide her family with the comforts of "The Lost Chord" and "The Minstrel Boy." Kitty was standing her turn at the loophole, leaning on her rifle and contributing the descant line to "Annie Laurie," when three horsemen flew over the top of the ridge and came careering down the hill at a breakneck gallop. Two of them were dressed in scarlet tunics.

A wave of painted riders on painted horses broke over the crest of the ridge behind them, firing their guns and whooping. The walls of the McLean house reverberated with answering gunfire from the barricades on either side, but Kitty didn't fire. The range was too far to accomplish anything but possibly aiming at the Indians and hitting one of the scouting party.

The Police horses hit the flats and charged straight on toward Fort Pitt, except for the one carrying the late Indian agent's nephew. Inspector Dickens had lent him Firefly, the fastest horse in the detachment's remuda. Instead of taking his chances at a straight run for the fort, he sheered off to angle toward the bush cover on the riverbank. A couple of the Crees swerved after him. The rest were steadily gaining on the two policemen.

Kitty heaved up her rifle and fired. The parlor was filled with thunderclaps and clouds of smoke as Amelia and Elisabeth came to the same conclusion about the range. One of Kitty's little brothers started screaming; another laughed and clapped his hands. Kitty waved the smoke out of her face and worked another shell into the breech. It was impossible to say whether any of them had hit their targets. A couple of the painted ponies were running with empty saddlepads, but there were thirty-odd rifles firing at the same time.

At the midpoint of the treeline there was a big man flourishing a war club that was somewhat like a field hockey stick with three butcher knives fixed into the blade. His face was striped with red and yellow and his long, black wavy mane—unusual in an Indian—streamed out behind him. Wandering Spirit.

Kitty fixed her sights on him. In the time it took her to take

aim, he shifted the war club to his left hand, clasped the slack
of his horse's halter between his teeth, drew out his rifle, braced
it across his left forearm, and snapped off a shot at full gallop.
Despite the roaring of gunfire all around her, Kitty heard the
lone clap of Wandering Spirit's rifle as distinctly as a solo voice
bursting out over a chorale. One of the constables catapulted
back over the withers of his horse. Kitty pulled the trigger.

When the smoke cleared, Wandering Spirit was still on his
horse. The second constable was only a couple of hundred yards
away from the barricade, but there was a young Cree gaining
on him, whipping his pony in at an angle to cut him off. The
policeman saw him coming and raised his rifle, swerving in the
saddle while still roweling the foamed ribs of his horse. Before
he could fire the two horses collided and went down. Both riders
somersaulted off the saddle, red tunic and beaded hunting shirt
kaleidoscoping. The policeman kicked free and ran for the fort.
He'd lost his hat. His crinkly, copper-colored hair burned in the
sunshine. His lips were drawn back from his teeth, and his eyes
were stretching their sockets. He was directly in front of Kitty's
loophole, although still a hundred yards away, running with his
right arm stretched forward as though she could reach out her
hand through the loophole and pull him in. Then he flung both
arms and his head back over his shoulders—hands clawing at
his spine—and the copper-mustached mask of terror was thrown
down and replaced by the grinning face and copper-wired braids
of the young warrior who'd rammed his horse.

Kitty rammed the bolt out and in and squeezed the trigger.
The rifle butt bucked back against her shoulder. Everyone else
in the fort seemed to be firing at the young Cree as well, but he
wasn't touched. He stripped off the constable's revolver belt,
scooped up his rifle, and skipped back on his dazed pony. A
few of the fort's defenders continued shooting at him, but he
was soon out of effective range where Wandering Spirit and the
others had fallen back after collecting their dead. The two who
had sheered off came back out of the bush leading Firefly. Wandering Spirit wheeled his horse and waved his war club, and the
whole pack went whooping back up into the hills, leaving a
black-and-white-dappled meadow with two red hummocks.

Kitty's eyes settled on the nearer one, a hundred yards straight
in front of her loophole, and she couldn't pull them off. It wasn't
an overtly gruesome sight. If it weren't that he was lying in a
patch of mud, he might well have been sleeping. Kitty's mother

said: "Don't stare, girls. Come away from the window." At that moment, one red-sleeved arm pivoted at the elbow, lifting a limp hand out of the mud.

Kitty shouted: "He's alive!"

Amelia said: "I saw it, too," and they both ran out into the courtyard.

Inspector Dickens was standing by the barricade telling Stanley Simpson: "There may well be snipers in the trees. . . ."

Kitty said: "Stanley, we saw him move," and pointed.

Stanley Simpson nodded. The inspector said hesitantly: "It may have been a vestigial contraction. . . ." Stanley grabbed the rim of the parapet and vaulted over. The garrison clustered up against the barricade to watch. He made it across the hundred yards of open meadow with no discernible evidence of snipers and crouched down beside the dead man with the waving arm. A ragged cheer went up as he hauled the constable to his feet and half dragged, half walked him to the barricade. A crew of other constables helped hoist him over into the safety of the fort, and then Stanley Simpson followed, breathing heavily. Kitty said: "Will he live?"

"He's shot up pretty bad, but not too bad. He's smart—played dead when that Cree was taking his gunbelt. Lucky for him there were a lot of bullets kicking up mud or the Cree would've made sure." Stanley went to join the hubbub around the wounded man—people were lifting the box off a buckboard to make a bed for him and scurrying around fetching quilts and bandages. Kitty looked at Amelia. From the expression on her face, the same thought had occurred to her now that the fireworks were over. Their father had given his word to Big Bear that their parley wouldn't be used as a ruse to launch an attack on the Cree camp. The three scouts galloping through waving their rifles might have seemed like exactly that.

Kitty was quite certain she could jump as high as Stanley Simpson, but a young lady in an ankle-length skirt doesn't have much room to maneuver. So instead of trying to vault over the barricade, she climbed up onto it. Amelia hissed: "What are you doing?" Everyone else was too preoccupied with the poor constable to notice.

"I'm going to make sure Papa's all right." She jumped down on the other side, almost losing her footing on the slick, half-thawed ground. There was a thump beside her, and Amelia took hold of her arm. For an instant she thought her older sister was going to try to hold her back, but it was just for comfort. They walked arm in arm across the meadow, setting a course that would angle them as far as possible past the red hummock of the second constable, who was most decidedly dead.

As they neared the base of the hills, Kitty began to hear the unmistakable orchestration of a large Indian encampment in an effervescent mood—dogs yelping, children squealing, women yelling, and men laughing and congratulating each other. She snuck a sideways glance at Amelia, who was sneaking one at her. They started up the slope staring straight ahead. It was too awkward trying to climb with linked arms, so they went hand in hand.

There was a rustling in the bush to Kitty's left. A Halloween figure with a green face and an empty eye socket leaped out in front of them. An optimistic corner of Kitty's mind tried to convince her that it was Stanley Simpson—he'd been known to take out his glass eye and grimace for the children on Halloween. But it wasn't Halloween, and Stanley Simpson wasn't that big. Nor was he in the habit of brandishing a feathered hand axe under people's noses.

Over the past couple of years, a strange and disorienting feeling had come over Kitty from time to time. Her mother, when she'd told her about it, had christened it her Alice in Wonderland feeling and said that when it came on she should just keep telling herself that it would go away. It came on with a vengeance now, and it didn't look like it was going to go away.

Amelia said: "*Wakiye, nistes,*" which was Cree for "Hello, older brother." The green-faced Cree looked confused.

Kitty said: "We have come to see our father, Straight Tongue," and they walked on past him.

After an uncomfortable instant when the back of her neck tried to grow an eye, Kitty heard him fall in behind them, murmuring under his breath in a baffled tone. Suddenly he laughed out loud and shouted: "Come look at this! Come see where the white men keep their courage!" They were soon surrounded by an escort of painted warriors uttering bloodcurdling ululations and contorting their faces horribly and making threatening gestures with their knives and laughing with delight when the white girls didn't squeal or flinch. Amelia's grip had cut off the circulation to Kitty's fingers, and it hurt her throat to swallow with her neck and chin held that rigid.

When they reached the edge of the camp, the parade was

swollen by a stream of women and children. Several of the young men took up firing their guns over Kitty's and Amelia's heads, the bullets passing close enough for their wind to ruffle Kitty's hair. An old woman said: "Aren't you afraid?"

Amelia stopped and held up her free hand. "Why should we be afraid of you? We have lived among you as brothers and sisters all our lives." There was an abashed silence, and then the green-faced cyclops stepped forward and said he would lead them to their father. The rest of the procession fell in behind, laughing and calling to their relatives to come out and see.

The parade marshal led them on a winding route into the center of the camp. In front of a large, vermilion-decorated tipi, Wandering Spirit and a dozen other arsenaled councillors were sitting in a circle. The furrow-faced little man leaning against a woven willow backrest was Big Bear. Beside him sat a bearded white man in a red-and-black blanket coat that didn't appear to have any bullet holes or knife slashes in it. Kitty's father rose to his feet, took off his hat, scratched his furry chin, shook his head, put his hat back on, and said: "Well, I'm damned."

"We were worried, Father, that when the scouts appeared it might have seemed that you'd broken your word to Chief Big Bear. We thought we might help you explain."

"As a matter of fact, I did become rather . . . intimately acquainted with the muzzle of Wandering Spirit's rifle, but eventually he saw that—"

"Straight Tongue was named well," Wandering Spirit pronounced sonorously. Which was a compliment not only to the named, but to the namer, who happened to be Wandering Spirit.

Kitty caught Big Bear looking at her from under his eyelids. The vague suggestion of an elevation of one corner of his mouth multiplied the wrinkles on his winter-apple face and radiated them upward. "Sunflower—did you bring me some of that good barley soup?"

Kitty's father sat back down in his place and picked up his pocket notebook. "I was just finishing writing a message for Inspector Dickens. You can take it back to the fort with you." He licked his pencil and opened the notebook.

Wandering Spirit shifted himself sideways and patted the opened space on the buffalo robe he was sitting on. "Come and sit. You two got more right to sit with the warriors than most of them big brave redcoats."

Kitty's father finished what he was writing and carefully tore two pages out of his notebook. A young Cree with ribbons in his hair snatched the loose pages from him, glanced over them, nodded at Big Bear, and handed them back. Kitty's father folded them over separately and gave them to Amelia. "This one is for your mother, and this one must go directly to Inspector Dickens. It explains the terms that Big Bear and I have agreed upon for the surrender of the fort."

Kitty's mouth dropped open, but before she could get anything out of it her father rushed on. "Of course it's up to Inspector Dickens to make the final decision, but I believe he'll see that this is for the best. I'd come down and explain the terms to him myself, but Wandering Spirit prefers that I stay here. All the civilians in the fort will become Big Bear's prisoners. He's pledged his word we won't be harmed. I've spoken to the prisoners from Frog Lake, and they've been well treated. Inspector Dickens and his troop are to abandon the fort and make their way down to Battleford."

Wandering Spirit said: "They can take their guns, but their horses are ours."

Kitty didn't have a wealth of experience in military tactics or reading poker faces, but it didn't take either to see that Big Bear was pleased at the prospect of tripling his stock of prisoners bloodlessly and that Wandering Spirit was pleased at the prospect of twenty un-Mounted Police blundering through the bush dragging their fine new rifles and crates of cartridges.

From the oversize banker's waistcoat Big Bear wore above his breechclout and leggings, the Chief extracted an immense, aged pocket watch. He wound the stem, glanced at the sun, and said: "We give you two hours to load up your wagons to travel with us, and for the Police to clear out. After that . . ."

Wandering Spirit said: "We'll rub out your fort before sundown. We can kill the Police like ducklings."

Kitty's father leaned forward toward her and Amelia and adopted the slow, precise tone of voice he used to explain things to their toddling brothers and sisters. "If Inspector Dickens agrees, tell Mother to pack the democrat with traveling rations and clothing as quickly as she can. And tell Stanley Simpson to seal up the inventory I've had him and the other clerks working on for the last two weeks and send it on with Inspector Dickens." Kitty nodded throughout to show that she was listening carefully, but she wasn't sure what he was trying to tell them.

Kitty and Amelia went back down the hill with their arms

around each other's waists for warmth. Part of the cold came from outside. The sun was starting its descent, and it was still too early in the spring for it to cast much heat except at its zenith.

Kitty said: "I'm sure Papa's doing the right thing, but I think Wandering Spirit's bragging. There may not be many of us, but we've all got good rifles and plenty of food. We could hold them off for a long time."

Amelia said: "Except for the water." There was no well in the fort; they had to haul their water in barrels from the river four hundred yards away.

Kitty said: "Inspector Dickens wouldn't miss it."

"You are a wicked girl."

"What do you think he meant, that mother should load the democrat 'as fast as she can'? Two hours is plenty of time."

"Maybe he meant that as long as it looks as though we're packing up as fast as we can, Wandering Spirit won't get angry if it takes a little longer."

"But there's no reason why it should. Maybe it has something to do with that 'sealing up the inventory.' "

Amelia said: "Stanley hasn't been doing any inventory I know of."

"Exactly. Maybe Stanley will know what it means."

By the time they reached the ragtag excuse for palisades, the mud between the shrinking drifts was reverting to crunchy black crystals. They first delivered the letter to their mother, who wasn't nearly as distraught as they'd expected. "Elisabeth saw you from the loophole, and we all ran to the windows and watched you go. I must admit it gave me a turn at first, but you're practically half Indian yourselves. Lord knows I'd sooner trust the Cree with you than some of Inspector Dickens's constables."

To deliver the note to Inspector Dickens, they had to cross the parade square, skirting around the overturned flatboat that had lost its race to be seaworthy before Big Bear appeared. Stanley Simpson had nonetheless continued with the routine of the last two weeks to give the other clerks something to do, boiling a pot of pitch to seal up the seams. . . .

Kitty suddenly stopped and yelled: "Stanley!" One Scots bluebell eye swiveled toward her, the other still stared ahead disconcertingly. "Father said you should finish caulking the boat as fast as you can. It has to be ready in two hours."

Inspector Dickens read to the bottom of the penciled message and snorted: "Preposterous! In the first place, the very notion of abandoning defenseless white women to . . ." Realizing that he was in the company of that very article, he aborted the graphic description. "In the second place, the notion that I would abandon a defensive position to march unhorsed cavalry over fifty miles of broken country teeming with hostiles . . ."

"Sir," Kitty interjected, "Inspector Dickens—the boat!" Inspector Dickens squinted down his nose as though she'd said "the white rabbit." "Don't you see, sir? My father promised that you wouldn't take your horses. He didn't promise that you wouldn't be out of reach in the middle of the river. As long as my father keeps his word, Big Bear will keep his."

"What? The word of a murdering . . ." Again he restrained himself from venting indelicately manly terms in the company of those whom his father had taught him were delicate women. But Kitty got the distinct impression that he was hoping to be persuaded.

It took somewhat longer than two hours to finish caulking the boat. The wagons had been packed within the first hour, but Kitty and the rest of the civilians kept running back and forth carrying the same bundles into the houses that they'd just carried out, in hopes that Wandering Spirit, looking down into the anthill of Fort Pitt, would get the impression they were scurrying as fast as they could. It was also hoped that he wouldn't notice that some of the scurriers were putting finishing touches on Inspector Noah's ark.

The sun was setting by the time every gap between the planks of the ancient hull had been given at least a lick and a promise. The soldiers of the Queen heaved it over onto its bottom, loaded in the entire contents of the ordnance shed, and formed a double-rank port and starboard while Stanley Simpson hitched two heavyset horses to the bow. The civilians pulled aside a wagon that formed part of the barricade on the riverfront side. Kitty thought there should be some exchange of good-byes and God-speeds, but the troopers who had danced with her at New Year's and her sister's birthday wouldn't look at her now. They obeyed the inspector's order to take hold of the gunwales and put their backs into it, the horses were whipped up and the four-hundred-yard boat-dragging race was on.

They were barely out of the starting gate when Wandering Spirit cottoned on and came charging out of the hills with two hundred warriors firing their guns. Kitty and the rest of the civilians could only stand on the broken barricade and shout their emotions. The season was a blessing and a curse—the boat skated and skimmed on the slick spring mud the troopers' boots slipped and slid in. The mud wasn't deep enough to make any difference to Wandering Spirit's horsemen. But the boat got to the riverbank before the Crees got within effective range. The Police crammed on board and launched themselves into the millrace current, poling against the ice floes like a centipede on a gravel slide.

The snookered Crees stood on the shore blazing away at the disappearing boat, then turned and charged into Fort Pitt. Wandering Spirit reared his horse up in front of Straight Tongue's family packed onto their laden democrat. He smiled with his teeth and said: "Out of all people, I should've been the one to know that Straight Tongue got his name from meaning exactly every word he says."

The McLean family and Stanley Simpson and the rest of the citizens of Fort Pitt were escorted up into the hills to begin their captivity with a night of snow crystals rattling against their tent walls. Big Bear had told his young men that they should leave off plundering the fort until tomorrow, so that any of the prisoners who hadn't been able to gather all their necessities together in the time allotted would have a second chance in the morning. It didn't come as a surprise to Kitty that they didn't listen to him. She took as a matter of course a fact that a lot of people from the east couldn't seem to grasp—that a Chief's authority wasn't the same as a commanding officer or an employer in white society. No matter how powerful and well respected a Chief of the Plains tribes might be—and in the North West those qualities were measured against the benchmarks of Poundmaker, Crowfoot, and Big Bear—he could advise but not command.

In the middle of the night Kitty was awakened by the raucous return of the plunderers. A new prisoner was thrust into the McLeans' tent. He had leaped off Firefly as soon as he'd hit the cover of the riverside willow thickets and crawled away to hide under an overhang on the bank. When night fell he'd snuck back to Fort Pitt and was confused to find it utterly deserted, until Wandering Spirit's young men came whooping over the barricades. He'd hidden in a barrel and then smeared his face with mud and tried to pass himself off as one of them, sidling his way through the sacking party. It hadn't worked, but the Cree had figured that if Kichee Manitou, the Great Mystery, had let him live through Frog Lake and the chasing down of the scouting party, who were they to kill him now?

In the morning the prisoners were allowed an hour in Fort Pitt before the tribe got on the move. The parade square was a mass of broken glass and torn calico. Every bottle of eau de cologne and Doctor Thomas's Electric Oil had been sucked dry. The ransacking was still going on. A parcel of warriors boiled excitedly out of Stanley Simpson's quarters and presented his spare glass eye to the cyclops who favored green face paint. He clapped his hand over his mouth in the customary Cree gesture of astonishment, worked the glass eye into his empty socket, and peered around expectantly. His Christmas grin sank into a scowl. He grabbed Stanley Simpson, pushed him against a wall, and showed him a microscopic view of the edge on his hand axe. "You think this is a good joke? It don't work!"

"Uh . . . it don't what?"

"I don't see out of it no better than no eye at all. What's the trick?"

"Oh . . . oh, well, you see, it's because . . . ahem . . . It's blue."

"Huh?"

"It was made to match a blue eye, like mine, and yours are brown, so . . ."

"Oh. I guess there's nothing you can do about that. I shouldn't've got my hopes up. Maybe I'll keep it in there anyway. Must make me look better even if I don't see better."

Kitty went into the house and found three Crees poised for action in front of the pump organ. Ghosts of music from a farther room had emanated when one of them happened to lean against the keys. She coaxed the bravest one into sitting down on the bench to show him there was nothing to be afraid of. He warily followed her instructions as to working the foot pedals and grinned at the pneumatic action. She pulled out all the stops and told him by signs and words to press the keys.

"The Lost Chord" and several of its brothers suddenly found each other in a crescendo that would have brought a blush to Herr van Beethoven's cheek. The organist recoiled as though he'd thrust his hands in a fire, hurling himself and the bench back on the floor. His friends sprang forward, shouting that the thing was the doorway to the cave of Machie Manitou—the dark side of the Great Mystery—and chopped the walnut cabinet to flinders.

Chapter 28

Madelaine Wilkie's sixteenth birthday had been celebrated at Fort Ellice. She was aware of the fact that her birthday wasn't so much a cause for a celebration as an excuse, and that the nomads of the plains never needed much of an excuse to haul out the fiddles and bash in the head of a keg of brandy. She'd once overheard Gabriel Dumont's father saying that the best gift the missionaries had brought the métis was the calendar of saints: "Back when I was a boy we were sometimes hard put to it to come up with a reason for a dance. Now you just ask the priest what saint's day it is, and off you go to celebrate St. Ralph or Saint Matilda." It had shocked her at the time, but she'd decided he hadn't meant to make mock of the Church but of himself.

Even though she could see her birthday party in perspective, it was still fun being the belle of the ball. Every young man in the vicinity came up with a gift of one kind or another. The entire season's stock of silk scarves and bead necklaces appeared to have been cleaned out of the trading stores. She could hardly wait to get sat down with the inventory ledger.

Her father had rigged up a long table with planks and sawhorses in front of the house. It was covered with platters of moose nose and beaver tail and buffalo hump. She drank enough wine to get giddy, or perhaps it was the dancing—as soon as one partner bowed his thanks, another was elbowing his way forward. And every birthday gift required a kiss. Her upper lip was sanded smooth by mustaches in varying stages of maturity and spikiness.

The sun had just set low enough for the bonfire to become the main source of light when the Dumont boys rode in, their moccasins still wet from swimming their horses across the river.

Isidor extracted a fiddle from a beaded bag strapped to his saddle and headed straight for the group sawing away in relative unison under the awning of a big old willow tree. Gabriel stood up in his stirrups to scout out the dancing ground, then climbed down and slowly worked his way around to where she was jigging with Moïse Ouellette.

Over Moïse Ouellette's bouncing shoulder, she watched the heads turn as Gabriel Dumont went by, watched his hand come up to wave in response to greetings or stretch out to shake hands proffered to him. The Dumont boys had become a reliable topic of conversation, particularly Gabriel. More often then not, when the bartering between her father and a prospective customer reached the inevitable pause of lighting pipes and shifting to tobacco talk from haggling, the customer would choose to exercise his prerogative with something like "Say, did you hear the story about Gabriel Dumont and the Blackfoot Chief?" or "Has anyone told you about the poor fool of a keelboatman that got drunk in St. Joe and swung an axe handle at Gabriel Dumont?"

He reached the point in the dancing mass where he could start angling his way in toward her. She shifted her gaze to a point over Moïse Ouellette's head, softening the focus so she could watch Gabriel Dumont approaching without appearing to be looking at him. He hadn't grown any taller, but he'd managed to grow a real beard—not a thick one, but at least it was composed of whiskers rather than wispy down. He appeared to have something inside his shirt, riding on top of his *ceinture flèche*, but given the generally lumpy and ungainly construction of his body, it was difficult to say for sure. Instead of waiting for the dance to end, he barged right up and said: "Hello, Moïse; hello, Madelaine."

Moïse stopped dancing, so she figured she might as well. "Hello, Gabriel."

"I brought you a present for your birthday." He reached inside his shirt, pulled out a battered, brown-covered book, and handed it to her. The title on the spine read, in English, *A Millwright's Guide to the Principles of Hydraulics*. "I heard you like books."

"Thank you."

"Didn't cost me nothing. I won it in a card game. Well, there they go starting another song. Do you want to dance with me, if you're finished with Moïse?"

Moïse said: "She's wore me out."

If anyone had cause to be wore out, it was Madelaine, but she sucked in a good, deep breath, smeared back the loose hairs plastered to her forehead, and took up the dance with Gabriel Dumont. The remarkable transformation that she remembered from the only other time she'd danced with him took place again more markedly. As soon as his body flung itself into active movement, its clumsy structure vanished into grace—grace in the biblical sense of a gift granted from some power beyond human understanding. His ugly excuse for a face lit up into a beam that melted her heart like a candlestick left standing on the hearthstone.

He squinted at her and hollered over the music and massed moccasin thumps: "Say—you look like you've been danced to death. Maybe you'd like to take a walk and catch your breath."

"I don't mind."

They negotiated their way through the dancers and out into the open. Now that his movements had been reduced to mundane walking, there seemed nothing out of the ordinary about him. She decided that there probably wasn't anything all that remarkable about the way he moved when he was doing something active, the effect was simply the surprise of seeing that ungainly body moving any way but clumsily. He said: "What say we go sit by the river for a minute? You could catch your breath, and I can have a smoke."

"I don't mind."

They were almost out of the firelight when her father called her. "Where are you going?"

"Just to sit by the river for a moment. I'm all out of breath from dancing."

"The factor's son's looking for you—finally worked up the courage to ask you to dance."

"I'll faint on him halfway through if I don't sit down and cool off."

"All right, but just a few minutes—people expect to see you at your birthday party."

"Yes, Papa."

"Hello, Gabriel."

"Hello, Monsieur Wilkie."

She sat down on a deadfall poplar that projected out into the river. Gabriel perched on a convenient boulder and set to work getting his pipe going. He wasn't very good at it yet. She scooped up a handful of river to drink and another to wash the sweat off her face. He said: "I got myself a new stallion that runs like the wind."

"Did you now?"

"Yup. Cost me a new gun and two kegs of powder. But I could afford it—I brought in three full carts of pemmican from last fall's hunt. My father says I should breed the stallion with my buffalo runner, since she's the one that paid for him." He sucked on his pipe. No smoke came out. He took it out of his mouth and held it as though he'd been intending to let it burn itself out and then light it again when he felt in the mood for a few more puffs. He said: "Must get suffocating for you here, having to stay around Fort Ellice all the time instead of going out with the hunt."

"I don't mind. I can go for a ride down the valley any time I like."

"That ain't far."

"Far enough."

"Hmm . . ." He pursed his mouth and squinted and nodded thoughtfully. "So, did a lot of people bring you presents for your birthday?"

"Some."

"And did they give you a birthday kiss, too?"

"Those that wanted to."

"I didn't get mine."

"I didn't know you wanted one."

He got up off his rock, put his pipe back in the pouch dangling from his *ceinture flèche*, and stepped toward her. She didn't get up. He bent down, put his hands on her shoulders, and angled his mouth in at hers. His mustache prickled. His lips were thick and warm. One hand moved across her shoulder to cushion the back of her neck.

"Madelaine!"

"Coming, Papa!" She went back up to the fire and danced with the Hudson's Bay Company factor's son. The music grew coarser and louder to carry over the whoops of the dancers. The party parted into two halves as various dancers became more interested in watching the wrestling. A very large male of the Tourond family had challenged all comers in one of the Plains tribes' wrestling games—the one where two men stood foot to foot, clasped right hands, and strained to throw each other off balance. Madelaine joined the ring of watchers as an excuse to get away from the factor's son.

Each bout didn't last long, and all followed the same pattern—a challenger would throw down his wager in front of Tourond, lock hands, and, after a moment of grunting, find himself on the ground. Big Tourond was almost as tall as Gabriel Dumont's father and uncles and big brother.

Madelaine ended up standing next to Gabriel Dumont. He said to her: "I could take him."

"You could brag you can fly, too."

The latest challenger was knocked off his feet, and his fat-bladed Green River knife added to Big Tourond's pile of booty. Gabriel Dumont pushed into the open space inside the circle and said: "My horse against yours and all the winnings you got piled up there."

Tourond blinked at him and then laughed. "I don't take candy from babies."

"Maybe you ain't in the habit of walking home, either, so I'll tell you what—even though my horse is worth twice as much as yours and everything you won so far tonight, if there's a good pair of moccasins in that pile, I'll let you keep them 'cause you're gonna wear through the ones you got on before morning."

"Come on, boy."

They set up with the outseams of their right moccasins planted against each other and their left feet braced behind them, clasped their right hands together, and stretched their left arms back for balance. Someone said: "Go!" and Tourond leaned forward and heaved, expecting, like everyone else, that his weight and height and leverage would hurl Gabriel back and end it before it began. Instead, Tourond's forward lunge stopped as though it had run into a wall, and the two of them stood frozen with their right arms vibrating. They moved into a stage of exploratory yanks and shifts with their right arms and their bodies, but their hands stayed locked together and their feet stayed on the ground.

On the far side of the circle, Madelaine saw Gabriel's big brother Isidor pushing his way to the front with his fiddle clutched under his arm. She focused again on the wrestlers. Tourond had decided to just straighten his arm and stretch it out to his right—given his advantage of reach, it would eventually pull Gabriel off his feet. Gabriel was fighting it, but inch by inch his arm was giving way. It was over in an instant. Gabriel's arm couldn't hold Tourond's arm back any longer, Tourond's arm shot out sideways, pulling Gabriel's along with it, and then Tourond doubled over with a scream and landed on his back.

Madelaine blinked back over what she'd just seen to try and make some sense of it. What had happened was that Gabriel had intentionally let his arm go slack and twisted his hand so that Tourond would either end up on the ground or with a broken wrist.

Gabriel came back toward her, grinning, flexing his right arm behind his back. He said: "I told you I could take him."

"I didn't say you couldn't. I said it was a waste of good air to brag about it."

He stopped dead, goggled at her, then his mouth popped open to let out a reply. Before he could think of one he was cut off by a shout from behind: "Clever boy's trick, boy, for a boy's game. You'd shit your pants in a man's fight."

Gabriel didn't turn around, but although he was still facing her, he no longer seemed to see her. His spine straightened and his shoulders dropped, leaving his hands dangling loosely in front of his thighs, and his little black eyes flared into light. When he did turn, it was like the flipping of a card—one instant she was looking at his eyes, the next at the tangled black thicket at the back of his head. Big Tourond stooped and came on with the firelight flickering off the cutlass blade of the Green River knife. Madelaine looked for Gabriel's big brother. He was just standing there with his arms crossed across his fiddle.

Tourond approached in a crouch, waving the knife in slow circles. The blocky little body in front of her suddenly exploded forward. As the knife came up to meet him, he grabbed the blade in his left hand and drove his right fist into Tourond's throat. Tourond staggered back. Gabriel hammered the heel of his fist against Tourond's chest, and the big man went down. Gabriel came down on top of him with both knees, then jumped back up in the air and landed with both feet on the elbow of the arm that held the knife.

Isidor was there now, grabbing Gabriel and pulling him back. "That's enough! You done him."

Madelaine moved forward in a dream. She took hold of Gabriel's left arm and looked down. The palm of his hand looked almost sawed in half by the knife blade. She unknotted one of the birthday silk scarves from around her neck and tied it tight around his hand. His eyes focused on her from a long way away, and he said: "Thanks. But don't worry, it'll heal."

The music started up again, or she began to hear it again. It wasn't the first time or the last that an evening's dancing involved a bit of blood on the floor. She would've expected to be used to it by now, but for some reason the rest of the night passed as disjointedly as though she'd never seen a knife fight before.

When there was no one left but the Wilkie family and those of the guests who'd chosen to curl up to sleep under a tree, her father said: "Well, I hope that shows you."

"What shows me?"

"What Gabriel Dumont did."

"Shows me what?"

"Have you got wool between your ears? The Dumonts are what they are—you couldn't ask for better men beside you on a hunt or in a war, but they're wild and always will be."

"I thought they were your friends."

"They are. But I keep my distance. Should be even more so for someone like you."

"Like me?"

"Madelaine, do I have to tell you I can't hardly write my name and you can sit down with a pen and ream off bookfuls in three languages? Or is it four?"

"My Latin isn't all that good."

"Well, if you don't want to say the same thing about your life, stay the hell away from Gabriel Dumont."

Madelaine's eighteenth birthday came in a plague year. There had never been one during her lifetime, but she'd heard her father tell stories of the smallpox epidemic that had turned the Assiniboine from one of the great powers on the plains to a minor tribe of isolated bands. This year it was the turn of the Plains Cree and, rumor had it, the Blackfoot in the far west. It began in the spring when a party of Crees showed up at Fort Ellice to trade buffalo robes and pemmican. Half of them had faces so bloated that their eyes were barely slits, and covered with sores like broken blisters. The Hudson's Bay Company factor barred the gates and warned them off, so they headed over to Jean Baptiste Wilkie's store. Madelaine's father stood in the doorway with a double-barreled gun and told them they couldn't come in. Madelaine watched them over his shoulder. One of them had picked up a piece of ice from the river that he kept rubbing over his face. As they turned their horses to move on, he threw it at the open doorway. Her father batted it away. When they were gone, he announced that he was closing the store and the family should pack together what they needed to spend the summer out on the plains.

They moved out the next day in three carts, with her father's string of saddle horses hitched behind. There were only a few stubborn patches of snow left, and the prairie was bursting open with wildflowers and rejuvenated green. Madelaine felt guilty about the joy of wandering freely through the spring, given the reason. They would stop for a few days or a week when they found a pleasant coulee to camp in and then ramble on. As the summer came on, the journey grew eerie. Once they passed by a Cree camp with no signs of life but squawking ravens and crows and a screaming from inside one of the tents that might have been human. Her father didn't swerve to go look, just whipped the cart horses into a trot. Once in a while they would see another party of travelers on the horizon. In any other year both parties would have angled toward each other and fired up the teakettle, but this year both would sheer off.

The one exception was a lone horseman who kept coming on. Madelaine's father reached back for his gun and settled it across his knees. As the rider drew closer, Madelaine could see he was métis, not Indian. She was accustomed to men who rode like they'd been born in the saddle, but there was something in the nonchalant ease of this one that put her in mind of a swallow turning cartwheels in the air just for the hell of it. Whether it was because of that thought or some detail of the oncoming silhouette, she knew it was Gabriel Dumont.

He reined in about ten feet in front of the lead cart house. "Afternoon, Monsieur Wilkie."

"Gabriel."

"I heard you was out on the plains, but I didn't figure on running into you. Your family all all right?"

"So far. And yours?"

"My mother went down last week. Not the smallpox—the TB."

Madelaine didn't find the way he'd said it offhanded, just direct and factual. Within it, she heard a just-as-direct acknowledgment of the fact that he'd cried over her grave and would again. Her father said: "I'm sorry to hear that."

"Everyone else is all right, so far as their health goes. Where you headed?"

"I was thinking we'd circle our way down toward St. Joe," which was what the métis called the little mission settlement of St. Joseph on the Red River. "If it turns out the smallpox has gone that far southeast, we'll just circle back and spend the summer out on the prairie."

"I'm going that way myself. There ain't going to be much of a hunt along the Saskatchewan this year, so I figured I'd throw in with the Red River hunt when they rendezvous in St. Joe. Why don't I ride along with you? An extra gun might come in handy—even if you skirt around the Sioux, the Cree are liable to do anything when they're this crazy with the sickness. And I'm sick to death of my own cooking."

Madelaine could tell her father didn't want to agree but couldn't come up with a good reason not to. Eventually he just nodded his head and flicked the whip to jog the cart horse back into motion. Gabriel Dumont twitched his horse's reins and fell in beside the cart. "Hello, Madelaine."

"Hello, Gabriel."

After the first few days he was more or less part of the family. He didn't appear to go out of his way to be ingratiating, and he didn't talk much, but he cobbled together bows and arrows for Madelaine's youngest brothers and sisters, and pretty soon they were following him around the campsite and calling him "Uncle Gabriel." Madelaine's mother didn't seem displeased when he struck off onto the plains one morning and came back with six fat prairie chickens. Even Madelaine's father didn't seem to mind sitting up late around the campfire telling Gabriel stories of the old days when he led the buffalo hunt.

They crossed a fairly recent trail made by several dozen un-shod horses and the dragging ends of travois poles. Beside it was a body in a beaded doeskin dress, slumped in the feeble shade of a waist-high boulder. Gabriel rode over to have a closer look. Madelaine's father reluctantly reined in the carts. Gabriel stopped his horse by the body and leaned down. The breeze carried a trace of his voice to Madelaine, speaking in Cree. He slid off his saddlepad, unfastened the water bag strapped behind it, and crouched over the body. After a moment he mounted up again without the water bag and rode back. He said: "They had to leave her when the fever made her crazy. But it turned out it didn't kill her, and I don't think it will now—the sores are all scarred over. But she can't walk no farther. Seems a shame she should beat the smallpox and then die 'cause she can't catch up. I can pick up your trail from here and catch up with you— probably four or five days. Don't worry, I got another set of clothes, so I can burn these and take a bath in a river.''

As the carts rolled on, she watched over her shoulder. He rode back to the boulder and dismounted. He picked the Cree woman up in his arms, stepped onto the boulder, and mounted his horse from there. He turned his horse and rode west along the Cree band's trail.

Four days passed in an unbroken routine. Every morning they would pack up the carts again and grind on in a southeasterly direction until the sun reached its height. Then they would stop to make their midday meal, unhitch the cart animals, and shelter in the shade of the carts until the sun wasn't spearing straight down at the tops of their heads. The grazing horses were un-hobbled and put back in harness to drag the carts on until there was just enough light left to make camp.

The fifth day passed with still no sign of Gabriel Dumont. On the evening of the sixth day they camped in a lovely little ravine where the fingertips of a peach-leaf willow tickled the back of a stream. As Madelaine was scouring out the skillet, she remarked to her father: ''Maybe we should stay here to-morrow, too, after so many dry camps out on the prairie. And the boys want to try to get some fish.''

Her father grunted, took his pipe out of his mouth and studied it carefully, then said: ''He would've caught up with us by now if he was going to. No doubt he came across a card game or a horse race around a keg of brandy.''

The next day she thought she heard a gunshot, but it was difficult to tell over the squeal of the cartwheels. She scanned the prairie but saw nothing moving except the shadows of the clouds. As they were setting up camp for the night, a voice called from the gathering gloom: ''Hello the camp!'' and Ga-briel Dumont rode out of the shadows with the body of an an-telope draped across his horse's shoulders.

He didn't ride on in, though, but stopped his horse just close enough for the light from the fire and the sunset to show him clearly. There were no marks on his face—other than the gouges and crevasses it was born with. Madelaine's father said: ''Took you longer than you figured.''

"Nope, I been right behind you for three days. Figured I'd wait to make sure."

Madelaine knew that he'd wanted to make sure the Cree woman's smallpox had been past the stage of contagion. She said: "She's all right?"

Gabriel nodded. "Her husband's other wives started filling her up with soup as I was handing her down off the horse."

He stayed sitting on his horse without coming any closer. Her father stayed standing by the fire with his mouth closed. Madelaine's mother heaved herself to her feet, stumped forward, took hold of one of the antelope's pronged horns, slung it down to the ground, and said: "You skin it, we'll cook it."

"Fair deal."

Given the skinning and carving, dinner was much later than if they'd just sliced off a few slabs of pemmican or peeled another dozen smoked whitefish off the mass in the barrel. But after Madelaine had wearily stripped off her dress and moccasins under the cart awning, and crawled under the blankets into the entangled human hearth of her younger sisters, she didn't sleep. After a long time of staring out through the wheel spokes at the stars, she told herself that if she didn't get up and walk herself to sleep, she'd still be staring at the sky when it turned light. Her younger sisters mewed and grumbled as she squirmed out from among them and peeled off one of the layers of blankets. She muttered soft-edged, wordless noises back at them, clutched the blanket around her body like a cape, and walked out toward where the field of stars met the black arc of the earth.

Bearded clumps of grass stalks hissed across her knees. Crickets sawed their legs together like high-strung fiddles. Nightwinds sighed across her skin. She looked back to make sure she could still see the pink glow from the embers of the cooking fire and the black blots where the cart bodies showed against the stars kissing the eastern horizon. When she looked ahead again, another black blot was rising up in front of her—about the size and shape of a yearling grizzly.

She clicked her throat shut just in time to kill the intake gasp. The shadow bear said: "You couldn't sleep, either?"

"I was just about ready to, but not after I've been scared half to death."

"I was trying to think of how to let you know I was here without . . . Would you rather've tripped over me? Well . . .

some sky, eh? Not a cloud, but you can see the new moon up there where the tail of the Big Bear gets cut off . . . see? . . .''

He raised his arm to point, but neither one of them were looking at the sky or his pointing hand. In the cold starlight his face looked even more like a knot of oak roots left out in the wind and weather for too long. She found herself shivering— even at the height of summer it didn't take long for the winds from the north to take back the prairie from the sun. He lowered his raised arm while he raised the other, put both hands on her shoulders, and kissed her for the second time. She felt herself sinking down among the sweet grass and sage. Her arms opened like wings to spread the blanket below them, then closed again to wrap around his back.

There was a harsh hissing sound, then a sharp crack like a gunshot. A hot iron seared across the blades of her forearms. She let go of the body above her as its spine snapped back in a bow, and a snarl like a cougar spat over her face. The crack sound came again, and she saw her father silhouetted against the stars, bringing his horsewhip down. Gabriel snatched it in midair and let the lash coil around his wrist—like grabbing the neck of a rattlesnake—and yanked on it as he rolled back across her thigh and kicked his feet up. There was a dull thump and a grunt, and her father sailed over him. Gabriel roared and launched himself forward, but she caught him around the legs and brought him down. ''Don't! Don't!''

She was naked on the ground between them. She curled up and covered her eyes with her hands. When the sounds of her own breathing settled enough to hear anything else, there was only one other sound—a wheezing, rhythmic rattle. She lowered her hands from her eyes to cover her breasts and looked up. Her father was sitting on the prairie with his head in his hands and the breath shuddering in and out of him. Voices erupted from the camp behind her. There was the sound of a horse approaching. She looked up and a hand came down out of the night, holding her dress. She took the dress and clutched it to her. The hand stayed there, open and waiting. She took hold of it. The campfire suddenly flared up.

She'd grown a good deal bigger since the last time he'd lifted her up on his horse, back in the summer of Le Grand Coteau, but then so had he. As she was hoisted into the air, she swung her leg around the horse's rump and came down behind the saddle, still clutching her dress in front of her. He clucked to the horse and it set off at a trot. She flung her arms around his waist and bounced along behind him. They rode through the darkness long enough for what had happened to sink into her. She told herself that at least her father hadn't been hurt and that she couldn't change it now. She tightened her arms around Gabriel Dumont and pressed her cheek against his shoulder.

He slowed the horse to a walk. The grassy sage smell of the prairie gave way to the resiny perfume of poplar and birch. Leafy branch ends trailed across her bare arms and legs. The moon came up over the trees. He stopped the horse and said: "This is a good place to camp."

She slid down, holding her dress-draped arm half in front of her. Without the warmth of his back pressed against her it became immediately apparent that the night had grown even cooler. She thought to turn her back to pull on her dress. Instead, she lowered her arm to let it slide to the ground, then squared her shoulders to look straight up at him, amazed at her own brazenness.

She could see his face quite clearly in the moonlight. He was sitting in the saddle with a kind of blank expression on his boulderlike features, slowly shaking his head from side to side. He said: "What a damned fool. All this time I thought I knew how beautiful you was from seeing you with clothes on."

She looked down at the ground, feeling the blush warming her cheeks. Then she looked back up at him and said: "You plan to stay sitting on that horse all night?"

His bedroll for summer camping consisted of one blanket, but they made do. In the morning she was startled awake by a gunshot. He was nowhere in sight, although his hobbled horse was still grazing placidly nearby. She got up and put on her dress. He came out of the woods with a fat mallard duck dangling from his left hand and his gun in his right. In the sunlight, she felt embarrassed about the things they'd done in the moonlight.

He came toward her holding up the duck and grinning. His moccasins made a squelching sound, and his hair and beard were dripping. He said: "Shooting's one thing and fetching's another."

She borrowed his knife and took the duck down to the stream to gut it and pluck it. By the time that was done he'd got a fire going and rigged up a spit with green willow wands. As the duck sizzled away, he said: "Sorry I ain't got a teakettle, but I figured on traveling light to St. Joe. I figure we should still head that way. It'll take at least a week for your family to get there, and maybe your father will have cooled off by then. Even riding two on a horse we can take it easy and still be there before them.''

A week of short traveling days and long nights took them through the Pembina Hills. They came out on the edge of the Red River Valley and stood looking down at the scattered métis cabins of St. Joe, currently surrounded by a city of tents and carts rendezvousing for the buffalo hunt. With the end of the journey in sight, Madelaine began to think of what was ahead of her. She had shamed her family, and it was hard to think of a commandment she hadn't broken. Maybe her family would take her back if she begged, or she could tag along behind Gabriel Dumont until he got tired of her.

He said over his shoulder: ''They got a store down there. Maybe you want to get a new dress and things before we go see the priest.''

''You're supposed to be dirty for confession.'' It tore out of her in a wet-choked voice that surprised her. It appeared to surprise him, too. He shot a perplexed glance back at her and then looked ahead again.

After a moment he shrugged his shoulders and said: ''I didn't think it was a rule that you had to make confession before getting married, but if you say so . . .''

''Who said anything about getting married?''

The perplexed glance he'd thrown back at her before was even more so this time—to the point where his black bead of an eye looked in danger of being crushed if the squinting lids and twisted eyebrow screwed any tighter. ''I thought when you left with me that meant that's what you decided.''

''*I* decided? Don't you have any say in it?''

His chest gave out that bearlike grunt that signified he'd encountered a quandary. He looked ahead again. After a moment he nodded firmly and said: ''You're right. I'll think it over.''

Her hands whipped around his throat and squeezed. He threw his arms up in the air and shouted in a strangled voice: ''All right! All right! I'll marry you!''

CHAPTER 29

There was to be a meeting of the Exovedate at the Letendre house at noon. Gabriel spent the morning on the other side of Batoche's Flats, in the cabin that was currently the war office. Its owner had gone north to bear and bring back messages to and from Poundmaker and Big Bear. Gabriel had spread out a web of scouts across the plains, some to keep him informed of what the government troops were up to and some to call in old debts. One of the scouts was Michel Dumas, who was currently leaning against the chimneypiece, his smoky blue eyes twinkling through his pipe smoke. He had obviously brought back a piece of news that he figured Gabriel would find amusing. Noon had passed, but Gabriel figured that whatever it was Michel was working his way round to saying in his own good time was more germane than the Exovedate.

"What they're planning," Michel said, "is to march out three columns of troops from different stops on the rail line. One from Calgary to go after Big Bear, one from Swift Current to go after Poundmaker's people in Battleford, and one from Qu'Appelle to come here. The column coming here is under General Middleton, who's the boss of the whole outfit. He'll have about eight hundred men and some cannons and a Gatling gun some American is trying to sell to them."

"Gatling gun?"

"It's a Yankee invention that fires hundreds of bullets by turning a crank."

"Does it work?" Michel shrugged. "What do you hear about this Middleton?"

"Big fat white man with a big fat white mustache. He's English; I mean English English, not Canadian English. They say he was very brave when he was young, but he ain't been in a war for thirty years. How I know all this, you see, is 'cause Jerome Henry and some of the other old fellows you used to

213

hunt with have gone and turned their coats and signed on with Middleton as teamsters and guides. The general, he's real happy to have people he can ask advice from that know the country. Like for instance, Jerome told him that it probably wouldn't take as long for his column to get here as he thought, because they would have more time to march in a day than he was figuring, because when they stopped for the night they wouldn't have to waste time putting out pickets and setting up defenses because—''

Michel had to interrupt himself and hold his breath for an instant, pressing his fist against his mouth, blue eyes bugging out as though the laughter were trying to push its way out around them. He managed to continue in a passably straight voice: ''Because our people won't attack at night 'cause if we're killed, our souls won't be able to find the Happy Hunting Grounds in the dark.''

''No!''

''Yes. That's what he told him.''

''He didn't believe it. . . .''

''Why not? It was straight from the mouth of the horse.''

But before Gabriel could start laughing, gunfire erupted outside. Both of them grabbed their rifles and went out the door. Down the slope from the church to the village, fifty or sixty Sioux warriors came galloping and whooping and firing their guns in the air. Their Chief followed at a more dignified pace. He trotted over to Gabriel, pointed at the bandage on his head, and said: ''Yeah, I'd heard they'd aimed to hit you in the vitals and ended up just shooting you in the brains. So—when do we fight and where and how many?''

''Soon and in a lot of places and there's a lot of them, maybe eight hundred.'' Chief White Cap didn't appear to be fazed. He and his Teton Sioux had fought white soldiers once or twice before, once at a place along the Little Bighorn River. ''Any trouble getting here?''

''Not much. When we came by Saskatoon a bunch of the Orange Men from there came out to ask us where we were going, but after they counted us up they saw we were going to go wherever we felt like. Then a little ways farther on we went past a farm and saw the people running out and running away without even putting their coats on. So I sent my son after them to see what was the trouble. He found them sitting in the snow with their bare feet on a blanket, a white farmer with his wife and children. They said they were Green people from Ire Land and when they saw a bunch of horsemen coming they thought it was the Orange Men from Saskatoon come to get them. They were very happy to discover it was just us red men. Anybody else come in yet?''

"Not yet. My brother's gone to bring our people from Fort à la Corne. Poundmaker's still keeping up his siege around Battleford, but he sent a message saying him and his warriors will keep sitting on their heels waiting to stand up when they get the word. I haven't traded any messages with Big Bear since he took Fort Pitt. But right now the best thing Poundmaker and Big Bear can do for us is to lure the white army into splitting itself in three. I got a council meeting to go to. There's a good place to put up your tents on the other side of those trees.''

The Exovedate was in the throes of discussing something that they shelved when Gabriel came in. He told them what Michel Dumas had told him and what that meant they should do. "The Canadian army's supplies and troops are all coming in by rail. If I took about fifty men or so southeast, we could put a barrel of powder under the rails and set it off under the first train that comes along. Even if we ain't lucky enough to get a troop train, it's bound to be carrying crates of rifles and ammunition. Then once they got the mess cleaned up and the track mended, we blow it up under another train in another place. They got five hundred miles of rail line out there, they can't patrol it all. But as long as they're trying to, they ain't coming here.

"Eventually Middleton's going to figure out that the only way he can get to us is to follow his plan of marching a column to Batoche—even if what we been doing to his trains means he don't have as many soldiers and supplies as he'd like. From Fort Qu'Appelle to here is two hundred miles of broken country that the general's never seen before and we know like our wives' bodies. All the way along their line of march we can hit and run like a wolf pack with a herd of buffalo. The first night we hit them they won't even have fortified their camp. Even once they learn to guard themselves they can't stop us sniping out of the dark. Middleton's so-called soldiers are mostly grocery clerks and farm boys from the east. After three nights without sleep they'll be at each other's throats.''

Riel said: "There are some facets you haven't considered.''

"I'm sure there are. But if one of them is that Macdonald might send us a telegram to talk peace, I'm going to tell you that the moment this telegram actually arrives I'll call off the war.''

''Have you considered that there may well be soldiers from Quebec in Middleton's column?''

Gabriel looked around at the other Exovedes to see if any of them understood why he should attach any special significance to that. He turned back to Louis and said: ''So?''

''They speak French the same as you or I.''

Gabriel's head started to hurt again. He propped his elbows on the tabletop and cupped his forehead in his hands. ''I don't care if they speak French or Cree or Chinese. . . .''

''If you knew them, you wouldn't wish to deal with them in such a fashion—to attack them by night from—''

''Well, if they knew me, maybe they wouldn't be coming here to kill my friends and family, but they are.''

''To attack them by night,'' Louis carried on as though there'd been no interruption, ''from ambush, as though we were in fact the brutal savages that Macdonald would portray us . . .'' The chestnut-maned head shook sadly. ''That is hardly civilized warfare.''

''Louis, there is no such goddamned thing as civilized warfare!''

''Our captain general's fiery nature is well known to us all. It is a great boon to us in the heat of battle, but not necessarily so when the situation calls for cool deliberation. I have been told in no uncertain terms that the help which will come to us in good time from certain quarters will only come if we hold here, to fight in defense of our homes against the forces of corruption.''

Moïse Ouellette said: ''Gabriel's the War Chief. Every Chief of the Plains tribes would tell you that once the warrior's tent goes up, the War Chief's in command.''

''I'm sure they would''—Louis nodded—''but we are not savages—or so we keep claiming. Our Chief is the Exovedate as a whole. It is up to you—those who have been chosen from the flock—to decide whether our army should launch themselves upon the enemy like fiends from hell or prove that we prefer the ways of peace until violence is thrust upon us.'' After some further discussion, the Exovedate voted to follow Riel's advice for the present, with the proviso that the captain general should keep himself and them informed as to the enemies' movements.

''Now''—Riel turned to Phillipe Garnot—''perhaps the *secré-*

taire would read again the resolution we were deliberating over when the captain general came in.''

Little Phillipe Garnot shuffled through his papers, cleared his throat, started to read in a gravelly whisper, then drank half a cup of tea and started over:

Resolved that the Canadian half-breed Exovedate acknowledges Louis David Riel as a prophet in the service of Jesus Christ the Son of God and only redeemer of the world; a prophet at the feet of Mary Immaculate, under the visible and most consoling safeguard of St. Joseph, the beloved patron of the half-breeds—the patron of the universal Church; as a prophet, the humble imitator in many things of St. John the Baptist, the glorious patron of the French Canadians and the French Canadian half-breeds.

Some of the Exovedes were enthusiastic, some weren't. Gabriel saw a 'pragmatic advantage to it. Father Moulin and the other priests were still refusing to hear confessions or give communion to anyone actively involved in the Exovedate or its army. If Riel was seen to be a prophet, it would be the priests who were in the wrong.

Louis said: ''If the resolution is to have any effect, it must be passed unanimously.''

Moïse Ouellette said: ''It's one thing for us to pass resolutions on how to hand out the rations we took from the stores, or whether we should carry the fight to the Police and all that kind of thing—but we ain't a council of bishops.''

It was pointed out to him that the Canadian army would certainly have marched out under the blessings and prayers of its own religious leaders, and that there was no denying the fact that the Police had been delivered into the hands of the Exovedate at Duck Lake.

Gabriel said: ''I'm remembering a thing Poundmaker said last year, when he suddenly quit being the missionaries' 'Good Indian.' He said that when he was young the Manitou used to give the people of the plains all they needed to live a good life. But then the missionaries came and told them there was a new god now and the Manitou was grown too weak to provide for his children. So Poundmaker and his people went over to the new god, and since that time the buffalo have disappeared, the antelopes and deer and even the rabbits have been just about hunted out, and the children are dying of hunger and cold. So Poundmaker decided he was going back to his old god because even if the Manitou's grown as weak as the whites say, he can't do any worse than the Christian god has.

"Well, we're Christians and always have been. But maybe Poundmaker's decision to go back to his old god still has something to do with us. Maybe our old god is the one we've had all along, only the priests and the bishops have moved away from him but Louis David Riel hasn't."

Moïse said: "All right, you talked me out of voting against it. But I still ain't been shown enough reasons to vote for it. Maybe that'll change, and if it does, I'll record my vote then. But for now"—he stood up out of his chair—"I'll step out the door while you vote." The resolution passed unanimously. Louis sat hunched on his chair with his hands clasped and his eyes shining.

Moïse poked his head back in and said: "We got a visitor."

Phillipe Garnot said: "The Exovedate is still in session."

"In my own goddamned house," a cracked voice shrilled behind Moïse, "I go where I please when I please." A shriveled old woman in a black dress and a fur coat pushed past Moïse. "Phillipe Garnot, you get your muddy moccasins off my table."

It wasn't technically her table, but her son's and his wife's. Arguing fine points with Mother "Batoche," though, was generally acknowledged as a pastime inferior to whacking your head with a hammer. Gabriel said: "I thought you were settled in at Fort à la Corne for the winter."

"I was. Xavier and his fool of a wife still are. Maybe they're content to leave their house sitting unprotected while *les maudits anglais* march in, but I'm not. Damned lucky thing, too, from the look of this place. Where's Madelaine? Why hasn't she boxed your ears? I came back with your brothers."

Gabriel went out into the spring sunshine and found Edouard and Eli standing on the porch. There was much back slapping and shoulder punching, although Edouard's part in the joviality seemed a bit forced. Gabriel didn't pay it much mind. Out of all his brothers and half-brothers and uncles and cousins, Edouard was the only one who appeared to bear any resentment that Gabriel had become Chief of the Dumont clan. Gabriel had accepted long ago that there would always be a strained undercurrent. When it came down to it, Edouard would always be standing at his shoulder. "So how many came back with you—

I mean besides this peach-fuzzed little child," cricking his neck back and shading his eyes to look up at his baby brother's chin.

Edouard said: "Twenty."

"*Twenty?*"

Edouard nodded.

"When are the rest of them starting out?"

"There ain't no 'rest.' "

"What? There's at least a hundred good men in and around la Corne. I told you to tell them all."

"I did."

"They said they'd fight!"

"So did you."

CHAPTER 30

When she heard the front door open, Madelaine expected Gabriel's voice to shout: "Before I take off my hat and put away Le Petit, did you give up waiting and eat my dinner?" But it was only Riel, who said Gabriel had to ride off somewhere and wouldn't be back till late. So they were six and a half at dinner: Madelaine, Louis, Mother "Batoche," Marie Angelique and Jean, and Marguerite, who was clearly showing the roseate beginnings of the third Riel child.

Marie Angelique fussed restlessly while her father said the grace. When he'd finished the grace and set to work carving the haunch of beef that Moïse Ouellette had dropped by, Marguerite said: "It may seem to you, Marie Angelique, that there are times when God doesn't have his eye on you. But you should know that He took particular care to make sure you were born—or to make sure your father was born, which amounts to the same thing.

"Long years ago when your grandmother was a girl at Red River, she thought she had a vocation to become a nun. Her mother was against it—not that she was against the Church, for she herself was the first Christian white woman in the west, and she'd spent many happy years as the housekeeper for Monsieur L'Abbé in Trois Rivière before she fell in love with the famous hunter Jean Baptiste Lajimodierre and followed him west. No, the reason your great-grandmama was against your grandmother becoming a nun is that in those days she would have had to go east to do so, and your great-grandmama didn't want her daughter to leave her. Then along came a man named Louis Riel. . . ."

"Papa's papa."

"Just so, Jean. He himself had been a seminary student until he came to understand that he was one of those who was made to serve God in other ways than being a priest. So, he wished to marry your grandmother, and your great-grandmama thought this was the answer to her prayers—her daughter would marry this good man and raise a family of her own instead of going away to the east.

"But your grandmother was willful and still insisted that she would become a nun. Then one day the girl who became your grandmother came out from mass and stopped on the steps of St. Boniface Cathedral because she saw something in the sky. The clouds opened up, and through them came the face of a man with a fiery beard who pointed his finger at her and said: 'You wicked girl—honor thy mother and father!' I know this is true because she told me this story herself. So, she became married to your grandfather, and now the whole world knows why it was that God sent one of his angels—or perhaps it was a saint—to tell her what she must do. Because her first child was the man who was destined to fulfill His sacred mission to the métis nation."

"Papa!"

"Just so, Jean. So don't you ever forget, Marie Angelique, that when your father is saying a grace or leading us in prayer, the eyes of God are looking down on us."

Mother "Batoche" said: "Here, Marie Angelique, you should have some butter on those potatoes or they'll stick in your throat," and slathered on a ladleful.

Long after the dishes had been cleared away and Marguerite had packed herself and the children off to bed, after Louis had gone up to his garret to write and meditate and Mother "Batoche" had gone yawning to her own room, Madelaine sat doing some mending in the kitchen with still no sign of Gabriel. She began to grow annoyed. If she'd been informed that he might be gone all night, she would have taken the opportunity to make

an overnight trip back home to check up on things and let Annie
know they hadn't forgotten she was alive.

It was too late to start now, and her eyes were getting tired.
She blew out all the lamps but one and went to the front door
to see if she could spot him riding in. She was about to give up
and take herself upstairs to bed when her side vision informed
her of a large, dark, shaggy shape hunched in a corner of the
veranda. He was sitting on Letendre's porch rocker in his old
black buffalo coat with Le Petit across his knees. She said:
"What are you doing out here?"

"Oh . . . just looking at the stars."

"Are you losing your mind, old man?"

"Hm?"

"They might call it spring on the calendars, but there's still
snow on the ground."

"Not much."

She went back inside and got a blanket to wrap around her
shoulders, then came out and squatted on the porch beside his
chair. The air still had the clarity of winter, the stars blazing like
the ice lamps of the angels. She packed her pipe and got it lit.
Gabriel said: "Moon should be coming up soon, what's left of
it. In a few more nights there'll be no moon at all, and the spring
storms clouding out the stars. . . ."

"Sounds like perfect weather for it."

"For what?"

"For the way you plan to deal with the Canadian soldiers."

"No, we ain't going to do that. Louis doesn't think it's the
way we should fight, and the rest of the Exovedate voted with
him."

"After you did."

"After *I* did? Who told you that? Why would I vote against
my own plan?"

"You gave him your vote the moment you asked him and the
Exovedate for their approval. Since when do you run a war by
asking your army to vote on what you should do?"

"The Exovedate ain't just a war council. It's more like the
government we had at St. Laurent. You didn't think it was strange
I should put things to a vote then."

She didn't reply. When it came down to it, she hoped Riel
was right. But a portion of her still wanted to scream that they
were in a war now, and their only chance was for Riel to get the
hell out of the way and let Gabriel fight it. She wondered how

much of that was just wounded pride that someone else's husband could be wiser and more adept at fitting his hands to the levers of the world.

Finally she said: "Maybe it's a good thing you got the Exovedate to clear things with. You got to admit, when your blood gets up you don't see much but the other fellow's throat. That's saved me and a lot of other people a lot of times—but maybe this time there won't have to be another Duck Lake if you wait."

It was his turn to let a lot of time pass before he spoke. When he did, his voice was soft and breathy: "Ah—there they are." The northern quarter of the sky began to shimmer. At first it was only a soft green iridescence, then it burst out in red and purple and blue dancing stalactites.

The door opened and Louis stepped out. He smiled at them, then at the sky, and said: "The banners of the army of the saints." He cocked his head toward the rocking chair. "My uncle Gabriel should rest if his wound is to be healed in time for the final battle."

Louis went back inside. Gabriel heaved himself out of the rocker, stiff joints cracking, and reached his hand down to help her up. She took him and the lamp into the kitchen to change his bandage. The seam across the top of his head wasn't getting any worse, but neither was it getting much better. Perhaps it was the normal rate of healing for a wound like that, but she'd grown accustomed to Gabriel's body regenerating itself abnormally swiftly. At least it seemed to be past any danger of opening up again, so she replaced the wadded dressing with a thin layer of gauze.

When she'd knotted the binding, Gabriel patted his hand around it and said: "Not so fat as it was."

"Your head?"

"Fat chance. Bet I can fit my hat on again." He went to the peg on the wall where his ridiculous little round-crowned, narrow-brimmed black hat had been hanging since Alexis rescued it from Duck Lake. He grinned at her from under the lumpy felt blob perched precariously atop the calico headband. She clapped both hands over her mouth, but the laugh came out her nose.

They were just finishing breakfast when the secretary of the Exovedate came by to announce that the river looked like it had cleared enough for the Batoche ferry to come out of its winter dry dock. Madelaine managed to deliver herself from the temptation to stand up and see if she really could put a dent in the crown of Phillipe Garnot's hat with her chin without raising her heels off the floor.

Gabriel went down to the river to supervise the launching of the scow and greasing of the cable. Mother "Batoche" went along to supervise his supervising. Riel went over to Phillipe Garnot's stopping place to convene a meeting of the Exovedate without the captain general. Madelaine took a broom to the second floor of the house, then climbed up to the third-floor garret that Louis had taken as his sanctum sanctorum, to sweep her way back down the stairway.

Dust danced in the blocks of sunlight coming through the gabled window. The floor could do with a good sweep, but she'd have to negotiate her way around the books and papers piled on the floor. The only furniture was a straight-backed chair and a small desk, above which he'd fixed the silver crucifix from the church to look down on him from the attic slant that wasn't exactly either a ceiling or a wall. Despite the jumbled stacks of books and sheafs of papers leaning against the legs of the desk, the desktop was a pristinely spartan arrangement of pen case, lamp, and a black pasteboard-covered notebook, the kind used for keeping monthly financial accounts.

She swept her way around to the desk and stood looking down at the whorled-brass, crucifixlike pen and ink case and the black book beside it. She shifted the broom into her left hand, put her right thumb down on the book to feel the pebbled cover, and idly riffled the pad of her forefinger along the striated layers of pages. Her fingernail stuck between two leaves, so she opened it.

The page in front of her was torn off halfway down. Above the tear, a studious and flowing hand had written across the pink-and-turquoise grid of account columns:

. . . the essences of milk that are in you. Change this base milk into a milk all-celestial, so that in drinking it I find a drink a thousandfold richer than all earthly drinks, so that in quenching my thirst I absorb a spiritual and divine liquor whose purpose is to create in me good blood, pure blood, the same blood which fills the heart of Jesus Christ resurrected and elevated to the heavens. O! my God, I firmly believe that Your power, through Jesus Christ Your well-beloved son . . .

That was where the page was torn off. With the broom leaned against her shoulder, she began to rattle through the leaves, picking out phrases wherever her eyes happened to light.

My ideas are right; they are well balanced. They are level, clear; and gloom is not in my thoughts. My ideas are a guide to my gun. My gun is true. It is the invisible presence of God that keeps my gun straight and true. . . . I saw myself in the mirror of justice: reason flashed in me: it flashed: it radiated on my face . . . I saw Gabriel Dumont. . . .''

Madelaine's eyes had already flicked on to the next page before the last phrase registered. She skipped back and read:

''I saw Gabriel Dumont. He was weak and ashamed. He did not look at me; he looked only at his barren table. But Gabriel Dumont is strong: he is strong in the grace of God: his faith will not be shaken: his hope and his confidence in God will be justified.''

There was a creaking on the stairs. Madelaine slammed the book shut and jumped back to her feet. The broom clattered to the floor. As she was scrabbling to pick it up, the little harvest-moon face of Marie Angelique poked over the top step. ''Auntie Madelaine, Mama asked could you please come and help her light the stove?''

CHAPTER 31

Gabriel came into the Exovedate meeting late, mud-streaked and tarry from getting Batoche's ferry back into operation. Moïse Ouellette was saying: ''So Tuesday, then, will be . . . ?''

Louis said: ''Viergaurore.''

Phillipe Garnot looked up from his minute taking and said: "And Monday is Christaurore."

Gabriel took his seat. Moïse said: "You just missed voting."

"On what?"

"The days of the week," Louis explained, "had been named after pagan gods. The next resolution"—passing a piece of paper to Phillipe Garnot—"is one which the Exovedate must pass unanimously if it is to have any power. The doctrine of eternal damnation, which the priests have preached at us all our lives, is a false doctrine—perhaps the most grievous of all the lies from the corrupt church of Rome. How could a God who is merciful and all-loving condemn any of His children to the fires of hell for eternity? There is a hell, of course, and sinners do suffer there—some for centuries. But when God decides they have been punished enough, He calls them up to heaven."

The notion appealed to Gabriel, and he was quite sure it would appeal even more to the wives and families of his soldiers who were being excluded from the sacraments. When the Exovedate had unanimously endorsed the new doctrine, Louis stood up with his hands clasped together and said huskily: "I knew . . . I knew that in the hearts of the rough and untutored hunters of the plains there was more gold than in all of Vatican City. God chose well when He chose the métis nation as the instruments of the mission to bring His strayed church back to Him."

The next item was the captain general's report on the news from Patrice Fleury's scouts. Nothing had changed since yesterday: Middleton's column had reached Humboldt, the telegraph station on the north edge of the Great Salt Plain, and were still camped there. Louis suggested that the general might well have received a telegram from Ottawa that altered the situation.

By the time the Exovedate adjourned for the day, Gabriel was hungry as hell and went looking for Madelaine to tell her his sufferings were beginning to feel eternal. As he walked across the meadow to the Letendre house, he saw that someone had saddled Starface and the gray pony and hitched them to the porch rail. But he had a more pressing question to attend to. He came through the door stomping the excess mud off his moccasins, dropping his coat and Le Petit onto a passing chair as he plaintively bellowed his way toward the kitchen. Madelaine ripped off half a wheel of bannock and handed it to him, saying

"Here, that'll keep you for a while," then reached for her coat. "We have to ride to your father's place."

"Is he sick again?"

"Not well. From the sound of things it doesn't seem likely to take him this time, but . . ." She was out the door. He held the bannock in his mouth while he shrugged his coat back on and picked up Le Petit, then tore off a chunk along the serrated line of his teeth and followed her out, chewing. Edouard and Eli went by as he was cramming the last chunk of bannock into his mouth to free his hands to check the cinch strap—Madelaine had saddled a lot of horses in her time, but Starface had a wide repertoire of tricks he could do with his rib cage.

Gabriel called out to his brothers: "Any more word about the old—"

"I told you!" Madelaine cut him off in a hissing whisper. "It isn't serious enough yet to worry anyone but us." He couldn't quite make sense out of that—Edouard and Eli were as much Aicawpow's sons as he was. And if it wasn't all that serious, why did they have to go charging out to see him, and why did she look so pallid and strained?

Edouard called back: " 'About the old' what?"

Gabriel forced down the whole pulped mass in one gulp and said: "What? I had my mouth crammed full. I just said 'hello.' "

Edouard and Eli looked at each other, shrugged, said: "Hello to you, too," and carried on toward Phillipe Garnot's log-shanty inn, which was now openly the tavern it had always been surreptitiously.

Madelaine had already started off, her bouncing hips not all that much narrower than the gray pony's. Gabriel finished checking the cinch—Starface hadn't fooled her after all—swung up onto the saddle, and trotted after her. He kept pace without gaining on the long slope up from the village to the church. If she didn't slow down, Starface could catch up easily on the plateau.

A couple of armed guards were standing uncomfortably in front of the rectory. Gabriel waved at them and shouted out some nonsense meant to keep up their spirits. He would have to make a point of pointing out to the rectory-guard squad that they weren't jailers. Unlike the storekeepers and other white prisoners in "Batoche's" cellar, the priests and nuns were free to come and go as they pleased as long as they didn't try to insinuate their influence where it wasn't welcome.

Gabriel let some slack into the reins and Starface happily stretched out his legs. Just before they caught up to Madelaine, she slowed the gray pony to a walk, which must have come as a relief to both. Gabriel slowed up beside her. They were out in the open now, between the vast purpling cavern of the sky and the first green shoots springing up through the mud and snow. He said: "What the hell's going on? This ain't the road to—"

"I lied about Aicawpow being sick again—or if he is, it's news to me. I had to get you somewhere we could talk."

"There's a nice fire in the parlor at Letendre's, and a bear rug in front of the hearth. . . ."

"What I want to say couldn't be said there. This afternoon, while the Exovedate was meeting at Garnot's, I was sweeping up the house. I went up to the attic where Louis's been writing things. On the desk was his journal, or account book or prayer book. . . . I started reading it."

"You *what*?"

"It was lying there. I was just wondering what he'd been writing. It wasn't like I was looking to find . . . ."

"Find what?"

"Gabriel . . . what they put Louis in the asylum for, he's managed to fight his way back from that far enough to be able to write good petitions for you. But they didn't cure him."

"So now you're a doctor?"

"I don't have to be a doctor to see that his book is filled with ravings, visions . . . ."

"Visions?"

"Yes. Of celestial milk, and of you and God knows what else."

"It's a private book. Louis talks to his book late at night. There just might be one or two things I might have said to you, or even you to me, in the middle of the night, that might sound a little funny if someone else was to drag them out in the light of day."

"Goddammit, Gabriel, I am trying to tell you that the man you're allowing to tell you what to do is insane!"

For a moment there was no sound but the puffing and thudding of their horses, the creaking saddles and the soft hunting-calls of the nighthawks overhead. Then Gabriel said: "Who won the battle of the Little Bighorn?"

"What?"

"You heard me."

"Sitting Bull. Well, along with Crazy Horse and Gall and . . . I can't remember all the other Chiefs."

"But the first one you said was Sitting Bull, just like everyone else always does. Sitting Bull wasn't within miles of where the fighting was going on. He never fired one shot at Custer's soldiers. All the time the battle was happening, Sitting Bull was in his tent praying and raving and seeing visions. But you and everybody else knows it was Sitting Bull that won the battle of the Little Bighorn."

She let go the reins to press the heels of her hands against her eyes. Her horse stopped as the weight of the reins dropped on his neck. She could hear his horse walking around in a circle to stand in front of her. She rubbed her hands down off her face and opened her eyes. He looked like she'd just served him a meal of rotten meat. He said: "When you ask a man to lead you, you're asking him to ride in front with his back toward you. It's real easy then to go to work with your honing stones and knife him from behind. But don't you ever, *ever* forget that the reason he's such an easy target is because you *asked* him to lead you." He put the heels of his moccasins to his horse and trotted back down the trail.

CHAPTER 32

Although the Exovedate continued to sit every day, Gabriel increasingly spent his daylight hours at the military headquarters cabin listening to reports from Patrice Fleury's scouts. General Middleton's column, heaving itself along as ponderously as the old walrus-mustached bull moose at its head, had left Humboldt to slog on across the Great Salt Plain. Three steamboats were freighting supplies downstream from Saskatoon to rendezvous with the troops but kept grounding themselves on sandbars and in backwaters of the South Saskatchewan. Big Bear's band had taken the Fort Pitt prisoners to Frog Lake. Poundmaker still had Battleford surrounded. The army columns from Calgary and Swift Current were steadily making their way toward Battleford and Frog Lake.

The timing was perfect for Poundmaker and Big Bear to head southeast to Batoche, leaving the troop columns to continue blundering northward to where they thought the hostiles were. Even though Indian encampments didn't move as quickly as soldiers unencumbered with women and children, they could fade through the bush and send mounted war parties ahead. Combined with Gabriel's soldiers, they could give Middleton the surprise of his life and then charge back north to deal with the other columns one at a time.

Gabriel made a halfhearted attempt to suggest it to the Exovedate and Louis David—just about everybody called Riel "Louis David" now, acknowledging the name he'd taken as a prophet. Everyone but Madelaine and Mother "Batoche."

Louis David was still adamantly opposed to fighting in any circumstances except the defense of Batoche. When it came down to it, Gabriel wasn't all that confident he would have been able to pull it off anyway. If he was Wandering Spirit or Fine Day—Poundmaker's War Chief—he might not have felt all that inclined to spring up at the behest of a métis "army" that had been doing nothing but squatting on their asses since Duck Lake. And he wasn't all that sure how much he could rely on Big Bear under any circumstances. Big Bear hadn't been fond of him ever since the time Gabriel rammed a rifle butt into his gut and told him: "If it don't come natural to you to talk civil, I can teach you how."

Madelaine said it was about time they went to take a look at their home. Gabriel was just as glad to get out of Batoche for a while; perhaps it would help dissipate this feeling that he was swimming through cold black soup.

They set off early in the evening, when the sun's slant across the table of the prairie cast a gold-dusted, thick light that would stay the same for hours. The trees were beginning to look like trees again. The dead gray grass had grown green again, sprinkled with pink and blue and yellow flowers. The sloughs were raucous with lusty ducks and crazy coots galloping across the water. In any other spring for the last thirty years, Gabriel would have taken the opportunity to unlimber Le Petit and pot dinner on the way home, but the thought didn't even cross his mind. Through the hour's ride from Batoche's Crossing to Gabriel's

Crossing, the only words he uttered were: "It's falling apart."
Madelaine didn't say anything.

The dogs barked them into the yard, leaping up against their
horses. Annie wasn't there, although someone had milked
Evangeline and done the other evening chores. Madelaine said:
"She must have already gone over to Uncle Jean's for the night.
I'll ride over there and bring her back."

Gabriel let Starface loose in the paddock to gambol with the
rest of the herd and went into the half-blue house with the joyous
dogs baying and carousing at his heels. He built a fire in the
hearth, lit the lamp over his billiard table, and rolled back the
tarpaulin. The hearth fire began to warm the room. The smell
of the felt and chalk and woodsmoke, the gentle clicking of the
ivory spheres, the familiar weight and rhythm of his own cue,
were comforting in a mechanical sort of way.

The dogs burst into a cacophony of barking and baying, and
the pack launched itself toward the door. Gabriel bellowed them
back and shushed them—bad enough that Madelaine should find
them indoors without being mobbed and mauled when she pulled
the door open.

Now that he thought of it, though, it was much too soon for
her to have ridden all the way over to Uncle Jean's and back
again. The dogs had scrambled back across the floor and lined
themselves up next to him. Some were standing stiffly with their
hackles bristling, some were squatting on their haunches or
pressing their bellies to the floor with their lips rolled up from
their teeth and their ears laid back. All were growling low in
their throats and staring fixedly at the door.

Gabriel turned down the lamp, set down his cue, picked up
Le Petit, and stepped back out of the light, levering a shell into
the chamber. The door jerked ajar, then creaked open slowly,
but no one crossed the threshold. In the shadows beyond was
one very tall shadow. A cracked wisp of a voice came out of the
night: "I haven't been keeping up with all the declarations of
the Exovedate, but I think patricide's still a mortal sin."

Gabriel growled to the dogs: "Go get him." They shot across
the floor in a boiling mass of teeth and fur and rattling claws
that transformed itself at the last instant into a batch of overgrown puppies slobbering over Aicawpow's hands and battering
the doorjamb with their tails.

Aicawpow shooed them out and closed the door. Gabriel
turned up the lamp, uncocked his rifle, and ducked under the

counter plank to see if any of the kegs would still make splashing noises when he shook it. He found one and poured out a couple of cups of brandy. In the light, the looming shadow looked even more spectral—gaunt, gray parchment stretched over the giant frame. Gabriel handed him a cup and said: "What the hell are you doing here? You should be flat on your back with your grandchildren feeding you soup."

"Does a man need a particular reason to visit his son? I thought maybe a nice, easy wagon ride in the spring air might do me good." He sipped at his cup, paused to *hah* out the brandy heat, and said: "So, when do we ride out to kill the English?"

"You're too old to ride anywhere."

"Is every man at Batoche's Crossing too old to ride?"

Gabriel swallowed a few ounces of brandy, let it settle, and said: "I think maybe you been talking to my wife."

"I can think of lots worse people to talk to. Where is she?"

"She went over to Uncle Jean's place to get Annie."

"Ah. You still haven't answered the question I started with."

"You know the answer. Louis David and the Exovedate believe we should wait and fight at Batoche."

"Ah." The old man nodded slowly, sucked in another taste of brandy, and flapped his cheeks against his toothless back gums. "Funny thing, I don't remember you having to ask any Exovedate how to lead the buffalo hunt all those years. I don't remember Louis Riel whispering in your ear how to fight the Sioux all those times you did it so good they finally asked us to make peace. I don't even remember the people shouting out 'Louis Riel' when Father André asked who should lead the government at St. Laurent—seems to me the name they shouted out was 'Gabriel Dumont.' I guess my memory must be getting as spotty as the backs of my hands."

"With all respect, Papa, you and I are ignorant buffalo hunters. There are a lot of things we don't understand."

His father drained his cup and shuddered it down. A flush was spreading outward from the wings of his long Sarcee nose, separating the gray of his skin from the gray of his beard. "Did you ever think there might be things Louis Riel don't understand? Since forty years ago at Red River, the Riels were always the first to shout about 'us half-breeds,' but the fact is Louis's father was only one-quarter Cree and his mother was white."

"So you think we should go around cutting open everybody's arm to see if their blood is the right color to be métis?"

"I think you should listen to what I say, not what you think I say. The fact is 'Louis David' was brought up in the town, to be a priest or a lawyer and live in the town. He don't know anything more about the prairie or fighting wars on it than you do about his books and his seminary schooling. If you ever do get around to start shooting at this army that's marching in on us, do you think their general's going to tell them not to shoot back until he can ask permission from some schoolteacher?"

"The whole Exovedate is in agreement with Louis David. You can't hardly call Moïse Ouellette and them 'schoolteachers.' "

"You think Moïse and them wouldn't follow you if you said it was time to fight?"

"Everybody's father thinks all the other boys should follow his son."

"Every father doesn't have a son who is Gabriel Dumont."

Gabriel picked up the keg and emptied the woody dregs into the bottoms of their cups. He said: "And what if I'm wrong? What if Louis's right when he says that if we only fight to defend Batoche, we'll get help from the Fenians and the métis south of the line, and from Bishop Bourget and the politicians in Quebec, and Macdonald will have to give in and make peace? What if I destroy all that by riding out to fight my own kind of war?"

Aicawpow's eyes and mouth grew round and wide. He creaked his head around to gape at the walls and the store shelves and the billiard table. "No wonder I can't make any sense out of this. I took a wrong turn on the road. This place looked like Gabriel's Crossing, and this looks like the inside of Gabriel's home, but it ain't. This is the home of some child who asks: 'What if I pull the trigger and miss? What if the horse bucks me off? What if nobody else stands up to back me?' "

"It ain't just me. . . ."

"It ain't you at *all*," slamming his dried old hand down on the counter plank with a slap that made the cups dance and the struts gasp. There was a noise in his chest, and he bent forward, wheezing and then forcibly slowing the rhythm of his breathing to long, deep drafts of air. He straightened back up and leaned his shoulders against the wall.

Given forty-odd years of gradual change, Gabriel didn't retain a clear picture of his father when he was young. But seeing him now in the dim edge of the lamplight, with the flush coloring his face and his black eyes shining, it was clear that what the old aunts had always clucked about Aicawpow's first son was true. In thirty years, Isidor would have been indistinguishable from his father at the same age. Old Isidor, as Aicawpow had been christened, shook his head and said hoarsely: "I don't know who you are, but you ain't Gabriel."

The dogs set up a clamor in the yard, accompanied by the screeching of cartwheels. Annie bounced through the door and leaned coquettishly across the counter to kiss Gabriel, then stood on her toes to peck Aicawpow's sandpaper cheek. Madelaine followed her in, shutting out the dogs and arching her eyebrows at the muddy pawprints on the floor. She looked up at Aicawpow and said: "You should be in bed."

"Your wife is making indecent proposals to me." They carried on with the form of old family jokes, but none of it helped.

Aicawpow stayed overnight. In the morning they loaded up his wagon and a cart with things to take back to Batoche: bags of flour, the tailings of the root cellar, the last keg of rum, clothes, blankets, half a dozen chickens trussed together, and the wheels to transform the jumper sitting beside the Letendre house back into a cart. There was some debate over whether Annie should come with them now—hinging on how many days they could safely gauge Middleton's rate of march to Gabriel's Crossing—during which Gabriel kept his mouth shut and his eyes on the ground. It was decided that Annie would stay on two days longer, loading whatever seemed useful and portable onto a couple of the freight carts ranked behind the barn. Madelaine or Gabriel would come back for her and the carts and Evangeline and the horses and dogs, who might end up filling some of One Arrow's warriors' stomachs if things didn't go well at Batoche. The pigs would probably have to be left behind to fill Middleton's soldiers' stomachs. The barn cats could fend for themselves, and God help the wandering looter who'd developed a taste for cat meat.

They hitched the cart horse to the tailgate of Aicawpow's wagon, the saddle horses to the back rail of the cart, and Gabriel climbed onto the wagon seat to take the reins from Madelaine. Aicawpow sat fuse-spined next to her, his teeth already gritted against the jolts ahead. They jounced wordlessly along the trail to Batoche's Crossing. The first meadowlark of the year was trilling. Finally Gabriel said to Aicawpow: "You know, you probably ain't going to be happy about this, but one night last winter old Ahsiweyin went and told me how you got your name."

"Did he now? Fact is, after fifty years and more I can't remember myself. Cree names—or Sioux or Blackfoot or any of them—don't hardly ever get given for some single reason. Seems to me one of the reasons they called me 'He Stands' was just 'cause in my young days when I stood up people tended to notice 'cause I stood a good two hands higher than anyone except your uncle Jean. And maybe partways they named me that 'cause in those days I didn't have a habit of running away from any kind of fight. And along with that, I never was a good talker like Jean was, so whenever we had to have words with some passing war party I'd just stand behind Jean trying to look mean while he did the talking. So they called Jean Skakataow, 'He Talks,' and me Aicawpow."

Gabriel laughed. "Like hell you never was a good talker. Ahsiweyin told me the real reason they gave you that name was that one time him and you and a couple of others found a keg of rum that had fallen off a trader's wagon, and when the keg was empty you were the only one could still stand."

"Ahsiweyin was always a notorious liar. But if he was telling the truth that one time, maybe I had a good reason to tell it different when you were growing up. The story Ahsiweyin told maybe ain't the best kind of story to tell boys who are trying to learn a notion of how to go about being a man. And if I did lie for that reason, it seems I chose right, because none of my sons has ever given me any reason to be anything but proud."

As they went past the church of St. Antoine de Padua, Gabriel wrapped the reins around his left hand and leaned his right on the brake for the long slope down to the village on the flats.

He'd become accustomed to the overcrowding at Batoche's Crossing. Over the last few weeks, white-clayed buffalo-hide tents and spruce-roofed dugouts had spread out around the cluster of buildings to house the overflow of métis and Cree and Sioux who couldn't be crammed into the cabins and sheds. But at the moment every dwelling appeared to have been abandoned in favor of milling about on the open meadow between the Letendre house and the row of stores that formed the business district of Batoche's Crossing. As Gabriel wrestled his little freight train down the grade, brake lever smoking and horses squealing, the shrunken figures in the village began to turn and point toward him. Michel Dumas came loping up the hill, shouting: "Where the hell have you been?"

"Back home, to get some things."

Michel smacked his forehead, rolled his cornflower-blue eyes, and said: "I should've thought. I rode right past there." He jogged along beside the wagon instead of taking hold of the cart rail to act as a drag as any sensible man would have. "I was coming to tell you Middleton camped last night at Clarke's Crossing."

"Goddammit, Gabriel," Madelaine said through her teeth, "Clarke's Crossing!"

Gabriel knew exactly what she meant. Although each branch of the métis assumed a divine right to roam anywhere they damned pleased between the Rockies and Hudson's Bay, they all had their home territories. The one centered around the Dumont clan was bounded on the south by a line through the narrows now known as Clarke's Crossing. It had been that way since Jean Baptiste Dumont elected to build a cabin for his Sarcee woman on the South Saskatchewan rather than take his winter wages back home to Quebec. General Middleton's soldiers had just kicked down their back fence and marched into their garden.

When the cartwheels reached the base of the slope, Gabriel reined in his father's wagon team and stood up. The beaded-buckskin and calico-clad crowd eddied around his knees. He knew them all. There was his sister Isabelle. There was her ancient father-in-law, Joseph Ouellette, the last man living of those who had walked their horses forward beside Mister Grant's toward the line of bayonets at Seven Oaks. There was Chief White Cap with his old brass-studded shotgun crooked in one arm and his shy-eyed young wife clinging to the other. There was old Mother "Batoche" in the black silk her rich son had bought her when her husband died. There was dark Edouard and towering, straightforward Eli and moccasin-burning Alexis. They were all looking to Gabriel.

He told Michel Dumas: "Tell all the captains that ain't in the Exovedate to meet me at the war house," then threw the reins at Madelaine and Aicawpow and jumped down. The mossy sod seemed to spring him forward toward Phillipe Garnot's shanty tavern, lifting him up across the front steps. The latch string jumped to meet his hand. He meant to ease the door open smoothly, but it crashed against the wall.

The Exovedate was gathered under a cloud of pipe smoke. They turned toward him crashing in. Riel started to stand. Gabriel said: "I'm riding out to meet Middleton."

Louis David swallowed his tongue and bit his teeth and said: "If the Exovedate chooses to vote in favor, I will take it as a sign from God that your way is right."

"You can go ahead and vote whichever way you please. I'm riding out to fight." Before Gabriel could say anything further, or Louis David could reply to what he'd said already, Moïse Ouellette was standing up and kicking his chair back, Albert Monkman was reaching for his rifle, Damase Carriere was yanking his coat sleeves over his arms, and little Phillipe Garnot was throwing his minutes book aside and checking the caps on a Colt dragoon pistol somewhat longer than his arm.

As he brushed past Gabriel toward the door, Moïse Ouellette muttered out of the side of his mouth: "About goddamned time."

CHAPTER 33

After weeks of waiting around Batoche's Crossing, the Army of the Exovedate wasn't prepared to leap immediately into the saddle and charge off. A good third of the army had to be called in from their farms to the north and the Duck Lake reserve. As it was, Gabriel wanted to wait until Middleton left Clarke's Crossing, where he appeared to be dug in for a few days' stay. The general was most obligingly dividing his own forces, ferrying half his troops across to the west bank under his second-in-command, Lord Melglund.

There was another meeting of the Exovedate, during which Louis David read out a series of passionate arguments against riding out to meet Middleton. "If my uncle Gabriel's wound were healed, I would more willingly consent to see him start out on an expedition of this sort. If anything were to happen to Monsieur Dumont, it would be an irreparable loss to the army and the nation.'' But none of the arguments dissuaded Gabriel, and the rest of the Exovedate voted with him.

The word came that Middleton had finally started north from Clarke's Crossing, his column and Lord Melglund's paralleling each other on either side of the river, marching along under a bright prairie sun with flags flying, bugles tooting, and gun crews cursing as they heaved the cannon wheels through the mud. In the amber light of dusk, two hundred métis, Cree, Sioux, and a smattering of white immigrants climbed onto their horses on the flats beside Batoche's Crossing. Wisps of evening mist were drifting in off the river. The horses had caught the mood and were stamping and tossing their heads.

Gabriel thrust Le Petit into the saddle scabbard and tugged on Starface's cinch girth, then turned to look for Madelaine. She was standing right behind him, holding up two beadwork-covered moosehide bands with dangling thongs. ''Here, I told you I'd make new ones.'' She knelt down and tied them on under each knee, bunching up the fabric of his trousers. ''How's that?'' He flexed both legs as far as they could bend and nodded, giving her his hand to help her back up to her feet. ''You just make goddamn sure you wear out these ones, too.''

He kissed her and pressed her soft-fronted, taut-backed body to him, breathing in her scent of smoked rawhide, body-musked silk, and kitchen herbs. He let her go, patted all four of her cheeks, and vaulted into the saddle to shame the young men into a show of jauntiness. The gauzy scraps of mist were coalescing into a single sheet hovering chest high. Above it floated disembodied horses' heads and the torsos of riders springing up out of the cloud. Bearded men in frayed slouch hats or smooth-faced men with feathers in their bear-greased hair were dipping their heads under the mist to kiss their children or stoically reaching out to take the guns or lances proffered out of the waves.

Gabriel wheeled Starface to face south and pranced him toward the base of the ridge. The bullet welt across his ass didn't seem to have inhibited his panache. Riel trotted his horse up alongside, holding the silver cross high to catch the last blaze of the sun. Behind them, the two hundred walked their horses out of the crowd of women and children and old men, shouting bold things to each other in half a dozen languages. Except for the thirty who'd been left with Edouard to guard Batoche, every man between the ages of sixteen and sixty was falling in.

Gabriel looked back over his shoulder and asked them in his

mind: How many of you, I wonder, will still be brave when the shooting starts? He whipped his horse up the slope toward the church and cemetery silhouetted against the gathering stars.

They rode at a hard lope along the corrugated plateau flanking the river. The night came down fast, but Gabriel didn't need much light along this trail. The heartbeat of the hooves behind became an undercurrent driving the decisions that had to be weighed. There would be scouts riding to meet them to tell him exactly, but he figured that Middleton's army would have camped for the night some miles short of Tourond's farm, which formed the halfway point between Clarke's Crossing and Batoche's. At the pace they were riding, they should reach Middleton's camp in plenty of time to hit them in the cold hour before dawn. Like a wolf pack with a buffalo herd, they could nip in and hamstring them and get the hell out before the soldiers got their boots on. Once the soldiers of the Queen had buried their dead and loaded their wounded onto their wagons and got their stomachs back up to march on, Gabriel's horsemen would be waiting for them in Tourond's Coulee.

Tourond's Coulee was a wonderfully deceptive place. Carved by Fish Creek winding its way into the South Saskatchewan, it looked at first glance like nothing more than a shallow, shaded dip in the prairie. Its tall jungle of birch and willows masked the fact that it was steeper and deeper than it looked, and that the road from Clarke's Crossing angled quite a ways along the floor of the cleft before clawing its way up the other side. Gabriel had a vision that Middleton's night-raided, bleary-eyed soldiers would never reach the other side.

After an hour's ride, Gabriel called a halt to let the horses breathe and let the horsemen fill their pipes and empty their bowels. Louis David called them all together to recite the rosary. The call didn't hold much appeal to Gabriel, nor to those of his soldiers who happened to be of the Protestant persuasion or had followed Poundmaker's lead in leaving Jehovah to go back to the Great Mystery. Gabriel's objections weren't on religious grounds but on the grounds that they had a long night's ride ahead of their night attack and the night was only so long. But since in a few hours the bullets would be flying around them all, they all knelt down—the veteran Catholics holding their horses' reins in their left hands to leave their right hands free to cross themselves—and mounted up again as soon as Louis David was done.

Michel Dumas came cantering to meet them with the news that Middleton had set up his camp at a place a few miles south of Tourond's Coulee. They rode on, sticking to the high ground. When they passed by Gabriel's Crossing, the dogs in the yard below and the corraled stallions sent up challenges that echoed faintly off the water.

At a farm a little farther along the road, Gabriel called another halt and killed a couple of steers. Several bonfires were burning by the time the rough butchering was done. Just as the last embers were being pissed out, and the last dribbles of beef juice were rubbed into beards, two riders galloped in from Batoche. "Gabriel! Edouard said to tell you there's a troop of cavalry coming at Batoche's Crossing along the Qu'Appelle road."

Gabriel couldn't make any sense out of that and said so. Why would the Police at Fort Qu'Appelle suddenly take it into their heads to launch a raid on Batoche when Middleton's army was almost there? The other possibility—that Middleton had managed to leave a cavalry troop hidden on the Great Salt Plain when the rest of the column turned west off the Qu'Appelle road—seemed even more unlikely. And a sneak attack by a lone cavalry troop didn't at all add up with the massed and stately progress of the Canadian army so far. Or perhaps Middleton was smarter than he seemed.

"Well, whether it makes sense or not, Gabriel, one of our scouts saw them and figures they'll make Batoche's Crossing sometime around dawn. Edouard wants you to send back thirty men, along with either you or Louis David to lead them."

Riel said: "We must all go back. Think of our wives and families huddled defenselessly. . . ."

"No! I set out to fight Middleton, and that's what I'm going to do." They argued about it for some time. In the end, Gabriel decided he could spare thirty men easier than the hours of night they were arguing away. Riel went back with fifty men, picking out most of the ones with good rifles. Gabriel rode on at the head of his hundred and fifty to attack an army of four hundred—eight hundred if Lord Melglund could contrive to get his column back across the river when the shooting started.

By the time they got to Tourond's farm, there was a barely perceptible breath of light along the eastern horizon. So much for a night attack. Perhaps it was just as well—Middleton would have no notion that they'd come to meet him until they sprang the trap in Tourond's Coulee.

Gabriel called a halt in the farmyard. Tourond had bundled himself and his family off to Batoche's Crossing the day the invading army reached Clarke's Crossing, but his cattle were still roaming the barnyard, and his rooster was performing a menacing dance in front of his sleeping harem. Gabriel told Michel to slaughter a bull and wring a few feathered necks to make breakfast. "But don't let anybody kill any more. Tell them a full-stuffed stomach only feels better than a half-full one until you get the fear pukes or a bullet in the gut. And don't let anyone go out along the road toward Clarke's Crossing. Maybe most of the Canadian soldiers can't tell the difference between moose tracks and horses', but they'll have scouts with them who can." Then he waved Moïse Ouellette and Eli and half a dozen others to come with him.

They picked their way down into the darkened coulee by a deer path, waded their horses across Fish Creek, and climbed up the south side. Keeping well off the road, they trotted along the edge of the riverside tree belt, listening and peering into the gloom. The sky to the east had softened from coal to charcoal. To the south appeared the distant glow of a watchfire. Gabriel told the others to wait for him and walked his horse ahead.

A few hundred yards ahead, a wooded knoll thumbed out onto the prairie from the bush along the riverbank. Gabriel climbed down off Starface and climbed up the knoll. The vague white gleam of the soldiers' tents covered enough land for several farms. The charcoal sky began to glow and then caught fire as the rim of the sun touched the horizon. A bugle sounded, then another and another. There was a drum tattoo of galloping horses off to his left. Across the open meadow to the north of the camp, a line of ragged shadows was chasing a pair of shadows. Middleton's scouts had finally spotted the spies who'd been shadowing the column since it left Fort Qu'Appelle.

Gabriel ran back to Starface and galloped him out into the open. The shadows ahead grew distinct outlines—half a dozen riders chasing two. The half dozen heard his horse, saw that he was closer to them than they were to the pair they were chasing, and veered toward him. He swung Starface around and charged back toward the trees. Once the bush cover closed around him, he turned Starface again, dropped the reins on his neck, flipped the holster thong off his revolver, cocked Le Petit, and waited. They thought better of pursuing him into the woods, though, and reined in. They turned their horses toward the two scouts they were first pursuing, saw they were long gone, and turned back to the bivouac disappointedly. Gabriel was at least as disappointed, but he had to admit that it was better for the surprise he was planning at Tourond's Coulee that the government troops' scouts should bring back a story of chasing off a few unidentified riders rather than bring back their dead draped across their saddles.

Gabriel rode back through the bush to where he'd left Moïse and Eli and the others, then they all rode back to Tourond's farm. Gabriel stood on the lip of Tourond's Coulee looking down while his soldiers stood around their fires in Tourond's farmyard dismembering roast beef and chicken and breaking eggs over their mouths. The red-and-black sky was brightening to pink and pearl gray. The next thing it was going to do was rain.

He pictured Middleton's column's progress down into the ravine and along the switchbacks of the road across the ford. Even with only a spring dusting of leaf buds on the poplars, Fish Creek was invisible. By the time Middleton's vanguard had got across the creek and reached the base of the slope up out of the ravine, most of his column would be inside the coulee. At that point, a strong force of dismounted men firing from cover could blow the front ranks to pieces. Once it sank into Middleton that he'd blundered into a trap, at the instant when he either ordered a retreat or tried to dig in and fight, a small force of cavalry that had stayed hidden on the south side of the ravine while the troops marched by could charge out from behind them. Just like buffalo in a pound, except that the government soldiers would have the option of throwing up their hooves in surrender.

Gabriel walked back to Tourond's farm and started picking out the riders who would hide with him on the south side of the coulee and charge down the roadful of soldiers. He figured he could only take twenty if the men on foot were to poleax the head of the column with their first barrage. The logical choices were those who had repeating rifles but had refused Riel's selection of them as part of the fifty he'd led back to Batoche. "Moïse. Michel. Phillipe Garnot." His eyes settled on "little" Eli, but then he thought of Isidor and decided to leave him with the hundred and thirty.

He'd just finished rounding out his twenty with several of White Cap's Sioux—maybe they didn't have much in the way of weapons, but they had experience—when one of the scouts that

Middleton's scouts had chased came galloping out of Tourond's Coulee. "They're marching out!"

"Did you stay the hell off the road?"

"Of course. I came across the meadow that—"

"Good. Now, here's what we're going to do. . . ."

By the time the marching boots and creaking gun carriages grew audible, Gabriel and his twenty were hidden in the bush under the south slope of Tourond's Coulee, within striking distance of the road. Gabriel and Moïse and Michel climbed up to the rim and peered through a border of rock cress and translucent-flowered kinnikinnik. The government troops still weren't in sight, but they could hear them singing in their flat Ontario English:

"We're gonna hang Lewis Ry-al from a sour apple tree. . . ."

What was in sight, though, was a batch of slouch-hatted irregulars stooped down pointing at the road with their horses' reins in their hands. Gabriel whispered: "What the hell are they sniffing at?"

Michel Dumas said: "Must be from chasing the cattle."

"From what?"

"Some of Tourond's cows had crossed over to this side of the coulee, so a few of our boys rode down the road to herd them back for supper."

"They *what*?" He clapped his hand down on the top of his hat to stop himself from shouting, promptly reminding himself of the half-healed furrow on the top of his head. Maybe the worst part of his knuckling-under to Riel's policy of nonviolent warfare was that so many of his young men had never had the chance to learn the lesson of the buffalo hunt and the battlefield. A few weeks of hit-and-run warfare would have taught them that if you want to keep on living wild and free, there's times when you have to do exactly what you're told.

There was nothing he could do about it now. The slouch-hatted irregulars—each of them more dangerous in this country than a regiment of redcoats—were climbing back on their horses and fanning out to take a closer look at the ravine. The ones splitting off east and west could peer into the coulee all day and see nothing but trees with new leaves, but the one in the middle was coming straight for where Gabriel's horsemen were hidden.

Gabriel scrambled back down the slope, grabbed the reins from the young Sioux holding his hand over Starface's nostrils, and hauled him hoof-sliding up the ridge. When they got to the top, the Canadian scout was barely thirty yards away. Gabriel jumped on the saddle and charged out at him. The scout turned and ran, but Starface gained on his horse quickly. Gabriel snatched Le Petit out of the scabbard and leaned forward. He had no intention of firing a shot. One good crack across the head would knock the scout out of the saddle, and when his friends came looking for him there was a good chance they'd assume that his horse had tripped in a badger hole. The scout was inexplicably obliging him by veering his horse off to the left, giving Gabriel the inside track.

He was close enough to see that the white-eyed rider's mustache was red under the caking of road dust when Moïse and Michel began to yell: "Gabriel!" He turned his head. Off to the left, in the direction the scout's flight was veering, there was a troop of about forty uniformed horsemen coming toward him. He reined Starface around hard, hearing the crack of their rifles, and fired a couple of shots over his shoulder as he galloped back to the coulee. He jumped off the saddle, slapped Starface down the slope, and threw himself down beside Moïse and Michel.

Behind the cavalry troop there were files of flags and marching men in red and green and black uniforms. The files spread out, closed ranks, and began to fire by the numbers, unlimbering their cannons to lob shells into Tourond's Coulee. Gabriel and his hundred and fifty were caught in their own trap.

CHAPTER 34

Gabriel snuggled the stock of Le Petit against his cheek and began to shoot back. At the first crack of smoke and the soothing bunt of Le Petit's brass heel mount against his shoulder, all thoughts of what should or shouldn't have happened vanished—they were in it now. The lines of uniforms were advancing in a broad front, cautiously at the center but unopposed on both wings. Gabriel never looked to see whether the man he shot at went down or not, he just picked his target, pulled the trigger, ducked down, rolled to another piece of ground, rose up, and picked out another man.

The cannons began to boom. To his left, the government troops were pouring into the ravine. The ones to his right were slowing down as they cleared the rim and came into the sights of Eli and the rest of the hundred and thirty at the bottom of the coulee. The ones directly in front of him were still coming on.

He'd got himself into a thicket. Branches and clumps of willow catkins were snapping off and flying away all around him, pattering down on his hat. He broke out through the back of the thicket and scuttled down the slope. There were only half a dozen of his twenty horsemen there. "Where are the others?"

"Gone back to join up with the big group."

Michel said: "Except one Sioux. He danced out in his paint to show they couldn't shoot him, and they did."

"Where is he?" Moïse pointed up the slope. "I'm going to get his gun and ammunition. Keep at them." Gabriel crawled up through the bush cover while Moïse and the others did their best to make the soldiers think twice about showing their heads over the ridge.

He heard a voice singing in Sioux and worked his way toward it. He found the Indian lying on a bald patch of the slope, with a hole in his belly and the first drizzling of rain splashing on his face, singing: "You can't count coup with a bullet, white man." When he heard Gabriel approaching, he shifted into his death song and forced his voice louder, then stopped when he saw it wasn't one of the soldiers.

Gabriel said: "I come to borrow your weapons for one of your brothers."

"White Cap came and took them already."

Gabriel looked down at the bullet hole through the blanket the Sioux had wound around his waist against belly wounds. "Think they've killed you?" The Sioux shook his head. A group of redcoats pounced out of the bush and came racing down the slope to finish him off. Gabriel rolled back under cover and dropped one of them, or perhaps the bullet came from Moïse and the others who'd shifted their attention to that quadrant. The redcoats ran back into the woods.

Gabriel scrambled back down to the remnants of his striking force. One of them shouted over the gunfire: "There ain't enough of us to hold them here! Let's join back up with the footmen across the creek!''

Gabriel couldn't argue. The south half of Tourond's Coulee was filled with uniforms working their way through the bush toward Fish Creek. Gabriel and his half dozen got there before them, splashing their horses across the creek and circling around to approach the hundred and thirty from behind rather than between their guns and the soldiers'.

As they started their cutback through the bush along the north edge of the ravine, they met a wave of men running in the direction of Tourond's farm and, presumably, the horses they'd left tethered there. Gabriel ran his horse in front of them and shouted: ''Where the hell are you going?''

''Where the hell do you think? Out of here. They got us trapped, and the cannons are finding the range.''

''They got no range to find, unless they can shoot through the ground. The only way they can shoot straight at us is if they wheel their guns right up to the rim, and they'd have to haul them a mile back to arc their shells up and in. I'm sure they're blowing hell out of Tourond's farm and everything around it, but they can't hurt you down here.'' He herded them back to join the others, but it became apparent that a lot of them had run out already. Of the hundred and thirty men he'd left on foot, he counted no more than forty-seven. Out of his original twenty horsemen there were now only fifteen.

The sixty-odd-strong Army of the Exovedate spread out as wide as possible along the north shore of Fish Creek so that any frontal assault would have to come wading. Eli and the other old hands—even baby brothers got to be ''old hands'' eventually—had gone to work in a businesslike manner, finding secure positions and squeezing off methodical shots at clear targets. But a lot of the younger men were close to panicked. It was hard to blame them; the new-green trees on the other side of the creek had just about disappeared behind gray blooms of rifle smoke, and every shot fired from this side attracted a swarm of lead bees to a honey bear.

Gabriel slid off Starface and moved to slap his bullet-welted rump back into the trees, but the horse was already long gone. Shouting out some nonsensical war cry to draw the younger men's attention, Gabriel ran to an unoccupied tree by the shallow depression of a deer trail and set to showing them how it was done—blazing away from behind a tree trunk whose girth was somewhat narrower than his own. Louis had been quite wrong in calling him fearless. Gabriel's insides were inclined to curl up like a porcupine at the prospect of a bullet entering them, just like everybody else's. But somebody had to set an example, and once you were in a fight the best chance you had of not getting shot was to shoot the other man first.

He called back to the wavering young men: "Come on, their bullets can't hurt you!" Which was technically true: a bullet wound didn't hurt until long after the bullet hit you, and a bullet that killed didn't hurt at all.

Gradually they edged forward to gather around him, taking tentative shots over the shore rocks and growing bolder. "Don't be afraid to take your time aiming—they can't see you till there's smoke from your gun. Pick out your shot and squeeze it off smooth, and *then* duck down like a scared rat."

The head of an immense black snake poked over the south rim of the coulee, then another and another until there was a line of snake mouths gaping down toward the north side of fish creek. The soldiers had wheeled their artillery forward. At that range, the bush and rocks and deer path trenches would be no better shelter from grapeshot than from the rain.

A man appeared in silhouette beside one of the snake mouths. Le Petit leaped up and spat, and the silhouette spun away. The men around Gabriel began to follow Le Petit's lead, slanting long shots up into the easy targets. Pretty soon the artillerymen didn't show themselves anymore. The cannons let off one ragged volley, tearing up the trees and spewing shrapnel into Michel Desjarlais, but that was all. Maybe one more blast of cannon fire would have finished off the Army of the Exovedate there and then, or maybe the entire Canadian artillery corps would have been wiped out when they stood up against the sky to reload and adjust their aim.

Hamstringing the artillery didn't change the fact that there were still hundreds of Middleton's soldiers against Gabriel's sixty. The narrow front that sixty men could cover still left hundreds of yards on either hand where the government troops could wade across the creek in safety and close in behind them.

Gabriel bellowed to his fifteen horsemen to follow and ran back to where Starface was waiting. Five of the other horses had been standing in a clump where one of the exploding shells had landed. Michel Dumas's white mare was screaming and trying to walk on three hooves. Michel put a bullet in her head and charged back to his place on the creekbank while the remaining fourteen clambered onto their horses. Gabriel led them along the north base of the coulee, galloping zigzag through the whipping branches, to hook around the troops who had already crossed the creek. A few soldiers fired at them as they went by.

Once there were no more uniforms showing through the leaves, Gabriel crossed the creek again, tethered his horse at the south wall of the ravine, and ran up to the top. He threw himself down on the rim of the plateau, breathing hard, to take a look. He'd come up on the inland edge of Middleton's line, which was anchored on the west by the east bank of the river. There looked to be a great deal of activity going on at the far end—Lord Melglund's column crossing over from the other side. If Middleton was smart enough to have brought along the ferry cable from Clarke's Crossing, it wasn't going to take long before the odds of twenty to three became forty to three.

Moïse panted up beside him with the other thirteen straggling behind. Gabriel pointed ahead, toward a hollow in the prairie that started a few yards out from the ravine and ran along the flank of Middleton's army. Moïse nodded. Gabriel stuck Le Petit through his cartridge belts, crawled on his hands and knees across the gap of open country, and dove into the hollow. It was only a couple of feet deep, but it was masked with a fringe of gooseberry bushes. He rolled to his feet and ran along hunchbacked, hearing the thumps behind of the fourteen métis and Sioux tumbling in after him.

At the far end he raised himself up on one knee and peered through the bushes. The troops in front of him were lounging about with their white pith helmets or pointless little gold-braided caps in their hands, waiting to be ordered in for the mopping-up. They had good reason to be sure of themselves, if all they were facing was one clump of resistance that they could easily engulf and overwhelm. Le Petit and his fourteen friends proceeded to show them otherwise.

Pretty soon, Middleton's army had realigned itself to deal with two fronts. After a lot of uniform tunics had been spoiled with diving chest down into the mud and a lot of gold-striped trousers soiled, after one misguided effort at a bayonet charge across a hundred yards of open prairie, the regiments facing Gabriel's handful settled down to pressing their noses into gopher holes and firing blindly. The important thing was that Middleton was no longer assuredly pouring his troops into the ravine.

Bluff and boldness certainly had a good deal to do with accomplishing that objective, but Gabriel wished he could take credit for the rain. Town-boy volunteers and parade-ground soldiers were bound to find it difficult enough to accustom themselves to getting shot at without being stuck out in the open in a freezing rain.

But when Gabriel reached around to the back of Le Petit's cartridge belt, all the loops he pressed flapped flat. Moïse and the others who possessed .44 rifles passed handfuls of cartridges to him on the assumption that he could make better use of them than they could. He could, but if the soldiers managed to work up their courage to try another massed charge, they weren't going to be stopped by pinpoint sniping.

A gust of wind from behind blew Gabriel's hat off. He snatched it up and checked it over to make sure it wasn't a bullet signifying that the government troops had managed to sneak around behind. Finding no punctures, he clapped it back on his head, snugging it down over the rim of his bandage, and then considered the fact that the wind was blowing toward the troops. That led him to poke his head up to make sure that several of those well-equipped fools in the bayonet charge were still lying where they'd been dropped. He squeezed a handful of the plants fringing the hollow and, sure enough, although the rain was steady and cold, it was the needling kind that worked its way through a man's coat and into his bones rather than the fat-dropped kind that drowned the grass. Among the new-green reinvigorated growth on the swath of prairie between the hollow and Middleton's wide flank, there was a lot of last year's bleached-out gray grass stalks and dry sticks of late-blooming brush.

Gabriel said: "Who's got powder?" One of the older Sioux grunted and handed him one of the world's last bull-buffalo powder horns. Gabriel said: "Wait here for me and save your bullets," then pushed his way out through a gap in the gooseberry bushes and elbow-crawled through the grass, dribbling out the powder in a line. It didn't last long. He shook out the last few grains, tossed the horn back toward the hollow, and struck a match. When he touched it to the end of the powder line, there was a flash of orange lightning and a long puff of blue smoke. The withered grass sputtered as the patina of mist hissed off it, then caught. Gabriel pulled up a few tufts of yellow

grass from behind him, shook off the rain, lit it from the rising
flames, and crawled along extending the line.

Although the spring-green damp slowed the fire's advance, it
helped increase the smoke. And once the wind had whipped the
flames up hotter they got moving pretty quickly, a broad front
of leaping flames and a black curtain of smoke thickening upward. Gabriel jumped up and chased the fire, blazing away with
Le Petit as fast as he could work the lever. He could hear the
gunfire from the soldiers ahead, but they couldn't see what to
shoot at any more than he could, and there were a lot more of
them for his blind shots to get lucky with. When Le Petit was
empty he emptied his revolver.

He caught up to the low line of flames, hauled in and held in
a deep draft of air, and jumped over into the smoke. The black
curtain thinned to gray as he ran ahead of the fire, eyes stinging
and lungs threatening to cave in. He could see the soldiers now.
They were running.

There was a dark blot on the ground in front of him. He
stooped down, hauled in a fresh gulp of air, and turned the dead
soldier over. His friends had already stripped off his cartridge
belt and taken his rifle. There was another black-uniformed lump
nearby. This one groaned as Gabriel rolled him over. He was a
baby-faced young man with a preposterous gold beard. His
glazed blue eyes cleared with terror when they saw Gabriel. The
other soldiers had taken this one's weapons, too; Middleton must
have issued an order.

The smoke was thickening; the fire was catching up. It was
slowing down as the rain gusted stronger and the wind weaker,
but it still had enough momentum to burn this far and farther.
Gabriel slipped his knife out of the sheath on his left hip, said
to the young soldier: "I'm sorry for you, but this is our home,"
then made the sign of the cross over him with his left hand while
his right did what Michel Dumas had done for his horse.

The soldiers who'd run away saw what was happening to the
fire and started back, firing as they came. Gabriel brought his
mouth down to the grass like a man drinking from a stream,
sucked in a cheek-puffing breath of relatively smokeless air, and
ran back to jump over the fire again. Moïse and the other fourteen in the hollow stood up when they saw him jogging across
the charred, steaming prairie. They were pleasantly surprised
to see him alive but disappointed that he'd brought no pilfered
guns or ammunition.

The fire was sputtering out but still had enough life in it to keep this end of Middleton's line busy for a while. The gunfire in the coulee was still going strong, interspersed occasionally by the boom and crash of cannon fire. Some of Middleton's artillery had pulled back to a stretch of wooded ground where they could carry on their range-finding experiments undisturbed. Gabriel pointed toward the trees. "I'm going to work my way in behind them and give them the idea there's another attack they got to turn and face. You stay here and keep it hot for them after they get the fire out."

The Sioux contingent sidled snake-eyed glances at each other. One of them shook his head at Gabriel and said: "If you leave here, we're getting out, too."

Moïse said: "Face it, Gabriel, we're all just about out of cartridges. What are you going to do, throw rocks at them?"

"All right. Then I'll just go show our friends down in the coulee we're still alive."

"Are you crazy? They're swarming like bees down there." But Gabriel was already out of the hollow and running for the edge of the ravine. He plunged into it, checked to make sure Starface and the other horses were still where he'd left them, and then worked his way through the bush on foot. The closer he drew to the firing, the more frequent grew the flashes of uniform colors and the clumsy thump of twig-crunching boots all around him. He dropped back and waded across the creek to circle up the north slope to come down on Eli and Michel and the others from behind. But once he'd got in behind them, he found himself hugging the ground in a thicket facing a sea of red- and green-clad backs. The soldiers had them surrounded.

Over the roaring of gunfire, another sound rose up, a high, quavery tenor. It grew stronger as other voices joined in: basses and baritones and in-betweens. Gabriel thought he recognized Eli's voice and Michel Dumas's. They were singing old Pierre Falcon's song about the day Mister Grant and the métis nation stood up to the white invaders at Seven Oaks—forty voices singing and keeping time with their rifles firing back at the eight hundred closing in on them. An unhuman voice joined in, trilling along on top of the melody. Eli had brought along his flute.

CHAPTER 35

Tourond's Coulee was a good deal farther from Batoche's Crossing than Duck Lake was, too far to hear the sound of rifle fire. But they could hear the cannons between the claps of thunder that had come with the rain.

Madelaine was holding Louis Riel's left arm. At the first distant cannon boom he'd knelt down in the parlor and started praying with his arms held out like a crucifix. After the first hour his arms had begun to tire and droop until finally he'd asked his wife to help him. Marguerite had taken hold of his right arm and asked Madelaine to take the left. They stood propping up his arms among the constant comings and goings of the wives and daughters and mothers of the men at Tourond's Coulee kneeling to pray with Louis David.

Edouard came in, but not to pray. He cut through the prayers rudely with: "Something's gone wrong. It shouldn't be going on this long unless the soldiers got them pinned down. Gabriel don't have enough men for a standing fight. We have eighty men here that could make the difference. . . ."

"No!" Louis wrenched himself out of his prayers, although he didn't alter his position. "The Police would find our wives and children defenseless."

"What Police? I sent out scouts along the Qu'Appelle road hours ago. If there was any troop of cavalry out there, they'd have come back and told us by now."

"They haven't come back to tell us that they *didn't* find an attack coming, have they? They may well have been captured or killed. We *must* defend Batoche." He closed his eyes again. "O! my God, for the love of Jesus Christ, for the honor of your Immaculate Virgin . . ."

Edouard turned around a couple of times, slapped his leg with his riding whip, and left. Madelaine called Annie over to relieve

251

her, reached for her close-woven woolen shawl, and went out into the spring rain.

She stood on the porch and listened. At first there was no sound but the hissing of the rain, the jingle of horses shaking the water out of their eyes, and the squealing of children chasing each other through the mud. Just when she was beginning to think it might be over, one lone cannon thud echoed faintly.

She lifted her shawl over her head, stepped off the porch, and walked up the long slope to the plateau above the village. It was a difficult climb. The new grass was slick with rain, the mud was slippery, and—no way around it—she was not as agile as she once was. Edouard and old Joseph Ouellette and a number of others were standing at the top, peering at the horizon and listening. The priests and the holy sisters were huddled anxiously outside the rectory, telling their beads and murmuring about "our poor métis."

She could hear the cannons more clearly up here, along with a soft, incessant popping noise that might be rifle fire or perhaps the drizzle pattering on Edouard's wide hat brim. Edouard was sucking on his mustache, alternately crossing his arms tightly and uncrossing them to run his fingers through his beard. Madelaine said to him: "I'm one of those defenseless ones you're supposed to be protecting, and I'm telling you that I would rather you go help my husband than sit on your heels here."

Joseph Ouellette said: "There's plenty of us who're too old to ride that can still remember how to fire a gun. And plenty of the young boys are— Hey, Alexis!" Gabriel's nephew slid off the shed roof he was peering from and ran forward eagerly. "You got a gun, don't you?"

"Not much of a one, Monsieur Ouellette, but it shoots pretty straight at short range."

Old Ouellette grinned. "He's a Dumont all right, eh, Edouard? Almost as tough as the Ouellettes. So *if* these Police come while you're gone to help Gabriel and Moïse, we can hold them off till you get back. If they do manage to break through to Madelaine and my old woman, on their own heads be it. But if Gabriel and the rest get taken or wiped out, we're all finished."

Edouard looked down at the Letendre house, took off his hat, ran his hand through his hair, put his hat back on, and said: "Well, I guess I'll have to interrupt his prayers again."

He started down the slope. Madelaine called after him: "Are you going to ask him again to give you permission?"

"I'm going to tell him that when my own flesh and blood are being shot at, I can't sit here."

All eighty of Edouard's defense force—the thirty who'd been left with him originally and the fifty who'd come back with Riel—went with him. They burst out of Batoche's Crossing like a watch spring wound to the point that its catch snaps.

The vague blot of brighter gray that denoted the sun above the cloud cover was already well on its way through its descent. Madelaine picked her way back down the slope. Annie was still holding up Riel's left arm; Mother "Batoche" had relieved Marguerite on the other. Marguerite was kneeling between Marie Angelique and Jean, their heads bowed against their tight-clasped little hands. Their white knuckles seemed to be radiating out from the white splotches where their foreheads pressed against their hands.

Madelaine went into the kitchen and boiled some eggs and cut some cheese and bread and poured some honey into a bowl. She had no desire to eat, but the children should. She managed to convince Marguerite to eat a few mouthfuls for the sake of the swelling that was already beginning to spoil the dainty midriff line of her peppermint-striped dress.

Alexis came running in, shouting that there were horsemen approaching along the road to Fort Qu'Appelle. Joseph Ouellette huffed in after him, lugging a shotgun that looked to be about the same vintage he was, and took up a position at one of the front parlor windows. He reversed his shotgun to butt the glass out of one of the panes, but Mother "Batoche" shrieked at him to wait until they could at least see who these horsemen were.

They turned out to be the scouts that Edouard had sent to look for the reported troop of Mounted Police or cavalry. They'd ridden halfway to Humboldt without seeing one living thing larger than a jackrabbit, with the exception of a herd of wild horses whose hoofbeats might have been mistaken in the dark for a cavalry troop. The scouts were extremely pleased that Edouard had gone and taken every man who could ride to help Gabriel, and extremely displeased that they'd come back too late to go with them.

The night came down. Clumps of stars showed the clouds breaking up. There was no more thunder from the sky or from the cannons at Tourond's Coulee. Riel continued to pray. Marguerite put the children to bed. Madelaine sat by the fire drinking tea and smoking her pipe between taking her turn at relieving Isabelle Ouellette or one of the other women holding Louis's arms, unceremoniously dropping the pipe or teacup or arm to run out the door whenever she thought she'd heard something.

Long after midnight, one of the tricks her ears were playing on her turned out to be true. Along with every other woman in Batoche, she stood watching the long line of horsemen wend their weary way out of the darkness, some of them two to a horse. One advantage to having Gabriel for a husband was that she was always the first to know. If he was alive, he'd be riding at the front of the line. He was.

He creaked down off the saddle and leaned back against his horse. He was covered in mud and soaked through, and he smelled like an old horse blanket cured in swamp water. She wrapped her arms around him and buried her nose in the hollow of his throat and thanked every saint in the calendar.

Alexis took hold of Starface's reins and said hopefully: "Should I take care of him, Uncle Gabriel?"

Gabriel nodded and then added in a hoarse whisper: "If you're wondering—we kicked hell out of them." As Alexis led his horse away, he leaned his weight off Starface's flank onto Madelaine's shoulder. She walked him up the steps, settled him onto a chair by the fire, and went into the kitchen to fill a cup with rum.

She could hear Louis saying in the parlor: "You must tell me what took place."

"I ain't slept for two days," Gabriel's voice growled back. "All that time I been riding or fighting. My head hurts like the bear that ate the stove. I can tell you tomorrow."

"I have been praying all that time. How could I sleep without knowing how those prayers were answered?"

Madelaine carried in the brimful cup and placed it in her husband's grimy hand, registering a disapproving glower from the prophet Louis David. Gabriel slurped in a good quaff regardless, sighed, and said: "Well . . ." Madelaine lowered her broadening hips onto the bearskin hearth rug and cocked her arm over Gabriel's knee.

He told it through up to the point where he was hiding in the thicket hearing the singing, by which time he'd reached the bottom of the cup. She went and filled it up again.

His voice had grown warmer and less hoarse. Steam was rising off his rain-drenched corduroys. "So, I saw I had no chance of sneaking through the soldiers to join up with Eli and Michel and them. So I snuck out and went back to the fourteen I'd left up on the prairie. There was only seven left—the Sioux had run out like they said they would. So I took my seven back across the coulee to Tourond's farm, or what was left of it after the cannons. I figured we'd get some food in us and wait for night, and then we'd come at the back of the soldiers and scare them off, or at least enough of them to open a gap for our men to get out.

"We heard horses. It was Edouard and his eighty. They wanted to go down into the coulee right away. I thought it'd be better to wait till dark, when we could really scare the shit right out of them. But one of the Crees convinced me different. He said: 'Uncle, you don't wait for tomorrow to rescue your friends.' "

He took another sip and smiled at the ceiling. "We came down that road whooping full-tilt and firing from the saddle. And those eight hundred soldiers in their pretty uniforms took one look over their shoulders at our raggedy-assed boys and ran like rabbits. They ran so far and so fast they left their camp on the other side of the coulee—big bonfire with a lot of guns and cartridge belts lying beside it, even their doctor's medicine box with three bottles of brandy in it. Wasn't enough for more than a swallow for each of us, but that swallow did taste good. I wanted to chase after them and keep them running, but Edouard reminded me that everyone was soaked through and chilled to the bone. So we went back to Tourond's and ate up the last of his beef and chickens and came home."

Louis said: "And how many . . . how many of our men were . . . ?"

"Four dead. That Sioux who'd danced out in the open guessed wrong that the hole in his belly hadn't killed him. We got two wounded—I don't think Michel Desjarlais's going to last long. A lot of the horses left at Tourond's got killed by the cannons."

Louis shook his head sadly and said: "Four men dead. Perhaps five."

Gabriel cocked his head toward Riel, slitted his eyes, and said: "That's right. And the number of Middleton's soldiers killed or wounded is upward of fifty. You prayed well."

"It is sad, though," Louis said in a tortuous voice, "that the prayers of a Christian should be answered by the death and suffering of other Christians.''

''Not near so sad as if this Christian had been one of them.''

Madelaine took him upstairs but wouldn't let him lay his head down until she'd changed the bandage on it. He was asleep before his body hit the bed. She wrestled him from side to side and up and down to peel off his clothes and to get the bedclothes out from under him to put over him. Then she undressed herself and crawled in. Remarkably, he woke up. Not for long, but long enough.

He slept through half the next day. She spent the morning helping with the wounded. They'd been bedded down comfortably enough in the back room of the store nearest the river, but no one had thought to clean their wounds or arrange a reliable relay of nursing volunteers.

When she came back to the Letendre house, Gabriel was in the kitchen eating everything in sight. She sat him down and gave him a third breakfast that wasn't raw like the first two, then they walked outside. The sun was egg-yolk yellow, and the earth was green. Everyone was out of doors, clapping each other on the shoulder and laughing. Gabriel wanted to look in on the wounded, but he couldn't walk three steps without someone jumping in front of him and shouting some grinning variation on ''Goddamn, we beat 'em, didn't we?''

During the interstices, he murmured to her: ''Not yet we haven't. But if it takes Middleton long enough to work up his courage, if I can get Poundmaker and Big Bear here soon enough, if Louis David's friends south of the line move quick enough, maybe . . .''

He started to laugh and pointed out one of their neighbors. ''I didn't think he was going to make it through last night. Not that any of their bullets touched him; he's way too smart for that. When the fight was getting started he found himself a little switchback in Fish Creek where he could stand in the water up to his chest with some rocks and reeds in front of him and fire away at the soldiers all day without them ever seeing where his bullets was coming from. The only things he didn't think of was that once he was in there he couldn't climb back out until the fight was over, and that the water he was standing in was snow last week. When we finally dragged him out you could've laid a side of beef on either side of him and they'd have kept good till next winter.''

Suddenly he stopped and looked at two young men wending their way through the celebrants. One of them was Michel Dumas's brother. "I wondered what became of them. They were with Eli and the others in the coulee, but they didn't come back with us." They saw Madelaine and Gabriel and altered their course toward them. "Why didn't you come back here last night like I told you?"

Michel's brother shrugged. "We slept over at my father's farm."

His partner cocked his rifle, pushed the muzzle against Gabriel's chest, and said: "Why did you run away and leave us to face the soldiers alone?"

Gabriel stayed stock still, apparently, but Madelaine could feel through the sleeve of his coat the muscles on his arm dancing under her hand. She didn't move her arm out of the crook of his, but she let it go limp so that it would fall away whichever way he chose to move.

Riel was suddenly between them, pushing the rifle barrel aside and saying: "Would you kill the one man who's saved us all?"

Gabriel didn't say a word, just turned and walked on with his arm still linked in hers. From the rock-hard feel of his arm and the stone cast of his face, she knew how much more of an effort it was for him to walk away than it would have been to pull a certain young man's head off.

PART FOUR

Riel was always the soft-spoken gentleman. But Gabriel—he was one hard man.
—"OLD TIMERS REMEMBER"
PRINCE ALBERT TIMES

CHAPTER 36

Kitty's eight brothers and sisters and her parents could barely all manage to cram onto their uncovered wagon at the best of times. With the addition of bundles of bedding, bags of flour, sacks of tinned meat, a voluminous old canvas tent, and Stanley Simpson, everyone but the babies had to take turns jumping down and slogging through the mud churned up by the horses and carts and travois in front of them. The order of march varied from day to day, depending on which families happened to be quicker at packing up their tent on a given morning. The one element that never varied was that the next family following the McLeans was Little Poplar's.

Little Poplar was a Cree Chief from the American side of the border who'd linked up his little band with Big Bear's during the years when Big Bear was the only Canadian Chief still wandering freely. Big Bear had put the McLean family in his charge. Little Poplar was a strutting kind of man who wore a big Stetson hat and a tooled gunbelt with two big Colt six-shooters. His nine wives were all sisters whom he'd married in ascending order as each emerged from childhood. He had a habit of saying that ten was a good, round number—fanning out the fingers of both hands by way of illustration and leering through them at Amelia.

Big Bear had set a steady course northwest since they'd left Fort Pitt. Kitty's father and Stanley Simpson had both concluded that he was heading back to Frog Lake, but neither of them could guess why.

When they stopped for the night, Little Poplar would amuse himself watching the white men wrestling their tents up while his nine wives attended to the women's work of making camp. He missed his entertainment on clear nights, when the McLeans would just spread out the tent canvas under the wagon and sleep curled together, some on the wagonbed and some on the bed below. Kitty's father would light the lantern and his pipe, prop his back against a web of wheel spokes, and read the children to sleep from one of the two books he'd salvaged from Fort Pitt: the Bible and *The Adventures of Robinson Crusoe*. His calm, warm voice would filter up through the floorboards along with the smoke from his pipe, and Kitty would find that it had become morning before she could quite make up her mind whether she could roll over without spoiling the story for her sisters and brothers snuggled against her.

Just when she'd become adjusted to the routine of winding through the bush all day and camping at sundown, it changed. The sky went from blue to mauve to burgundy, and still no one called a halt. Over the spires of spruce trees a taller spire appeared. Stanley Simpson murmured: "That'll be Frog Lake Church." They passed by a few scattered houses that were now just gaping rib cages of charred beams. The church appeared to be the only building that hadn't been burned.

Stanley Simpson suddenly said: "Look away to your left, girls!" Kitty naturally looked to her right. There was a blackened body of a man tied to a tree. His bloated flesh puffed out around the ropes. The ravens had eaten his eyes, and someone had stuck a pipe in his mouth for a joke.

They camped for the night in and around the ruins. Kitty's father learned that the dead man was one of the mission's two priests and that the remnants of the other were also on display. He went to the council tent to ask Big Bear that the bodies be decently buried. Wandering Spirit promised he would see to it, then went out and threw the bodies into the cellar of the church and set the church on fire. It burned all night, shooting steeples of flame at the stars. The McLeans' tent was set up a good distance from the church, but the roaring of the fire and the festivities around it kept them awake.

In the morning they packed up groggily and fell into line. As their wagon rolled past the smoking mound of rubble, Wandering Spirit rode up and called to Kitty's father: "Straight Tongue—buried 'em pretty damn good, eh?"

At midday they reached the shore of Frog Lake, and it was announced that they would camp here. From the protracted haggling over tent sites and the relatively elaborate preparations, Kitty assumed that this wasn't going to be just another overnight camp. She spent the afternoon helping with the tent, converting the democrat into overflow sleeping quarters and gathering firewood. By evening their lakeshore campsite was part of a settled village of a thousand Plains Cree, Woods Cree, and Saulteaux, segmented into factions around sub-Chiefs like Little Poplar and Wandering Spirit, all under the nominal leadership of Big Bear.

Kitty's mother was dishing up another tinned-beef-and-flour stew when Mrs. Simpson hove into view around Little Poplar's tent and walked over to her. Kitty wasn't quite sure that she trusted Mrs. Simpson, née Pelagie Dumont. Although she was married to the Hudson's Bay Company trader James Simpson—no relation to Stanley—she was also Gabriel Dumont's sister. She was the only woman of the Frog Lake settlement that the Cree hadn't widowed. She was an immense fat woman whose moccasins never made a sound.

Mrs. Simpson padded up to Kitty's mother and said: "What are you going to do about your daughters?"

"My daughters?"

"That's what I said. I don't mean the little baby ones, I mean those three," gesturing at Kitty and her older sisters. "Now that we're going to be camped here for a while, the men are going to have time to think about other things than getting their tents packed up and herding their horses along. The widows and girls from Frog Lake don't have to worry. My husband and a couple other métis bought them from Big Bear for thirty horses and some money. But your daughters don't belong to no one."

"They do! They belong to themselves. And to us—their family, and my husband and I."

"Uh-huh." It didn't sound like an agreement so much as an assessment. "That ain't such a good place for Straight Tongue to get put in."

"Big Bear promised that—"

"Big Bear ain't everywhere. Maybe I'll talk it over with my husband. We got some good friends among the Woods Cree." And she lumbered away. For someone who was supposedly a prisoner, she seemed to come and go as she pleased, and no Little Poplar had been assigned to watch her.

Not that the leash kept on the other prisoners was all that short. In the ensuing days, Kitty discovered she was free to roam about the encampment, in between helping her mother try to fashion edible meals with one pot, one skillet, an open fire, and a very limited pantry. Like every other family in the camp, they were expected to feed themselves out of the supplies they'd carried with them and whatever they could hunt or gather. Since

Kitty's father and Stanley Simpson weren't allowed guns, they couldn't do much hunting.

One afternoon Kitty wandered out along the lakeshore beyond the last tents in the village. No one called out to stop her. She supposed they considered it unlikely that she'd try to escape alone across several hundred miles of primeval bush and rock and prairie. She came to a marshy creek mouth that was bright green with foot-high leaf stalks growing out of the shallows. At first she thought she must be mistaken; she couldn't possibly have found a bed of cattail shoots within a few minutes' walk of a village from which several hundred Indian women went on foraging expeditions every day. Maybe there were a number of women who already had their eye on them and were just waiting for them to grow a little taller. If that was the case, there were going to be a number of disgruntled Indian women.

She took off her shoes and stockings and hiked up her skirt, partly to keep it out of the water and partly to make a shopping basket. The water was cold at first. The rocks on the creekbed were slimy, and the pellety muck between them squelched up between her toes. But the sun was hot, the trees were alive with courting songbirds, and the family was going to be delighted when she came home with a very tasty variation from tinned beef, salt pork, and flour. Her grandfather used to call cattail shoots "cossack asparagus," a phrase he'd picked up while he'd been expanding the Hudson's Bay Company's territory into Russian Alaska by the simple expedient of building forts where they weren't supposed to be and then claiming he'd misread his maps.

She picked off the first fringe of shoots and waded out farther, hiking her skirt higher as the water lapped above her knees. She heard a noise on the shore and turned to look. A horse and rider had walked out onto a mossy hummock. The sun blazing through the leaves was directly behind the horseman's head; she could only make out a vague silhouette that danced and shifted against the searing yellow light. An unnaturally husky voice called out in Cree: "Sunflower, would you like to come riding on my horse?"

Suddenly she felt queasy. She tried to say: "No, thank you," but no sound came out, so she shook her head. He turned his horse and walked it down the slope of the hummock, circling to come out onto the flat rock where she'd left her shoes and stockings. She could see the rider now—a barrel-chested warrior with brass cartridge casings weighing down his sidelocks. He was dressed in a rust-splotched black shirt, the hacked-off remnants of one of the dead priest's cassocks.

The sound of the hoofsteps changed from moss-muffled thuds to a harsh clatter on the rock and then to splashing as he waded his horse out toward her. She wanted to wade away from him, but she didn't trust her legs; she couldn't feel them from the knees down.

He stopped his horse beside her. The fringed seam along one thick, buckskin-clad thigh was directly in front of her eyes. She couldn't raise them to look up at his face. "Don't you want to come riding with me, Sunflower?" His voice had settled deep in his chest.

She blinked to clear her eyes, managed to disengage the rhythm of her breathing from the galloping of her heart, and dragged her eyes upward. His eyes and mouth were wide slits, with one corner of his lips raised in a hint of a leer. She opened her mouth to speak, then found she had to swallow a couple of times to work the knot out of her throat. She said: "A big man like you could pick up a little girl like me with one hand, so what does it matter what I want?"

His mouth dropped down into a straight line, then drooped into a frown. He looked down at her a moment longer, then turned his horse and walked it back out of the lake and into the trees. She stood where she was, wiping her cheeks with the hand that wasn't holding up her skirt, waiting for her knees to stop doing their imitation of the trembling aspens. Her mother's voice called her name. She turned to move in that direction, discovered that her legs still weren't working, and ended up sitting down in the lake.

Her mother and Amelia and Elisabeth fished her out and recovered the floating cattail shoots. By the time her feet were dry enough to put her shoes back on, the story had been told and her mother's concern had been mollified enough for the scoldings to proceed. Kitty promised that she'd never venture out beyond the edge of the camp again.

In the evening, Mrs. Simpson came once more, this time with several Woods Crees. She said: "Straight Tongue, these three will each take one of your daughters to stay with their families overnight. They'll bring them back in the morning. Tomorrow night they'll sleep in the tents of a different three families, and so on like that until this is over."

Kitty's mother started to protest, but her father cut her off.

"That's very kind of you, Mrs. Simpson, and of your friends. I trust my daughters won't be too much of a disturbance to your households." It was the inauguration of what Kitty and her family grew to refer to as the Indian Protective Society.

Big Bear and the other Chiefs spent every day wrangling inside the council tent or, when the weather allowed, in front of it. On clear days, Kitty would sometimes hover on the edge of the circle and listen. She heard nothing but grandiose speeches circling the same questions. The Frog Lake Chiefs appeared to have no clearer idea than their prisoners of what Poundmaker's Cree and Assiniboine were up to at Battleford or the métis at Batoche's Crossing. Consequently, their councils consisted of endless variations on "Well, if that happens instead of this, we should do this instead of that."

Then on one day two separate sets of messengers arrived. The first was heralded by flashing mirror signals from the hills to the east—the scouts that Big Bear had sent out toward Battleford. The other was a lone métis who rode in from the south, still damp from swimming his horse across the North Saskatchewan.

Kitty was inside her family's tent, sewing together a long rent where the skirt of her dress had snagged on a thorn, when Amelia ducked in and offhandedly mentioned the messengers. Although she hadn't stitched through to the hem yet, Kitty bit off and tied off her thread, buttoned her dress back on, and hurried outside, wending her way through the ebullient bustle of the camp. There was an outburst of gunshots and whooping from the direction of the council tent that was still going on when she got there.

The warriors surrounding the circle of Chiefs were just settling back down and reloading the guns they'd fired off in the air. A métis she'd never seen before was sitting with a smug smile wrapped around his pipe stem. Kitty judged that he'd just finished delivering his message, and the Cree scouts were about to give theirs.

They'd seen the Canadian army column on its way to break the siege at Battleford. They described a long, broad river of bright uniforms and bayonets and rumbling artillery carriages. They said that Poundmaker had already packed up his people camped in front of Battleford and faded into the hills.

When the scouts had delivered their report, Big Bear murmured over his shoulder at the warriors leaning in toward his willow backrest. Four of them sprang up and ran in the four directions through the camp, shouting that everyone was to assemble in front of the council lodge. Big Bear leaned back and looked at the clouds while the entire village full of warriors and women and children and dogs flowed in and settled down around him.

The friskier dogs and children were cuffed or shamed into a semblance of silence. The last yowlings faded as Big Bear rose up to the full height of his withered, weathered bones. He clasped his blanket cloak across his chest with his left hand to leave his right arm free to gesture, like a senator in one of the illustrations from *The Lays of Ancient Rome*, and said in a voice six times his size: "Back in the days when I was young, I fought the Blackfoot. I fought them long and hard, and I believe I fought them pretty well."

From the murmurs behind her, Kitty guessed that this was roughly equivalent to a veteran of the Light Brigade saying: "We were known to do the occasional bit of charging."

"But as I grew older, as the whites poured into our country with their guns and smallpox and coughing sickness, as our young men and the young men of the Blackfoot continued killing each other with no gain to either tribe, I saw that the only way was to make peace. Poundmaker and I sat down with Crowfoot, and we agreed that we would stop fighting each other and stand together against the whites. But we would not stand against them by the ways of war. Although we would not lie down peacefully in front of their iron roads, we would fight within the bounds of peace—in the councils and the treaty talks and, as I chose for myself, to refuse to settle on a reserve until the terms were as good as we could get.

"But now I see that the other Chiefs here are no longer for peace. Now the soldiers are coming, and I think now we will no longer be able to choose any way but to fight them as best we can." He stopped and stared off into the distance—not over the heads of the crowd or the crowns of the trees, but through them. Then he unlatched the clasp on his change purse of a mouth again. "Two summers ago, when I was south of the Medicine Line, I had a vision. I saw a spring break out through dry ground and bubble up higher and higher. It wasn't water; it was a spring of blood. I put my hands over it to push it back down, but it burst between my fingers. I couldn't stop it.

"My words no longer have any meaning in this council, so I

will no longer come to speak here. I will stay with you to the end, but I am your Chief no more.'' He folded his right arm down inside his blanket, then turned and walked away.

Their new Chief was Wandering Spirit. His first decision was that they should break down the camp and get back on the move immediately. In among the bustle of packing up the wagon again, Kitty tried to get someone to tell her what all this meant. Not even her father seemed to know. Finally she asked Mrs. Simpson, who had long since bundled together her and her husband's traveling gear and was sitting on the bundles puffing her pipe. The cold black eyes looked at Kitty from a long way away. ''What it means is my brother finally woke back up.''

CHAPTER 37

In the fifth year after Madelaine Wilkie became Madelaine Dumont, there had been an event unprecedented in métis history. It happened in late spring, when the hunters who'd wintered in the Touchwood Hills gathered together for the summer buffalo hunt. Over the past few years, more and more métis had been putting up wintering cabins in the Qu'Appelle and Saskatchewan country rather than traveling all the way back to Red River or White Horse Plains.

After a winter in a cabin in the hills, Madelaine found the crowd intoxicating. Not that she'd minded the isolation when Gabriel was there, but more often than not he was off hunting or trapping or stumbling across a marathon card game in some other hunter's tent. The swirl of the spring rendezvous distracted her from the niggling notion that her father had been right about Gabriel Dumont. Not that Gabriel was ever harsh or cruel to her. It was simply the fact that in his world a good wife was less important than a good horse or gun or run of cards.

Boys started running through the crowd, calling out that it was time to elect the Captain of the buffalo hunt. Two hundred hunters and their families assembled in front of a rocky knoll that old Joseph Ouellette had selected for a podium. He would run the election and then give up his place for this summer's Chief. Madelaine looked around for Gabriel and found him standing behind her with his arms crossed. She said: "Who do you think?"

He shrugged. "Lots of good men here to choose from."

He was right. There were several old hunters—although not as old as Joseph Ouellette—who were still spry enough to take an active part and had led many hunts in the past. Aicawpow would have been numbered among them if he hadn't gone back to Red River to take up living with his new wife. And there were plenty of men of the next generation who'd already been successful Captains once or twice or who were due to take a try at it. Gabriel's brother Isidor was almost old enough to be included in that group but would likely be seen as needing another few years' seasoning.

Joseph Ouellette began to speak. After much shushing among the crowd so that his cracked old voice would carry, he started over: "First thing is electing the Captain in Chief so's I can get down off here. I don't want to hear no more'n five names to vote on, so think before you shout."

There was a pause, then someone called out: "Gabriel Dumont!"

After she got over the shock, Madelaine craned her neck around to try to see whose voice it was. Someone on the other side of the crowd shouted: "Gabriel Dumont!" Another man repeated it, and then another, and then it was a general roar.

When it had died down, Joseph Ouellette cackled: "Okay, I got my five names. Let's see, there's"—numbering them off on his fingers—"Gabriel Dumont, and Gabriel Dumont, then Gabriel Dumont . . . Gabriel Dumont . . . and then there's . . . uh . . . I forgot the last name. . . ."

"Gabriel Dumont!"

"Oh! My memory ain't what it was. Let's get on to the voting. . . ."

"Gabriel Dumont!"

When he could make himself heard again, old Ouellette said: "Maybe I'm wrong, but it sounds to me like them other four ain't got a chance. Where are you, Gabriel?"

Gabriel didn't walk past her as much as he was propelled by back-slapping hands. He took Joseph Ouellette's place on the knoll and stood nodding awkwardly at the applause and shouts of approbation. Madelaine stared around in disbelief at the leathery hunters and their families expressing their delight that they'd just elected a twenty-five-year-old man to lead them out onto the plains. Not that she doubted he could do it, but it had never occurred to her that there were so many people who saw the same things in Gabriel that she did.

Gabriel slipped into the captaincy like an old pair of moccasins. When the morning line of march was held up because one family was being lackadaisical about hitching up their carts, Gabriel was there bodily wheeling the carts out of the line so they'd have to fall in at the tail end and eat dust. When the hunt failed to find the herd after ten days and the Captain of Ten who was guide for the day said they should strike southeast into the Cypress Hills so they could at least get some elk to keep from starving, there was Gabriel pointing northwest, and a day's march in that direction brought them to the herd. When two hunters strayed too far and got caught by a raiding party of Blackfoot, Gabriel was on his horse so fast that by the time the others had caught up with him he had already taken a Blackfoot scalp and was hanging the body from a tree as a warning. The next day he made a free run for the widows and orphans, killing more buffalo than both the dead hunters would have. When a young hunter's old trade gun blew off, mangling two fingers, his friends automatically called out for Gabriel, and it was Gabriel who poured a cup of rum down him and then whacked off both fingers with one sweep of his knife. But it was Madelaine who stopped him from wrapping up the stumps with his dirty neckerchief and bandaged them with clean cotton instead.

Leading the hunt brought a change in him that gave her hope that her father might have been wrong after all. Not that he suddenly turned into a model of Christian virtue, or that she wanted him to; it was just that he had more important things to occupy himself with than playing cards and getting into knife fights. When he sat up late around the campfire drinking, it was to ask advice from the old hunters, and it was Gabriel who'd say: "Well, it's getting late, and we got to make an early start. . . ." But the most remarkable aspect was that he started talking to her, asking her whether she thought the pemmican making was going fast enough to make another run tomorrow, or whether Calixte Tourond was old enough to be given Le Petit's most recent ancestor.

When they assembled for the fall hunt, Gabriel Dumont was elected Captain again. But the first snow found Madelaine back in the cabin in the Touchwood Hills and her husband off trapping or hunting or roaming wherever his horse's nose pointed.

In December she began to suspect she might be pregnant, then grew sure of it as January went on. She didn't say a word to Gabriel for fear that, like the last time, she would lose it before it was even the recognizable beginnings of a child. She stayed inside as much as possible, going about her days' work slowly and gently, and every night she prayed to the two Marys—the Holy Virgin and her own name saint, Magdalene—to let her baby live.

Gabriel went away on a hunting trip that stretched into two weeks—perhaps he'd hunted up a few card games—and the stack of kindling he'd chopped for her ran out. She bundled herself up warmly and took the hatchet out to the woodpile. Taking it easy, letting the weight of the axe head do the work, she trimmed frozen branches off frozen trunks until she judged she had a pile big enough to start three mornings' fires and then went to work breaking them up. She was raising the hatchet again when her insides exploded. She had just enough control left to hurl the hatchet away before she was flung down in the snow with her body curling itself around the convulsions inside it. The pain grew worse, pushing itself downward. She saw that she was lying by the corner of the cabin. She took hold of one of the projecting log ends and pulled herself up into a squat with her legs braced wide. Howling and rolling her forehead back and forth against the rough-cut wood, she gave birth. The pain subsided to the point where she could feel the wet warmth seeping in through the sides of her moccasins. She lowered one hand to unfasten her skirt and then laddered herself upright hand over hand on the steps of the corner logs.

The cold helped revive her. She stepped out of her skirt, stooped down to roll it loosely together, and carried the bundle into the house, supporting herself with one hand against the wall. She set the bundle down inside the door and stumbled over to the corner where Gabriel kept his keg of rum. After half a cup a blessed numbness set in. She put on her spare winter skirt, took her snowshoes off the wall, and carried them and the bundle back outside.

She trekked as far into the bush as she could go and found an old birch tree with a fork in it as high as she could reach. She wedged the bundle in the tree, crossed herself, and said a prayer that the souls of the other babies in limbo would be kind to it. Then, as an afterthought, she took the copper hoops out of her ears and wedged them in among the folds of wool.

Back in the cabin, she built up the fire, scooped out another cup of rum, dragged a buffalo robe over in front of the hearth, and rolled herself up in it. When she woke up it was dark and the pain was still there. The worst of it was the realization that the reason her prayers hadn't been answered was because she hadn't been praying for the baby's sake, but in hopes that a baby would make her husband more aware of her.

Two days later Gabriel came home. She could hear the jingle of his harness bells long before he appeared. She opened the door and stood leaning on the frame, hoping that it would look as though she were leaning nonchalantly rather than propping herself up. Strangely, when the *carriole* appeared around the shank of the valley, he was riding in it rather than running along on snowshoes.

He climbed out awkwardly, with one hand cupped against the chest of his voluminous blanket coat. He said: "I brung you a present—although you only have to keep it for a while." One side of his chest began to move and throb, and a muffled squall came out. He pulled open his coat and showed her a little wisp-haired, brown baby who was currently very annoyed.

He reached in as though to pull the baby out. "No! Come inside." She slammed the door behind him and turned to see him holding the shrieking, red-faced thing out to her. It was trussed up in a beaded moosehide moss bag, with only its head protruding. She put it down on the table and unlaced the bag. It was a girl. The moss packed around her was soaked and stinking. Madelaine said: "Cut a strip off a blanket. Go on!" and cupped the dirty little creature against her breast, jogging her up and down in her arms and crooning. Amazingly, the shrieks abated a little.

Gabriel came forward with a strip of blanket cloth. Madelaine swaddled the baby up in it and sat down by the fire. Gabriel said: "Her name's Annie. Her mother is—was—Marie Hélène Desjarlais. She had Annie at Red River and then came west, where there ain't so many civilized people to turn their noses up. Couple of nights ago Marie Hélène got hold of a bottle of gin at Fort Ellice and went for a walk on the river. I figured maybe we could look after Annie for a while until we can find one of Marie Hélène's family or someone else to take her.''

Madelaine felt sick. Gabriel had gone on a lot of ''hunting trips'' last year, as well—sometimes as far as Red River. It would only take one twitch of her arms to throw the baby into the fire. Gabriel went on: ''I been feeding her on flour and water. . . .''

''On *what*?''

He looked down at the floor. ''Well, I couldn't think what else to . . .''

The squalling had died down to a kind of plaintive mewing. One tiny hand fumbled up and took hold of Madelaine's lower lip. Annie gurgled and sighed and fell asleep in her arms.

When spring came, Gabriel was again elected Captain of the hunt by acclamation. Once again, once the caravan rolled out, Gabriel became a Chief to his people and a husband to her, but this time it only pointed up to her the reversion that would inevitably take place when the hunt was over. He spent more evenings in their tent than in the past, but she was sure it had more to do with Annie than with her.

This year the wanderings of the buffalo herd meant the hunt ended nearer to Fort Pitt than Fort Carlton. On the first day of trading Gabriel insisted she come along with him. She strapped Annie in her cradleboard, slung it over her shoulder, and walked with Gabriel across the trampled meadow between the roistering tents and the Hudson's Bay Company trader's store.

People called out greetings and jovialities in Cree and Michif and Scots-accented French—to Gabriel, not her. She had become one of those drab-clothed, anonymous lumps of métis women herding their broods along in the wake of their men, except that the only children she was going to drag along behind her husband were other women's. Gabriel shouted boisterous jokes back and laughed while she plodded along with her head down.

Then someone did speak to her—a thick-armed Cree warrior ambling by on a speckled horse. He said: ''*Waugh*, Big Legs— I'll give you a brass bead to spread them wide for me.''

Gabriel's hand shot out and fastened around the Cree's right wrist. Madelaine stopped and stood stonily. Gabriel said: ''Did you say something to me? I didn't hear you clear.''

The Cree said through gritted teeth: ''I didn't say nothing to you, Gabriel. I was talking to her.''

Instead of dragging the Cree off his horse or roaring an insult that would make him jump down of his own accord, Gabriel said matter-of-factly, almost gently: "Her and me are never apart. What is done to her is done to me," then let go of the purpling wrist.

The Cree put his hand in his armpit and rode on. Madelaine was about to say something acerbic about the fact that they were never apart unless Gabriel had somewhere more interesting than home to go to, then realized that wasn't what he'd meant.

Inside the trader's store she muttered perfunctory replies to his questions as to whether they should buy two yards of this cotton or three and whether she liked those earrings. When it was all stacked up on the counter, she said to the trader: "You got a garden out back; are you selling any seed potatoes?"

"Never have, but I guess I could."

"I want two bushels."

Gabriel said: "Two bushels! By the time we eat our way through half of one the wild parsnips'll be ripe."

"Did I say anything about eating them? If we head straight back from here to the Touchwood Hills and plant them around the cabin, we'll have ten bushels by the time we get back from the fall hunt. Or don't you remember getting hungry around last March?"

"Well, what if we decide we want to winter somewhere else instead of going back to that old place?"

"Then you can put up a wintering cabin anywhere you want, and while you're chopping and building I'll go back to the old place and dig up our potatoes."

Gabriel rolled his eyes and exhaled in exasperation for the benefit of the trader and the other customers. But as they walked back to get a cart to load up with their cloth, tea, lead, gunpowder, and two bushels of potatoes, he put his arm across her shoulders and a continuous rumbling sound came out of his chest. She wasn't sure if he was laughing or humming.

CHAPTER 38

The piece of ground where Xavier "Batoche" Letendre had chosen to establish a ferry service was shaped roughly like the bowl of a much used wooden spoon dipped toward the river as though to skim off all the money floating down. The inside of the bowl horseshoeing the village on the flats was a quarter-mile grade of forty-five degrees—cracked and runneled by dry run-off gulleys, furred over by stands of poplars and thickets of saskatoon berry. For the last couple of hundred yards it eased to a much more gradual slope before bottoming out in the flats nestled into a bend of the river. Perched above the village was the church of St. Antoine de Padua with its mushroom-shaped bell tower. Perched on the cap of the bell tower, like a gnome on a toadstool, was Gabriel Dumont, with his legs crossed under him and his chin propped in one hand, sucking the tailings out of his pipe.

There was no sound up there but the whistle and hoot of the wind charging full-tilt across the plains to try and buffet him off. He'd been sitting there since first light, and now the sun was high enough to show a ribbon of blue between its lower rim and the horizon. He was trying to see the slice of the world spread out below him from two directions at once: from the village of Batoche on his left hand and from the prairie plateau on his right that General Middleton's army was going to come marching along.

Middleton had yet to move an inch north of the place where his soldiers had run out of breath running south from Tourond's Coulee. But he would eventually, and Gabriel no longer had any choice but to stand and meet him here.

Gabriel knocked his pipe out on his knee, swiveled around, and uncrossed his legs to stretch his feet down to the peak of the roof. He edged his way down the long, shingled slope—sliding as much as crawling—until the toe of one moccasin butted happily against the top rung of the ladder. When his feet clutched terra firma, he turned and walked to the rim of the bowl and looked down. Below him, every man, woman, and child at Batoche's Crossing was gathered within the crescent of shadow that was thinning in the sun. On their shoulders they held axes, picks, mattocks, spades, lengths of rope, and—here and there—the leather ribbons of teams of draft horses. Gabriel stood looking down at them, feeling the weight of all of them pressing on his shoulders, until the faces began to angle up toward him. He called out: "The Captains of Ten and Chiefs," and beckoned with his arm.

His pitiful dozen Captains of Ten started up the slope, along with White Cap and One Arrow, Louis David Riel, Phillipe Garnot in his capacity as recording secretary, Madelaine, and Mother "Batoche." Madelaine stopped halfway up the ridge and pointed toward the river. The people at the base of the slope began to do the same. Gabriel turned and looked. Wheeling in over the river was a starched-white, frothy cloud that arched down gracefully to settle on the water, bobbing calmly like a field of overblown water lilies. The pelicans were home, putting a seal on the spring. It was a good omen.

When his captains and headmen and -women were arrayed in front of him, Gabriel said: "I don't know how much time Middleton's going to give us—a few days, at least. I think he's the kind to stop and rub his ass a long time after it's been kicked. But just in case, we'll start by doing what's most important and then add on to it if he gives us the time. I want to dig rifle pits in along the rim, from the church to where the road comes over. We're going to need logs to lay in front of each rifle pit, but I don't want to cut down any of the trees along the hill—they're going to be good friends to us. So I want two captains to start taking down trees on the riverbank and hauling them up here: Moïse and Edouard.

"But before you go, I want you and all the other captains to watch out for something. Everybody is going to try to help. Some of the old men and some of the women won't do nothing but hurt themselves trying to help with this kind of work, but they'll be good help at some other things I got in mind. When you see someone who ain't up to it, you just tell them Madelaine's got something she needs help doing. You don't have to shame them, and don't guess without watching—'cause the fact is some of them old men can work us into the ground. And so can''—pointedly not looking at his wife—''some of the women.''

Madelaine said salaciously: ''Just because I've been known to work *you* into the ground don't mean . . .'' Nobody seemed quite certain how to respond to that, except Mother ''Batoche,'' who burst into cackles of wheezing laughter and finally had to have her back slapped.

Moïse and Edouard went down to work. Gabriel turned to Madelaine. ''Louis David's arranged to get the prisoners taking turns looking after our wounded, so you don't have to worry too much about that. What you and Mother ''Batoche'' can start doing instead is going around from house to house and gathering all the loose metal. Especially the lead—there's a lot of people using old tea chests for clothes trunks. You can put some of the old men to work melting down the lead for bullets, and the boys too young to swing an axe can still swing a hammer to break up the other metal into pieces small enough to fit in a shotgun. They shouldn't mind being asked to break something.''

They started down the slope. Gabriel called after them: ''And get together all the sacking and straw and old clothes you can find. And needles and thread.'' Madelaine looked back at him quizzically. He winked. ''You'll see.''

As he turned back to his captains he said, half to himself, ''I don't know whether our worse problem is ammunition or guns to put it in. Half them old shotguns ain't been fired more than once a week for twenty years.''

Chief White Cap said: ''There's an old man I brought along with me who in all his life never learned to shoot or hunt good enough to kill a cow in a farmer's field. But he's lived rich and kept seven wives, because he knows how to fix guns. Not like a white blacksmith, maybe, but he can do medicine with wire and a hammer and bits of tin cans as good as the white god's medicine after they killed him on the cross.''

Louis David crossed himself and murmured to the sky: ''I'm sure there was no blasphemous intent to compare the work of mortal hands to the Eternal.''

''I didn't say eternal, but at least as good as three days.''

Phillipe Garnot shook his head. ''No, three days was the time between the crucifixion and the resurrection. From the resurrection to ascension was forty-two days.''

White Cap shrugged. ''Sometimes his guns last that long.''

Gabriel said, ''Come on,'' and stepped to where the prairie

ended and the slope down to the flats began. "This'll be the first one. Here . . ." He dug the heel of his moccasin into the ground on the near side of a stand of saw grass, then walked ten feet farther along and kicked another notch. "And here. Between there you dig straight down knee high, and then straight back until the floor meets the slope. We'll stake down two logs one on top of each other in front and pack the space between the twists of the bottom log and the ground with the ground you dug out. But don't go filling in the spaces between the two logs—the good thing about the fact that trees don't grow exactly straight is that they'll give you natural-born loopholes. And make sure that with all that digging and chopping you don't go disturbing any of this," flapping his hand through the curtain of high grass and sage. "It's going to stop the bullets a lot better than the logs and dirt."

The older men nodded; the younger ones looked at each other sideways. They'd figure it out for themselves eventually. The best way to stop a bullet from hitting you was to stop it from being aimed at you. The prairies were deceptive even to the people who grew up on them. A course of several decades could begin to teach you to be able to read the tiny gradations of shadow and color that showed where an apparently translucent scraggle of brush had a large, dark object behind it or where a flat stretch of distant meadow had a gulley down its middle wide and deep enough to hide an army. The rifle pits were going to look naked and obvious from behind, but the town- and farm-bred soldiers of Middleton's army would see nothing but a placid swath of waving grass and wildflowers and birch and willows, out of which blossomed the occasional windblown puff of smoke. Excluding, of course, the things Gabriel was going to want them to see, which was going to be Madelaine's job.

Gabriel carried on along the rim of the bowl, sketching out the borders of rifle pits and appointing one of his captains in turn to each dig. By the time he'd run out of captains he'd worked his way halfway around the bowl, stopping at a little gulley that ran straight east out onto the prairie, paralleling the Carlton Trail. Louis looked back along their course at the men, women, and children hacking busily at the appointed sites and said: "Do you think that will be enough?"

"No. But if Middleton starts out tomorrow morning, they'll have to do. Now I don't think he will—not tomorrow or the next day or the day after that. But better we should build a skeleton first and then fill it out if we have the time, just in case I'm wrong. Once these ones are dug and built, we'll dig a few more between to fill them out and then start working our way down the slope behind them—a rifle pit here, a badger hole there . . .'' He found himself grinning. ''Come along, I'll show you something.''

Louis David and Phillipe Garnot trooped along behind as he bounded down the slope. Halfway down, he braked to a halt, flapping his arms to maintain his balance against the momentum, then wheeled around and dropped down to the ground. Lying on his belly with his chin on his fists, he beckoned the other two to adopt the same position—not that Phillipe Garnot needed to go out of his way to bring his field of vision close to the ground. Louis David inspected the ground suspiciously and found a relatively mudless patch of grass to lower himself onto.

Gabriel stared straight ahead up the angle of the slope, through the green-yellow haze of ground cover to the blue and white above the sharp-cut horizon line of the crest of the ridge, chortling to himself and waiting for the other two to see it. After a moment, Louis David cleared his throat and said: ''Well?''

''Well, what do you see?''

''I see some spring flowers, some bushes, the sky . . .''

''What I see,'' little Phillipe Garnot said with a smile in his voice, ''is a shooting gallery.''

Louis David made no noises of illumination. Gabriel said: ''Look, Louis David—from the moment they come over that ridge they are silhouetted against the sky, and all they can see in front of them is spring flowers and bushes and grass blending against spring flowers and bushes and grass. So if they do manage to keep up enough courage to charge across La Jolie Prairie up top, the moment they get close to the rifle pits on the rim, we get the hell out and run back to the rifle pits down here and let them come. In the time it'll take them to run down the hill, my cross-eyed grandmother could drop half a dozen of them—and another dozen when they break and run back for the top. In fact, I hope they do break through our front line quick—'cause from there on, Phillipe's right—they're marching down a quarter mile of shooting gallery.''

Instead of laughing and applauding, Riel stood up, brushed off his checkered coat, and said: ''Now I have something to show you.''

Gabriel followed him back up to the side gully that marked

the cutoff of the arc of rifle pits. Just north of the gulley was the line of the Carlton Trail, bisecting the bowl and the village inside it. Louis David pointed north along the continuation of the ridge scooping down to meet the northern hinge of the horseshoe bend of the river around Batoche's Flats. "All along there we have no defense works at all."

"We don't need them. Middleton's a straight marcher. If he was going to attack from the east, he would have marched along the Carlton Trail. But since he's coming from the south, when he hits our south wall he's just going to keep ramming his head against it till he knocks himself out. Oh, he might try a little stab at a bit of a side attack, but as long as we got enough men in the gulley to drive it back, he'll go back to his straight lines."

"How do you know?"

"How do I know?" It was like being asked: "How do you walk?" "I know because . . . because of how he ran his army at Tourond's Coulee, and how he did his march from Qu'Appelle . . . because I spent twenty-five years fighting Sioux and Black-foot War Chiefs . . ."

"These are not Sioux or Blackfoot."

"I know that. But after fighting a few wars you learn to read the other side—whether it's a War Chief or a general, it's still a man with a certain way of thinking."

"But how can you be certain?"

"Well, you and everybody else here better pray I am. 'Cause if Middleton ain't a horse with blinkers, he's going to see he's got all the open country anybody could want"—sweeping his arm out across the eastern horizon—"to march around in a cir-cle and come at us from behind."

"My thoughts exactly. Which gives us all the more reason to extend our defenses all the way around Batoche rather than sim-ply fortifying our front."

"Goddammit, Louis!" Gabriel tore off his hat and threw it on the ground. "If we had the time and the hands, I would build a twenty-foot stone wall all around us and make it ten feet thick to stop the cannonballs—but we don't! When you play cards you don't get handed the whole deck to pick out the cards you want; you got to play with what you got dealt. And that means some-times you got to bluff and guess what the other man's thinking. The only hope we got of standing up to Middleton head-on is throwing everything we got in front of every move he makes.

Stick to your praying and let me do the fighting, for Christ's sake.''

Riel had a temper of his own. Since the days at Red River it had been well known that he would react to the slightest contradiction with a spewage of lava and burning ash. But this time he merely puckered his eyebrows and mustache sadly, stooped down to pick up Gabriel's mangled hat, dusted it off with his coat sleeve, and handed it back to him. Without looking directly into Gabriel's eyes—just close enough for Gabriel to see the gray irises misted over—Louis David patted his shoulder tentatively and said: "We shall take it up with the Exovedate. You present your position, and I'll present mine. The will of those chosen from the flock shall decide which is for the best."

CHAPTER 39

Around midafternoon, Madelaine decided to absent herself from her tin snippers and potato-sack sewers for long enough to look in on the wounded. Not that she didn't trust the prisoners who'd been appointed to look after them. White or not, this wasn't a race war, and most of the storekeepers and Indian agency translators had been part of the South Saskatchewan community for years. She trusted them to look after their wounded neighbors as best they could, but none of them were doctors. Not that she was, either, but half a lifetime married to Gabriel had given her a certain amount of experience with cuts and scrapes and bullet holes and bandages.

She stopped in at the Letendre house on the way, to wash the dust and soot off her hands. Old Mother "Batoche," in the widow's black she'd worn as long as Madelaine had known her, was reveling in the possession of her daughter-in-law's kitchen. "No, no, don't you worry yourself about dinner, Madelaine. You just keep ahead doing what you're doing outside, and I'll take care of—"

"I ain't worrying about it at all. I just came in to scrub some of this muck off before I go visit the wounded."

"Wait, I'll come with you." She rummaged out a bucket from the back pantry, set it on the floor, and raised up her spindly arms to heft down the iron soup pot in which she'd been rendering down the remnants of last night's chickens. "Boiling my old bones," as she called it. Madelaine tried to help. "I can do it, dear. There, it's lighter already. Don't worry about the floor, a little chicken soup'll do it good."

Madelaine did manage to persuade her to let her carry the bucket over to the store where the wounded had been bedded down. They passed by the Widow Letendre's son's store along the way, with the guard lounging in a patch of sunlight to make sure the prisoners who went over to look after the wounded didn't try to go anywhere else. One of them was coming out of the riverside store as Madelaine and Mother "Batoche" were going in, one of the few Madelaine wasn't acquainted with, carrying a rolled-up bundle of soiled linen.

There were only two wounded left who hadn't either died or got up and walked—Francois Boyer and Michel Desjarlais. Madelaine had to count the months up several times before she could convince herself that less than a year had passed since Michel Desjarlais and his family had stopped at Gabriel's Crossing on their way from the farm the Prince Albert Land Company had stolen from them. Mother "Batoche" resumed charge of the bucket, knelt down beside Francois Boyer, and started ladling soup into him. "Open wide. That's good. You'd be Calixte Boyer's boy. Yes, your great-uncle Maxime married a Sioux woman, I remember—don't scald your tongue, dear—and nobody wanted to trust her, because she was Sioux, of course. You'll have to open wider than that if . . . That's better, mmm. Yes, and they had nine children, I remember, and the youngest ran off with a protestant. . . . Oh, let it dribble. You can lick it off when you get hungry again. Open wide. . . ."

Madelaine had proceeded to Michel Desjarlais, who was much the worse off of the two. He'd taken a crack of shrapnel across the side of his head from a shellburst in Tourond's Coulee.

She bent over him. "Michel?" His eyes moved toward her, but whether intentionally or just lolling slackly she couldn't say. His jaw inched up and down, but only a formless sigh came out. Yesterday he'd been able to wink at her and murmur a few words.

She inspected his bandage. There was blood seeping through. Yesterday the wound had looked to have closed. The bandage was fresh, though, so she decided she'd do more harm than good by peeling it off to look at the wound.

The sheet underneath him was rank and old; the prisoners had only changed the top one. There was no fresh linen in sight, but there was a stack of clean blankets in a corner. Better scratchy than dirty. She fetched the top one off the stack and raised one of the top corners of the mattress—the dry straw inside the ticking crinkling between her fingers—to free the sheet so she could start to work it out from under him. She saw something shiny under the corner of the mattress. She picked it up. It was a thin, triangular sliver of slick white bone.

"Mother 'Batoche' . . ."

"Yes, dear?"

"I have to go see Gabriel. When you've done feeding Francois there's no need to worry yourself about Michel—he's sleeping, and I don't think he could eat right now anyways."

"Just as well, it saves me filling another bucket. Open wide, Francois."

The air outside was filled with bustle—hammering, singing, harness jingling, and the biting of axes and shovels. Madelaine only heard it distantly. She had to keep swallowing to keep her gorge down. She walked across to the base of the slope, looking for Gabriel. He was halfway between the entrenchers on the plateau and the bustlers on the flats, digging a hole with Edouard and Eli. She climbed to within hearing distance of them and stopped.

Without expending any more discernible effort than any of the other digging crews, their comparative rate of sinking into the ground was like a badger to a pack of hounds. The Dumont brothers had worked and fought and hunted together for so many years that the instant one of them started to step back from a root tangle that his spade couldn't chop through, one of the others was already handing him an axe. They kept up a running stream of interjected, well-polished taunts and self-mockeries, unbroken by any need to communicate verbally about the task at hand. Every now and then, though, there was a small hitch, when a series of well-worn jokes faltered where the fourth was supposed to come in or when one of them reached over his shoulder for an implement that wasn't being handed to him.

Madelaine called: "Gabriel." He straightened up, downed his shovel, climbed out of the hole, and stumped stiffly toward her, trailed by the commiserations for his advanced age that were his first inheritance from Isidor. Madelaine had seen three-legged dogs who'd learned to run just as fast as before. So would the Dumont brothers, if they were allowed to live long enough to adjust.

When Gabriel got close enough she opened up her hand and said: "What do you think that is?"

He looked down at the palm of her hand, plucked the white sliver off it, held it up to the sun, and squinted at it. He shrugged. "A piece of bone?"

"A piece of Michel Desjarlais's skull."

His face grew steadily darker as she told the story. He dug an opening in the earth with the toe of his moccasin, dropped in the sliver of bone, and covered it over. Forty-some years of mass and confession hadn't altered his pagan conviction that a man went to his next life without the pieces of him that hadn't been buried. He said: "Which one of them was it?"

"I'm not certain it was any of them. Maybe that sliver had been hanging by a hair and just fell off when the bandage got changed. But it does seem like . . ."

"Yeah, it seems like. All right, you'll have to pick out some of the women to take care of the nursing. The prisoners'll stay locked up from now on."

"Are you sure of that?"

"Yeah, I'm sure. Even if this might just've been an accident, better not to take the chance."

"I meant 'are you sure' you can give that order? I thought it was Louis David's order that the prisoners should do the nursing?"

His lips curled back from his side teeth and his fist came up, but he ended up just letting out a long breath through his front teeth and rubbing the crooked bridge of his nose with the back of his fist. He said: "I'm sure. White Cap's Sioux have wanted to kill the prisoners since they got here. After this . . . I'll just tell Riel that if the prisoners don't stay locked up, I won't be responsible for their lives."

"Uncle Gabriel!" Annie came running up the slope carrying the first of the scarecrows that Gabriel had set Madelaine to organizing: a straw-stuffed burlap head and torso dressed in a green hat and an old flannel shirt with its sleeves tacked to a broomstick pretending to be a gun. It looked about as lifelike as a brass duck.

Gabriel looked it over and nodded approvingly. Madelaine said: "I know most of Middleton's soldiers are town men and farm boys, but they'd have to be stone blind to be fooled by . . ." She was going to say "this thing," then realized Annie might take it as an insult to her work, so she amended it to: "These things." Annie looked insulted anyway.

Gabriel said: "Let's see," and carried it up to the half-dug trench where Edouard and Eli had decided that as long as he was going to rest his back they would, too. "Go on up to the top and see how it looks from there." Edouard and Eli climbed out of the hole as Gabriel jumped into it and propped the dummy at one end.

Madelaine walked up the hill with Gabriel's brothers, shaking their hands off her elbows. When they got to the top they turned around and looked down at the rifle pit. Gabriel had knelt down at the opposite end from the dummy and adopted the same pose, pointing Le Petit in place of the broomstick. The diffusing haze of high grass and sweet clover turned them both into colorless shadows, with the exception of the bright green of the manne-quin's hat. But it was still painfully obvious that one of them was a man and the other a straw-stuffed scarecrow.

Gabriel shouted up at them without breaking his pose: "Well, what do you think?"

Madelaine murmured: "Who's going to tell him?" With so many things that had to be done and so few hands, they couldn't afford to waste time on an idea that wasn't going to work, no matter how fond Gabriel was of it.

Edouard said: "I think you should."

But before she could, the dummy stood up, climbed out of the rifle pit, waved his green hat in the air, and shouted: "Hard to tell sometimes who's the dummy, ain't it?"

One advantage to mass excavation sites was that a lot of loose clods of earth tended to pile up. She picked one up and heaved it at him. Unfortunately it's always difficult to judge ranges ac-curately on a downgrade, or she would have caught him beam on as he bent to exchange the green hat for his beloved battered black. It was late in the night before he finally got her to admit that "Yes, all right, it was a good trick. Got any more?"

But instead of reveling and chortling, he sank into a silence as thick as the moonless dark and then said: "Let's hope so, 'cause the fact is we ain't got much else."

CHAPTER 40

Gabriel was nervous about the other side of the river. If Middleton carried on with his original plan of marching in two columns, and ferried back the troops who had come across to help him at Tourond's Coulee, they could set up guns on the west bank when they got to Batoche's Crossing and shell the rifle pits from behind. So Gabriel picked out four of his Captains of Ten to establish themselves on the west bank and patrol to the south, under the overall command of Albert Monkman. Monkman was about the same age and size as Eli, which gave him the same steady temperament of a dog too big to bark for barking's sake.

Riel crossed over with Albert Monkman's contingent to ride with them on their first day's scouting. Gabriel was just as happy to have him out of the way so he could proceed with the digging-in without benefit of advice. Louis David's opinion as to the best disposition of the rifle pits had, of course, prevailed in the Exovedate, given that the only reason Gabriel could articulate to support his own point of view was: "Because it feels to me like they're going to keep on coming at us from the south." By the time Louis David had got through his eloquent delineation of the reasons he disagreed, Gabriel had been left doubting his own perceptions.

Consequently, half the entrenching crews were busily fortifying the northeast approach to Batoche's Crossing. It still seemed to Gabriel that it was a wasted effort to build anything more than a few trenches anywhere north of the Carlton Trail, but the fact that it seemed that way to him no longer seemed as valid as it once had.

The work was progressing as a kind of frantic holiday. It was the time of year when every human being on the prairie always burst into activity: digging their fields to put in the new seed, galloping over the plains to inspect the trails for the cart trains, oiling their guns for the goose hunt. This spring found them once again digging and galloping and oiling their guns.

Gabriel found it a pleasure to be chopping logs and shoveling earth instead of waiting and debating. He kept being interrupted by messengers and scouts galloping in from all four quarters of the compass. The news they brought was up and down. Big Bear's Crees had finally uprooted themselves from Frog Lake and were on the move in the direction of Batoche's Crossing. "Big Bear's Crees" were, in fact, "Wandering Spirit's Crees" now, which might be for the best. Whether the old man liked it or not, he had served the purpose of drawing together an army for Wandering Spirit to lead.

There was good news from Fort Edmonton. About sixty métis hunters from that vicinity had been spurred by the story of Tourond's Coulee to saddle up and start east. They could be expected to reach Batoche's Crossing in a week or so. But Poundmaker—damn his eyes—had skipped back to his reserve with his Crees and Assiniboine in the hope that his bloodless siege of Battleford would define him as a relatively Good Indian.

At the end of the day, Gabriel stepped back from staking a two-log breastwork in front of a rifle pit, cricked his back straight, looked at the sky, and crinkled his face to think. His stomach and the angle of the sun said it was time for supper. The days were growing longer, maybe long enough that he could stop and eat now and still get in a few more hours' work before dark; or perhaps it would be better to keep on working till the light was gone and eat then. He kicked his ponderations into what Madelaine called his "beard-scratching gait" and looked down at the village to see how long the shadows were getting.

The ferry scow was coming back across the river, carrying one saddle horse and one man other than the ferryman. Although Gabriel couldn't have said why, he knew it was Riel's horse, and he also knew that something was wrong. He buried his axe in a log and stumped down the hill.

He reached the dock at the same time as the ferry. Louis David's jaw was screwed grimly tight. Gabriel said: "What's happened? Lord Melglund's troops crossed back over?"

"No. And they show no signs of doing so, or of any intentions to break camp yet—at least none that could be discerned from across the river.'' None of that sounded particularly grim. Louis David combed his fingers through the chestnut ringlets of his beard and said: ''That man is going to betray me.''

''What man?''

''The man in command on the other side of the river.''

''Albert Monkman? Who said so?''

''I know. He is trying to encourage his soldiers to desert.''

Gabriel went back and saddled his horse, slid Le Petit into the scabbard, and trotted down onto the docked ferry. He didn't dismount or speak, just pointed at the far shore. The ferryman cranked him across—Batoche's ferry worked on a clever arrangement of hand crank and cable rather than oars. Gabriel had been meaning for years to convert his own scow to the same motive power. Maybe Phillipe Garnot would get around to it.

When they docked on the western shore, Gabriel said: ''Wait here,'' and rode up the bank to the cluster of log houses where Albert Monkman's soldiers had billeted themselves. Some of them were lounging in the last of the sunlight, some of them were putting up tents, some were scaling and gutting a netful of fish. Gabriel told the loungers to bring everyone outside and sat waiting on his horse. Albert Monkman came out immediately and asked him what was going on. ''You'll see. Wait till everyone's out here.''

When they were all assembled, Gabriel cracked his jaw to unleash his addressing-the-troops voice and said: ''I want to ask you a question. Has anybody been trying to talk any of you into running off or going over to the enemy?'' There was a generalized shuffling and shrugging, with a murmur of indistinct vocalizations, but no one stepped forward to volunteer an answer. ''All right, you better go ahead with your supper. It's been a hard day's riding for all of you. I don't think any of you should go out riding again tonight.'' He turned Starface around and trotted back down to the waiting ferry.

In the Letendres' kitchen, Madelaine and Annie were sitting down to supper with the Riels and Mother ''Batoche.'' Gabriel poured himself a bowl of Mother ''Batoche's'' chicken soup, which was more like chicken stew once she'd got through stirring in split peas and dried corn and husked barley and some bright green bits Gabriel didn't want to know about. Between mouthfuls, he told Louis David about his one-sided conversation with the west bank contingent. ''I don't know what's been going on over there, but something.''

"I told you—Monkman is planning to betray us."

"Who told you?"

Riel's eyes gleamed. "No man told me. I know. We will both cross back over and confront them." He stood. "Excuse me." Gabriel wiped his mouth and followed him out. On the way to the ferry they passed Moïse Ouellette and Michel Dumas, who were pointing at each other's horses and saying disparaging things that would lead to a race and a lot of money changing hands when things returned to normal. Gabriel called to them to come along.

The river was low; even the melt-off from the Rocky Mountains had flowed past by now. The cog-driven scow rattled and splashed through the darkening water. The men on the western shore were picking the bones out of grilled whitefish with their fingers. Louis David walked into the largest of the dockside houses and called for an assembly. All who could crammed in after him; the rest pressed around the open door and windows. Gabriel let Riel take the floor and stood back with Le Petit in his hands and Moïse and Michel at his shoulders. It felt eerie and strange to be standing there weighing his rifle on the pads of his fingers while his eyes weighed the movements of men he'd been standing up with all his life.

Louis David said: "My friends, I know that someone has been trying to convince you to desert. You refused to answer directly when the question was put to you by Monsieur Dumont. Our uncle Gabriel is too honest a man to make accusations without evidence that he can see or hear. But there are other ways of hearing and seeing." His eyes settled directly on Albert Monkman and stayed there, although his voice remained at an oratorical level. "Rest assured that I will come to the truth of this, even if I have to have the man I suspect shot before any of you will speak up."

There was a silence long enough for Gabriel to begin to wonder who Moïse and Michel would side with if their friends told Louis David to shove it up his fart hole. Then Patrice Fleury said: "It's true. Albert Monkman tried to talk me into deserting."

A younger voice called through one of the unshuttered windows: "He said the same thing to me, too."

Riel nodded like a schoolteacher whose slowest pupils finally got something right and said: "We must bring this before the Exovedate."

Gabriel pointed at Albert Monkman and Patrice Fleury. "You'll come back across the river with us. And whoever it was that yelled through the window—sounded to me like Garçon Abraham Belanger."

The seven of them crossed back on the ferry without speaking, except for the occasional exchange along the lines of "River's low for this time of year, eh? Like my old grandfather used to say—bitter winter, little snow."

A meeting of the Exovedate was immediately convened at the Letendre house. Marguerite and the children were shooed upstairs while Madelaine, Annie, and Mother "Batoche" retired to the kitchen. Patrice Fleury and the youngest man of the Belanger clan extrapolated to the Exovedate on what they'd said on the other side of the river: Albert Monkman had been encouraging them and the rest of his soldiers to get the hell out before the Canadian army got here and killed them.

Albert Monkman, twisting his hat in his hands, was called to account. He said hoarsely: "It's true I said those things. But it wasn't for the reasons it sounds like. Everyone was telling me that Louis David has powers, that there are spirits who watch out for him and tell him things. I didn't believe it, but I wanted to make sure. I thought that if he was a prophet, then he would know what I was saying, even if no one told him. So now, you see, I know, and now I have to believe it."

Louis David sat blinking at him. Albert Monkman stood waiting. Riel maintained his authoritative posture and expression but showed no signs of pronouncing judgment. Gabriel waited a while for Louis David to speak, then spoke himself: "Michel—tie up his hands."

Michel Dumas yanked a handful of thongs off his elaborately fringed coat and started forward, braiding them together. Albert Monkman stepped back and looked at the walls, but he had no way out. He said to Gabriel: "Are you going to kill me for giving Louis David a chance to prove he's a prophet?"

"Whatever you might have been saying to yourself in your head, you must've had in your heart to do what you said. So I'm going to lock you away with the other prisoners we can't trust."

When he told the story to Madelaine as they were readying themselves for bed, she said: "Riel was over there with them all day. Somebody must have let a word slip, or Albert looked guilty and he guessed."

"I don't think so. I believe he had a revelation."

She didn't reply. He was about to push her to do so when there was an eruption of drumming on the door downstairs, then the crash of the door flying open and a male voice shouting inside the house for Gabriel Dumont or Louis Riel to show themselves.

Gabriel was out of the bed, snagging his revolver along the way, and through the bedroom doorway without pausing to reach for his trousers. Louis David and Marguerite emerged from their room, Marguerite carrying a candle. Marguerite's hand went to her mouth, and she looked away as Gabriel snatched the candle out of her hand and moved to the landing, noticing in passing how interestingly the candlelight illuminated her foaling young breasts.

Whoever it was in the dark at the foot of the stairs had gone silent. Annie and Mother "Batoche" appeared farther down the second-story hallway, huddled around a lamp. Gabriel waved them all back and started down the stairs with his left arm extended straight out to hold the candle as far away from him as possible and his right elbow clutched against his ribs, cocked to spring the pistol into play. A man in a bowler hat and a fur vest appeared at the base of the stairs. He was one of the gallopers Gabriel had sent to try to get Poundmaker off his ass. Gabriel said: "Man, you just came this close to getting shot. . . . Matter of fact, maybe I should shoot you anyway."

"I saw the house was dark, but I thought you wouldn't want to wait to hear. What's happened is that—even though Poundmaker'd gone back to his reserve and left Battleford to the soldiers—they still came after him. He didn't even have any scouts out, so he had no idea until they started shelling his camp at dawn and three hundred soldiers came charging."

Gabriel sat down on the step, heedless of splinters, set the candle down on one side of him and his revolver on the other, and buried his eyes in the palms of his hands, letting out a sick sigh. Although he'd been quite willing to strangle Poundmaker for trying to shuffle out, it was understandable that Poundmaker—like all other good Chiefs—would think first of the people he was directly responsible for. Gabriel had tried his damnedest to make Poundmaker understand that the only hope his people had, from the first shot they'd fired at the Police in Battleford, was to keep on fighting until the government made peace. There wasn't much consolation in being proved right this way. Poundmaker couldn't've had more than a couple hundred ill-armed warriors, along with their wives and children and old men, in the tents the dawn cannonballs had torn into.

Something soft hit Gabriel in the back of the neck. He looked around and found that Madelaine had thrown a blanket down to him. He picked it up and wrapped it around himself as the messenger added: "He was camped at Cutknife Hill."

Gabriel nodded mechanically and grunted to show he'd heard, then jumped back to his feet. "Where? They jumped him *where*?"

"Cutknife Hill."

"No. Nobody could be that stupid."

"Only a full colonel in the Canadian army."

Louis David started down the stairs, saying: "What is the significance of Cutknife Hill?"

Gabriel turned around to explain it, but Madelaine's voice floated down from the landing: "It didn't used to be called Cutknife Hill. They rechristened it thirty years ago, after a famous Sarcee War Chief named Cut Knife. He'd snuck up on a little band of Crees who were camped there and jumped them at dawn. The Cree Chief was a young man called Poundmaker. He kicked Cut Knife's ass up one side of the hill and down the other 'til the Sarcee ran."

"I see. And the pagan belief in Poundmaker's 'medicine' would have it that—"

"I don't know from medicine, but I'm sure Gabriel'd tell you he'd be glad to give odds to anyone that wanted to lay down money to learn to play billiards on Gabriel's own table."

Gabriel said to the messenger: "What happened?"

"Poundmaker and Fine Day kicked Colonel Otter's ass up one side of Cutknife Hill and down the other until the Canadian soldiers ran. Fine Day wanted to chase after them and rub them all out, but Poundmaker thought it was better they should pack their traps up right away and get started for Batoche's Crossing. I figure since they're moving their whole camp it'll take them a week or so to get here. But there's no doubt Poundmaker figures the only chance they got now is to help us fight."

Gabriel sprang down the stairs, whirled the courier off his feet in a bear-hug jig, set him back down, and dragged him by his vest hem to the door. "Get out there and tell the story to everyone who's still awake. Keep on going around and telling people till they start telling it to you first."

By that time they were through the door and out onto the

veranda. Gabriel let go of the messenger's vest and watched him go. There were a few fires still burning, with crouched shadows murmuring across them, and a few houses still showing light through their windows. Gabriel went out onto the steps so he could empty his revolver into the air without putting holes in the porch roof, laughing and whooping. Maybe, after all, just maybe . . .

CHAPTER 41

A tent city had grown up on the open meadow between the Letendre house and the little row of stores fronting the Carlton Trail. With the invading army on the move toward Batoche's Crossing, it was decided that the tents should be moved to the other side of the tall birch thicket behind the stores. There was a cleared space on the riverbank there, courtesy of Edouard Dumont, who'd spent portions of the past few summers chopping out the trees and undergrowth with the intention of plowing a second barley field.

Madelaine put up a tent there among the others. Not that she had any intention of moving out of the Letendre house, but if and when the Canadian artillery started lobbing shells around Batoche's Crossing, she and Gabriel and Annie and Mother "Batoche" might appreciate the option of a less conspicuous place to come in out of the rain. When she'd gone to fetch Annie from Gabriel's Crossing, she'd made a point of piling their old clay-whitened buffalo-hide tipi skin and its skeleton of poplar poles onto the top of the cartload. She'd wondered at the time whether it was silly to bother with the poles when they could always chop down new ones, but they turned out to have been an inspiration. What with the crews felling trees to front the rifle pits, and several hundred people chopping down saplings to hold up their own tents, there wouldn't have been much left to choose from. It would get even worse once Poundmaker's people and the others got there. But then Gabriel had given her the notion that when that day came, General Middleton's army was going to get chased all the way back to Saskatoon, and the people at Batoche would have the whole sweep of the prairie to divvy into campsites.

She spent the afternoon gathering together all the spare bedding in the Letendre house and piling it up in the parlor with a minimal selection of her own cooking things and other bare necessities for living in a tent. When they were all together, she picked up an armload of quilts and blankets and walked across the meadow and through the woods. She was almost at the tent door when an undefined something kicked the trip wire of one of her five senses. She stopped in her tracks and looked around and smelled and listened.

It turned out to have been a sound, from inside the tent. Now that she had concentrated on hearing, it was unmistakably the sound of two voices panting monosyllables in syncopated harmony, accompanied by a rhythmic rustling. Although there wasn't much in the way of articulate vocalizing to go on, she identified the voices immediately. Her first impulse was to dip a bucket in the river and give them a dose of the prescribed treatment for coupling dogs that got stuck together.

Instead of going to find a bucket, or flinging the tent flap open, Madelaine stood in place, chewing her teeth and hugging the bundle of bedclothes. In a few days, Michel Dumas might very well be dead. And so might Annie—stray bullets and cannon fire had been known to kill the innocent before. Even if both of them came through the fighting unhurt, what kind of a world might they find themselves condemned to live in if Middleton's soldiers succeeded in breaking through Gabriel's line of rifle pits?

Madelaine turned away and left Annie and Michel Dumas to whatever joy they could find in each other. The tipi next to theirs was the Riels', donated by a family who were making do under their patched old spare tent. She ducked into the Riels' tent and dropped her stack of blankets beside the entrance. There was no one at home. The Riels' two battered traveling trunks had been set up as bedsteads, with layered buffalo robes and blankets spread out in front of them. Something gleamed in the middle of one of the beds—the polished-brass pen case sitting on top of the black notebook.

She made a halfhearted effort to convince herself to go back out into the sunlight, then she let the door flap close behind her and crawled across the still-green grass of the tent floor to Louis's journal.

What had been the last entry when she'd looked in it before was now about halfway through. Since then, he'd taken to dating each entry as a relatively strict day-by-day diary. The shortest entry by far was for the day when Gabriel decided he was riding out to meet Middleton whether the Exovedate liked it or not, which read in total: "April 23. I awoke with a start."

On the next page was: "April 25. The Spirit of God has displayed me Middleton's great cannon; it is knocked over. It is unhealthy because it aims its thrusts against the throne of God. The barrel is severed from the butt . . . O my God! You Yourself have broken in two the barrel of this big gun. Complete this rupture . . . that it be a mortal rupture . . ."

She skipped ahead and read: "O my Métis Nation! You have long offended me with your horse races . . . This is why the Eternal Christ said yesterday that while sparing you I killed your horses. The Eternal remembers the sinful attachment you have for your horses . . . O my Métis People! I punish you lightly. All I ask of you is humble obedience."

Madelaine skimmed on, reading wherever her eyes happened to light:

"The Spirit of God placed me in a carriage with Michel Dumas. He was departing for the United States. . . . I said to him: 'Think of me as an Example Tibi.' I took my leave of him. . . . I saw an engorged, flowered serpent following after him. . . . I have lived miserably in the United States among snakes, among venomous vipers . . . wherever I set my foot I saw them wriggling. . . . The United States is Hell for an honest man."

"The Spirit of God gave me to see the Métis Nation in the likeness of a woman. . . . Her face . . . showed the irrefutable scars of much base carnality. She had turned herself away from me for too long."

Since the moment she'd heard the first gunshots from Duck Lake, Madelaine had been afraid of what would happen to everyone she loved if the Army of the Exovedate lost the war. She was suddenly as afraid of what would come next if they won.

"I thank you, Lord, a million thousand thousand times for having spared my life in the two battles we have fought. . . . O grant me the most perfect repentance, so that in casting from me all bad thoughts, I merit that the battle goes well for me, without an accident, without a wound, without receiving the merest . . ."

She yanked the page over to keep from tearing it out, which she would have if she'd read any more of Louis's fervent prayers that he continue to not suffer a scratch while Gabriel rode out to fight with the bandage on his head seeping blood and Isidor lay in the ground with a fist-size hole through his chest.

The air in the tent had inexplicably grown thicker and staler, to the point where Madelaine had to put her hand to her throat to stretch it wide enough to get in enough oxygen. The squirming black lines had to be pinned down one by one and consciously translated into words. A sibilant, dry hiss rattled softly in the small bones beside her earlobes.

It was the sound of the tent flaps sliding apart. An aghast voice hissed: "What are you doing?"

Madelaine dropped the book and half turned, half fell from her crouch on the tent bed. It was Marguerite—galvanized doe's eyes flaring from Madelaine to the book on the bed and back. She demanded again: "What are you doing?"

"I . . . I brought in some blankets . . . and I saw this book lying here. . . ." Madelaine didn't much care for the notion that she should be under any obligation to explain herself to any woman half her age, but it was her own damned fault.

Marguerite stole a look back over her shoulder, then licked the pad of her lower lip with the tip of her little pink tongue and whispered: "What does it say?"

"Say?"

"Yes—Louis's book . . ." Marguerite seemed to be endeavoring to keep her voice hushed, but it quavered, like that of a child who's been determined to be good and then stumbles across her big sister with her hand in the jam jar. "What has he written in it?"

"A lot of things. Mostly prayers."

"Could you . . . would you read me one?"

Madelaine tried to think of a way out of it, then picked up the book and opened it. She skimmed across both leaves, hoping she wouldn't have to turn the page or make something up, and lucked onto: "O my God, do not punish the Métis Nation. For the sake of Jesus, Mary, and Joseph, be merciful toward her. See how she is charitable, how she is gentle and easy to lead. Weigh favourably, O my God, the good works the Métis Nation performs for Your greater glory, for the honor of the religion, for the salvation of souls, for the betterment of society.''

She closed the book. Marguerite stood soundlessly mouthing the last few phrases to lodge them in her memory, awed by a glimpse inside the altar she was privileged to serve. She smiled at Madelaine as though they were now united in some sort of benevolent conspiracy, swallowed to find her voice, and whispered: ''Thank you.''

Madelaine put down the book, picked up her stack of bedding, and stooped back outside, leaving a couple of blankets behind to cover her reasons for coming into the Riels' tent. Now she had no choice but to carry on into her own tent. She made as much noise as possible, thumping her moccasins down heavily and fumbling with the door flap. She could have saved herself the performance. Annie was alone now, sitting in the shaft of sunlight through the smokehole, combing out her glossy hair. ''Hello, *Maman*—I just came in to arrange the bedding.''

De-arrange it, you mean, passed through Madelaine's mind, but she didn't say it. It was one thing to decide to be tolerant under the circumstances and another to let Annie know that she knew. Somehow she'd become surrounded by people and things she couldn't speak to or of.

She spoke to herself a great deal as she strode back along the path through the woods to the Letendre house and went about the rest of her tasks for the day. She reminded herself of what Gabriel had told her—she wasn't a priest or an alienist to pass judgment on the validity of Louis's visions. She told herself that forty-five years on this earth ought to have taught her that it didn't ask whether she understood things before making them real. Nonetheless, when Louis came in for dinner she found her heart pumping out red ice.

But a moment later, Gabriel made Riel fade into the furniture, simply by standing hunched in the doorway with his arms crossed and his eyes on the floor while Annie shooed the children to the table and Marguerite and Mother ''Batoche'' unspitted the sizzling piglet. Madelaine said: ''What's happened?''

''Hm? What do you mean?''

''Don't play coquette with me—what's happened?''

''Oh. Well . . .'' He pushed off from the doorway and shambled forward. ''Supper's on the table.'' He took his chair and bowed his head while Louis said the grace. When it was done he crossed his arms again and continued to stare at nothing while slabs of crackling pork and jelled scoops of last year's choke-cherries slapped onto other people's plates.

Madelaine paid no attention to her plate, either. "Don't pretend nothing's happened when any blind fool can see something has. Tell me."

His oakroot shoulders heaved up and down. His arms wound themselves more tightly around each other, and his eyes rooted themselves to a knothole in the tabletop. "They reached our place today. They burned it. They took the horses. They killed the chickens and pigs and ate them. They stole everything there was to steal. They ripped up all your clothes for rags. They broke up your washing machine and shot the pieces full of holes."

She felt raped. But what she said was: "The factory that made my washing machine is still making them. I can sew more clothes. When they burned down all our buildings they can't have burned all the trees that we can cut down to build new—"

"They didn't burn all our buildings. The stables and the barn they pulled apart so they could use the boards to make a floating fort out of the *Northcote*."

"The *Northcote*?"

"Their fire canoe," which was what the Indians called steamboats. "They built walls all around the deck so they can float down behind us and shoot us in the back."

Her mind's eye saw a picture of an anchored steamboat filled with soldiers firing into the tents along the riverbank. She said: "So that's what it is."

"What what is?"

"*That!*" Revolving her hand in his direction to denote the obvious. "The thing that's got at you—it's that you don't know what to do about the *Northcote*."

"Who said I didn't? We'll just line up on both sides of the river and shoot hell out of her as she comes around the bend, then drop the ferry cable to trap her and keep on shooting holes in her like a cheese until they run up a white flag or we've killed them all. Either way, it ends up with us rowing out the ferry scow to load up all their guns and ammunition."

"Then what is it?"

"What's what?"

"I give up. Mother 'Batoche,' could you pass me them cold turnips to go with my cold pork?"

Gabriel pulled his hands out of his armpits and clasped them between his knees. He said to his thumbs: "Pig-fucking sons of shitting bitches stole my billiard table."

Jean and Marie Angelique dropped their spoons and their jaws. Marguerite's and Louis's eyes caromed back and forth off Gabriel, their children, and each other. Mother "Batoche" opted for gumming her knuckles instead of her dinner. Madelaine looked at Gabriel's furious pout and started to laugh.

His eyes shot a murderous glance at her. Then he threw back his shoulders, rocking the chair onto its hind legs, and roared out rolling peals of beer-barrel laughter, alternately slapping both hands on the table—cutlery bouncing—or against his chest to pound some breath into his lungs. She stopped laughing before he did and just sat staring at him and wondering how many more times her old bones could stand to have it proved that they still didn't know how much they loved that ugly bastard.

Long after the crickets had gone to sleep, the night stayed alive with shovels and axes and torchlight. Madelaine lay in bed alone, delving for some bedrock under her evaporated sense of time—had she been lying sleeplessly for hours or slipping in and out of dreams? Was the sky outside the window growing grayer, or had her eyes grown sensitive to starlight in the minutes since she'd peeled off her dress and warmed the bed? The ice that had crystallized around her heart as she'd read further into Louis's black book was still there, but the sunrise would bring Middleton's soldiers regardless.

The entrenching sounds faded away. There was a whisper of moccasin leather on the stairs. The door creaked open. To let him know she was awake, she said: "You done enough with the breastworks?"

"Huh?"

"Have you done all you can with the br—" at which point he launched himself on hers.

Perhaps thousands of men wouldn't have stooped so cheap, and thousands of women wouldn't have whooped and giggled, but he did and she did. In the midst of it he suddenly broke away from her and stood. She said: "What . . . ?"

"Ssh!" He stood staring out the gray window. Far away there was a soft, high, vibrant bugling. Gabriel buckled on his revolver and cartridge belt and reached for Le Petit, murmuring: "Well . . . if we can hold them for a day or two, if Poundmaker or the boys from the west get here in time . . ."

"Or Louis's friends south of the line—the Fenians and—"

The silhouetted, boulder-necked head snapped around at her so fiercely that she cut herself off. It slowly revolved back to face toward the dawn. In a growly whisper, the bear's chest said: "There ain't none. It was all in Louis David's mind." He went to the door and turned. "Tell you what, old woman—if you keep your head down when them cannonballs are going over, I'll keep myself greased so the bullets slide off. I love you." He was gone.

CHAPTER 42

Alexis was standing on the porch steps holding the reins of Gabriel's horse—saddled and bridled and twitching its tail in the dew-bright morning. Gabriel patted his nephew on the shoulder and swung up onto Starface. Edouard and Eli, Moïse Ouellette, Michel Dumas, and a dozen others walked their horses toward him. The rest of the population of Batoche was fumbling stiffly out of their houses and tents, banking up the fire under the teakettle, checking over their shotguns one last time.

Gabriel sent Michel Dumas to collect one of the Captains of Ten and take up a position at the ferry cable. "But don't lower it till I tell you. If they see what we're up to too soon, they'll back water and pull their ass out before the jaws close on it." Then he turned Starface and led his fifteen horsemen at a gallop up the hill and past the church. At the southwest corner of the cemetery fence he reined Starface to the right and then to a halt as they came to the edge of the cliff down to the river.

A mile or so upriver, the black smoke of the steamboat puffed over the trees. Far out on the open prairie to the southeast, the long, dark, winding snake of the army column crawled forward. The fire canoe was coming on fast, whistling shrill signals.

Gabriel had figured that Middleton's plan would be to bring up the troops and the steamboat simultaneously. It was a good plan and would have put Gabriel in an awkward position—trying to fend off an attack from two sides at once—if only somebody had thought to mention to the general that the current of the South Saskatchewan picked up a good deal of speed in the stretch between Gabriel's Crossing and Batoche's.

The smokestacks came into view, then the pilot house and the upper deck. A shell of sandbags and planking had been built up all around both decks, with loopholes to fire through. They couldn't very well wall up the windows on the pilot house, though. Behind the stern wheel waddled two long, squat barges loaded down with bales of fodder, barrels of rations, and crates of ammunition. Gabriel couldn't really have asked for much more in the way of cooperation. The poor pilot was not only stuck with trying to maneuver an unwieldly, overloaded steamboat through difficult waters, he was being asked to do it with two barges in tow.

Just above Batoche's Crossing there was a bend where the river kicked along like a millrace. It was a tough run for a pilot at the best of times. Patrice Fleury, who'd replaced Albert Monkman as commander of the west bank contingent, had been instructed to place his soldiers along the bend. Gabriel led his horsemen down into the willow thicket on the east bank of the bend. They dismounted and worked their way forward, planting themselves behind convenient trees or shore boulders. Gabriel could see no sign of Patrice's snipers on the opposite shore, but that was as it should be.

The *Northcote* was whistling frantically for some reassurance that it hadn't shown up for the party all alone. As the blunt prow nosed into the bend, Gabriel called: "Kill the helmsman first!" and let fly with Le Petit at the crown of the wheelhouse. The thicket around him exploded with smoke and gunfire. Puffs of smoke bloomed from the trees on the western shore. The wheelhouse walls spat splinters and instantaneously became covered over with pockmarks.

The barricaded decks erupted with answering rifle fire, killing lots of rocks and bushes. Gabriel had been informed by his friends in the baggage train that the *Northcote* was garrisoned with C Company of the infantry school. They were getting an education.

Like the others firing from the riverbank, Gabriel began to alternate his fire between the wheelhouse and the returning fire from behind the barricades. Unlike them, he interspersed his shots with nasty grumblings at Madelaine. Any other woman in the North West Territories would have been quite content with barns and stables faced with any old scrappy planking—but oh, no, *Madelaine* had to have inch-thick seasoned birch. . . .

Whether the pilot had been killed or had just pasted his belly to the deck with his arms over his head, the *Northcote* drifted rudderless. She bumped her nose against a sandback, the current swung her sideways, and she floated downstream beam-on with the barges scissoring against her sides.

Gabriel ran back to his horse and galloped along the shore with C Company's bullets buzzing past him. He rounded the bend flailing Le Petit over his head, bellowing at Michel to drop the cable. What with the gunfire and the screaming of the whistle, Michel of course couldn't hear him, but how much brains did it take to figure out that this was the signal?

Finally the cable began to inch down slowly. Gabriel reined in his horse and watched the agonizing ballet of the descending cable and the drifting steamboat. He could see that it was already too late for the cable to catch the hull, but if it could get low enough in time to trap the deck housing . . .

The middle layer of the wedding cake edged safely under the lowering blade of the cable. There was still the pilot house—if the boat was built solidly, the whole thing would have to stop when the top layer stopped. The cable caught against the rim of the wheelhouse, stretched, then slid up over it. With a screeching crash of sparks and cinders, the smokestacks tore loose and fell down on the graduating class of the infantry school. The *Northcote* and her barges nuzzled downstream blossoming flames.

Horsemen appeared on the far shore in the gap of the Carlton Trail. One of them rode out onto the landing stage and waggled his rifle over his head. Gabriel trotted onto the eastern dock and pointed Le Petit downstream. Patrice waved back to show he understood, then turned his horse and led his soldiers after the *Northcote*, firing from the saddle.

Gabriel walked Starface back off the dock. Michel Dumas came loping and grinning from his cable squad, crowing: "Guess we showed them, eh?"

Gabriel looked down at him. Standing in moccasins, Michel wasn't much shorter than Gabriel on horseback. It wouldn't have constituted all that much of an unfair advantage just to lean out from the saddle and bash him across the head with Le Petit. But maybe it was his own damned fault for not giving the signal soon enough, and at least the *Northcote* was out of the fight—provided Patrice could keep them convinced that turning around and steaming back to set up a crossfire wasn't wise.

The brass voice of bugles bounced down over the ridge around Batoche. Gabriel hauled the reins around so hard that Starface screamed. He whipped the braided leather reins against the tender place where the bullet had welted his rump at Duck Lake and charged across the flats to the base of the ridge.

Alexis was waiting there. Gabriel threw the reins to him while yanking his feet free of the stirrups and swinging over the saddle. He hit the ground running and sprinted up the slope. It was a long quarter mile, about thirty degrees for the first third and then sharply angling steeper. By the time he got to the top his heart was thudding in his eardrums and his lungs had been ripped open. He stood at the top gasping, vaguely registering the fact that Edouard and the rest of his *Northcote* shooters had picketed their horses and were taking up positions among the others who had walked up from the village. Old Joseph Ouellette was calling to his son to come join him in his rifle pit. "I got a kettle of your mother's tea—burn the ass off a skunk."

Gabriel looked out over the long meadow called La Jolie Prairie—a gently rolling plain dotted with poplar bluffs and shallow saddles of willow marsh. Half a mile to the south, the army column was separating into different colors as the regiments lined up beside each other. The bugles blew and the soldiers started forward—eight hundred and some odd of them against Gabriel's hundred and seventy.

The métis in the rifle pits were crossing themselves and murmuring prayers. The Cree and Sioux were singing competing war songs. Gabriel called out in French and then in Cree and Sioux: "Anyone fires a shot before I do gets my first bullet." Louis David appeared halfway down the hill behind them, holding the silver cross high over his head.

Gabriel walked a little ways out onto the prairie and picked himself a spot behind a low tangle of cranberry bushes. He lowered his left knee onto the ground and planted his right foot flat, working the heel of his moccasin back and forth to build up a little ridge of earth and grass roots behind it. Once he had effectively turned his body into a swivel base for Le Petit, he crossed himself and recited the little prayer he had made up after the priest had blessed him and the Riels at Fort Benton.

At about three hundred yards, the whole massed front of the

army came to a halt. They were within range of Le Petit, but knocking down one or two of them with long shots wasn't going to accomplish anything. One of the gun carriages was unhitched from its team, and a small cannon was wheeled forward. Gabriel didn't believe that any of the soldiers of the Exovedate or their log breastworks had been seen through the masking grass, but any fool could guess that the place where the horizon dipped down to Batoche was a good place to hide an army. If it made Middleton feel better to lob a few little cannonballs over their heads before coming on, that was all right with Gabriel.

But what came out of the little gun was a rattling hailstorm of bullets, chewing up the ground in front of the rifle pits and grinding the sage bushes into powder. Gabriel flung himself flat and hugged the earth. When the Gatling gun stopped firing, he sprang back into his firing position, shaking bits of shattered cranberry twigs out of his eyes. There was a roar from eight hundred throats, and the gold-trimmed uniforms surged forward, racing for the privilege of being first to take revenge for the friends they'd buried at Tourond's Coulee.

"Run hard," Gabriel murmured at them. It was farther than it looked, and they were weighted down with guns and bayonets. He drew a line across the meadow from the bell tower to the Carlton Trail and waited, snuggling Le Petit against his cheek. As the first boot crossed the line, the red tunic above it got a new buttonhole.

Every shotgun and rifle in the trenches behind him fired at once. The first thunderous volley gave way to a thinner, sharper chatter as Gabriel and Edouard and the few others with repeating rifles levered frantically through their cartridge chambers to make up for the muzzle-loading going on around them. When the smoke cleared, the face of the invading army had altered like the flipping of a card. Some of the bold fronts had become backs bounding away, some of them lay shattered and screaming in the tall grass, some of them had found themselves a molehill or a gopher mound to hide behind and were settling into a desultory snipe-and-duck at the puffs of smoke and stuffed dummies that were the only enemy they could see.

The important thing wasn't that this particular advance had been stopped in its tracks, but that the character of the fight had changed. What Gabriel had been most afraid of was a headlong charge by Middleton's entire army, which his ill-armed hundred and seventy wouldn't have a hope in hell of stopping. The government troops had consented to play Gabriel's game now, and he was quite content to keep on being the dealer until the buffalo came back, or Poundmaker and the others joined in, or the Army of the Exovedate ran out of ammunition—tomorrow or the next day.

Without taking his eyes and rifle sights off the swatches of color and twitches of grass fronds that the natural pallet and wind currents of the prairie couldn't account for, Gabriel called over his shoulder: "Anybody hit?"

Moïse Ouellette's father called back: "They killed four of us."

"Four?" He'd thought they'd be safe in the rifle pits.

"Four of our stuffed brothers," the old man cackled back. "Gotta get a tourniquet on this one before he sawdusts to death."

Gabriel waited for the laughter to subside, then called out: "Edouard?"

"I hear you."

"Take your ten and some of the Crees over to the trenches along the trail, quick." There was no reply. He didn't expect one, any more than he expected to have to say it twice.

Some fool policeman who hadn't learned anything from Tourond's Coulee fired a shot from exactly the same location he'd fired another one a moment earlier. Le Petit had a word with him without disturbing Gabriel's train of thought—he was sending Edouard over to the east side of the ridge because he figured Middleton was going to probe in that direction to see if Batoche's defenses were as strong there as the west side and the center. Maybe the general was smart enough to figure out that a powerful response from the east would mean that they were thinned out in the west, but Gabriel didn't think so. He had to bank on the general having no idea just how few men there were in the rifle pits. It was one thing for Gabriel to plant spies in Middleton's column and quite another for any government spy to smuggle himself into an army that was made up entirely of interrelated clans and families and tribes who considered anyone they hadn't known for twenty years a stranger.

Maybe the Canadian army couldn't be snookered with card tricks. There was no end of maybes. But now they were the kind of maybes that Gabriel could gauge as well as any man alive, not the kind that could paralyze him.

The Canadian artillery began to boom, whistling shells into the river and the houses on both sides of Batoche's Crossing.

They couldn't put a scratch on the entrenched men killing their infantry, but they could blow hell out of their wives and families. Gabriel decided not to think about it. Madelaine would have killed him with her bare hands if he'd led a rout down the ridge to see if she was safe.

Ahead and to his left, a regiment of infantry was fixing bayonets to take their general's stab at the east side of Batoche. Gabriel turned his attention in their direction, inserting a bellyful of fresh cartridges through Le Petit's brass gills.

CHAPTER 43

Madelaine was sitting in the kitchen putting the final touch on a dummy—painting blue stripes on its pie-shaped face in imitation of the gaudy Sioux and Cree up in the rifle pits. Mother "Batoche" was punching bread dough, with her eyes trained in the direction of the gunfire as though they could see through the walls. Marguerite was doing her best to soothe her children's fears while patently on the brink of flying into her own hysterics.

The world had changed since Madelaine was a child. By the time she was as old as Jean and Marie Angelique, she'd already lived through several occasions of crouching inside a circle of Red River carts while arrows and musket balls whistled by. No one ever grew out of the fear, but you did learn that it helped if you kept your hands busy and did your best to chatter away in a level voice, if you tried to at least keep from fanning the fears of those around you. She said: "Jean? Marie Angelique? Would you help me? I need a couple of little fingers to dip themselves in the pigment here and paint some bright stripes on the face of our sackcloth friend." Soon they were at least partially immersed in competitive artistry and the tactile joys of fingerpainting burlap.

The front of the house exploded, or seemed to. There was a splintering crash, and the roof joists rattled against each other.

The children screamed and ran to their mother, smearing blue paint down her skirt. Madelaine ran out of the kitchen. There was no sign of damage. She opened the front door.

A corner of the porch roof was torn away. At the end of a trail of timber shards and shattered shingles, a new furrow had been plowed across Madame Letendre's garden patch. The grass smoldered where the cannonball had come to rest.

Women and children and the men too old to fight were streaming out of their houses and running for the woods along the riverbank. The Caron house was tilted sideways over a jagged gap in one wall. The wailing and screaming carried above the clatter of rifle fire from the top of the hill and the roar of the cannons.

Marguerite shouted from behind her: "Let me through!" and came charging at the doorway with Marie Angelique under one arm and Jean squalling in the other, doing her best to run despite the double load and her voluminous skirts and the four months' swelling in her belly. Madelaine stepped out of her way and snatched Jean as she went by. Mother "Batoche" came out tucking her hair under her shawl. They joined the rout toward the river.

As they passed by the Sauvé house, a cannonball went through it from one end to the other, spitting out through the south wall to churn into the earth with a geyser of sod bits and smoke. Madelaine stopped and called over Jean's squalling: "Mother 'Batoche'—do you think old Norbert . . .?" Mother "Batoche" looked at the Sauvé house, then laughed and jigged her thin chin up and down. Madelaine handed Jean to her and ran to the Sauvé house as Mother "Batoche" carried on toward the river, clucking at Jean not to be afraid of a bit of noise and smoke.

Madelaine threw open the door. Toothless old Norbert Sauvé was hunched over the table with his back to her, spooning up mush with his right hand while his left held a half-woven Assumption sash for further study. From the alignment of the holes in the walls, if he'd been leaning back in his chair when the cannonball whistled through, it would have taken the top of his head with it.

Madelaine automatically shouted: "Norbert!" but kept on hurrying toward him without expecting a response—he'd been stone deaf since he still had a headful of teeth. She shook him by the shoulder. He was startled into dropping his spoon. When he saw who it was, he grinned jovially and picked up his spoon again to use it as a pointer for the clever pattern he was weaving. She yanked him out of his chair and turned him around. He was irate for an instant, then his eyes found what she'd come to show him and grew as wide as the new holes in his walls. She tugged him toward the door. He pulled free to reach back and grab his half-done sash with its dangling, multicolored cat-o'-several-dozen-tails waiting to be braided in, then lit out the door at a pace she could hardly keep up with.

A plume of black smoke was rising from the other side of the river. One of the houses among the cluster on the west bank was belching flames from its roof. As Madelaine's eyes lingered on the fire, it threw up a shower of burning beams as another red-hot cannonball dropped in. If the homes on the far shore were in range of the Canadian artillery, then so were the tents that she and the others were running for. She decided there was nothing she could do about it except pray that the gunners couldn't see the tents through the trees.

As she puffed along toward the little rank of storefronts and the dubious safety of the trees on the other side, she remembered the two wounded men in the back room of the store nearest the river. She slowed down, calling herself several varieties of fool for even entertaining such a thought—she was no more invulnerable to cannonballs than they were—then swerved toward the store.

Francois Boyer had got up on his feet, barely, and then fallen to his hands and knees. Michel Desjarlais hadn't moved. She might just as well put a bullet in their heads as settle them to sleep in a tent through the still-frosty nights or move them back and forth with every barrage. She said to Francois: "There's a little cellar under Phillipe Garnot's stopping place. I'll help you over there and come back for Michel."

"No—take him first. I might be able to make it on my own."

She doubted it, but she went over to Michel's bed anyway. She wasn't sure if she could carry him on her own, but Francois was in no shape to help. She looked down at Michel Desjarlais and reconsidered her chances: in the days since she'd found the sliver of bone under his mattress, he'd wasted away to translucency. He didn't appear to hear the cannon bursts. She put her hand to the side of his throat. It was cold, and there was no pulse. She said: "No need to wait for Michel. We can bury him tonight," and put her shoulder under Francois Boyer's armpit.

The sound of the battle was eerily muffled by the clay walls of Phillipe Garnot's cellar. She ferried down half a dozen lamps and lit them. One would have been enough for light, but not to take the edge off the dank underground cold. As she was lighting the last, there was a thumping on the floor overhead, and two of Gabriel's soldiers came struggling down the ladder carrying Damase Carriere. Damase was one of the Exovedate and, like Gabriel and his brothers, one of the few men still young enough to fight but old enough to have grown up when the country was still wild and free.

Damase was cursing a cobalt streak, and his right leg looked as if it had grown a new joint between the knee and ankle. His cursing was more in outrage than pain. In the midst of the battle for his nation's life, charging along behind Gabriel with bullets and cannonballs whizzing around them, Damase had caught his foot in a badger hole and wound up at the bottom of the ridge with a broken leg.

Madelaine sent one of the stretcher bearers upstairs to steal one of Phillipe Garnot's kegs and the other outside to hack down a poplar sapling. She pumped Damase full of rum, told them to take a good hold on his shoulders, then fastened her hands around his right ankle and yanked hard. He screamed and passed out. Once the leg was reset and the splints bound on, he woke up long enough to tell her: "If they can't kill Gabriel with all the chances he's giving them, they can't kill nobody."

Up on the hill, Gabriel was crouched on La Jolie Prairie, looking over the situation. To his right, the churchyard stood between the two armies. Something white flapped out of the church door, and Father Moulin emerged, waving his surplice over his head. A red-coated officer and a squad of infantrymen marched forward to meet him. Le Petit came up, the sights quivering across the diminutive figure of Père Caribou—as Father Moulin had been rechristened for his notion that the métis should replace the buffalo hunt by forging north into the Land of Little Sticks to hunt caribou. Although Father Moulin and the soldiers were three hundred yards from him and the air was filled with the sound of gunfire, Gabriel heard each word of their conversation echoing through his mind:

"How many are they, Father?"

"Less than two hundred, and they don't have much ammunition. . . ."

Gabriel's finger pressed against the trigger. His hands were shaking and his lips had pulled back from his teeth. His forefinger ached to squeeze a hair's-breadth farther, but he made it go slack and slowly lowered his rifle.

Behind the scattered snipers that made up Middleton's front line, the bright red-and-green garden of the regiments he was holding in reserve began to nod toward the east. Gabriel rubbed his eyes to clear away the acid Father Moulin had thrown in them, then looked again to try to see what the troop movement might mean. He leaped up and ran back for the crest of the ridge, with the soldiers' bullets disintegrating grass stalks all around him. His previous acquaintance with their marksmanship at Tourond's Coulee suggested that he was quite safe at any range farther than ten feet, provided they were aiming at him.

He skidded over the rim, thudded sideways into the nearest rifle pit, and found himself gazing up into the multihued, befeathered, and bemused visage of Chief White Cap. White Cap said: "Fight best with your feet in the air?"

Gabriel pointed east and said in Sioux: "Take your whole bunch over to join Edouard and make as much noise as you can." White Cap's sky-blue-streaked face was replaced by the sky. Gabriel rolled back onto his feet and lit out westward, running lopsided against the grain of the ridge, shouting for his riflemen to follow him. He'd culled a kind of flying squad out of the few who had repeating rifles, such as Moïse Ouellette and Michel Dumas. Michel might not be capable of thinking for himself beyond "I think I want breakfast," but he was a good man in a fight. Almost as good as Damase Carriere, whose "rifle" was a rusty shotgun but was such a steady-hearted old berserker that Gabriel had naturally relied on him to fill out his aces—until the damned fool had gone and tripped over his own moccasins.

The eastward shifting of Middleton's reserves had suggested that Edouard had done a good job of throwing back the probe on that side—so much so that Middleton thought that's where their major strength was. Middleton's west flank, ending where the ground dropped away to the river, was anchored by the artillery.

A wooded gulley poked into La Jolie Prairie between the church and the cemetery. Gabriel crashed through the tangle of birch and willow and flung himself down on the tip of the ravine. Moïse and Michel and the others thumped down around him. A hundred yards across the churchyard, General Middleton's big guns were booming and bucking and spewing smoke. Interspersed among the shirt-sleeved gunners, a smattering of red-tunicked infantrymen leaned on their bayonet shafts or covered their ears. In between the cannon volleys, Gabriel could hear that the gunfire from the eastern quadrant had grown substantially louder, augmented by wolfish ululations. Anyone who'd been through one skirmish on the old days of Plains Tribes warfare knew that the bloodcurdlingest war cry ever uttered wouldn't put a scratch on a rabbit, but the green-and-black-uniformed regiment detailed to help guard the guns was quick-marching off in that direction.

Gabriel thumbed back the hammer on Le Petit, picked out a mustachioed gunner who was just about to yank a lanyard, and pulled the trigger. The bark of Le Petit was instantaneously echoed and amplified by the rest of the pack in the gulley. The redcoats and white shirts wavered, dropped, squealed, ducked behind their guns, and turned their attention from the distant targets they were faced toward to the nearby woods on their left. And then they did something that caught Gabriel completely by surprise. They turned and ran like hell.

He had hoped to give them an intimidating kick in the side. It had never occurred to him that an artillery emplacement that had been happily lobbing shells into a village full of women and children would be so shocked at anyone being so rude as to shoot back at them that they'd run off and leave all their cannons and shells and powder unprotected.

Gabriel blinked a couple of times, decided that his eyes were taking in the truth, then sprang up and ran for the guns. Within the first two steps he'd already formulated what would happen once he reached them. Moïse and Michel and the others following him would each scoop up a keg of powder, and he would commandeer a keg to lay a trail of gunpowder from the battery's remaining pile of powder kegs and explosive shells. One sulphur match would rub out Middleton's entire artillery corps.

But when he was halfway through his third step, the ground in front of him went mad with bullets spitting up feathers of dust. He turned his ball-of-the-foot-forward step into a heel-down backward kickoff and dove back into the bush as the Gatling gun devoured the vegetation.

A quick roll call of his fingers and toes and of the other men hugging the gulley brought Gabriel to the happy conclusion that no one had been hit. But there was no denying the unhappy conclusion that the damned Yankee invention had saved the general's bacon and artillery. There was the consolation that from now on the gun crews would be devoting as much of their attention to looking over their shoulders as loading, firing, and computing elevations.

Gabriel bounced to his feet and led his squad at a lope back down the gulley and around to the rifle pits at the center of the line. As the sunlight turned red and stretched a long, purple shadow from the barrel of Le Petit, Middleton's army retreated. Gabriel sent his last few cartridges at their backs to keep them honest, then sagged forward across the birch log fronting the rifle pit. Moïse Ouellette was slumped beside him, grinning and gasping. Moïse managed to catch enough breath to croak out: "We did it."

"For today."

About a quarter mile beyond the cemetery, the soldiers of the Queen were piling up ramparts and digging in. Much closer, bright-uniformed squads were bustling in and out of the church and rectory, bearing stretchers with their dead and wounded. The soldiers and the holy fathers and sisters appeared to be quite cozy.

Moïse heaved himself upright and declared in a wispy voice: "Dinnertime," gesturing weakly at the village below.

Gabriel shook his head. "Not for me yet. Come nightfall I got some words to have with some people up here. Guess I better climb down and get some more cartridges, though."

Moïse reached into the pocket of his corduroy coat and came out with a handful of cartridges. "Forty-fours?"

Gabriel nodded, and Moïse dropped them into his hand. There were only about a dozen, but that should do it. If he got cornered, there was always his revolver.

CHAPTER 44

As the evening came down, the guns up on the hill grew mute, encouraging the timider or wiser residents of Batoche's Crossing to emerge from the hidey-holes in the bush or under the riverbank where they'd been crouched all afternoon. Madelaine and Annie and Mother "Batoche" had spent the afternoon out in the open in front of their tent, pan-frying *galettes* over the fire, stacking the crisp flatbread on rocks to cool, and chasing off the dogs, magpies, and flies. As Mother "Batoche" had said when Madelaine arrived to find her and Annie manning their outdoor bakery: "Whether they beat the English or not, they'll still be hungry."

A few of the men from the rifle pits began to trickle back through the gathering darkness, weary and dirt-caked but jubilant. The Cree and Sioux camps began to reverberate with drums and singing. Mother "Batoche" said: "They can't aim their cannons at night, can they?"

"I don't think so."

"Then we might just as well spend the night under a roof and cook a good meal in the kitchen."

As they were loading the *galettes* into flour sacks and dousing the fire, Alexis came trotting along the bank with his aged bird-gun propped across his saddlepad. He'd been told he was too young to fight in the rifle pits and had been dispatched to keep track of Patrice Fleury's running fight with the *Northcote*. "Is Uncle Gabriel here?" Madelaine shook her head and pointed toward the ridge, where an occasional gunshot cracked the night.

Alexis's eyes gleamed and he wheeled his pony in that direction. Madelaine lunged out and grabbed his bridle. "Oh, no, you won't! You'll come with us back to the house and wait there. If Gabriel ain't on his way there already, he will be soon." He climbed down sulkily and walked his pony along beside them. "What did you come to tell him?"

313

"The fire canoe's gone. After we chased 'em past here, they anchored where the river widens up again, down by Uncle Isidor's . . ." He remembered and crossed himself, murmuring, "Mercy on his soul. . . . Patrice Fleury and them couldn't shoot through their barricades," he continued, "but kept them from climbing out to fix their smokestacks. I guess they finally gave up, 'cause they pulled up their anchor and started off downstream while there was still light. Guess that's that for them."

In the light of the rising moon, shadowy figures were trickling out of the woods, heading hopefully for the places where they'd left their houses this morning. Miraculously, although a few corners had been knocked off and a few walls had holes in them, they were all still standing—with the exception of the pile of rubble where Madame Caron stood weeping. Madelaine went over to her and put an arm around her shoulders. Madame Caron looked up at her, sniveled, wiped her nose, and said: "At least we neither of us got no more damned floors to scrub."

There was a crowd gathering in front of the Letendre house. The sheering-off of the porch roof had provided Louis David with a patch of moonlight to stand in—there would be no bonfires tonight. He told the throng in front of him: "What more proof could we ask that God will keep His promise to His people? The hosts of darkness that sought to overwhelm us have been driven back, and though their bullets flew as numerous as blades of grass, not one found its mark. Can there be any doubt left that the hand of God protects us? That the priests' refusal to give us religious solace means that they have abandoned God, not that God has abandoned us?"

Madelaine went inside and helped Mother "Batoche" fire up the oven for *tourtières*. There was still no sign of Gabriel, although the sudden absence of Annie suggested that Michel Dumas had come back. Marguerite brought Marie Angelique and Jean into the kitchen and sat them down on either side of Alexis while she helped with the cooking. Both children were soon nodding under Alexis's arms, drinking in the smells of venison, sage, onions, and pastry baking together, occasionally prying open their eyes long enough to announce that they weren't sleepy yet.

Once the *tourtières* were in the oven, Madelaine boiled up a pan of fat to make *beignes croches* from the leftover dough. Louis David finished his exhortations and climbed up to his garret. Edouard and Eli staggered in and pounced on the pile of *galettes*, washing down the powdery crusts with black tea—two swallows per cup. Madeleine said: "Where's Gabriel?"

Edouard looked at Eli with hooded eyes and let out a guttural sigh. Eli shrugged, raised his soft brown eyes to hers, and said: "Gabriel's gone Gabriel." Early in her marriage, Madeleine had learned that the Dumont family lexicon contained the verb phrase *to go Gabriel*. It appeared to have originated with Gabriel's crazy uncle.

Edouard said: "He's sneaking around the woods outside their camp, making sure they don't get much sleep or get to warm themselves at their campfires."

"Or even get to strike a match to light a pipe," Eli added, "if I know Le Petit."

Madeleine looked in the oven. "Hot *tourtières* soon."

They both shook their heads sadly—Eli because he'd have to start immediately if he was to ride up to Aicawpow's where his family was staying, show them he was still alive, get a couple of hours' sleep, and be back by morning; Edouard because hell was going to freeze over before he'd slack off for more than a moment while Gabriel was still out there fighting.

Edouard stood up and shoved a few *galettes* in his coat pocket for Gabriel, wrapping up a handful of *beignes croches* in a bit of cloth for the other pocket. He said: "Gabriel asked me to bring him back some cartridges, and a surprise he said was wrapped in a green blanket."

"Upstairs. I'll get them." She shut the oven door from his drooling eyes. "If you're not back when the *tourtières* are done, you can always have them cold tomorrow."

Edouard said: "We might have a lot of things cold tomorrow."

Gabriel was prowling through the shadows in the moonlit churchyard. He didn't see or hear any sentries, although the soldiers had been carrying their wounded friends into the church all through the afternoon. He skirted the patches of light from the rectory windows and made for the door of the church.

There were low voices inside. He raised the latch and began to ease the door open. There was a sudden sound of scuffling and skittering—they'd seen the door move. He flung it the rest of the way open, jumping in with Le Petit poised to fire from the hip as the door bounced back from the wall.

Father Moulin was standing in front of him with his hands

clasped under his white spade beard and his chipmunk-cheeked, Oriental sage's visage fixed in a kindly smile. Over the cassocked shoulder, Gabriel just caught the tail end of a flash of garments disappearing through the door beside the altar rail. It was a flash of black and gray and white, though, not bright uniform colors.

Gabriel's eyes circled the inside of the church, found no one else, and returned to Father Moulin. "Where are they?"

"Where are who, my son?"

"If I'm your son, my mother's soul's got a lot to answer for, and so does yours when your time comes. Where are the soldiers?"

"Back in their camp. You know where that is, if the gunshots I've been hearing weren't imagination."

"I saw them carrying their wounded in here."

"So they did—and carried them back to their camp at the end of the day." Gabriel pushed him aside with his rifle barrel and started down the aisle. "Don't you trust me, Gabriel?"

"Why wouldn't I? Just because you hold parleys with our enemies and attend to their wounded while you turn our own people away . . ."

"Would you have me drive dying men from the church door? And I have turned none of our people away—it's they who have turned away from the church."

Gabriel vaulted over the altar rail, kicked open the vestry door, and thrust in Le Petit. The candlelight showed two kneeling nuns, who gasped at him and then ducked their lips down to their bead-wrapped knuckles and swiftly murmured what they obviously expected to be their last prayers.

Gabriel stalked back to the altar, took a candle, and threw open the cellar trap. He quickly lowered the candle into it and snatched it back out just as quickly. If there were scared, armed, wounded soldiers down there, odds on they would have fired. He lowered the candle again and peered down the cellar stairs. There was no one there. He knew there was nowhere else to hide inside the church, since his hands had helped dig the cellar and raise the rafters.

He closed the trap, put the candle back, and headed for the door. Father Moulin demanded: "And what would you have done if they were still here—kill them?" Gabriel didn't bother to reply. One or two wounded soldiers would have provided a better bargaining tool than all the other prisoners combined. But if they had insisted on fighting to the death, of course he would have killed them.

There was the possibility that they could be hiding in the rectory. Gabriel was quite sure Father Moulin was hiding something. But he didn't have time to take the rectory apart plank by plank. As Gabriel stepped back out into the night, Father Moulin called after him: "Gabriel? . . ."

Automatically he slipped sideways out of the light from the doorway before stopping to reply. "What?"

"It is not too late. There is more joy in heaven for the return of the strayed one than for the ninety and nine. . . ." Gabriel walked away.

While Gabriel was at the church, Moïse Ouellette and a couple of White Cap's Sioux had kept up the occasional sniping over the army camp's barricades. The Sioux had run out of powder and were reduced to bows and arrows. But when it came down to it, bows were probably more accurate than their ancient HBC guns and were definitely more effective for arcing shots over ramparts.

Gabriel found a piece of high ground and joined in. There wasn't much to shoot at anymore. As soon as darkness brought the sniping, the soldiers had quickly doused their cooking fires. Not even a candle showed. The poor soldiers must have had nothing for supper but cold biscuits and dust—the dust because the general had decided to erect his camp in the middle of a plowed field.

Gabriel settled for firing a few blind shots into the gloom beyond the vague shape of the wagon-and-earthworks wall. They must have had some effect, for a number of soldiers suddenly charged out in a sortie. All they got for their trouble was a few minutes of blundering around in the bush, enlivened by a few arrows and fiendish laughter from the Sioux.

As the moon lowered itself into the arms of the trees, Gabriel went to find Moïse and the Sioux. "I figure that's enough for one night. Better save your ammunition and get some rest for tomorrow."

Moïse said: "What about you?"

"I got someone I'm supposed to meet at moonset."

He slipped back through the bush to the churchyard, then skirted the picket fence around the cemetery until he came to where the ground dropped away to the river. He settled down with his back against a fence post and watched the stars ripple on the water far below. There was a whisper of leaves behind him, and a large body lowered itself to squat beside him.

"Evening, Gabriel."

"Evening, Jerome. Care for a smoke?"

"Don't seem healthy to show a light tonight."

"For them, not us." Gabriel packed his pipe and proffered his tobacco pouch. Jerome Henry never had to be asked twice. He'd grown fat and used to his creature comforts in the years since he gave up the buffalo hunt for driving freight carts and guiding. And it didn't look as if the army had been forcing him to live on hard rations during the last few weeks.

Gabriel said: "You keeping your head down?"

"Oh, there ain't been much sniping over on the baggage train side. Funny thing, that." He passed the pouch back to Gabriel and struck a match. The flamelight over the glowing pipe bowl showed a round, furrowed face with a wreath of beard framing the jaw—rather like a Quaker storekeeper, if you didn't look too close at the eyes. "You got 'em spooked pretty good. Middleton sent Lord Melglund back east halfway through the day."

"What for?"

"Some say to send telegrams from Humboldt, to the Police in Battleford and Prince Albert, telling them to get their asses down here and give the general a hand. Some say to take the railway all the way back to Ottawa so there'll be someone there to talk against the screaming for Middleton's scalp when he retreats from here. Some say Lady Melglund sent a telegram telling him to get back home before he gets hisself hurt."

"What do you say?"

"Me?" As though he hadn't expected such a question, Jerome puffed on his pipe for a moment to reconsider the opinion he'd no doubt formed hours ago. Gabriel waited patiently. Jerome Henry might look like a middle-aged cherub, but anyone who knew him knew he was about as guileless and quick to commit himself as a ten-year-old badger. "Well, I say a man don't pack up his valet and cook and wagonload of camp gear to take a jaunt over to Humboldt—and anyways, the civilians holed up in Battleford and Prince Albert'd never stand for the Police pulling out on them. I say the general didn't come out here expecting a fight—he figured on rolling right over you and riding home to get his knighthood. I say whatever Lord Melglund's been sent east for, a few more days like today'll be about all the general's got the stomach for—he's already making noises about how the damned politicians gave him a wrong idea of how many rebels there was and should have sent him more troops. I say you just about got him snookered."

Gabriel shook his head in wonderment. If the news went back to Ottawa that eight hundred soldiers couldn't beat down the rebellion, Macdonald would have to talk treaty. Jerome said: "One big problem—some of the militia captains ain't too happy with the general. They say they could clean you out fast if he'd let them charge full out. I figure one good mass ass kicking'd make 'em ponder considerable on the wisdom of that."

"The minute I get enough men and guns to do that with . . . Some night soon you better make sure you got a barrel to hide in."

"When? Any news of Poundmaker or— Evening, Edouard."

"Jerome." Edouard squatted down between them, setting aside the blanket-wrapped bundle—about the size of a man's leg—that Gabriel had asked him to bring back from Letendre's attic. He pulled a couple of frayed-edged *galettes* out of his coat pocket and handed them to Gabriel. "Thought you might be getting hungry."

Jerome poked at the bundle. "What you got there?"

"Oh . . . just a little something I found at the Duck Lake store. You better be getting back before the sky lights up."

"Won't be sunup for hours."

"This country's full of surprises." Once Jerome was on his way, Gabriel picked up the bundle and let the memory in their moccasin soles guide him and Edouard back through the black woods to a spot halfway between the soldiers' encampment and the rifle pits. Gabriel unrolled the blanket. Inside it was a rocket with a stick and a fuse poking out of its bottom. They argued over whether it was the air-exploding kind or the military kind—called a Congreve rocket—that was made to explode when it hit the ground, and then they argued over projected trajectory. They compromised in the time-honored family tradition: Edouard sulkily knuckled under to what Gabriel had wanted to do in the first place.

When Gabriel put the match to the fuse, it didn't sputter alight. It flared up instantaneously. Gabriel and Edouard squawked and flung themselves to the ground as the rocket fizzed out sparks and shot into the air. They rolled over, smothering the embers on their clothes, then sat up with their mouths open as the rocket exploded into a sunburst of red-and-yellow flame above the soldiers' camp. Every tree and bush for half a mile flared alive, then disappeared again in the dwindling light of the rocket's descending fragments. There were panicked gunshots and shouts from the dozing Canadian army.

In the last light from the shower of fire, Gabriel looked across at his gawking brother. They both collapsed laughing. Maybe the rocket hadn't inflicted any physical damage on Middleton's soldiers, but it sure as hell gave them something to think about.

Gabriel and Edouard accompanied each other as far as the crest of the ridge and then split off as Edouard headed for his farm north of the ferry and Gabriel angled down the slope toward Letendre's house on the south side of the flats. He was halfway down when he heard whispering voices and the rustle of cloth. He dropped flat on his belly. Two black gaps in the field of stars grew larger as they walked down the hill toward him, murmuring fiercely at each other. One voice was his sister Isabelle's—Moïse Ouellette's wife. The other was a female voice he knew but couldn't place.

"But if he was to get shot and die unshriven . . ."

Isabelle said: "Louis David says—"

"He says a lot of things," the other cut her off. "Do you think Father Moulin doesn't pray that we will allow him to be our priest again?"

The hem of a skirt brushed Gabriel's nose. He stifled the sneeze, eyeballs popping.

"If Father Moulin was a true servant of God, he wouldn't turn away when we asked him for—"

"Are you quoting *Pope* Louis David again?"

The voices grew indistinct; Gabriel sat up and waited for them to fade completely. Although the wound across his head had long since calcified into a puckered scar, it now began to throb softly. When the voices melted away, he made several grunting attempts to heave himself back to his feet. He finally made it and staggered on down the hill, arguing with himself over whether he should be congratulated for not falling asleep while he was prone in the grass or whether he had and was only dreaming.

The Letendre house was in darkness. Gabriel lit a lamp in the kitchen and rummaged the cupboards. Madelaine came down the stairs with an old shawl draped over her faded flowered flannel nightgown and unplaited graying hair, looking about as

drab as a spring sunrise. She fed him half a cold *tourtière* and
led him upstairs.

He closed his eyes but didn't sleep. When the red-shot black
lining his eyelids softened to pink-veined gray, he rolled his head
off her shoulder and his ass off the bed and reached for his
cartridge belts, hat, and rifle.

Through the riot of waking water birds in the willow marshes
and the trilling of meadowlarks out on the plain came the sound
of Middleton's buglers blowing reveille. Gabriel ran his hand
through a clump of broad-bladed grass and wiped his face with
dew. Riel had climbed up to the barricades before him. His eyes
were unnaturally glossy, and his complexion had the sheen of
melted candle wax. After the last twenty-four hours, Gabriel
figured he probably looked pretty damned otherworldly himself.
Riel said: "What do you think will happen today?"

"They'll try to run over us. We'll try to stop them."

The Army of the Exovedate straggled up the ridge, yawning
and scratching themselves and making jokes about *La Rababou*.
Rababou was a Michif word for a gossipy chatterbox. Michel
Dumas had christened the Gatling gun *La Rababou*. Gabriel
called: "Edouard! Take your ten soldiers and—"

"Eight."

"Eight? I thought no one got hit yesterday?"

"No one did. But where I had ten yesterday I got eight today."

Gabriel wondered how many of his other Captains of Ten had
woken up that morning to discover they were Captains of Eight,
or Seven or Five. The *rabobous* the priests had cranked into
action—like the one he'd heard talking to Isabelle last night—
were doing a better job for Middleton than the Gatling gun.

The cannons began to boom again. The day passed much the
same as yesterday, except that the government troops appeared
to have lost a good deal of steam. Their thrusts against the line
of rifle pits were about as enthusiastic as a fox attacking a bull
moose.

The third day blended into the second. Gabriel hadn't slept
more than an hour of the past seventy-two. The crease across
the top of his head had become a constant explosion of red and
green and purple. The only separation between one skirmish
and the next was when the barrel of Le Petit began to burn his
hand. He no longer tried to encourage himself and the others

with the notion that the odds were going to tip at any moment, as soon as feathered or slouch-hatted horsemen appeared on the northern horizon. Without one bullet wound worth mentioning, his hundred and seventy had been whittled down to ninety. He didn't even think anymore about the snowy day when he'd asked the congregation if they would stand up with him to fight for their rights. It was Gabriel Dumont against the British Empire.

CHAPTER 45

In the darkness, Madelaine slipped out of the house and threaded her way through the pigpens and chicken coops toward the slope up to the rifle pits. Gabriel was out there somewhere, seeing to it that the soldiers stayed behind their earthworks for the night.

Keeping close to the woods along the riverbanks so that her silhouette would blend into the matte background, she began to climb the hill. Halfway up, her forward foot came down on air. She began to fall face first into a hole she couldn't see. She managed to fling her weight sideways so that she *whumped* down on the damp grass of the hillside instead of plunging headlong into one of Gabriel's trenches.

She walked more carefully after that. A barred owl boomed at her from his hunting perch in the woods to her right. The frogs and crickets peeped and fiddled a descant to the steady murmur of the river. Despite the bruises where her elbow had insinuated itself between her rib cage and the earth, she found herself feeling unreasonably happy. She finally pegged it to the fact that it had been three days since she'd last heard voices other than those of guns or human beings.

The field of stars jolted down toward eye level, showing that she was nearing the crest of the ridge. A mushroom-shaped, starless vault pointed out the bell tower of the church. The church was dark. The windows on the side wall of the rectory threw yellow squares of lamplight on the grass, but the ones flanking the front door were dark. Madelaine knocked tentatively.

The door was immediately opened by one of the holy sisters. "Madame Dumont! Come in, come in."

"I didn't want to wake anyone. . . ."

"No one's asleep. Father Moulin just thought it best to leave the front door dark so no one would be seen. He'll want to see you."

Madelaine was a bit thrown off, and even a little miffed, that her midnight visit should be taken so matter-of-factly. As she followed the sister down the corridor, she learned why. In every one of the priests' cells or common rooms opening off the hall-way, there was a woman or a married couple in earnest conver-sation with a priest or a nun.

At the end of the corridor was a closed door. The sister escorting her knocked. It was flung open by Father Moulin, who had a bandage on his head. "Did I or did I not tell Sister Ber-thilde that I was not to be . . . Oh, Madelaine . . ." His testi-ness dissolved into an ingratiating smile. He looked back over his shoulder at Michel Dumas's tiny old mother perched hunch-shouldered on the lip of a chair. "Madame Dumas, perhaps you might like to speak with Sister Mary Ignatius for a while? . . ."

Madelaine started to protest that she could wait, or talk to one of the other priests, but Father Moulin was adamant, and Madame Dumas was accommodating. The sister took the old lady's elbow, Madelaine was shunted onto her chair, and Father Moulin closed the door. She indicated the bandage on his head and said: "Are you hurt, Father?" As soon as the words were out of her mouth, she told herself they were lamebrained—he hadn't tied a bandage around his head for decoration.

"Not badly. A bullet came through the church, but it was so spent it barely scratched the skin. You can tell Gabriel it proves my head's as hard as his." He sat down on the only other chair in the room, which had been pulled out from behind the writing desk to make for more intimate conversation, and clasped his hands behind his beard like a fur muff. "I didn't mean to sound gruff at the door. I'm afraid we're all not at our best. The whole night long is a steady stream of parishioners, and we can't sleep in the day for the guns. . . . What did you come to see me about?"

"Well . . . it's Gabriel. . . ." Of course it was Gabriel, she told herself sourly, just as all the conversations in the other rooms had begun with "It's about Michel, Father," or Moïse or Patrice or Phillipe. "You know he didn't start this war to get anything for himself. Whatever the government did or didn't do over the years, Gabriel could always find a way to take care of himself and me and his family. He's in this because of other people. Is it a sin for him to try to be his brother's keeper?" She wished she'd chosen to say it another way, since it only pointed up the fact that the first effect of Gabriel's standing up to fight had been to get his brother killed.

"Of course it isn't. Of course I know, and God knows, as well as you do yourself, that Gabriel's heart is nothing but generous. But generosity can be misguided and used for sinful purposes."

"Doesn't it seem wrong to you that a man who had nothing in his heart but concern for his friends and neighbors—even if you think he picked a sinful way to try to help them—doesn't it seem wrong that if he . . . *dies* out there on that hill just past the church steps, no priest will give him absolution or pray for mercy on his soul?"

Father Moulin stroked his beard and gazed with pursed lips at a table leg. Then he clucked his lips apart and said carefully: "He's in your hands, my child. We're all in your hands. Gabriel may be the rock our people here cling to, but you're his rock. In the small hours of the night, the hours of doubt—even Gabriel has moments of doubt—the right word from a loved one can turn the stubbornest of men. You could stop this war."

Madelaine got up and went to the window. There was nothing to see except the highlighted fragments of a broad-boned, broadbeamed, speckle-haired old woman in the black depths of the glass and the little image of the priest behind her. She said to Father Moulin's reflection: "You didn't know us when we were young. Maybe Father André told you how it was. For the first years after we got married, the words I heard over and over were 'Poor Madelaine,' no matter how soft people thought they whispered them as I went by.

"Here I'd ended up shackled to this wolf of a man who spent his money on whiskey and'd just as likely disappear three days and nights playing cards. . . ."

She turned around to tell him the rest to his face. "But a strange thing happened over the course of years. For one thing, it got obvious that I wasn't ever going to give him children, and he could have walked away from me with the blessings of the

Church and taken up with any of a thousand bright-eyed girls who wouldn't mind marrying the Chief of the buffalo hunt who owned a ferry and a freight business and whose name meant respect from Hudson's Bay to the Rocky Mountains. But my Gabriel never had one thought to do that. I haven't heard anyone whisper, 'Poor Madelaine,' since long before the Canadians bought this country. So if you or the Pope or anybody else wants me to do something that might ever make me hear people whisper: 'Poor Gabriel,' you can go to hell.''

CHAPTER 46

At the dawning of the twelfth of May, Gabriel Dumont climbed the ridge above Batoche and turned at the top to look back toward the west. On the river, a white flotilla of pelicans was spread out in a line among the gray wisps of mist, herding fish into the shallows. He could see a long way across the rolling plain beyond the river, many miles unmarred by any straggling line of Indians on the move or file of métis horsemen. Maybe they were out there, just beyond the point where the poplar bluffs and willow ponds blended into the grass, although the eye had the illusion it could still see details all the way to the horizon. Or maybe they had already crossed the river and were coming through the woods to the north. The one place they definitely weren't was Batoche's Crossing.

Michel Dumas came up the hill yawning and winding his rifle two-handed behind his back to work out the kinks. He squinted toward the army camp, rasped his fingernails across his stubbly cheeks, and said: ''Still out there, are they? You'd think they'd get tired of marching back and forth and getting shot.'' Moïse Ouellette and his father climbed up next, the old man with a moosehide bag slung on the muzzle of his muzzle-loader like a bindle stiff. ''What you got there, Grandfather—your medicine bag?''

Joseph Ouellette growled back: ''There's medicine and there's medicine," climbing down into the nearest rifle pit. He squirmed his spindly buttocks back and forth to make a hollow in the ground, experimentally propped his back against the wall of the trench, decided that was as comfortable as he was going to get, and dumped the contents of his bag out beside him. It made an ankle-high mound of pebbles, pewter buttons, bits of rusted nails, fragments of smashed crockery, and broken glass. He shook his powder horn against his ear, nippled in a miserly pinch, and scooped up a handful of pebbles and nail ends. "What the hell, eh? Worked for little David."

Michel Dumas grunted: "Middleton ain't no Goliath."

Moïse said: "Probably outweighs him."

La Rababou started chattering again, and the soldiers marched out. Gabriel went back to trying to outguess Middleton, charging from one rifle pit to another with his flying squad. On the slope behind, Riel continued to parade his silver cross up and down, and the bullets continued to veer around him. When the soldiers had turned tail again, he ran up to Gabriel and said: "I am going to send one of the prisoners to tell Middleton that if he continues to fire his cannons at a village full of women and children, we shall kill the hostages!"

It seemed a bit late in the day for threats, but Gabriel muttered: "Do what you like."

At noon, the government troops retired behind their barricades for lunch. The morning's maneuverings had brought Gabriel back to the west side of the ridge and the rifle pit where Joseph Ouellette had set up shop for the day. Moïse was there as well, along with Michel Dumas and little Phillipe Garnot with his huge Henry rifle. They were munching on *galettes* and palming up river water from the buckets that Alexis and the other almost-men were running up the hill.

Moïse studied his half-eaten *galette* distastefully and said: "When this is over, the next person that offers me a piece of frying pan bread gets the butt of my rifle between the eyes."

Gabriel said: "At Le Grand Coteau, the first time I ever found myself shooting a gun at people who were shooting at me, the worst part was the hunger. We'd dug rifle pits out about two hundred yards from the circle of carts, and when I first climbed into the hole my father pointed out to me, I thought what I oughta be concerned about was that there was two thousand Sioux against seventy-seven rifles.

"But as the day wore on, I started to notice what was truly

important. With nothing but open prairie between us and the carts, and the Sioux coming at us all day, it wouldn't be safe to go back and ask our mamas for a bite to eat until dark. Long summer day.

"I'd stand up to fire across the sacks of pemmican piled in front of the hole, then drop back down and hug my belly and whine about the hole my stomach was chewing. It wasn't 'til halfway through the afternoon that it finally sank into my head that the pemmican sacks I was shooting over was sacks of pemmican."

He waited for the laugh. What he got instead was Michel Dumas saying: "Huh?"

"What 'huh'? I ate my ramparts."

Moïse gave out a wistful croak, swallowed a couple of times, and said: "Plain pemmican or berry pemmican?"

"Berry pemmican."

Moïse drooled some more and moaned: "Blueberries or saskatoons?"

"Saskatoons, I think."

"Oh, good—I hate saskatoons."

"There ain't no goddamned difference!"

"Even a drunken Blackfoot can taste the difference between blueberries and saskatoons."

Gabriel growled: "My grandmother was Blackfoot."

"I thought she was Sarcee." Moïse turned to his father. "Ain't the Dumonts always been Sarcee?"

"Same difference now, since the Sarcee joined the confederacy. Except for the language. Let's see now . . . that was back before me and Mister Grant beat the English at Seven Oaks, and Gabriel's grandparents would have got together some time around—"

Gunfire interrupted him. Gabriel peered out through the gap where the eccentric twists of the two birch trunks forming the barricade provided loopholes. Red-and-gold uniforms were dog-trotting through the churchyard, pausing to methodically demolish the cemetery fence so the rear ranks could charge through without breaking stride. Le Petit dropped a couple of them, but they kept on coming. Between shots, Michel Dumas yelled: "They're crazy! Edouard's boys'll cut them to pieces from the side."

"With *what*—bits of gravel and rusty nails? Come on!" Gabriel rolled back out of the rifle pit, ran down the slope, and slid into a virgin rifle pit where the base of the ridge met the flats. Michel and the others had followed him—Joseph Ouellette trailing behind because of his stiff knees and his insistence on scooping his bits of gravel and rusty nails back into his bullet bag. He panted into the trench just as the front rank of soldiers crested the ridge.

Gabriel emptied Le Petit into them. He hardly had to aim; they filled the sky and had a quarter mile of hill to run down. They screamed and threw up their arms and fell and rolled toward him, tripping up the booted legs around them, but the rest kept on coming. Halfway up the slope, someone in a rifle pit— it looked like Calixte Tourond—fired the ramrod of his muzzleloader into a soldier's leg. A batch of bayonets came down and pried Calixte out. He sprang up like a jack-in-the box and flew backward, the soldiers yanking their bayonets free.

As Calixte bounced down the hill, Gabriel shouted to Moïse and the others: "They'll kill us like rats in these holes!" and lit out.

Near where the Caron house used to stand, a fold of the riverbank pushed a knob of high ground up on Batoche's Flats. Gabriel ran straight for there, reloaded Le Petit, and set to work slowing the uniforms' downhill momentum. Although they didn't stop, they began to stall and slow up.

He was peripherally aware of a man with a muzzle-loader taking up a position beside him, standing up to squeeze off each shot methodically, as though the buzzing in the air were worth less notice than blackflies. When Le Petit had to be loaded again, Gabriel spared a sideways glance to see who it was and then immediately reamed himself out for the unnecessary waste of an instant's attention to the job at hand. Of course it was Joseph Ouellette.

The waves of red and black and gold kept breaking over the ridge and washing downward. Here and there a little point of resistance jutted into the tide but invariably was swept around and blotted out. Moïse and Michel and Phillipe and a few others of Gabriel's braves had come up to join him on the knoll. On the other side of the meadow, a few guns were firing out of the store windows and the blacksmith shop. They were the last.

Gabriel shouted over the gunfire: "Old man—we can't stay here!"

"Wait just a minute so I can kill another Englishman. Here—

I ain't got no back teeth left." He handed Gabriel a pewter button that was too wide to fit down the barrel of his shotgun.

Gabriel put the button in his mouth and bit down to turn the circle into an oval. He handed it back, not so much saying as exhaling: "All right," then lowered his hand to his hip and finally did what he'd been anticipating since the moment the first bugles blew four days ago—he slipped the holster thong off the hammer of his revolver. "I guess we might just as well die here."

CHAPTER 47

Madelaine and a smattering of the bolder women from the riverbank edged forward through the woods to see what the sudden crescendo of shooting and shouting signified. The government soldiers were pouring down the hill and onto Batoche's Flats. They were all over the Letendre house, firing out of the second-story windows toward the little row of stores that formed the village. Gunfire from the store windows, and from a wooded knoll near the river, was slowing the charge to a crawl.

Suddenly the front ranks of soldiers all fell down. It was explained an instant later when the Gatling gun let loose from behind them, raking the storefronts and Phillipe Garnot's stopping place and everything in between. Madelaine turned to run. A spruce bush beside her exploded, spewing out needles and bits of bark. She threw herself down flat, hugging the ground as the bullets went over. The surface of the river looked as though it were under a spring rain.

La Rababou grew quiet. There was a massed roar and the thudding of hundreds of heavy boots running forward. She looked back over her shoulder. A few Sioux and métis were scrambling out of the back windows of the stores and the blacksmith's shop and running for the trees, trying to keep the buildings between their backs and the oncoming waves of soldiers who were shooting as they came. A gold-braided officer with a sword in one hand and a pistol in the other charged through the doorway of Phillipe Garnot's stopping place and immediately flew back out again with his gold frogging shattered and smoking. The front rank close on his heels swerved around his body, surged inside, and dragged out Damase Carriere, beating him with the butt of his old shotgun and kicking at his splinted leg.

While they were working Damase over, a couple of their friends commandeered the gray pony out of Phillipe Garnot's corral, and another found a length of rope. They tied one end of the rope around Damase's neck and the other to the horse's tail. Then they whipped the pony into a gallop, chasing it around the houses and sheds of Batoche with Damase bouncing behind.

There was no more gunfire in and around the village, except for the occasional whooping soldier shooting in the air. In front of Letendre's store, a mounted officer was herding a troop of infantry into a line. They fixed their bayonets and turned toward the tents along the riverbank. Madelaine decided it was time she got the hell out of there, but as she scrambled back to her feet, she saw something on the ground behind a deadfall to her left. It was a small child, lying face down. She tried shaking his shoulder, then rolled him over. He might have been Isabelle Ouellette's youngest, but it was difficult to tell now—*La Rababou* had finally managed to hit someone.

On the other side of the meadow, Gabriel shifted Le Petit to his left hand and emptied his revolver into the soldiers charging up the face of the knoll. They ran out of steam and fell back to think it over. But before he could reload, old Joseph Ouellette gave out a grunt, rammed his shoulder into Gabriel's, and slid to the ground. Gabriel bent over him. The bullet had taken him through the neck; his eyes were already glazing over.

The soldiers started edging forward, working up their courage for another charge. Gabriel said: "Thank you for your courage, old man, but I don't want to make it easy for them." As the bright tunics surged again up the front of the knoll, Gabriel dove off the back and rolled down into the tangled belt of forest on the riverbank.

By evening, the village at Batoche's Crossing was doing its best to make up for the skyful of low-hanging clouds that had blotted out the sunset—fluming up rolling spheres of flame as the roofs fell in. Not all the buildings had been fired. The general and his staff had had enough of sleeping under canvas.

Gabriel was working his way north through the spruce-scented thicket beyond the gap of Edouard's field. The light of the house fires and the caterwauling of the redcoats barely penetrated.

There were vague scrabblings in the bush all around him—the surviving defenders of Batoche were settling in with their families for the night under cutbanks and bushes before continuing their flight north. Gabriel stopped and gazed up at a ragged jackpine branch clawed against the violet sky, trying to guess where he was and gauge whether it was far enough from the soldiers' new bivouacs to risk a yell. He decided that even if they did hear, they weren't likely to come blundering through the tangled dark to look for him, more's the pity. He unhinged his jaw to turn his chest cavity and skull into an echo cave and bellowed: "Madelaine!"

He waited. A pair of nighthawks scythed between the river and the clouds.

"Gabriel!"

It came from some ways ahead and to his right, where the river jogged east after Isidor's place. He moved in that direction, weaving through the alder thickets by feel. He stopped when he could hear her crashing through the bush toward him. She missed him by a good twenty yards, bulling her way through the bush like a blind black bear. He called: "Here!" The splinter of vegetation swept louder, building to the crescendo of a full-bosomed thunderhead that rammed him chest high, knocked him off his feet, and landed on him like the mother of all herds going over God's buffalo jump.

She said: "You're not hurt?"

"Not up till now."

"Come along." She climbed to her feet and tugged at his hand. "I've got Marguerite and Jean and Marie Angelique. There's a spruce grove with a lot of moss. . . ."

"Louis David?"

"No. No one's seen him. Look at you! In your shirt sleeves—there's going to be frost. . . ."

"What about you? You ain't exactly dressed for a blizzard. And Marguerite and the little ones—I bet they didn't bring their winter coats."

"We'll be fine. We can all spoon up like sled dogs."

"Who knows how many nights we'll have to spend out here?

We're gonna need blankets, at least. I'll go get some. You wait back with the others. I'll find you.''

Gabriel backtracked toward the tipi village that had attached itself to the village of Batoche's Crossing. When he'd skirted around it in the dusk, it had been empty, but as the path took him back past Edouard's place, he could hear the soldiers roistering as boisterously among the tents now as around the burning buildings.

Just north of the cluster of tents, there was a grove of old poplars that formed a colonnade with crowning caps of leafed branches whispering high overhead. Since Duck Lake and the banishment of all the people of Batoche from the church up the hill, Louis David Riel had gathered them together in this grove at sunrise and sunset to pray and sing hymns. The tree at the head of the grove had become a kind of shrine. Fixed to its trunk, at the height of the farthest upreach of Gabriel's arms, was a muslin-draped piece of cardboard that had once been the side of a box of Little Chief Tinned Peaches. A chromo of the Sacred Heart was pinned to the cardboard with several of the tin stars used to label Star Brand Plug Tobacco.

Gabriel was halfway across the grove when someone stepped out of the shadows on the other side. Over the amalgamated murmur of river splash, sighing poplar leaves, and choirs of soldiers singing campfire songs around the embers of houses, a wispy remnant of Riel's voice said: ''How could God let this happen?''

''How could we let this happen?''

''We are . . . defeated. What do we do now?''

''Now? We die.'' Gabriel kept on walking toward his destination, which Louis David happened to be standing in the path of. Within the melting, burning, four-nights'-sleepless, bone-scraped landscape of blue shadows and orange flames, Middleton's soldiers and Louis Riel bled together into one obstacle. Gabriel couldn't say why—he couldn't say much of anything at this point. But he did find himself saying, in a voice whose fierceness would have surprised him if there were enough left of him to surprise, ''You must have known from the beginning it'd end this way.''

He had approached close enough now to see appendage movements: Riel's head jerking down and his arms coming up to cross his wrists behind his neck—like a run-out bull waiting for the axe. Gabriel said softly: ''Marguerite and the children are with Madelaine''—pointing northward—''in a spruce grove. They're all safe, but the frost'll kill them if they got no blankets to sleep in. Just keep heading north along the riverbank and wait with them for me. I'll bring some blankets from our tent.''

''No!'' Louis's hand snaked out toward Gabriel's elbow but then jerked back before touching, as though a spark had cracked out across the gap. ''You mustn't! The soldiers will kill you!''

''They can't kill me. They been doing their damnedest all day. Keep walking north about a quarter mile and call for Madelaine.''

Gabriel walked on south along the riverside path, as though walking to his outhouse. It didn't cross his mind to skulk through the bush. The fires of Batoche grew brighter as the sky grew darker. As the trees thinned out ahead of him, he could make out the light of a bonfire among the tents. He switched Le Petit to his left hand and tugged his knife out of its sheath.

The site Madelaine had chosen to pitch their tent was about twenty yards from the mouth of the path. The bonfire was at the other end of the tent village, surrounded by soldiers comparing souvenirs. One soldier was standing guard in front of Gabriel's tent, leaning on his rifle and gazing sourly at the revelers around the bonfire. Gabriel came out of the woods and walked straight toward him. The soldier glanced at him once, then went back to watching the souvenir hunters—just another of the half-breed mule skinners going about his business. It would have been a smart ploy on Gabriel's part—gambling that the soldiers would hardly expect one of the rebels to come nonchalantly strolling out of the bush—if he'd planned it. He was past caring.

He'd covered about half the distance when the soldier glanced back at him, becoming aware that the half-breed's line of march was to him rather than past him. He still showed no sign of alarm—probably rehearsing his pidgin French for ''I got no tobacco to spare'' and ''The rum's all gone.'' But then a sudden flare-up of the bonfire gleamed on the foot-long blade in Gabriel's right hand. The blue eyes bugged agog at the knife, then came back up to Gabriel's face and bugged wider. At the next instant the soldier was fumbling frantically to turn his leaning post back into a weapon, opening his mouth to yell toward the bonfire, and Gabriel was leaping forward, swinging Le Petit with the fullest extension he could stretch into his left arm. The tip of the barrel caught the soldier across the temple, and he went down like a poleaxed steer before the alarm yell left his mouth.

From inside the tent, a male voice called hesitantly: "George? George, are you . . . ?" and the tent door flapped open. Whether George was being asked whether he was "there" or "all right" or something else remains a mystery. Because as the second soldier crawled out of the tent—with the crown of his uniform cap pointing straight ahead to clear the low doorway—Gabriel spiked the knife straight into the back of his neck. The blade stuck fast, but Gabriel just held his arm stiff and waited for the jerking and bucking of the dead man's nerve spasms to pull it free. As the body fell, he kicked it aside to clear the doorway. It landed across George, who grunted in his sleep.

Gabriel pushed the door flap aside with the barrel of Le Petit and stooped through the opening. If there were more soldiers inside, he would kill them or they would kill him and that would be that. But there were none. He wiped his knife on his pants leg, put it back in its sheath, and scooped up as many blankets and quilts as he could hold in his arms—pressing them against his midriff with Le Petit clutched in both hands.

When he came back out, George was moaning softly and dully pushing one hand against the inexplicable deadweight that was making it hard to breathe. Gabriel waddled off toward the woods, pregnant with blankets. Just before he reached the mouth of the path, a scream of horror ripped through the campfire jollity behind him. He waddled on.

By the time he reached the spruce grove where Madelaine and the Riels were hidden, the night chill had set in. Not that he felt it himself, but they had only been sitting and waiting, and he could see the children shivering. Louis David was shivering as well—huddled against a boulder with his elbows between his knees—but it was hard to say if that was from the cold.

Gabriel peeled his fingers from around Le Petit, dropped the blankets and quilts in a pile, flexed his stiff arms, and said: "Where's Annie?"

Madelaine said: "I don't know. She got away safe. There's a lot of widows with children, she might be helping one of them."

Gabriel handed her a quilt from the top of the pile and said to Riel: "The rest will have to do for you and your family."

"No."

"What?"

"My uncle Gabriel is ever generous"—his uncle Gabriel had to strain his ears to make words out of the shred of a voice— "but there are barely enough blankets for you and Madelaine."

"A quilt and each other—we'll be fine. There's four of you and only two of us."

"No. We couldn't possibly . . ."

He was finally prevailed upon to take the blankets, but he wouldn't take any of the quilts. Madelaine picked up the quilts and said she'd found a bed-size hollow carpeted with moss and spruce needles. Gabriel said: "Good. Go there and keep warm. I'm going back to get some food."

She could say more with silence than anyone he'd ever met. Finally she broke it with: "Suicide's a sin."

"Tell that to the soldiers."

"I'm not hungry."

"The children are."

She let out a long breath and said: "There's a bag of dried meat in the tent, and a sack of flour. I'll look around here while you're gone and find where the women with children are hiding."

The soldiers had all cleared out of the tipis, leaving the bonfire to die on its own. When he'd brought back the food and given it to Madelaine to distribute, there were a few particularly timorous families who hoped they could be escorted farther north before settling in for the night. He asked Madelaine to wait for him in the spruce hollow: "If the soldiers manage to work up the courage to come out tonight, and if they was to find you and try to blame you for what I done—tell them that if the government couldn't make me behave, they can't hardly expect you to."

But he couldn't evade forever the moment when they were wrapped together in the dark and he had no tasks left to stand in front of him. He could tell from her breathing that she wasn't sleeping. After a long time, he said: "I can't help but think . . . that if it wasn't for me, you'd be lying safe and warm in your own bed in your own home."

"I am."

CHAPTER 48

Marie Angelique and Jean were hungry in the morning. So was everybody else, but the children hadn't learned that there are discomforts in life that won't change no matter how much you beg; they can just be lived through. And if they're not lived through, of course, they cease to be discomforts.

Madelaine was surprised, though, by how well they managed to hold it in, only letting out the occasional little mewing sound from where they sat rocking together with a blanket wrapped around them. She took Gabriel's hat down to the riverbank, rinsed off as much of the sweat and grime as possible, and brought it back with its crown full of river for Marie Angelique and Jean to slurp up little handfuls so they'd have at least something in their stomachs—last night's dried meat and flour hadn't gone very far among all the hungry mouths. Marguerite managed a trip down to the shore on her own, even though she was obviously terrified by Gabriel's offhand announcement that daylight would bring the government troops out combing the woods.

All in all, Madelaine was also pleasantly surprised by how stoically Marguerite was bearing up—considering that this was probably the first time in her life she'd woken up with no prospect of breakfast and armed men beating the bushes looking for her. Perhaps she'd just been shocked dumb by what had happened to her husband. Louis David was rocking back and forth like the children, lips murmuring soundlessly in fervent conversation with himself or one of the other saints.

The instant that that sarcasm tagged itself onto her train of thought, Madelaine regretted it. It was a bit like backhanding a heartbroken child because its weeping has grown annoying. The world that had collapsed around Louis David was hers as well, and Gabriel's.

Gabriel's state of mind was even more alarming to her, although for entirely different reasons. After a half night's sleep,

336

he'd woken up with the lights in his eyes rekindled, looking dirty and dangerous and moving with a grim energy. He was sitting cross-legged on a cushion of moss, counting the cartridges left in the bag after filling the loops on his cartridge belt. The only articles she'd scooped up in her flight from the soldiers had been her tobacco pouch and pipe and his sack of cartridges.

He dumped the cartridges back in the bag, pulled the drawstring shut, wiped a last speck of grease off Le Petit, then sprang to his feet and walked toward her. He handed the bag of bullets into her custody and said: "First thing is to find some horses. A lot ran off from Batoche while the shelling was going on, and a lot more when the soldiers opened the corrals. If I can't find some strays, I'll steal a few off Middleton's pickets. Been a while since I had a chance to do some horse raiding."

Riel suddenly jerked his head up with a kind of awed surprise. "Do you think we can escape?"

"Escape? It's them that'll want to escape. We still got a few dozen good fellows in the bush. Even without them, I think I can make it unpleasant for big-footed fools stomping around in my garden."

Riel shook his head, lowering his eyes and his voice. "It's over."

Gabriel's eyes and voice stayed level and terrifying. "Maybe for you it is. They killed my friends and burned my house and chased my wife out into the woods like an animal."

Perhaps if they had been alone, she would have tried to argue with him; but not with the Riels here. And in his present frame of mind she probably wouldn't have accomplished anything except make him angrier. He turned his attention from Riel to her and said: "You should be safe here till I get back. Their scouts'll be real slow and wary about working their way in through the bush. I'll bring back some horses and some food."

She said: "Be careful," without much hope of it.

When he was gone she found herself a patch of sunlight near the river and sat smoking her pipe with a blanket shawled over her shoulders. She couldn't seem to get warm. Marguerite and the children came and perched on a deadfall nearby. Madelaine resented the intrusion. After yesterday she was no longer obligated to keep up the pretense of a common bond. Mixed in with all her other emotions about the fall of Batoche, there was an element almost of relief. Now that the hopes of the community along the South Saskatchewan were shattered, she didn't have to be concerned with anyone except herself and Gabriel.

The Riel brats were squeaking like an ungreased gate in a windstorm. Their mother was even more aggravating, with her ridiculous attempts to distract their attention from their bellies: "Do you hear that bird cheeping, Jean? What kind of a bird do you think that is?" The shadows under Marguerite's eyes were such a fervent blue, they would have turned White Cap's gaudiest warrior green with envy. The swelling in her belly had belled out far enough now to signify a child, rather than the amorphous lumps of red gelatin that had broken Madelaine's heart three times.

Madelaine knocked her pipe out, shrugged off the blanket, and heaved her old bones up on their feet. "Come on, you two. It's way too early in the year for wild parsnips, but there's a rise in the ground over there I bet's perfect for last year's bearberries. Careful over the rocks, Marie Angelique. Lucky for us the plains grizzlies got all killed off years ago—in the old days you wouldn't dare go looking for bearberries without at least three men with guns. And even then, there was this one time when my father and Mister Grant and your uncle Gabriel, who was barely bigger than a boy then . . ."

Gabriel went all the way through the tree belt to the edge of the plains without coming across any other remnants of the Army of the Exovedate. They must have all gone farther north in the woods or taken refuge in the farms along the river. He was skirting along just within the fringe of bush cover when he heard a horse nicker.

It was somewhere out on the prairie, down in one of the coulees out of sight. To look for it, he'd have to venture across open ground. He thought of crawling forward through the tall grass, then decided to hell with it and walked straight out with Le Petit cradled in the crook of his arm. For one thing, he'd only seen one army patrol all morning, and they'd been far to the south. For another, the mood of last night hadn't left him entirely—if they saw him, they could take their chances.

He did make a point of walking softly, though, for fear of scaring the horse. For that matter, there was no guarantee that the horse wasn't one of a cavalry troop hunting for him. He reached the edge of the coulee and looked down.

It was a lone horse, unsaddled and unbridled, nibbling away at a succulent patch of new grass. It didn't seem possible, but by all the signs—the white blaze under the floppy forelock, the three white stockings, the habitual placid expression of a horse that could barely rouse itself to plod across a barnyard, and the puckered furrow across the hair on the right flank—it was by God old Starface. He opened his mouth to call him, then noticed that the wind was gusting from behind, bending the grass stalks and asters over the lip of the coulee. He closed his mouth and smiled to himself and waited.

After a moment, Starface suddenly jerked his head partway up—strands of salad like a goatee on his lower jaw—then shook his head and lowered it again, reaching for more breakfast while still chewing the last mouthful. Then his widened nostrils caught the message on the wind again. He peered sideways, stretched his lips back from his teeth, and arched his neck to whinny out a horse laugh.

Gabriel climbed down the slope, mostly by sliding on the heels of his moccasins, clutching at passing willow shafts to keep his balance. Starface had gone back to his breakfast, affecting a blasé, jaded attitude. But he did putter his lips together when Gabriel put his hand on his neck.

More decades than Gabriel cared to count had passed since he'd last ridden a horse bareback and bridleless. But if there was any horse that owed him the benefit of the doubt . . . He grabbed a handful of neck mane and vaulted aboard. Starface nipped at his ankles for form's sake, then carried him up out of the coulee.

A distinct scent of sizzling beef came wafting over the prairie. Perhaps it was so slight as to pass unnoticed on any other day, but at the moment Gabriel could taste it all the way down into the pit of his stomach. He followed his nose north and back into the bush. In a bowl under a poplar ridge, Alexis was helping Eli butcher a steer. Mother ''Batoche'' was ministering to a cooking fire. Phillipe Garnot and his wife were impaling chunks of bloody beef on green willow wands fenced around the glowing bed of coals. Salivating around the edges were a dozen barefoot children—Garnots and strayed Ouellettes and other flotsam. As Gabriel walked his horse into the clearing, Eli didn't look up from his hacking but muttered loudly: ''Yeah—figured you was too mean to kill.''

''Seen Edouard?''

''Not since yesterday. Seen Riel?''

''He's back with Madelaine and Marguerite and the children. I should take them something to eat.''

Mother "Batoche" shrieked: "Not yet, unless you want worms."

Gabriel had never heard of anyone getting worms from rare beef, but he wasn't about to start a fight with Mother "Batoche." He looked around at the barefoot children. It was perfectly standard practice for them to go unshod from the time the last snow patch melted until the ground froze again. Gabriel could remember squelching mud through his toes as the best rite of spring. But usually they wouldn't be doing this kind of extended running over broken ground until the gradual progress of the summer had given them a chance to build up calluses. The older children were trying to set an example by sitting stiff-necked and tight-lipped with their cut and bleeding feet extended in front of them.

The steer's hide was laid out bloodside to the sun. Gabriel slid off his horse, snicked his knife out of its sheath, sliced the legs of the cow-hide into strips, and cut the strips free. He flipped the hide over, waved the children forward, and—starting with the youngest—stood them on the dappled hide and cut outsize ovals around their feet. Around the rim of each oval he made slits to thread the strips through. By the time there was nothing left of the steer's skin but thumb-size triangles, every little foot was laced into a crude approximation of a fur-lined moccasin, with the still-moist insides on the outside. All except Alexis, who was a Dumont and would tough his way through anything that didn't kill him.

Mother "Batoche" announced that the beef chunks looked black enough to suggest they weren't raw in the middle. Gabriel took off his shirt to make a bag for half a dozen of them, then squatted almost to the ground to get enough spring in his aging knees to jump onto his horse. He just made it. He called to Eli: "Your family's safe?"

Eli nodded. "Should be all right at Aicawpow's. I was working my way north to there when I came across this bunch chasing some poor dumb maverick steer."

"Well, I'll look for you there. Tell the old man me and Madelaine are still alive."

There was no sign of anyone around the spruce grove. He realized that the sound of Starface's hooves approaching wouldn't be discernibly different from that of a cavalry scout. He clucked Starface to a halt and hooted like a whippoorwill—which Madelaine would know damn well wouldn't sing in broad daylight.

She came out of a cranny where a skirt of spruce boughs pressed against a rock, brushing off clinging bits of twigs and dirt. Her cheeks were caved in and roweled, and there was a gray tinge creeping into her skin that he didn't like the look of. He said: "Where's the Riels?"

"Gone to Jean Delorme's farm. Louis figured they'd put up Marguerite and the children and he'll go back into the woods."

"You shouldn't have let him go."

"How could I stop him? I gave him my gun, that was all I could do."

"You gave him *what*?"

"My revolver, the little twenty-two."

"In the state of mind he's in?"

"Don't be ridiculous. He's far too religious to ever think of shooting himself. I don't know if he could bring himself to shoot anybody else, even to save his children, but at least he's got it if it comes to that." She gestured at his vest-clad torso. "Sun get too hot for you?"

"I needed a food sack. Come on." He slid off Starface's back, took her hand, and led her to a spot on the riverbank where a willow tree's overhang covered the shore. Hidden under the rippling green curtain, they savored their time crunching through crusts of charcoal to the spurts of hot beef juice inside, washing it down with handfuls of sweet-flowing river water. When all six chunks were gone, Gabriel took off his vest, shook the crumbs from the tablecloth, and turned it back into a shirt. Belching happily, he climbed to the spruce cave and brought back the quilts, spreading them out beside the willow pool.

What with their first stomachful of warm food in thirty-some hours, and the accumulated short rations of sleep, they both dozed off. When they awoke the sun was bending to the west, and Madelaine looked a little healthier. They decided they should move on farther north before nightfall. They spent the night in a hazel thicket by a slough, grateful for the night chill that kept the mosquito hatcheries from opening for business until later in the year.

Gabriel drifted for a long time along the border of sleep. The air was sweet with the resin of balsam poplar and cedar bushes. Nightbirds and crickets, and the gentle rustling of high grass and spring leaves ruffled by the breeze, melded into a lulling, constant murmur. He was ashamed to discover a portion of himself dreaming of an escape to somewhere where he and Madelaine could spend a safe summerful of sweet-scented nights under the stars and sun-soaked days lolling by a fishing pond or stalking venison. He reminded himself that the war wasn't over.

They were awakened by a blaring mob of waterbirds all pulling their beaks out from under their wings at once to discuss the dawn. Gabriel said: "I could kill a couple of them for you, and you could roast them up while I'm out scouting."

"Do you think it's safe to build a fire out here in the open?"

"Since when couldn't you build a smokeless campfire? Or maybe it'd be best for us to start moving right away, and work our way north to Aicawpow's. You'd be safe there. If the soldiers do go there, they'll be looking for me, not you."

"What about you?"

"I'll fix myself a few little dens in ravines to hole up in when I need to sleep. There's a lot of farms where if I was to come calling in the middle of the night they'd give me a bite to eat. And it's a good time of the year for hunting."

"What will that accomplish?"

"Roast grouse, rabbit stew . . . ."

"I meant the other hunting you're planning to do. What good will it do to kill more soldiers? Everyone's run away."

"Not everyone. And those that have will start coming back when they see how easy it is to pick off the redcoats and stay free. We can get down to fighting this war the way we should've from the start."

She sucked her upper lip in between her teeth and gazed off at the horizon. After a moment she murmured: "Maybe it's best I go to Aicawpow's."

There was a lot of open country between their hazel pond and Aicawpow's farm. Gabriel put Madelaine on Starface and followed along after them, keeping to what cover he could, jogging hunched over through the tall grass, putting out a burst of speed whenever the gap between them threatened to open up wider than a hundred yards. He had a twinge of horror for an instant when he wondered whether he was guarding his wife or using her as bait, but he dismissed it.

When the chimney of his father's house came into view, Gabriel stopped and crouched down. Middleton could have put a watch on the place. There were plenty of poplar bluffs where scouts with spyglasses could hide. He called after Madelaine in a voice just loud enough to carry across the distance between them: "I'll come see you tonight." She didn't reply or turn to look back, just made a cupping and closing motion with her hand behind her waist, as though taking hold of his hand.

He waited and watched as she walked the horse into the yard, as Aicawpow's youngest son by his second marriage left off splitting firewood and started toward her. When Aicawpow's winter-oak-tree frame stooped out through the doorway, Gabriel turned and started back. He kept up his hunched-over, cover-hugging dog trot until his father's house and outbuildings had blended into the prairie behind him. Then he straightened his spine and let his legs stretch out into an easy, rolling lope, Le Petit bouncing loosely in his hand, wolf eyes scanning the horizon for the silhouettes of horsemen.

CHAPTER 49

Madelaine was sitting on a rocking chair in the sunlight in front of Aicawpow's house, discussing with the old man the question of whether his son was losing his mind, when the government soldiers rode into the yard. Only one of them was in uniform—Inspector Gagnon of the Mounted Police, and his brass buttons were hidden under his waist-length beard. He was the only policeman she'd ever seen who managed to keep the silly little pillbox hat perched on his head without tying it down.

The cavalry troop that trotted in behind him was dressed in an eccentric amalgam of dust-colored, sun-bleached work clothes and weather-shaped slouch hats. They lounged loosely in their saddles like the cowboys they were. Inspector Gagnon translated for "the Major"—a leather-and-wire construct with a droopy gray mustache. "General Middleton has declared a general amnesty for all except the active leaders of the rebellion—on the condition that you surrender up your weapons. The ringleaders will be judged on a case-by-case basis, and a fair trial is guaranteed for all."

Aicawpow creaked painfully up off his chair and said in French: "I'm too old to have done any fighting."

Inspector Gagnon translated that to "the Major," who muttered curtly through his mustache. "The Major says they found the bodies of men a lot older than you in the rifle pits at Batoche."

"Well, maybe they *looked* older. . . . If I give up my hunting guns to you, how can I feed my family?"

"The Major says you appear to have a lot of cows and chickens about the place. Not to mention pigs, he says, by the smell. The Major will give you a receipt, in the Queen's name, for all confiscated weapons. You can get them back as soon as the ringleaders are in custody." The upshot was that Inspector Gagnon and two of the cowboys climbed off their horses and rummaged through Aicawpow's house, emerging with an antediluvian flintlock musket and a double-barreled fowling piece with a thong-bound cracked stock.

One of "the Major's" troop flipped open a receipt book. "The Major" told him coldly: "Just scribble a bunch of naughts and crosses over it and we can get on to the next . . ."

"I think that will hardly do," Madelaine said in English. "We'll require a signature from Inspector Gagnon and the officer in charge, and a written description of each piece of private property you're expropriating."

"The Major" hooked his hawk nose around to point at her and said: "You speak English."

She blinked back at him blandly and said: "No."

"The Major's" eyes batted like a heliograph. A couple of the cowboys laughed. He shushed them with a glance and then turned back fiercely to her and Aicawpow. "You people had better start getting it through your heads that you've just been defeated in a treasonous uprising against your Queen and country. Today the whole damned district is filled with poor, simple farmers who didn't take part in the rebellion—but someone did, and don't fool yourselves that we aren't going to find out every last one. Sergeant"—turning to Inspector Gagnon—"take down that woman's name."

Inspector Gagnon—or Sergeant, they never could make up their minds—maintained a straight-ahead gaze at the interesting eaves of Aicawpow's house and drawled: "Oh, I don't think we'll have to write it down to remember. And I don't think she'll try to tell you her husband had no part in the rebellion. Her name is Madelaine Dumont, AKA Madame Gabriel.''

The cowboys suddenly stopped slouching. A number of them discovered an urge to scratch their shoulders with their chins or to allow their horses to turn in a circle. A cursory receipt was filled out quickly. Inspector Gagnon handed it down to her, muttering in French: ''You are a very, very wicked woman.'' ''The Major's'' troop trotted out of the yard in double file, eyes flicking from side to side and hands surreptitiously loosening their sidearms in their holsters.

As the hoofbeats faded, Aicawpow waved his hand to catch the attention of Gabriel's half-brother working at the chopping block, then nodded his head. The boy pried up a corner of the woodpile and came forward blowing sawdust off a repeating rifle and the lovely long-barreled shotgun that his father's two oldest sons had given him for his seventy-fifth birthday. Aicawpow told him: ''For now maybe you better wrap them up in a blanket and dig a hole under one of the cow stalls.''

Madelaine reloaded her pipe and handed her tobacco pouch across to her father-in-law. They sat smoking in silence and soaking up the spring sunshine for some time. Then Aicawpow popped the pipe stem out of his mouth and sighed in a pebbly voice: ''The worst thing there is is for your grown children to die before you. Isidor was bad enough, but at least that was in a war—oh, yes, murdered under a white flag, but still part of a fight for something. If Gabriel was to go down now, when there's nothing left to fight for . . .''

''He thinks if he keeps on fighting, others will join him.''

''He's wrong. Hell, once Edouard and Eli have quit, he should know. Eli's took his family back north, and Edouard's loaded his on a couple of carts to cut southwest through the badlands and get across the medicine line. Not that it'll make any difference to Gabriel that he'll have to fight alone.''

''He's coming here tonight. Will you try and talk some sense into him?''

''I don't see how I can if you can't. The only time he ever listened to anyone more'n you was that little while when Riel had him hypnotized, but that's over now. Isn't it?''

She dismissed Louis David with a snort. ''But I can't tell Gabriel about this kind of thing. A long time ago we made a deal: he don't try to tell me how to add up the ledgers or write a letter, and I don't try to tell him how to ride a horse or fight a war. You're about the only man he knows who's fought more wars than he has."

One of Gabriel's half-sisters came running from the direction of the riverbank, pointing her arm back over her shoulder and shouting for them to come and look. Aicawpow craned himself out of his chair, grunting with each unfolding joint. Madelaine was suddenly alarmed at how stiff and emaciated he'd become. She'd thought that his painful rising to address "The Major" had been a performance. The immenseness of his bones was deceptive; it took more than a second look to see that there was nothing there but calico-clad bones and parchment. He walked with a punctuating wheeze; only the length of his legs made it a healthy pace.

What his daughter wanted them to see was on the other side of the river, where the riverbank folded up on itself to form a high crest about halfway between Aicawpow's farm and Batoche's Crossing. A large group of horsemen—Madelaine guessed about fifty or sixty—were standing in their stirrups, looking downstream toward Batoche. From that vantage point they should be able to see the white flags flying over the houses. They turned their horses to the west and began the long ride back to their homes around Fort Edmonton.

Aicawpow stood watching them go, brittle arms crossed tightly and black eyes burning. He said huskily: "Goddamn. Even with all that, he still almost beat them."

Madelaine said: "What about Poundmaker? And Big Bear?"

"They'll do the same as what we just saw, if they haven't already. They were coming to join Gabriel's army, not be it."

Sometime between midnight and dawn, a deep voice boomed out inside Aicawpow's house: "If I was a Sioux, I'd sure be having a fine scalp dance."

Madelaine climbed out of her jury-rigged bed in a corner and came to the table, where Gabriel was lighting a lamp. Aicawpow shuffled out of his bedroom, grumbling: "What the hell happened to my dogs?"

"Same thing as used to happen to mine when you came calling. They licked my hands and wagged their tails and went back to sleep."

Madelaine stoked up the fire to make tea and rummaged through Aicawpow's wife's pantry. Gabriel said: "I heard Moïse Ouellette's got a letter from Middleton to give to Riel. Anybody know what's in it?"

"We ain't seen Moïse." Madelaine put a slab of cold duck pie down on the table, and Gabriel descended upon it. Then she went to fix the tea, determined to keep out of the way of Aicawpow's attempt to talk sense to his son.

Aicawpow began with an offhanded "Kill many of them today?"

Gabriel shook his head and spoke between mouthfuls. "They had about two hundred horsemen out looking for me, but I was in behind them. I watched them for a long while from a hill, figuring on knocking over any that strayed from the main bunch, but none of them did. All day long I been picking up ammunition. Amazing what people will drop around a battlefield."

"So tomorrow you'll get started on the killing?" Gabriel nodded and chewed. "How many do you figure you'll get before they kill you?"

"They won't. And once a few others join in with me . . ."

"No one will."

Madelaine set a cup of tea in front of each of them and said: "Edouard's already started south to escape to the States," then reminded herself that she'd decided to keep her mouth shut. •

Gabriel looked from one to the other of them, picked his teeth with his tongue, sipped his tea, smacked his lips, and went back to munching up the crusty rim of duck pie. Aicawpow said: "You almost won it for us. No man could've done more."

"I can try."

Aicawpow cocked his elbow on the tabletop, aimed his forefinger at his son's nose, and said: "Now you listen to me. I'm proud you haven't given up, but if you stay around here just to kill people, you're going to be thought of as an idiot."

Gabriel wet his finger to mop up the crumbs, downed the rest of his cup of black tea, and again looked from his wife to his father and back again. Madelaine took his cup away to refill it. When she brought it back, he said: "So you figure I should give myself up so they can give me a fair trial before they hang me?"

Aicawpow said: "Don't be stupid. You should get the hell out of here and across the line like Edouard. Once you're out of the Canadian government's reach, you can wait and see if maybe they'll stop howling for your blood after a while."

"Maybe Edouard can do it, but . . . I hate to be the one to have to tell you, Papa, but not all your sons grew up as well known as some others. If Edouard and his family get spotted out on the prairie by some Police patrol, the odds are good he'll be able to convince them he's just Jean Baptiste from Lac La-Biche goin' sout' for da fishe. But there ain't a lot of Policemen or volunteer cavalry that don't got at least some picture in their minds of this ugly excuse for a face."

"They have to see you before they can recognize you. You can stick to the ravines and broken country—you don't have a family to cart along with you like Edouard."

"I got a wife."

Madelaine said: "I could go down later on in the summer with one of the freight cart trains and meet up with you at my brother's place in Montana. God knows I've done longer trips on my own when I used to take your furs in to Red River while you were out with the spring hunt. And it might help throw them off your track—as long as I'm still here they'll think you might be."

Gabriel shook his head. "I'd rather go down fighting than running, and that's all that'd come of it. Seven hundred miles across the prairie with every policeman and soldier in the North West looking for me . . ."

Aicawpow said: "You did it last year, and that was with two buggies and a wagon."

"No, then it was just the regular patrols, and they were only sort of looking for me—'Oh by the way, Corporal, if you happen to run across Gabriel Dumont . . .' Now it's all the Police and the whole army, and they really want to find me."

"Do you think so?" Madelaine wasn't having much luck sitting on her tongue. "If you were a couple of Mounted Police out on patrol and you saw a speck on the horizon that you thought might be Gabriel Dumont, do you think you'd ride real hard to catch up with him?"

"Maybe not—but they could ride real hard to tell one of the patrols of thirty or forty that wouldn't be far away."

"If I believed that any son of mine couldn't ride from here to the Rockies and back without getting spotted by a bunch of white cavalry, I'd tie a sack over my head and ask someone to throw me in the river."

Gabriel looked from one to the other of them again, scratched his beard fiercely, and told the ceiling: "And I thought twelve to one at Tourond's Coulee was bad odds." He lowered his eyes to his father. "All my life I've followed your advice. Maybe I want to do it this time. But first I have to go see Moïse Ouellette and find out what's in that letter from Middleton. If that don't change anything . . . well, I got a good horse in your paddock, but I'll have to borrow a saddle.''

Aicawpow drew in his chin, rocked back in his chair, and sucked in a grimaced hiss of air. ''Hey, your wife didn't say nothing to me about borrowing nothing. . . .''

CHAPTER 50

Moïse Ouellette and Gabriel's sister Isabelle had surprised a clutch of soldiers mounting a dawn raid on their henhouse and were avidly bargaining market prices with the ranking officer. Le Petit could have easily drilled a hole in every uniform from the gooseberry bush in the Ouellettes' cow pasture that Gabriel was crouched behind. Instead, Gabriel waited for the soldiers to leave, waited until Moïse and Isabelle were chortling over the handfuls of coins they'd just got for two scrawny pullets, then leaned up and tongued out an awkward imitation of the ricochet cry of a killdeer. Moïse raised his head. Gabriel repeated the call—again, an approximation that would only fool a town man.

Moïse suddenly remembered he'd been meaning to check those loose shingles on the outhouse roof. He climbed up, stood up, idly scanned the horizon, and then waved Gabriel in. As Gabriel came into the yard, Moïse climbed down and Isabelle called over one of their adolescent daughters to take his place and keep watch. Gabriel kissed his sister and assured her that Aicawpow and Madelaine were both fine, then he and Moïse sat down with their backs against the front wall of the house while she went inside to make tea.

Moïse passed Gabriel his tobacco pouch and said: ''Yup, they been combing the woods pretty good for you.''

''Not good enough.'' He added, winking, ''But maybe soon a few unlucky ones might stumble across me.'' The Moïse he'd known all his life would have laughed, or at least grinned ap-

preciatively. This one just stared somberly at the ground between his moccasins.

Gabriel dipped his pipe in Moïse's tobacco and said: "Yup,
wouldn't take very many of us to raise holy hell in their camp
some night."

"I gave in my rifle."

"You what?"

"What choice did I have? It was either that or leave my family
alone while I hide in the bush hugging my rifle until the soldiers
catch me and kill me."

"They couldn't catch my cross-eyed grandmother."

"There's over eight hundred of them, Gabriel! And a lot
more'n that when the Police come down from Prince Albert. It
don't matter how thick their boots and their brains are, they're
eventually gonna stumble over anyone that's trying to hide from
them. They told me if I gave in my gun I could stay here and
get the fields seeded, and in a few weeks they'll come and take
me and the other Exovedes down to Regina for trial."

"Trial for *what*? For defending your homes from the same
government that's going to judge you for it? The government
has sheared you like sheep, and now you're all baa-ing along
wherever their dogs want to herd you."

"It's different for the rest of us, Gabriel. We got to try to save
what we can for the sake of our children."

"I thought that's what we started this for."

Isabelle came out carrying three tin cups of tea, took one
look at her brother and her husband, then set two of the cups on
the grass between them and carried the third back inside. Gabriel gave Moïse back his tobacco pouch, lit his pipe, sucked in
a swallow of tarry tea, and said: "I heard you got a letter for
Riel, from Middleton."

"It's written to Riel, but it's meant for you as well."

"What's it say?"

"It promises if you give yourselves up you won't be harmed
by the soldiers, and the government'll give you a fair trial."

"Like the trial you'd give a skunk in your henhouse. Well,
give me the letter and I'll hunt through the woods for Riel."

"I already gave it to him."

"What did he say?"

"He said it seemed like the best thing to do."

"What did?"

"To give himself up."

Gabriel didn't believe him at first. It seemed so patently obvious that even if the Moïse Ouellettes and Phillipe Garnots might stand a slim chance of a fair hearing in John A. Macdonald's courts, Louis Riel had no chance at all. When Moïse finally convinced him that Riel had taken Middleton's promises at face value, Gabriel snatched up Le Petit and sprang to his feet. "Where did you leave him?"

"There's nothing you can do for him now."

"I can tell him not to shove his head in a noose!"

"You're too late. Whether you're right or not, he's already sitting in Middleton's camp with the whole army guarding him. As soon as he read the letter he said he was going straight in to surrender."

Gabriel lowered his head. It seemed that everything he did was too late. Moïse added: "Next time the soldiers come by, they're bound to want to know if I got the message to you, and what you had to say in reply."

"You tell them . . . tell Middleton I still got ninety cartridges to give to ninety of his men."

He turned his back on Moïse and stalked into the riverside woods. As soon as he was well away from the Ouellette farm, though, his stride lost its purpose and he sat down on the riverbank. The pelicans were soaring. A song sparrow twittered from a clump of wolf willow.

He wondered if the morning when he left Louis David sitting shattered on the riverbank to go and find some horses would be the last time they met in this life. If only he'd come straight to Moïse's yesterday the instant he heard about the letter, instead of amusing himself with shadowing the soldiers who were hunting him, he might have been able to save him. He had never expected that Louis would do anything drastic without taking some time to work up to it.

Come to think of it, Moïse's story didn't make any sense. It was utterly unlike Riel to make such a momentous decision without a lot of prayer and meditation, and once he did come to the decision he would certainly want to say good-bye to his wife and children instead of marching off immediately for Middleton's camp. Moïse had always been against Louis David in the Exovedate, and now he had lied to keep Gabriel from talking Louis out of going to his death.

Gabriel was about to charge back up the Ouellettes' farm, when another reason occurred to him for why Moïse might have lied. The past few months might have suggested to him that the odds weren't so much on Gabriel talking Louis David out of surrendering as on Louis talking Gabriel into it.

Gabriel began to laugh. It didn't seem to him like much more than an under-the-breath chortle, but he guessed he must have laughed a lot longer and harder than he'd thought, given the tears rolling down his cheeks.

A whippoorwill called in daylight. Gabriel swiveled in that direction and returned the call. Alexis came out of the bush. Gabriel said: "You shouldn't be roaming about with the army scouts out—they're jittery and blind enough to shoot at anyone."

"I ain't 'roaming about,' I got sent to bring you a message. And these," producing a bag made out of a flour sack corner. It turned out to be filled with a few *beignes croches*. Gabriel patted a stump beside him, and they sat munching while Alexis got on with his message. "Aunt Madelaine said you'd be coming by Uncle Moïse's today. He told me you'd gone this way. The message was that there's so many soldiers watching Aicawpow's farm that it ain't safe for you to go there, even at night. If you want to get a message to them or get something from there, I'm small enough to sneak past any soldiers. Or if they do catch me, they won't care about a boy lost in the dark going to his great-uncle's place to borrow a horse to ride home. And the soldiers wouldn't know Starface from a moose."

"Uh-huh—did you just happen to mention this horse business as a 'for instance,' or is it something your aunt Madelaine said?" Alexis squirmed ingenuously. Gabriel laughed. "Come on—we got a long walk through the bush and probably a lot of diving into gopher holes along the way."

Nightfall found the two of them napping in a cave where the river had eaten away the bank under the roots of a big old willow. Gabriel woke up and nudged Alexis, and the two of them wormed their way up through the bush to where they could see the tip of Aicawpow's chimney blotting the stars. Gabriel stopped and whispered to Alexis: "If you hear the least sound of a voice, or a horse stamping, or metal clicking, you shout out in your highest-pitched voice: 'Don't shoot, I'm just a poor lost boy.' Now, do you remember every word of the messages to your aunt Madelaine and my father?"

"Yes."

Gabriel believed him. Like most people of illiterate traditions, Gabriel was constantly amazed at the feeble memories of those who considered themselves educated. Alexis hadn't spent enough years in the mission school yet for his natural faculties to become corroded.

Gabriel waited as Alexis crawled onto the dark meadow and disappeared. They had arranged to rendezvous under the unmistakable silhouette of a lightning-blasted pine tree about a mile north. But Gabriel stayed where he was, waiting for the sound of a gunshot. If one soldier fired into the dark toward Alexis, Gabriel was coming out with both guns blazing.

He waited through half again the time it should've taken Alexis to reach the farmhouse, then he slunk back into the bush and started north. When he'd been crouched beside the twisted tree for half an hour or so, he heard voices out on the plain—several deep ones and a lighter one. They faded out. A horse approached. Starface trotted into the starlit clearing, and Alexis climbed down off the saddle. It wasn't one of the battered old spare saddles that everyone accumulated over the years; it was the harness equivalant of Le Petit. Alexis said: "Aicawpow said to tell you first off that he's too old to ride anymore anyways."

"I heard voices out on the prairie."

"Well, I snuck by 'em on foot easy enough, but they were bound to hear the hoofbeats. I told 'em the story Aunt Madelaine made up, about getting lost and borrowing a horse to get home. They patted me on the head and told me not to soil my diapers if I heard an owl."

"Did you pass on my messages?"

"I told Aunt Madelaine you'd said: 'Wait till there's a cart train heading to Montana, don't try to come on your own—I can live through a couple extra weeks of waiting.' "

"And what did she say?"

" 'I might not.' And I told Aicawpow you'd said to tell him: 'If you die before I come back, I'll kill you.' He said something back to tell you. I can't figure it, but I'm pretty sure I got the words right. . . . Maybe I got it mixed up."

"What did he say?"

"I think he said: 'Tell Gabriel I got good reasons to be proud of all my children. But he's the only one ever made me wonder whether his sainted mother's virtue might've been tried too hard by a better man than me, on one of them nights I was out muskrat hunting.' Does that make sense? Maybe I didn't get it right."

Gabriel couldn't find a voice to reply. "Well, anyways . . . Aunt

Madelaine said to tell you one more thing. 'I'll make you a deal, old man . . .' I'm just telling you her words, Uncle Gabriel— 'I'll make you a deal, old man, if you get your ass there in one piece, I will, too.' "

Starface was butting his nose up against Gabriel's chest, eager to go. Gabriel put his foot in the stirrup. Alexis's "Uncle Gabriel!" didn't come until he was halfway up to the saddle, so he couldn't pause to hear the rest until he was mounted with Starface stamping impatiently. "Aunt Madelaine said she couldn't send any more'n this if the soldiers were going to believe my story." He reached into his shirt and handed up a half dozen *galettes* that had been riding on his *ceinture flèche*.

Gabriel stuffed them in his own shirt and opened his mouth to say some kind of thanks and farewell to the next generation's budding Gabriel or Aicawpow or Mister Grant. But the only words that would come out were a croaked "I'm sorry." He gave Starface his head and plunged into the night.

He rode south along the ragged line where the riverside woods met the plains. When he got close to the plot of land that Aicawpow owned today and some white Canadian might own tomorrow, he wrestled Starface to a walk so that the hoof thuds wouldn't be loud enough to alert the soldiers. The course he'd mapped out was to hug the curtain of the woods along the river until he'd got halfway between the scouts watching Aicawpow's place and the bulk of the army camped at Batoche's Crossing. Then he'd cut east at a gallop. The remaining hours of darkness should give him plenty of time to hook around the main camp and be long gone to the south before the dawn brought enough light to make him and Starface anything more than distant hoof-beats in the night.

Starface had barely hit his stride, though, when a voice called out: "Gabriel!" and there was the sound of hooves galloping after him.

While his left hand took the reins and spun his horse around to face the voice, Gabriel's right hand was spiraling Le Petit out of the scabbard and cocking it in midair. "Gabriel!" came again, and this time he recognized the voice. Michel Dumas coalesced out of the shadows—hatless, coatless, and weaponless—bouncing on a horse as much taller than Starface as Michel was to Gabriel. "Moïse told me you're heading across the line."

"Ssh! I'm going to try. What happened to your fancy new rifle?"

"I lost it when they chased us out of Batoche. Picked up a good horse, though. I been thinking of trying the run to the medicine line. But trying it alone, without a gun for hunting or fighting off the Police . . ."

"Ain't going to get much chance for hunting. Got any food?"

"Two *galettes*!"

"Two magic beans, Mother!" Michel looked miffed at Gabriel's laughter. "Well, what the hell, Michel—odds are they'll chase us down and kill us long before we starve to death."

They worked up quickly to a gallop, Gabriel holding Starface in so as not to leave Michel's long-legged stolen stallion behind. Michel called jovially across the hoof drumming and the gap between them: "Funny thing, ain't it? Just exactly a year ago almost to the day."

Gabriel was about to yell back: "Since when?" when he realized Michel meant the last occasion they'd set off south to Montana. Gabriel growled back: "Ride—don't talk."

PART FIVE

Gabriel knows the prairies as a sheep knows its heath, and can go anywhere blindfolded. They'll never catch him.

JOHN ANDREW KERR

CHAPTER 51

Kitty was taking her turn stirring the soup made from the last of their dried peas and flour when she felt an icicle go down her back. She turned and saw Little Poplar, sporting his twin six-guns and resplendent Stetson, strutting toward their tent. Fanned out behind him came half a dozen feathered thugs with muddy eyes and stony smiles. He walked up to Kitty's father and said: "It's time your daughters were married, Straight Tongue. A Chief as big as me should have a tenth wife," leering sideways at Amelia. "Sunflower and the Quiet One will go to my warriors."

Kitty's mother let out a strange little sigh. Kitty looked over and saw her mother's eyes rolling up and her body starting to sag sideways, but she couldn't get there in time to break her fall. Fortunately, she had crumpled onto a patch of ground cedar instead of the rocks beside it. Kitty knelt down and propped up her mother's head and shoulders onto her lap, fanning her face with her hand.

Little Poplar took another step in toward her father and hissed nose to nose: "Do you give that your blessings, Straight Tongue?"

"Of course I don't."

Kitty's mother came back to herself and began to raise her head off Kitty's lap just as Little Poplar drew out one of his long cavalry pistols and shoved the muzzle into her husband's beard. The clearing echoed with the impossibly loud double click of the pistol being cocked. Her head fell back into Kitty's lap again.

One of the reasons that the cocking-back of the pistol's hammer seemed unnaturally loud was that it wasn't the pistol—it was the hammer of a huge old flintlock musket with a sawn-off barrel. Blue Skybird, one of the Indian Protective Society that took turns adopting Kitty and her sisters overnight, was standing about six feet to Little Poplar's right, aiming his homemade blunderbuss at a point about a handsbreadth above the twin holster belt.

Little Poplar turned his head in that direction without shifting the pistol mouth from under Kitty's father's chin. Blue Skybird said calmly: "You shoot Straight Tongue and I shoot you."

Little Poplar said: "This has got nothing to do with you."

"I say it does."

They held like that for a moment, then a hunch-shouldered old man shuffled out from behind the other Plains Crees and tugged on Little Poplar's arm. "Come along, grandson." They went away. Kitty's mother suddenly squawked and rushed to rescue the soup from burning.

That evening, Kitty's father chose to read from the Bible rather than *Robinson Crusoe*. The passage seemed to be one Kitty had heard before—about a bird as a messenger or servant of God.

The camp had halted its ellipsoid wanderings through the bush to hold a thirst dance in an attempt to remeld the factions that had been splitting wider apart since Big Bear had stepped down as Chief. A huge thirst dance lodge—bent saplings and interwoven boughs enclosing an arena two hundred feet across—had been erected on a flat meadow near the campsite. From a tall pole erected in the middle flew a faded Hudson's Bay Company flag—the Union Jack with *HBC* emblazoned across it in gold.

The day the thirst dance lodge was ready happened to be a date celebrated in every latitude around the world. Kitty's father had been keeping careful track of the passage of days since the surrender of Fort Pitt and informed the other prisoners that it was the twenty-fourth of May—the Queen's birthday. They spent the morning working over their bush-tattered rags of clothing to approximate a festive appearance. Kitty's mother opened their last three tins of peaches. At noon they all gathered together to toast Her Majesty in thin, cold tea and to sing "God Save the Queen," "Land of Hope and Glory," and "The Maple Leaf Forever."

Wandering Spirit emerged from the thirst dance lodge in his ceremonial costume of beaded white antelope skin and lynx fur hat with its five white eagle feathers—each of which stood for a white man he said he was going to kill. He stalked over to the impromptu choir trying to raise "Rule Britannia" above the thunder of drums. "What are you singing for?"

"It's the Great Mother's birthday today."

"Oh! That's good, that's good. We will sing a song for her, too. You see"—pointing at the flag floating above the thirst dance lodge—"we still remember the good days when the Great Mother and the Company were the only white powers here. We have no quarrel with her, only with her under-Chiefs in Ottawa."

Amelia said: "You've hung the flag upside-down. That's a very bad omen."

Wandering Spirit slitted his eyes like a lynx and looked up at the flag, then whirled and went back into the thirst dance lodge. The drumming and chanting broke off and was replaced by another Cree song, this one expressing thanks and praise and wishes for a long life to a great Chief.

A rider came pounding in, braids bouncing, and shouted at the Cree guarding the prisoners: "The Police are coming! A thousand of them!" Kitty knew full well there weren't a thousand Police in the whole country, but to the natives of the territories any redcoat was "Police."

The scout jumped off his horse and ran into the thirst dance lodge. The drumming stopped abruptly, and the warriors came pouring out. All the prisoners were herded onto the open meadow, where they became the hub of a vast circle of Cree women and children and old men—the theory being that "the Police" wouldn't shoot at where the white hostages were. They'd just got squatted down there when the orders changed again. Now they were to break camp immediately and move north with the warriors toward a place called Frenchman's Butte, which Wandering Spirit had decided was better-suited to make a stand.

Within an hour the entire massed village was trampling the bush under a wide swath of horses and travois and wagon wheels, leaving a trail like a stampeded herd of buffalo. They reached Frenchman's Butte at dusk, and the prisoners were put to work with the warriors digging trenches by fire- and moonlight. Kitty levered away at the root-tangled earth with a long-handled shovel that had been part of the stock of tools distributed by the farm instructor at Frog Lake.

When the dawn light came she was leaning on her shovel beside her father, looking out over what their night's work had wrought. The face of the butte was now pocked with shallow, bush-masked trenches. In front of it stretched a broad, deceiving sweep of bright green meadow—deceiving because it was actually a spring-soaked muskeg bog. If the pursuing column tried a frontal charge across it, they would find themselves mired in a sucking marsh. The soldiers would become a field of bright red targets wriggling helplessly within easy range of old trade guns and bows and arrows. There had been a corduroy road across the bog, but the Cree had torn out all the logs to reinforce their trenches.

Wandering Spirit ordered the prisoners to be escorted back to a clearing behind the butte. As she stumbled along somnambulantly, Kitty thought she heard her father's voice whispering in Cree, promising a thousand dollars if someone would sneak close enough to the advancing soldiers to shout out the message that the prisoners were still alive. It was only another thread of sound in the indistinct fabric of dream voices, ragged breathing, and the thumping of her leaden feet.

When the herders stopped prodding them, Kitty sank onto a luxurious rock skin of fallen spruce needles and was almost asleep when a storm broke. Wandering Spirit came looming like a thunderhead, bellowing for "Straight Tongue," trailing in his wake the lesser storm clouds of other Chiefs and warriors. "Straight Tongue—you broke your word! You promised to stay with us to the end, and now you try to bribe my warriors to help you sneak away. If I can't trust you alive—I've never known a dead man to betray me."

The war-decked council had spread out in an arc, flanking Wandering Spirit and hemming in the prisoners. Kitty saw, or thought she saw, a flickering magic-lantern picture over Wandering Spirit's shoulder. On a rocky knoll, a blanket-caped, shriveled figure seemed to be hunkered against a spruce tree, watching. Big Bear.

Kitty's father said: "I never asked anyone to help us sneak away."

Wandering Spirit snorted. "The man you tried to bribe will tell the truth. First—does anyone have anything they want to say on Straight Tongue's side?"

It was obvious that "anyone" meant anyone except Straight Tongue's fellow prisoners. Cut Arm, the Woods Cree's Chief, stepped forward. Behind him, idly angling his eyes from side to side, stood Blue Skybird. Cut Arm said: "I only got one thing to say for Straight Tongue."

Wandering Spirit said: "Say it."

"I'll kill the first man that says a word against him. Well, that's about all I got to say."

Cut Arm stepped back. Wandering Spirit tried to glare him to death with no discernible effect, then called out for the warrior whom Kitty's father had tried to bribe. No one answered the call. Wandering Spirit turned in disgust and stalked back toward his defense works.

Kitty sank back into sleep, or slipped into a pleasanter dream. She was awakened by the sound of nearby explosions and rifle fire and shouting. The rest of the family were sitting up, looking off in the direction of the battle. Kitty's father said: "It won't last long. No matter how cleverly Wandering Spirit arranged matters, they can't stand against cannon fire." But they did, all through the morning and into the afternoon.

At one point, Big Bear wandered back from the vicinity of the battlefield and told the McLeans: "We're killing a lot of them. The Gun That Shoots Twice makes a lot of noise, but they can't aim it to hit anything."

Kitty's mother finally gave in to the fact that they weren't about to be rescued and made a pot of oatmeal. Oatmeal and dry biscuits were about all they had left. As the sun was sliding out of the yellow bar of the spectrum and into the red, the cannon fire redoubled. The crash of the shellbursts was now mingled with screams. Kitty's father said: "They've got the range now." A few warriors trickled back, looking over their shoulders, and soon it was a full-scale flight. The prisoners were swept up in the waves of running warriors and their wives and children. After a mile or so, one of the scouts that Wandering Spirit had delegated to lag behind came galloping and shouting that the "Police" weren't pursuing them—in fact, the artillery barrage that had chased them out of their trenches had been set up to cover the white army's retreat.

The Crees' flight slowed to a walk and then stopped. The warriors looked at each other in disbelief and then began to laugh and sing. The only ones who didn't join in the celebrating were Big Bear and Wandering Spirit.

It was decided they would push on up a nearby hill before nightfall. While the rest of the camp was collecting itself, Kitty's father asked her mother to rummage out a bright-colored rag and a pen. He surreptitiously scribbled something on the flyleaf of *Robinson Crusoe*, tore it out, and slipped into the bush, sauntering out just as the camp lurched back into motion.

Kitty had thought they'd been traveling hard before Frenchman's Butte, but the days that followed proved her wrong. They were forcing their way through dense bush country now, wading across waist-high creeks and heaving their shoulders against the spokes of the democrat to help the horses haul it up muddy slopes. It seemed impossible that the bright-uniformed cavalry behind them couldn't catch up with this straggling mass of scarecrows cutting trail, but there wasn't so much as the sound of a distant bugle.

One evening, Kitty was helping her father unhitch the horses when two warriors walked up and took hold of the bridles. "Our horses were killed in the fight with the Gun That Shoots Twice. When the time comes to fight again, we'll need horses."

From then on all the McLeans walked, except for Kitty's two baby brothers, who were carried by their father—one in his arms and one strapped to his back. It was a blessing in a way that they had almost no food left to carry. The Crees weren't in much better straits for provisions. When they'd been camped at Frog Lake, Kitty had kept the younger children occupied by conducting a census of the camp's dogs. They'd come up with a grand total of four hundred and eighty-two. Now there wasn't a dog in the camp—all had been sentenced to serve as traveling rations or had added up their own census and skipped off into the bush.

The Crees and their prisoners were fighting their way through a mosquito-humming thicket one afternoon when the rearguard shouted that they could see the Police. There was a general panic and surging ahead. Kitty's father handed off the toddlers to their mother and stepped aside into the bush. Kitty followed him. By now, things had become so disorganized that they were allowed to worm their way back through the thicket while the Crees charged on by. Looking out from the edge of the thicket to the far side of the ravine they'd just passed through, Kitty saw swatches of bright British red moving through the mottled green. She said: "I can see them!"

Her father's head jolted around. He pointed his finger at her and said: "Go back and join your mother and the others." Then he stepped out into the open. Kitty stayed where she was. Her father unfurled his handkerchief and waved it over his head. The red tunics suddenly disappeared behind puffs of smoke. The appearance of the smoke puffs was followed closely by a crackling sound, and then the foliage was mulched with bullets. Kitty was frozen between throwing herself back farther into the thicket or jumping forward to her father. A broad brown arm shot past her head, grabbed the back of her father's collar, and yanked him backward. Kitty scrambled along behind as Cut Arm dragged her father out of reach of the soldiers' bullets, her father going bug-eyed and fighting to get his fingers inside the collar that was choking off his windpipe.

Cut Arm finally decided they'd reached safety and let go. Kitty's father lay gasping for breath, the blue tinge gradually leaving his cheeks. "Sorry, Straight Tongue." Kitty's father waved off the apology. Cut Arm turned to look across the ravine. "Well, that proves what I been saying all along—they ain't going to stop now till they've killed us all."

They caught up with the tail end of the fleeing women and children and gradually fought their way ahead toward the rest of the family. Kitty could just see her mother and older sisters through the multicolored waves ahead, and Stanley Simpson carrying her baby brothers, when a swatch of wet leaves squirted out from under her foot and her knee went down on a rock.

Her father knelt beside her. "Are you all right?"

"I think so . . . but it hurts."

The packed mass of people and horses was stalled behind them, eddying around her prone body and squeezing itself slowly along the open fringe of broken path. Little Poplar looked down and said: "Get on the move, Straight Tongue."

"She's hurt!"

"I said get on the move."

Her father helped her up. She managed a couple of steps, but the pain was too much. The knee buckled under her again. She was crying with fury at her failure to overcome it. Her father bent over her again. She knew she was too sturdily built for him to carry. Little Poplar pushed him away. "Can't you hear, Straight Tongue? I said get moving."

Cut Arm's oldest wife was there between them. "Go on, Straight Tongue, I got a horse to put her on. We'll catch up with you." Kitty's father looked a question at her. "I'll take care of her, you got my word. And my man could take care of *that*"—jerking her thumb at Little Poplar—"before breakfast. Go take care of the rest of your family and don't worry."

Kitty was lifted onto a sprung-ribbed pony's withers behind the crossed poles of the travois it was dragging. Cut Arm's oldest wife, plodding along beside, raised the ragged remnant of her skirt above the hurt knee and pressed her fingertips against the joint in various places. Some points made Kitty wince, some didn't. "That's good, Sunflower—a day or so without walking on it and you'll be back to outrunning all them men that want to chase you."

The course of the tribe's flight led toward Loon Lake. There was a ford at the mouth of the lake. But by the time Cut Arm's family reached there, the sun was going down and it was too dark to cross safely. Kitty's family were already on the other side. Cut Arm said to put up the tent here and cross over in the morning.

At dawn, Kitty was half dreaming and half aware of the loons howling on the lake and the whitethroats peeping their "Sweet Canada-Canada-Canada . . ." when a lightning bolt rammed into the earth next to the tent. The children screamed. Cut Arm sprang up, grabbed his rifle, and ran out wearing nothing but his loincloth. Kitty got to the door flap before Cut Arm's wives, so she was the only one who saw his feet and shoulders instantaneously reverse themselves—legs flinging up in the air while the nape of his neck hit the ground. There was a big red flower where his face had been.

The scattered rifle shots accompanying the cannons solidified into massed volleys. Wandering Spirit rallied his warriors into a ragged line, and they fell back slowly between the oncoming redcoats and the fleeing women and children. In the open stood the hunched and wizened figure of Big Bear, taking no more notice of the storm of bullets than a barrister with a serviceable umbrella takes of a drizzle of rain.

Kitty ran through the still-gray dawn and flickering shadows. Whether Cut Arm's oldest wife had been right in her prognosis, or whether it was just fear, yesterday's insurmountable pain in her knee was now just a numbness. Along with the other squawling and running women and children, she splashed into the ford and churned her way through the chilling flow toward the far shore.

She was close enough to reach out and grasp one of the brown hands extended over the shore rocks when she looked back over her shoulder. The ford behind her was foaming with women and children carrying those too young to keep their heads above water. Back among the tents, Wandering Spirit's rearguard was fighting and dying. Along the shore, a naked Cree boy two or three years old was toddling back and forth bawling with his eyes slit tight against the gunfire and his tiny hands bobbing in front of his chest like a gopher's.

Kitty heard herself say: "Oh, no," but she wasn't sure whether it was a lament for the child or a demand that she not do exactly what she'd already started doing, which was to turn around and fight her way back against the current of water from her right and human beings head-on, both of which threatened to sweep her off her feet.

She reached the shore she'd just left, scooped up the wailing boy—naked baby fat warm against her sodden breast—and crooned at him in Cree between the chatterings of her teeth: "Ssh! Ssh . . . you're safe now," as she waded out again. But this time there was no longer a panicked herd for her to blend into. She was only halfway across the channel when a red-hot iron boot kicked the side of her neck. She felt her head spinning sideways, felt the buffered punch of her ear hitting her shoulder, felt the flaring heat of the dawn strike her yellow hair. A faraway bass voice shouted in English: "For God's sake don't shoot— it's one of the McLean girls!" She wasn't sure whether she was stumbling across the sucking current or floating with it, but she did know that the voices she was moving toward were the ones shouting in Cree.

CHAPTER 52

By nightfall the Crees and their prisoners had once more left the soldiers far behind. Kitty stumbled along in a red haze, holding a damp rag against the side of her neck. Rags were easy enough to find, it was just a question of tearing a piece off the rags they were wearing. One of the old Cree women had chewed up some leaves to close the scratch where the bullet had grazed her.

When they camped for the night, Kitty's mother sat her down against a tree with a blanket wrapped around her and boiled some water for the last of their tea. Along one of the creeks they'd crossed, Kitty's father had managed to chase a fish into the shallows and scoop it out with his hat, but that was all there was to eat.

As the fish was being rendered down into soup, one-eyed Stanley Simpson came back from listening in on the council of Chiefs. His face looked as if it had been modeled from plaster of paris. He said: "They've decided that five whites have to die to make up for Cut Arm and the other four Crees killed this morning." They just stared at him. "This isn't spur-of-the-moment anger like the time before; they've had all day to think about it. It doesn't help that it's exactly five, just like Wandering Spirit's five feathers."

Kitty's father said: "Who?"

"You—they said Straight Tongue is the only white big enough to be a fit exchange for Cut Arm. Me. And three others—they hadn't made up their minds."

Kitty looked dumbly at her older sisters to see if one of them would tell her she was hearing things. They were casting the same look at each other and at their parents. It didn't seem possible, after all they'd lived through together in the last six weeks, that it could end with vindictive arithmetic. Four-year-old Duncan stamped on the ground, squinted his whole face, wiped his nose and eyes with the back of his hand, and squeaked: "We mustn't let those darned Indians see us cry!"

The family laughed. It wasn't much of a laugh, and it had an edge of hysteria to it, but Duncan was right. There wasn't anything they could do to stop the Crees from killing whomever they wished to kill; all they could do was face it as best they could.

Several of Wandering Spirit's warriors appeared and herded all the prisoners toward the council lodge. The blanket-wrapped bodies of Cut Arm and the other four were laid out on the ground. All the Chiefs sat facing them, except Big Bear, who was hunkered on a mossy outcrop with his twelve-year-old son crouched beside him. As the prisoners were herded into the clearing, the entire rest of the village drifted in through the bush and stood silently among the white columns of birch trunks and poplars and the belled skirts of evergreens.

Kitty's father walked forward to the bodies and looked down at the one that had Cut Arm's rifle laid across its blanket shroud. He said: "Cut Arm was a good friend to me." He went on to tell of what he'd known of Cut Arm in the past—of his ferocity in battle and generosity in peace. From there he enlarged it to speak of the friendship that had existed between the Cree and the white traders for centuries, and of the compassionate and forgiving nature of the Great Mother Across the Water.

When he was done, Wandering Spirit said: "All you say is true, Straight Tongue. You have always been a good friend to us. If Cut Arm had died in a battle, his spirit would have crossed over singing. But your people came upon us with no warning, hoping to slaughter us in our beds." He looked down at the ground and muttered: "This is a sad way for a friendship to end." Then he beckoned to the executioners.

Before the appointed warriors could step forward, Louison Mongrain stood up. He was the métis whom Cut Arm's people had elected to take his place as Chief. He said: "I would like to say something about Cut Arm. He was a man that always kept his word. He promised that he would kill the first man that harmed one of the white prisoners. Cut Arm can't keep his word on that anymore, so I figure it's up to me to keep it for him. So that's exactly what I'm going to do."

Kitty felt a kind of shifting of the forest, as though the trees were all getting up and changing places. She looked around the clearing. It was the people among the trees who were shifting. There wasn't much actual movement, but what had been one large Cree band an instant earlier was now very clearly separated into Wandering Spirit's people or Little Poplar's or those who still defined themselves as Cut Arm's band. All the men were holding guns or knives or war clubs. Louison Mongrain stood facing the six warriors who were set to do the killing. Over his shoulder, Blue Skybird's eyes swiveled lazily across the tableau.

Wandering Spirit said: "If anyone's got a right to speak for Cut Arm's wishes, I guess it's you." He waved away the executioners.

The fish soup was just about boiled away. No one in the family complained when Kitty's mother filled the pot back up with water and started all over. The Indian Protective Society appeared to have disintegrated—no one came to take Kitty and her sisters off to separate tents for the night. Just as they were all squeezing into their worn-thin old tent, Louison Mongrain appeared and handed Cut Arm's rifle and cartridges to Kitty's father. "You might need these tonight."

It was a clear night with a full moon. The rising of the moon threw the clear-etched silhouette of a man with a rifle approaching the back of the tent where Kitty lay pretending to sleep. Her breath caught in her throat. But the shadow didn't grow any larger. She lay waiting for him to advance closer so she would have a good reason for alarming the rest of the family. But the man appeared to be content for the moment just to gaze down at the back of the tent.

Kitty edged toward the tent wall, pressed the side of her face against the ground, and very slowly raised the canvas hem just high enough for one eye to see out. There was a man with a rifle standing there, but he wasn't looking at the tent; he had his back to it. It was Louison Mongrain, keeping watch. She let go of the tent wall and crawled around her brothers' and sisters' feet toward the doorway. From the murmured complaints and "Kitty, what are you doing?" the only ones sleeping were the toddlers and infants. When she reached the doorway where her father lay, his hand came down on her shoulder and he whispered, "Don't go out there."

"I just wanted to look." She parted the door flaps. "See?" The moonlight showed the tartan-blanketed back of Blue Sky-bird, sitting cross-legged with his flintlock scattergun resting on one knee. By the time she'd worked her way back to her own blanket, the information had been relayed through the whole family. They all slept like winter bears.

In the morning the tents were broken down and they were on the move again. Big Bear's tribe had degenerated into a straggling snake several miles long, winding through the bush to no apparent purpose. Kitty's mother—hollow-eyed and staggering mechanically like a wound-down watchwork doll—tripped over the elbow of a pine root and sat down heavily. Kitty reached down to help her up. Her mother batted her hand away and shrieked: "No! I'm not walking another step!" A curious crowd of their captors began to gather and look on. Kitty's mother turned on them from her knee-hugging position on the ground. "Go ahead and kill us or torture us or eat us and get it over with! I won't kill myself or my children for you with walking and starving!"

Wandering Spirit and his coterie of warriors forced their way through to the front of the crowd. Kitty said: "I hope you big, brave men are proud of yourselves! You've succeeded in breaking a woman's heart."

There were murmurings among the Crees and then scurryings. Several women scuttled away and came back with a twist of flour or tea leaves or a sliver of dried meat, piling up the offerings in a mound beside Kitty's mother. Wandering Spirit announced that this looked like a good place to camp for the night. Kitty's mother got a fire lit and mixed together a kind of floury pot-luck stew in the frying pan that had been bouncing against Kitty's back since they'd had to abandon the democrat.

There was another council of the Chiefs and headmen. Wandering Spirit announced that he was stepping down as War Chief because he no longer believed that they could fight this war and win. Little Poplar volunteered himself to take Wandering Spirit's place and outlined the master strategy he'd been nurturing since Frog Lake. They would ride to Prince Albert and capture the fire canoes there, then chug downriver, killing all the whites they met along the way until they got to Ottawa, where they would kill the government.

In the red light of evening, the McLean family were half dozing around their campfire, sighing over their first filled stomachs in weeks, when Wandering Spirit wandered out of the shadows. He sat down on a rock next to Kitty's mother and stared into the flames. In the turmoil and panic of the last weeks, Kitty hadn't noticed until now the erosion of Wandering Spirit. The bold warrior galloping down on Fort Pitt with his black curls streaming in the wind had become a caved-in old man starting at shadows. Tufts of white caught the firelight among his raven waves of hair.

After a moment, he said hoarsely to Kitty's mother: "The white god—will he forgive the men that did the killing at Frog Lake? I don't mean me. There's no hope for me. But the others, the ones that just lost their heads after all those years of seeing their children starve and the Indian agents turning their faces away . . . do you think the white god might judge them kindly?" Kitty's mother told him that the white laws would judge them by their acts, but the white god would look into their hearts when the time came.

In the morning the camp didn't move on. Instead there was another council. Kitty's father was sent for. Kitty and Amelia trailed along behind him and watched from the edge of the circle. It was clear that something had changed. Although Big Bear still occupied his observer's position, although Wandering Spirit looked no more forceful than he had the night before and showed no signs of trying to resume his War Chief's status, the eyes of all the others kept sliding in their direction. Except for Little Poplar, who glowered at a fixed point in the air.

Wandering Spirit gestured Kitty's father to sit beside him. "Straight Tongue, it's been decided that the only choice we have is to make what peace we can with the Police. The problem is, even though we're all agreed we have to take whatever terms they offer, we can't trust them anymore to keep their word. And we can't trust their Chiefs in Ottawa. But we know we can trust the Great Mother. You are a good friend of hers. . . ."

"I am *what*?"

"She knows you."

"She certainly does not. No more than any of her other several million subjects."

"You are good friends with her children, then."

"Not at all. Not that I wouldn't be proud to be, but . . ." He trailed off in the face of the first active gesture that Big Bear had made in a council circle since the day he'd told them he was no longer their Chief. One crabbed brown hand reached down inside the oversize banker's vest and plucked out a flash of white light.

Amelia clutched Kitty's arm and hissed: "It's—"

"I know." It was the silver snuffbox engraved with the name and crest of the Marquess of Lorne, "With Gratitude to W. J. McLean." Their mother had buried it along with other family treasures in the courtyard of Fort Pitt while Inspector Dickens's troopers were caulking the ark.

The snuffbox was passed around the circle to Wandering Spirit, who weighed it in his palm in front of Kitty's father's eyes. "This is yours, isn't it, Straight Tongue? The Great Mother's son gave it to you, didn't he, from one good friend to another?"

Kitty's father rubbed his face as though trying to scrub his mouth off. "It is mine, and . . . but . . . the Marquess of Lorne is not the Great Mother's son. He's the husband of one of the Great Mother's daughters." Wandering Spirit shrugged at the splitting of hairs. "During the time when he was Governor General of Canada, he toured the North West and I helped guide his party for a short time. He gave me that in the same way you might give an end of tobacco to a stranger who loaned you his horse."

"Any man who once loaned me his horse is a good friend to me forever."

"Yes, but . . . but . . . He's only the husband of one of the Great Mother's many, many, many daughters. And even if I could get him to speak to the Great Mother, although it's true that she rules over all of us, she rules through''—he fumbled for terms, then rolled his fingers around the circle of Chiefs—''the *council* of the North West Territories, which is under the council in Ottawa and the council across the Stinking Water . . .''

Kitty watched her father looking from Chief to Chief in hopes that one of them would understand and explain to the others. She saw the Chiefs and warriors looking at each other with a grimness that suggested they understood all too well. Blue Sky-bird leaned across to thud his hand down on her father's knee. ''What we're trying to tell you is if you can get us an honest truce, we'll take it. But if all we can get is promises from liars, we might as well go down taking as many of them down with us as we can.''

Big Bear rose up to his full five feet and padded across the circle to Kitty's father. ''It's like this, Straight Tongue: we're going to set you free to go to the Police and get the best peace for us you can. We trust you for that. If me and a few others have to go down to give them their revenge, we'll do that for the sake of our families. But if the Police are going to kill our families anyway . . .''

''What about my family?''

''They go with you.''

Kitty watched her father grappling with the several teams of horses hitched to different corners of him. Finally he said: ''All right. I'll go and talk to the army . . . 'the Police.' If they won't listen to me''—tapping his forefinger on the lid of the snuffbox in Wandering Spirit's hand—''I promise you I'll get a message to this man.''

The exhalation around the circle was like that of a group of blizzard-lost hunters seeing a square of yellow light among the swirling white and black. Big Bear's pipe-stem bearer came forward with the sacred bundle. After the ceremonial unwrapping and lighting by Big Bear, Wandering Spirit took a few solemn puffs and then offered it to Kitty's father, saying: ''I think this is what you want.''

''It is.''

Amelia ran back to tell the rest of the family, so that when Kitty and her father sailed in—Kitty bearing the pipe-stem bundle that had been given to her father in trust to hand to the Police—clan McLean and all the other prisoners were primed to mob them. To put the seal on it, Wandering Spirit strode from one end of the camp to the other, wearing face paint and full ceremonials, proclaiming that as of next morning all the prisoners were set free. He passed by the McLeans on his way back to his own tent, still using his declamatory voice. But now the message had changed. ''Anyone that wants to see Wandering Spirit for the last time, come now.''

The entire village flowed down toward Wandering Spirit's tent. In the open space in front of the vermilion-daubed cone of white buffalo hide, Wandering Spirit stood alone—except for his black-eyed wife beside him in her fringed doeskins and fierce stillness. Any other Cree man with Wandering Spirit's status as a provider and contempt for missionary rules would have had several wives, but he'd never wanted another.

Wandering Spirit swept his hand up past his hip and extended his fist to the four directions. Sun flared off the blade of the knife he'd snicked out of the sheath as he'd raised his hand. Amelia started to let out a shriek as she realized what was coming next. Kitty dug her fingers into Amelia's shoulders, but whether it was in empathy or to shut her up she wasn't sure. Wandering Spirit plunged the knife into the left side of his chest.

He was still alive when the McLean family trudged past his tent in the morning on their way back down the trampled trail toward the soldiers who'd chased it into being. The knife had missed his heart. His spitting and growling howls, like a wounded lynx, had reverberated across the camp all night long. The last words Kitty heard before the woods closed in were ''Good joke, eh, Kichee Manitou? When I thanked you for making me a hard man to kill, you didn't tell me there might come a time I'd want to die!''

•The woman whose baby Kitty had saved had told her where two canoes were cached on Loon Lake, which would save them fifteen miles of walking around the shore. She'd also told her of a food cache on the south shore. They sang around the campfire that night, stuffed with bacon and bannock and army hardtack and corned beef.

They still had a long tramp ahead of them to Fort Pitt, where the pursuing column was bivouacked. On the morning of the third day, Kitty was helping Stanley Simpson pack up the tent when they heard a low rumbling noise. A wagon appeared on the ridge above them, with two armed, bearded men on the driver's bench. Kitty's father said: ''Good morning!''

The driver said: "Are you McLean?"

"I am the man who is commonly known as Mister McLean."

The driver's partner muttered sideways: "Commonly known as 'the man who surrendered Fort Pitt.' "

The driver said: "Word came you'd been set free. We got sent out to meet you." On the back of the wagon was a large crate crammed full with new clothes and shoes in various sizes. They rummaged through it giddily, squealing at packets of perfumed soap and five-cent papers of hairpins. Clutching their treasures, Kitty and her mother and sisters chased each other giggling through the woods to a bend in the creek they'd camped beside, while her father and brothers and Stanley Simpson marched to another bend downstream. They all left their rags hanging in the trees.

They rode in the wagon the rest of the way to Fort Pitt. Over the trampled embers of the fort a tent city had been erected, the lanes between the rows of white peaks rainbowed with uniforms. Kitty and Amelia went exploring. As they passed by two soldiers smoking cigars in front of their tent, Kitty overheard one of them say: "Don't look to me like they had too rough a time of it. Looks more like they just come back from a Sunday school picnic."

Kitty turned around and said: "I would like to see you go through such a picnic and come out smiling."

CHAPTER 53

When Annie had reached eight years of age, Madelaine had pretty much given in to the notion that the girl wasn't just a temporary addition to the family. And it looked like they were finally going to have a home that wasn't temporary. Gabriel had staked out a piece of land at a place on the South Saskatchewan where the Hudson's Bay Company used to moor a leaky little scow for the benefit of travelers and put up a long, low, clay-plastered log cabin. There was no land office to register it with, but that would come as soon as the Canadian government got around to organizing its new territories.

He spent their first winter there building a new scow, big enough so that passengers' horses wouldn't have to swim along behind as they had in the past. In the spring she painted him a sign to nail up at the place where the Carlton Trail divided, then went to work putting in a garden.

They were just finishing up dinner one evening when old Joseph Ouellette rode in. While Gabriel pried the lid off his latest batch of hop beer, Monsieur Ouellette said to her: "I found a couple of robust boys that ain't old enough to hunt yet, but Gabriel said you're the one I should talk to about divvying up the money."

"Money?"

"From the ferry."

Gabriel came forward balancing three dripping tin cups, saying: "I figured if this ferry business is gonna have a chance of working, it's gotta keep running while we're gone." He took a healthy quaff, puckered, swallowed, and muttered: "Got to find somewhere I can get barley that ain't green."

She said: "Gone where?"

"They're rendezvousing for the buffalo hunt next week. You didn't think I was going to spend the whole summer rowing a boat, did you?"

She hadn't, exactly—she'd thought he'd probably intersperse it with putting up an icehouse and a smokehouse and maybe breaking some ground to put in a bit of barley of his own. She said: "I got a garden to take care of."

"You already got it planted."

"Not hardly. I want to get some more seed from Fort Carlton. And then there's the weeding, and keeping the deer and gophers from eating it as it comes up."

"Monsieur Ouellette can do that." Monsieur Ouellette looked dubious. "Besides, one day's run on the buffalo hunt will bring us in more food and more credit at the Company store than a whole summer's gardening."

"You're right. You go on the hunt and I'll stay here and look after the garden. There'll be plenty of women on the hunt who'll be glad to make pemmican for you."

The little black eyes shot a glance at her like burning coals. He downed his cup and went back to the barrel. Madelaine went to tuck Annie into her bed in the corner. Gabriel and Joseph

Ouellette were launching into an evening of trading old stories and singing old songs. It wouldn't be the first time Annie had slept placidly rocked on the waves of boisterous bass voices. But when Madelaine went back to fill her cup, she could see that tonight was going to be different. There was a nasty edge to the tall tale Gabriel was telling, and the voice he was telling it in. He was sluicing down the beer as though he'd bet Le Petit that he could drink the barrel. Gabriel was "going Gabriel," and there was nothing she could do to stop it.

After Joseph Ouellette had staggered out to find his horse, Gabriel turned to her and slurred slowly: "So . . . so now you'd rather spend the summer with your garden than with me."

"Don't be foolish. But if we're ever going to get this place established, we can't both be out on the plains all—"

"This *place*!" He grabbed one of the chairs he'd made over the winter and threw it against the wall. One leg broke off. "This goddamn *place* is what matters to you? Why don't you fence it around and put a ring in my nose?" He spun away from her and stuck his arm halfway down the beer barrel to refill his cup.

She said: "You never had any trouble going off on your own from any other place we lived. Oh, but that was different because *you'd* decided to leave me on my own."

He took a step toward her and stopped. He stood with his head sunk between his shoulders and his breath snorting in and out, like a buffalo bull about to charge, slopping beer out of the cup vibrating in his hand. Then he turned and butted his way out the door, flinging it shut with a crash that shook the house.

In the sudden silence she could hear a soft snuffling sound. It was Annie, coiled up in her buffalo-robe bed like a woolly caterpillar with a burning twig thrust at it. Madelaine went over and squatted down beside her, making soothing sounds and rubbing Annie's back. "There's nothing to be afraid of, little rabbit."

"But he . . . Uncle Gabriel . . ."

"You mustn't ever be afraid of your uncle Gabriel. He makes a lot of noise when he gets angry, but you know he wouldn't ever hurt you, or me. Never, never, never." The squeaking sounds went away, although the snuffling continued. Annie curled herself around Madelaine's knee. Madelaine stroked the silky head of hair that had yet to coarsen with age. "Whenever you get frightened of your uncle Gabriel, Annie, try and remember that he can frighten anyone, and that's exactly why you never have to be afraid of him. He's too strong.''

As she waited for Annie to fall asleep, Madelaine thought over what she'd just said. Even back in the worst drunk nights when Gabriel was young and wild, he'd never raised a hand to her, and she'd learned to take it for granted that he never would. Maybe she should worry that when he ''went Gabriel'' she could bully him with impunity, because the only man who'd ever scared the hell out of both of them was Gabriel Dumont.

The little bundle of warmth clasped around her knee and thigh had gone limp. Madelaine edged away, got up, and went outside. Underscoring the peeping of crickets and tree frogs, and the murmur of the river, there was a bass-range snoring. He had lain down, or fallen down, under the awning she'd added on for a summer kitchen. She went back inside to get a blanket and curled up beside him. In the morning he said: ''Guess I better whittle up another chair leg.''

She went with him to the hunt rendezvous. Over the last nine years the election of the Captain of the hunt had become a formality and then had been dropped completely. Madelaine sat on her horse watching the carts fall into line. When the whole half-mile-long caravan was set to go, it had to stand in place while the Captain of the hunt trotted over to Madelaine. Gabriel said: ''Well . . . you better get in one damned good garden.''

''You better make damned sure them women making your pemmican is doing just that.''

He kissed her and turned his horse to the west. She watched until the dust and axle screams had faded, then turned her horse back toward Gabriel's Crossing.

The wild strawberries were ripe when he came home. Besides the string of empty carts he'd unloaded at Fort Carlton, there was one cart filled with pemmican and fresh meat and one that was filled with a lumpy object covered with canvas. He stood looking out over the meadow to the south of the house, nodding his head and saying: ''Hmmm'' until she kicked him and said: '' 'Hmmm' what?''

''Huh? Oh, I was just thinking maybe that meadow wouldn't be a bad place to start. . . .'' And he yanked the tarpaulin off the plow loaded onto the cart. By the time he had to go off to lead the autumn hunt, he'd broken three acres to seed next spring.

CHAPTER 54

The duty officer was filling out a requisition form for more requisition forms when a sergeant stamped in and saluted. "Sir! The patrol's come back with two prisoners, sir."

"What are they charged with?" With the influx of lawyers into the territory over the last few years, the duty officer had weaned himself of the habit of asking: "What are they guilty of?"

"I'm not sure if they're charged with anything, sir."

"Pardon me?"

"As a matter of fact, sir, I'm . . . uh . . . I'm not really sure if they're prisoners."

"Have you been drinking, Sergeant?"

"No, sir! I—"

"First you come in here and tell me the patrol's brought in two prisoners. Then you say you don't know if they're charged with anything. And now you say—"

"Sir—it's Gabriel Dumont. Sir."

The duty officer stood up, put the pen back in its stand, reached for his hat, and headed for the door. The sergeant fell in behind. The patrol was gathered around the trough at the end of the parade square, where two rumpled saddle tramps were watering their horses. The saddle tramps had their backs to the duty officer, but one of them was exactly the kind of commanding figure he expected of the man who'd welded a raggle-taggle collection of half-breeds and Indians into a force that whipped a modern army eight times its size: a head taller than the surrounding troopers, straight-backed, with double-axe-handle shoulders tapering down to a horseman's waist. His traveling companion was squat by comparison, wearing a shirt and trousers made out of the same checkered cloth and a funny-looking little black hat with the brim turned up all around—just the sort of loyal, comical errand boy that all heroes came equipped with.

As the duty officer approached the watering trough, the patrol troopers and off-duty loungers stopped gawking and came to attention. "At ease." The two civilians turned toward him. One look at the scoured-boulder features and the black flares in the eye slits, and the duty officer knew it was the short one who was Gabriel Dumont.

The duty officer introduced himself. The tall half-breed said: "Me, I'm Michel Dumas. This here's my friend Gabriel. He don't talk much English." He did say something, though, in the French-Cree patois of the half-breeds—a resonant growl rumbling out of his chest. "Gabriel wants to know if you bluebellies—uh . . . Americans—got anything against us for fighting the Canadian government."

It was an interesting question. The duty officer took it to the colonel, who telegraphed it to General Terry in St. Paul. General Terry passed it on to General Schofield in the Chicago headquarters of the Missouri division. General Schofield handed it up to the adjutant general, who tossed it to the Secretary of War, who bounced it to the Secretary of State, who carried it gingerly into the Oval Office.

While all that was going on, Gabriel and Michel were undergoing a grueling incarceration in the stockade at Fort Assiniboine—stuffing themselves with commissary beef, posing for photographs with their guns and horses, lounging of an evening on the stockade veranda accepting guzzles from soldiers' whiskey flasks while Michel translated Gabriel's answers to the questions about Duck Lake and Tourond's Coulee and the Battle of Batoche.

"Is it true you shot the hat off General Middleton's head?"

"Maybe someone did, but it wasn't me. If Middleton had ever come in range of Le Petit, it wouldn't have been his hat got shot off."

After four days of stretching their shrunken stomachs back to normal, a telegram arrived from Grover Cleveland, President of the Republic of the United States of America: "The military forces have no authority to arrest or detain them. They must therefore be released from military arrest."

Gabriel made Michel translate that several times until he got it precisely. As they were trotting out of the fort gates, waving back at the troopers crowded onto the sentry catwalks, Michel laughed: "Well that's that, eh? We're free in the land of the free."

Gabriel grunted: "I wouldn't nod off yet. This here 'Cleveland' was real careful to say just that the army didn't have no cause to arrest us. He left it open that he could still send the sheriffs or police after us if Macdonald finds a way to squeeze him."

"What does he care about John A. Macdonald?"

"Who knows? It's a big world, and Macdonald's government is part of the biggest empire in it."

Four days' easy riding through the Bear Paw mountains and across the Missouri took them to Spring Creek, where Madelaine's brother lived. They'd left Fort Assiniboine with their saddlebags stuffed to bursting with U.S. Army rations, which turned out to be fortunate because in the whole four days Gabriel didn't see one living creature bigger than a squirrel or a crow. Unregenerate old heathens like White Cap or Big Bear, or Poundmaker in his backsliding phase, would say that it was because the white hunters had no respect for the animals they killed, never thanked them for sacrificing their lives to feed their two-legged brothers, never prayed that the deer or buffalo tribe would forgive them and return. Without compromising his own religion in the least, Gabriel had a notion that the old heathens wouldn't be far wrong.

Madelaine's brother welcomed them into his home, and his wife set to work fattening them up with fried meatballs and dumplings and gooseberry pies and blueberry puddings drowned in heavy cream. Not quite up to Madelaine's, but . . . any tent in a blizzard, as the priest said to the Blackfoot girls.

After a few days of loafing and burping, Gabriel grew restless. He didn't expect that Madelaine would roll in until the leaves were turning. He saddled up Starface again, and he and Michel rode off to Fort Benton and then to Helena. People thronged into the taverns or craned their necks out of windows to get a look at the half-breed general. People he'd never met before handed him wads of dollars contributed from unasked-for door-to-door subscriptions. Newspaper reporters bought him drinks and hung on every word Michel Dumas translated in response to their questions. Gabriel began to suspect that it was true what the Canadian settlers in the North West always said: the Americans were crazy.

Edouard and his wife inched into Helena on a splint-wheeled wagon layered high with household goods and children. Gabriel and Edouard clapped each other on the shoulder and gazed into the corners of each other's eyes with that arm's-length warmth they'd settled on before Eli was born. Because Edouard had actually left Batoche before Gabriel, he didn't bring with him the one thing Gabriel longed for almost as much as Madelaine—news.

But other refugees began to trickle in—that faction from Batoche, or Poundmaker's band or Big Bear's who felt safer throwing themselves onto the winds of blind fate than on the mercy of the Canadian government. They informed Gabriel that everyone who hadn't taken the run south had surrendered, all except Big Bear and Horsechild, the son who refused to leave him. The entire Canadian army plus the North West Mounted Police were now directing their energies toward capturing one wandering old man and a twelve-year-old boy.

They also told him that Marguerite Riel and her children were safely ensconced at Louis's mother's home in St. Boniface, that the mass trials were scheduled to start in Regina in July, and that Louis was held in custody at the Police headquarters there. Gabriel went back to Madelaine's brother's place, counted up the donated money banked in a moosehide bag under the bed, and began to formulate a plan. The news from the next trickle of fugitives confirmed it. Big Bear had finally surrendered to a detachment of Police the pursuit troops had left behind to guard a supply depot—"The only three white men in the whole North West that weren't looking for him." What that meant was that Middleton's job was done. The Canadian army was packing up and heading back east for the triumphal processions. Their last casualty of the rebellion was the colonel who'd led the charge into Batoche against the general's orders. He'd died of a fever on the steamboat ferrying his regiment down to the railhead.

Gabriel took a number of dollars out of the bag, left the rest in the care of Michel Dumas, bought a few twists of tobacco, and rode north into Gros Ventres country. The Gros Ventres were noticeably more hospitable than they'd been a year ago. He was feasted and feted and handed on from one Chief to the next like a medicine bundle, telling the same stories over and over across different council fires to please his hosts. Not that Gabriel was averse to a bit of reveling in his own exploits, but at the moment he was more interested in talking to the Gros Ventre Chiefs about other things: the best route for slipping across the Medicine Line without attracting the attention of cavalry patrols, the best places to hide relays of horses . . .

He left a bit of money and tobacco with each Chief, as a kind of down payment against the hour when it came time to buy horses and the services of Gros Ventres warriors to watch over them. To his surprise, the Chiefs seemed to regard his money and tobacco as a token gesture sealing the upcoming loan of the horses and young men they meant to give him for free. It gradually sank in that anyone with a lick of sense could see that the recent war north of the line was likely going to prove the last occasion when the old, free ways put up anything like a fight against the invading armies of the east. The Gros Ventres wanted to be able to say they'd had a part in it.

When he rode back into Helena it was a dry, bright, dusty day. A dozen or more saddle horses were hitched to the rail in front of the tavern favored by the local métis. Gabriel had never seen more than two or three there during daylight hours. He reined Starface in beside them, climbed down, and slid Le Petit out of the saddle scabbard. Back along the South Saskatchewan he would have left it there without a twinge of doubt that it would still be there when he came out—even if that wasn't until they closed the bar—but Montana was somewhat farther along the road of civilization than the North West Territories.

There was a lot of ebullient Michif bubbling out through the open doorway. Gabriel stepped across the threshold onto the sawdust and paused to let his eyes adjust from the sunlight. At a pair of pushed-together tables in the corner, Michel Dumas was holding court, waving his big arms and sputtering: "Nine hundred of them there was! And barely fifty of us in Tourond's Coulee. I says to Gabriel, I says . . ." The other chairs were filled with métis farmers and hunters from around Helena, all with fixed smiles on their faces and full glasses in front of them. The fat bartender was standing next to Michel with a tray under his arm. Michel dug some coins out of his pocket and handed them over without looking at them or interrupting the flow of his story.

Edouard was leaning on the bar. He swiveled his head toward the doorway but didn't say anything. As was perhaps inevitable with Edouard, his expression on seeing Gabriel walking in on this was an inextricable alloy of genuine sympathy and gloating.

Gabriel padded his moccasins across the sawdust to Michel. The bright blue alcohol-lamp eyes came up. "Gabriel! I was just telling them how we—"

"We'd better talk," gesturing at the doorway.

"You bet. Pull up a chair. Barman, bring another—"

Gabriel clapped his hand onto Michel's meaty shoulder. Michel dragged his attention back from the fat man behind the bar. Not trusting himself to speak, Gabriel just nodded his head toward the doorway. The blue eyes snapped wide. "Oh!" Michel shushed himself, sidled his eyes back and forth slyly across his broad-beamed field of vision, and whispered: "Never know who might be listening, eh?" Then he winked and stood up, booming out: "Well, sure, Gabriel, I'll be glad to take a look at your horse's off hoof and see if he needs a new shoe after your long hunting trip."

Gabriel turned and walked out, tossing Le Petit to Edouard on the way. Once outside, he went around to the muddy alley between the tavern and the dry-goods store next door and waited there. Michel finally managed to negotiate his way off the board-walk and followed Gabriel around the corner with the exquisitely delicate balance of a veteran drinker.

"What're you buying drinks with, Michel?"

"Huh? Oh, I don't buy much. I buy a round, then somebody else buys one and somebody else buys another. . . ."

"Yeah—just enough to get you going, and then it's drinks for the house all night long. Ain't that how it is? Every night since I been gone, ain't it?"

"Come on, Gabriel. . . . After half a year of getting shot at and running from the Police and—"

"Where's the money bag?"

"Back with my gear at the Wilkies'. You don't think I'd go and bring it to a place like this, do you?"

"No—you just fill your pockets from it every morning before you come here. Anything left in it?"

"Of course there is! Lots!"

"How much?"

"I don't count up every penny like some grocery clerk."

"Whatever's left, I'm taking it. You don't spend another penny."

"That money ain't just for you! It was given to *us*!"

Gabriel drove the heels of both hands up against Michel's chest, bouncing him back against the clapboard wall of the saloon. "I'll tell you what it ain't for—it ain't for pissing away buying drunks to play hero to."

Michel started forward, saying: "Now you look here—"

Gabriel threw him back again. "I am looking, and lucky for me I didn't eat nothing for breakfast."

"Don't you push me!" The overgrown blue-eyed boy came off the wall cocking his fists. Gabriel stepped back and braced his feet gratefully; it would be so kind of Michel to give him a good excuse. But instead Michel slowed down like a man wading into deep water, and his fists unfurled. "Just . . . just don't . . . you don't have to go pushing me, Gabriel."

"Maybe not, so long as you don't have to go drinking our money away. We're going to need it for other things."

"Since when were you a teetotaler?"

"Since never. But there's a lot of people'd love to have us prove we're just a bunch of drunken half-breeds. Have some pride."

A sound came from the street that wouldn't have caused their heads to turn if they were still back home, where the unholy shrieking of the ungreased wooden axle of a Red River cart was just a natural part of the aural landscape of summer. They went out of the alley to have a look.

All along the boardwalk, white storekeepers and farmers were gritting their teeth and covering their ears as the cart ambled by. The man holding the reins was gaunt-cheeked, goat-bearded Patrice Fleury. Leaning on the side rails behind him were two copper-skinned, black-haired women—a lithe young one and an older one who was considerably broader in all directions.

Gabriel walked out onto the street. He was vaguely aware of Michel disappearing back into the tavern behind him, but Michel Dumas and all other trivialities had suddenly been relegated to the very distant background. As Gabriel's path and the cart's intersected, he took hold of the top side rail with both hands and vaulted over. Then he was pressing Madelaine down across the stacks of traveling gear, and she was batting at his hands and laughing and squealing: "At least wait long enough that we can sell tickets!"

He got back on his feet and pulled her up onto hers, swaying with the motion of the cart. Patrice Fleury glanced sideways at him and muttered: "Long ride no water, eh?" Gabriel punched Patrice's hat down over his eyes and kissed Annie on the cheek.

Madelaine said: "I thought you were going to be waiting at Spring Creek?"

"I thought you were going to wait for a freighter's cart train?"

"Patrice offered to bring us down here himself."

Gabriel turned to Patrice. "It's that bad up there—that you figured it was better you and your family go on the run?"

"No. They're waiting for me back home. I got to turn around and head right back anyways, if I'm going to be in Regina in time to go on trial."

"That's a hell of a lot of eating dust just for our sake."

"Don't thank me—thank your wife and her sister." Madelaine's sister was Patrice's wife. In Patrice's place, Gabriel probably would have come to the same decision: fifteen hundred miles of roadless prairie was a lot less daunting than two Wilkie girls.

By that time, Patrice had clucked and whip-tapped the cart pony into angling off the street and up against the boardwalk. Gabriel climbed down and raised his arms to help Madelaine over the railing. Either he was growing stronger or she'd lost some weight. Annie clambered down and murmured without looking at him: "Uncle Gabriel, is Michel . . . ?"

He nodded toward the saloon door. "In there. Go on in, we all got good reason to be thirsty." The American women didn't seem to show up in saloons much; it would be a healthy change for the American men. Patrice Fleury followed Annie inside. Gabriel paused on the boardwalk to get a good look at Madelaine. The disturbing gray tinge he'd seen creeping into her skin after Batoche was there again. "You don't look so good."

"That's a hell of a nice welcome."

"You look beautiful, idiot. I mean you don't look so well."

"It's just the traveling. Couple days' rest, I'll look sixteen again."

"I hope not. I'm a lot fonder of women than girls."

"How many?"

He arched his eyebrows and pursed his forehead as though trying to add them up, then reached out to usher her to the doorway. Instead of laughing at him, though, or punching him, she dug in her heels and held him back. "Gabriel . . ." The big black eyes absorbed his, and the big brown hands gently took hold of his forearm. "Aicawpow."

He started to say: "What about him?" but before the words passed his lips he knew. He looked away from her as the breath grunted out through the bridge of his nose. It wasn't a gasping blow, just a soft thump like a jackrabbit's foot kicking his stomach. "How did it happen?"

"He just went to sleep one night and didn't wake up."

"Well . . . well . . . he was an old man. He had a good long run at it, no question." He didn't voice the fact that whatever time Aicawpow might've had left certainly wasn't lengthened by the death of one son and the others on the run from the Police. Madelaine would have felt obligated to make noises pretending it wasn't so. He crushed her hand into the crook of his elbow and walked her inside.

Patrice Fleury and Annie were occupying a lone table. Michel Dumas was nowhere to be seen. Gabriel called the barman over and restrained himself to one glass of whiskey. He would've liked to say: "I just heard my father's dead, bring me a couple bottles," but given the lecture he'd just given Michel . . . When the glasses were emptied he said to Madelaine: "How'd you like to tell that barman in English we want to buy a bottle to take away with us? I seen a place among some trees by the river where we could put up a tent. . . ."

"My brother said they had a room to put us up in."

"He does—but I bet he wants his family to sleep tonight. Less'n you're real stuck on this notion of selling tickets. . . ."

CHAPTER 55

Madelaine woke up coughing. She tried to muffle it and keep still, so as not to wake up Gabriel, but the convulsions in her chest pulled her upright fighting for breath. Gabriel put his hand on her back. When the coughing passed, he said: "How long has that been going on?"

"It's just natural from seven hundred miles of eating dust. I can feel it starting to go away already." She pushed away the blankets to climb off their buffalo-robe camp bed and attend to the fire. But first she pulled on her dress. Last night Gabriel had shown every sign of finding her saggy old body aesthetically pleasing when it was prone in the moonlight, but there was no point in giving him too graphic a demonstration of the effects of gravity.

They were camped in a stand of cottonwoods, which didn't grow back home. An unfamiliar kind of warbler was singing over the blackbirds' rasping croaks. As she built a fire on last night's embers, Gabriel got up and buttoned on his trousers. He left his shirt off, though, apparently unconcerned with the effects of gravity. The fact was, there wasn't much on him to sag. She would have to fatten him up.

In between repositioning the stones around the fire and crumbling tea leaves into the kettle he'd filled from the stream, she watched him moving around the campsite. The bit of a pot left on him was from feast and famine, not fat. There was a battered look to his arms and torso, with old white scars etched here and there and patches of the puckered skin of age that disappeared when the muscles underneath were called into play.

She tried to imagine herself feeling this same interior melting looking at his body thirty years ago when it was fresh and smooth and characterless, and couldn't. She didn't think to carry that line of thought through to the possibility that he might feel the same way about hers.

They spent the morning lounging around the fire, eating thick slices of bacon and stacks of pancakes slathered with her sister-in-law's blackberry jam, talking over what they should do to reconstruct their life. Madelaine said: "I brought the money that's left over from selling the ferry."

"That'll help."

"Tomorrow or the next day we could go to the land office at Fort Benton and find out about the American laws on home-steading. If we can get a little piece of land and put a cabin up, we can get through the winter on your hunting."

"There ain't much left to hunt."

"We won't need much for just the three of us."

"Three?"

"Have you forgotten about Annie?"

"I thought her and Michel . . ." She wasn't conscious of her face adopting any particular expression in response to what he was starting to say, but what he saw in it made him grimace and suck his breath in through his side teeth and say to the sky: "Yeah, I guess you're right."

"If it turns out we don't have enough money, we could always get a message to somebody back home to sell off our land and send us the money—if the government ain't taken away our title. But I think it'd be better to hold on to it if we can. Maybe in a few years the government'll let us go back." Gabriel shook his head emphatically. She said: "You never know," but didn't press it further.

He said: "Everything you said sounds like a good plan. But it might have to wait till next year. Your brother said we could spend the winter at his place. You see, there's something else I'm going to have to do that'll keep me from being able to use this summer getting a place of our own ready for the winter."

"What's that?"

"Rescuing Riel."

It took a moment for her ears to convince her mind that that was really what they'd heard, and another moment to disentangle her stomach and lungs and heart so she could speak relatively evenly. "Rescuing Riel from what?"

He looked at her as though she'd asked him, "What's blue and spread above the earth?" "From the Police!"

"He gave himself up of his own accord."

"Because he believed he was going to get a fair hearing. Once they finish their pretend trial and tell him they're going to hang him, he'll be ready for me to break him out."

"They might not decide to hang him."

Gabriel snorted and rolled his eyes.

"It's true! The law says if he wasn't sane, they have to put him in an asylum—they can't hang him or put him in jail. The rumor is that's what his lawyers are going to try."

Gabriel chewed on his thick lower lip for a moment, then shook his head. "You didn't see Louis's face when he was telling me about his days in that asylum in Quebec. He'd rather hang than live out his life in a place like that."

"He wouldn't have to live out his life there. If the government can get him safely put away in an asylum for a year or two, everybody's blood will cool down and they can let him out without the Orangemen going crazy."

Gabriel sucked on that notion for a while. "Maybe. Maybe. And if it comes down to it, it'll be a hell of a lot easier to break him out of an asylum than a condemned cell. We'll see."

They settled in at her brother's house for the duration. Their lives settled into a pattern of going into Helena every day or two for news, murmuring with the other exiles around a back table in the tavern. From time to time, Gabriel went off on lone hunting trips along the Judith River or north into Gros Ventres country. She didn't ask him how far north. Sometimes he actually brought back a mule deer or a brace of geese.

They were walking along the boardwalk one day when Gabriel vanished. She heard a thump and looked down. He was lying on his side as limp and boneless as a child fallen into sleep while falling onto its bed. She flung herself to her knees beside him and wrestled his shoulders onto her lap. "Gabriel! Gabriel!"

His eyes flickered. "Huh? What . . . ? Oh. Happened again, eh?"

"*Again?* What do you mean 'again'?"

"It's just a little bit of . . ." He was smiling dismissively and rising to his feet with an elaborate precision of movement meant to give the illusion that his equilibrium wasn't rocky or his vision hazy. "A little bit of a hangover from the crack across the head at Duck Lake. It don't happen hardly at all anymore. Just every now and then I fall down and then I get back up again."

"What if it was to happen while you were riding? Or walking along a riverbank?"

"I bounce pretty good. And there's nothing like a cold ducking to wake you up fast."

"You're going to see a doctor. There's a doctor's got a sign up down the street. . . ."

"Am I, now? And how's that cough of yours that was going to go away as soon as you got the road dust out of your throat?"

"Fair trade. I'll go see the doctor when you do."

"You're a hard woman. Though not everywhere. . . ." He reached out to pinch her left breast. She slapped his hand away, after the fact. "All right, we'll go see this doctor today, after we step into the saloon to have a drink to brace ourselves and see if anybody's waiting for me with some news."

There was someone waiting for Gabriel in the tavern, but not with news. A tall, nattily dressed man, with brilliantined curls and a horseshoe mustache, was helping Edouard hold up the bar. As Madelaine and Gabriel came in and headed for their table in the back, Edouard nodded significantly in their direction. The tall man bounced off the bar and moved to intercept them. "Mister Doo-mont! I'm Major John Burke, representing Colonel William F. Cody—Buffalo Bill's Wild West! I'd consider it an honor to buy you a drink."

Gabriel said: "I speak English like a loon walks. *Parlez français?*" Major Burke shook his head. "Bungee? Ojibway?

Dakota? Blackfoot? Michif? Cree? Well—my wife, she translate."

"Ah—Mrs. Doo-mont! A great privilege." The hand slid in
and out of hers like raw liver. "Would you be so good as to inform
your husband I'd consider it an honor to buy him a drink?"

"So long as you'd consider it two honors to buy us both one."

He did, adding in another for himself and downing it even
faster than Gabriel, calling for another round before the empty
glass hit the table. "Now, Mrs. Doo-mont—no doubt your husband's heard of Buffalo Bill Cody?"

She translated that to Gabriel. He said: "Does he mean the
Cody that brags he killed ten thousand buffalo by sitting up on
hills a quarter mile from a herd and picking them off with a
Sharps rifle? Tell him to tell his friend Cody that if he wants the
métis to call him 'Buffalo' Bill, all he has to do is go out one
time on his horse and charge through a stampeding herd with a
musket in one hand and a powder horn in the other and come
out the other side with his white trousers still white. . . . No, I
guess you can't tell him that—thanks to 'Buffalo' Bill and his
friends, there ain't no herds to charge into no more."

Madelaine's translation to Major Burke was: "My husband
says: 'Who hasn't heard of Buffalo Bill?' "

"Well, Buffalo Bill has heard of your husband. Colonel Cody
thinks—he *knows*—that the crowds who've thrilled to the sight
of Sitting Bull and Little Sure Shot Annie Oakley, from the
crowned heads of Europe to the democratic masses of Chicago,
will thrill to the sight of the Hero of the Half-Breed Rebellion.
Now, I'm prepared to offer your husband a contract. . . ." He
mentioned a staggering number of American dollars. Madelaine
converted them into pounds sterling in her head and still thought
maybe she should ask how many people they wanted Gabriel to
kill.

As she translated the proposition to Gabriel, though, she could
see his expression calcifying into "Tell him to piss in the air and
catch it in his mouth." She reminded him: "We're going to
have to live off something, Gabriel."

He looked down at the table. Suddenly she saw one of Riel's
visions made flesh in front of her: "I saw Gabriel Dumont; he
was weak and ashamed and staring at his empty table." She
opened her mouth to say something to undo what she'd wrought,
but before she could find words he looked up at her with eyes
like polished coal and said: "How much would he pay to put

me in a cage like a bear and roll me around with his circus?"
He downed the rest of his whiskey. Major Burke called for another round. The fierce light in Gabriel's eyes dimmed out. "All right. Tell him I got things I have to do this summer. Maybe next year."

When she'd translated that, Major Burke raised the offer, then upped it again when Gabriel shook his head. Michel Dumas was suddenly hovering over their table. "I couldn't help but hear what . . . If Gabriel won't go, I will."

Major Burke looked doubtful. "It's hardly the same thing, but . . . there's always a place in the show for a man that can ride and shoot. I'd be willing to take him on your husband's recommendation."

Madelaine told that to Gabriel, who shrugged. "Tell him Michel can ride and shoot at least as good as Buffalo Bill."

"My husband says his friend Michel rides like the wind and can shoot the eyes off squirrels."

"Fair enough. Why don't we step over to the bar there, Mike. Mrs. Doo-mont, your husband can expect to hear from me again," with a wink and a grin. "Once I'm fixed I don't shake off no more'n a bulldog."

When Major Burke had made his exit, leaving Michel Dumas showing off the embossed business card and offhandedly computing travel time to Chicago, Gabriel muttered darkly at her: "What are you going to tell Annie?"

"I'm going to tell her to circle it on the calendar as her lucky day. Now drink up, we've got a doctor to see."

They had to wait while the doctor bandaged up a surly-looking cowboy with a fancy six-gun rig. The bandaging took longer than it should, what with the doctor chortling fit to choke and gasping out at Madelaine and Gabriel: "Can you beat that? Shot himself in the foot! In thirty years I never seen the beat of it. Says he was hunting gophers. . . ."

The doctor seemed strangely embarrassed about examining a husband and wife together, but since Gabriel couldn't answer diagnostic questions in English he didn't have much choice. The doctor's verdict on Gabriel was that the bullet had cut an artery that was slowly reknitting. The blackouts came when his brain grew short of blood, but they would grow steadily less frequent until they stopped completely once the artery was healed.

It was always difficult to gauge exactly how much English Gabriel could follow, especially when it was delivered with an

American accent, but Madelaine had no doubt he'd picked out the word *tuberculosis* in the doctor's diagnosis of her. The word was as familiar to the métis as "smallpox" to the rest of the Plains tribes. It was the word that had killed his mother. As she was buttoning up her dress, Gabriel said: "So what's he say?"

"Oh, he says I got a little shadow of TB, but it'll go away just like your fainting." The expression on his face bordered on skeptical, but he couldn't ask the doctor.

As they were on their way out the door, the doctor called after them: "Ma'am! You got to take in mind that both of you are nigh on fifty years old. The fact that either of you is still alive at all after what you've been getting up to over the last year is just about the damnedest thing I ever . . ." He began to chortle again. "No, I guess it's the *second* damnedest thing I ever seen—next to that cowboy shooting himself in the foot."

Some days after Major John Burke headed back east with Michel Dumas in tow, a second stranger came nosing around the taverns in Lewiston and Helena looking for Gabriel Dumont. Madelaine was reading and translating from the *Fort Benton Record*'s record of the beginning of the trials in Regina when a lanky man with red hair and black eyes approached their table and said in Michif: "My name's James Anderson. I seen you a few times before, Monsieur Dumont, up around Fort Edmonton, but we never met. It'd go over real good with my family when I get back home from this freight trip if I could tell them I sat down with Gabriel Dumont and bought him and his wife a drink."

Gabriel shrugged as though it wouldn't bother him unduly. James Anderson sat down, called to the bartender, and then tapped his finger dramatically against the TREASON TRIALS COMMENCE! "Damned government's going to take its revenge."

In a voice so weary and defeated that Madelaine had to look twice to make sure who it was, Gabriel sighed: "Well, from the very first gunshot it was bound to come out this way, I guess. It was a sad mistake from the beginning. My mistake more'n anybody else's; Riel never wanted to fight. I can't but feel bad for those that couldn't escape like I did."

"You didn't escape to much," James Anderson said indignantly. "Goddamned government stole everything you had."

"Well . . . well, we escaped with our lives," flabbily patting his hand on Madelaine's. "Me and my brother Edouard have been looking to get a couple of little pieces of land, out around the Turtle Mountains, where we can tend our own gardens and live out our last years with the family that's left to us. Ain't that right, Madelaine?''

It was the first she'd heard of it. The Turtle Mountains were in the Dakotas, the opposite direction to that in which his hunting trips had supposedly been taking him. She smiled inanely and sipped her gin.

"Yes, yes,'' Gabriel went on, nodding somberly. "With a bit of hunting and a few root vegetables, maybe a few head of cattle . . . Well, thank you kindly for the drink, Monsieur . . . Andrews?''

"Anderson.''

"Forgive me, my hearing isn't what it was,'' creaking up off his chair as though he'd aged twenty years since morning. He didn't say another word until they were rolling out of town on her brother's buggy. Then he began to laugh low in his throat and said: "Not very good at it, are they?''

" 'They'?''

"Oh . . . might be the North West Council, or the Police, or maybe even Macdonald himself. Place is so chock full of spies . . .''

"Maybe he was just who he said he was.''

Gabriel looked at her slantwise and chewed his cheeks with his back teeth.

The Montana newspapers kept up their regular reports on the trials north of the line. They could peddle a lot of papers on the sensation of that Riel fellow who used to teach school down the road reincarnated as the apex of a pyramid of treason, murder, rebellion, and foreign intrigue. Madelaine and Gabriel and the other exiles learned through dry sidebars that Moïse Ouellette and all their other friends and relatives on the Exovedate had pleaded guilty to treason felony and had been sentenced to penitentiary terms of three to seven years, including Albert Monkman, whom the Exovedate had locked up as a traitor. Big Bear and Poundmaker got the same. Big Bear's son was too young to go to prison, so they'd put him in a reformatory. Wandering Spirit and six other murdering hostiles were sentenced to hang. During all the years when Big Bear was the last prairie Chief who refused to sign a treaty, one of the terms he'd held out for was that anyone on his reserve who was convicted of a capital crime would be shot rather than hung.

The trial of Louis Riel dragged on and on. His lawyers sent many telegrams to Montana and to Ottawa, asking Gabriel to come up and testify that he had started the war against Louis's wishes and asking the government to guarantee him safe conduct to give his testimony. Gabriel agreed, but John A. Macdonald refused. Gabriel said: "Maybe I should go anyway. Just because they won't promise in writing don't mean there ain't a chance. . . ."

"*I'll* give you a guarantee!" she shrieked at him. "I guarantee John A. Macdonald'll dance a jig the day you cross the line. The French in Quebec are screaming that they'll hang Macdonald if he hangs Riel; the Orangemen in Ontario are screaming that they'll hang him if he doesn't. If you go north, Macdonald can hang you to please the English and let Louis go to please the French."

Gabriel's response was to go off on another hunting trip. He came back looking thinner, but with a bounce in his movements and a return of that old, eager mannerism of tasting the air through his teeth. There was a kind of delirious, buoyant sheen to him that scared her. Although she wished that the story he'd told James Anderson was true, and prayed that Louis's trial would end in a verdict that made Gabriel's mad plan unnecessary, as long as Gabriel had something to run at he didn't have to look back at what he was running from. She was no longer sure whether she had more dread of the moment he loaded up Le Petit and saddled Starface to ride north across the line or of the moment he gave it up and stopped moving forward and let them all catch up with him—the corpses of Isidor and Aicawpow and all the rest, and the faces of all those men condemned to live their next few years in cages far from their families. She knew that there was no just reason he should feel responsible for the chances they'd all chosen to take, but she also knew Gabriel.

The verdict of the jury in the Riel trial was guilty—with a unanimous recommendation for mercy. The judge's mercy was that the prisoner be held in the Police guardroom until the eighteenth day of September, when he would be hanged by the neck until dead, "and may God have mercy on your soul." But Louis didn't hang on the eighteenth of September. His lawyers launched a fleet of appeals and convinced the government to appoint a commission of physicians to determine whether he was sane. While he was being prodded and probed in the Police cell in Regina, Marguerite gave birth to their third child at his mother's home three hundred miles away. It was a boy who only lived a few hours.

Autumn came on sooner than Madelaine expected. Although they were a good deal farther south than the South Saskatchewan, they were also a good deal higher up on the slope to the Rockies. The cottonwoods turned gold. The powder-blue leaves of the big sagebrush trees dried to powder and were blown away in fragrant fragments mingling with the snowflakes carried down with the wind off the mountains.

The trickle of refugees from the north had dried up long ago. Those who hadn't taken advantage of the gaps left in the immediate wake of the war were either enmeshed in the processes of the law or aware of the fact that the Police were watching them for any suspicious movements. Except, of course, for those whose diligent service in the government cause put their loyalty beyond question. . . .

"Afternoon, Gabriel."

Madelaine jumped and looked back over her shoulder at the voice coming out of the air. Gabriel didn't twitch from methodically fixing the wheel of her brother's eggshell-bodied buggy; he just drawled: "Afternoon, Jerome. If you plan on surprising anyone, you oughta keep the hell off the skyline. Now, if you was to climb down off your swaybacked excuse for a yellow horse and clamp your hands onto the left side of this while Madelaine keeps hold of the right, in a minute or two I'll probably have nothing better to do than sit and pass the time of year with you."

Once that program was accomplished, Madelaine negotiated her way into the kitchen and excused herself around her sister-in-law's dinner preparations to make a pot of good black tea. By the time she lugged the kettle and the cups out to the copse of alders fringing the yard, Gabriel and Jerome Henry were deep in tobacco and news. Jerome was laughing: "Will Jackson—excuse me: Joseph Honoré Jaxon—kept carrying on so loco he embarrassed his guards. They finally got so sick of him pissing himself, they just stripped his clothes off and found his legs were all striped blue from where the dye on his prison union suit had run."

Madelaine poured out the tea. Jerome clapped his hands together and said: "Well, you'll want to know about the trials and all."

Gabriel said: "We got that news already. They got a telegraph and newspapers down here—and Madelaine can still read as good as ever."

"All right, then I'll tell you what they wouldn't put in the newspapers. Let's see now . . . First off—you know why Moïse Ouellette and Phillipe Garnot and them pleaded guilty?"

Gabriel grunted: "I wondered. Guilty of defending their homes. . . ."

"The government lawyers told them if they didn't plead guilty to treason felony, the government'd charge them with straight treason and hang them. Mind you, maybe you'd be happier if you'd stayed up there and gone to jail with them. At least you'd be close to the love of your life." Madelaine raised an eyebrow at him. "His billiard table's in Stoney Mountain Penitentiary."

Gabriel said: "I guess they figured if they couldn't catch me, that was the next best thing."

Jerome turned his bland storekeeper's visage back to Gabriel. "Could be—but they weren't going to put you in jail anyway, they would've hung you along with Wandering Spirit and the others. They stood all seven of them in a row on this hanging machine, singing their death songs with the ropes around their necks. All except Wandering Spirit. He sang a love song for his wife."

They sat sucking their pipes for a moment, and then Jerome began to laugh. "Big Bear's trial—when they were reading out the charge to him . . . The charge was 'Rebellion against the Crown,' but in Cree it came out as 'Knocking Off the Queen's Hat.' So Big Bear kept getting more and more confused and finally started yelling at the translator: 'I didn't even know the Great Mother had a hat, and if I did, I wouldn't steal it!' So the next one to come up was One Arrow, and the lawyers thought it'd translate better if they said 'attacking the Queen's fundamental authority,' but that got turned into 'stabbing the Great Mother in the bottom.' "

Once they'd caught their breath again and wiped their eyes, Gabriel said: "And what about Riel? Have you heard anything about what's going on with them doctors?"

"Well, his lawyers keep trying to put across the notion that he wasn't sane and responsible, but they keep running up against the same wall."

"Yeah," Gabriel grunted. "Macdonald won't stand for it."

"That ain't it at all. Riel won't stand for it."

For the next ten days, Madelaine didn't see much of Gabriel. It was probably just as well, since when they were together she had to try to live on shallow breaths to keep the coughing and the pink froth from welling up. On the eighth of November he came galloping into her brother's farmyard like a shooting star. He jumped off Starface, handed her a crumpled piece of paper, and charged on into the house.

It was a telegram, addressed to the bartender in Helena. "Sane STOP November sixteen STOP." Gabriel came out of the house unfolding another piece of paper. Madelaine said: "November sixteenth?"

"That's the day they're going to hang him."

Within a few minutes he was out behind the barn with a score of leathery men watching intently as he drew a diagram in the dirt, copying from the piece of paper. Madelaine sat against a fence post, sucking the life out of her pipe. Her nieces and nephews were on shed roofs or at the hayloft door, keeping watch.

"Uncle Gabriel! Someone's coming!"

It was Edouard. Madelaine stood up and came forward as Gabriel grabbed hold of his bridle and hollered: "How many?"

Madelaine felt a twist in her stomach when she saw Edouard's face. It was the first time she'd ever seen him look at his brother without a trace of rivalry complicating his empathy. Gabriel shook the bridle and said: "Come on! How many are there?"

Edouard unpuckered his mouth and the corners of his eyes and whispered: "Three hundred."

"What?"

Edouard swallowed the sand in his throat. "Three hundred."

"Goddammit, if you can't remember a simple message right . . . !"

"That's what it says," drawing a folded telegram from his shirt pocket.

Gabriel snatched it from his hand. "You don't read English any better than I do! Here—" He thrust it at Madelaine.

The telegram read: "Three hundred STOP Circled around it like red ripples in a pond." After she'd translated it, Edouard said softly: "Gabriel, the whole goddamned North West Mounted Police are waiting for you."

"It can't be. . . ." Gabriel let go of the bridle and looked down at his drawing in the dirt—two rectangles for the guard-house buildings, with a walled square in between and a dot in one corner for the scaffold. "There's no way they could've been warned."

One of the leathery men said: "None of our people would talk."

"Well, somebody did!".

The other men stood glancing at each other sideways or study-ing the toes of their moccasins. One of them murmured to Ga-briel without looking up: "I'm sorry, Gabriel, but three hundred . . ." He shook his head slowly, then turned and headed for the line of saddled horses hitched to the fence rail.

Gabriel kicked the ground, scuffing out a corner of the guard-room, and bellowed: "Nolin! Charles goddamned Nolin! It had to be. I'll kill the son of a bitch!"

Madelaine said: "It wasn't Nolin."

Gabriel wheeled on her: "Who else could've told them?"

"Louis told them."

"What?" He squinted at her, turtling his head forward.

"Don't you remember? In the newspaper story on his last speech at the trial? He said: 'And Gabriel Dumont on the other side of the line—do you imagine that Gabriel Dumont is inac-tive?' "

"Why shouldn't he say that? He knew I wouldn't abandon him."

"Of course he knew that! That's why he made damned sure there'd be enough guards to stop you!" She was quite sure she shouldn't even be thinking any of this, much less saying it, but she was past caring. She was definitely past caring about Louis Riel. After all the blood had soaked into the ground and all the smoke and ashes had blown away on the wind, the only person who'd got what he wanted was Louis David Riel. "You don't get to be a saint without getting martyred."

Gabriel came at her with his fingertips clawing the air and his teeth and eyes sparking like misaligned gears. Before he reached her he stopped and lowered his head and turned and waved her away, muttering: "That's crazy." He sat down on the ground with his hands spread-eagle against either side of his head, as though to press it back together. "Don't talk like that of the dead."

CHAPTER 56

Gabriel had lived through a lot of hard winters, but none as hard as the winter of 1885–1886. Not that the Montana winds were near as fierce as on the northern prairies, or the foothills cold nearly as cruel, but there were other elements. For one thing, he had never lived on charity before. With all the tact and hospitableness in the world, he and Madelaine were too old to adjust easily to living in someone else's house. Her brother had given them a small room of their own. Annie slept on the floor in the parlor when she was there, but that wasn't often. She was being courted by an American named Will Hamilton, who wasn't nearly as dashing and handsome as Michel Dumas, or as big and strong and charming, but he had his points.

As hard a winter as it was for him, Gabriel figured it was harder on Madelaine. At least he could get away from time to time on hunting trips. It was cold, rough work, but there's nothing like camping in snowdrifts to keep your mind focused on the immediate present instead of wandering into the past. The winter had driven the bighorns down from the high country, and there were still a few elk to be found.

When spring came, he and Madelaine were finally able to lose themselves in the pragmatics of the plans they'd made the summer before—pursuing the details of squatters' rights in the Sun River country; debating nickel-and-dime differences between this axe or that shovel. Neither of them ever referred to the fact that a year ago they would've laughed at such amounts, both of money and land.

The blossoming of the spring brought a flush back to Madelaine's cheeks and a brightness to her eyes. Gabriel sometimes wondered if she wasn't a bit too flushed and too bright. There was no denying that she was coughing less frequently—at least when he was around.

They were coming back from town one day in her brother's

fancy buggy. The hillsides were bright with wildflowers. The air was drenched with the sweet resin of balsam poplars and cottonwoods. The horse had been infected by the mood and kept tossing his head in an effort to sneak his teeth around the bit, surging out of his trot whenever Gabriel let an inch of slack into the leather ribbons. Gabriel chuckled at him and wrapped the reins around his hand to keep them taut. Can't blame a horse for trying.

Madelaine pointed up at a spattering of white froth floating high overhead against the blue. "See the swans?"

"Pelicans."

"Swans! Look at the long necks stretched out."

"Ain't necks, it's their beaks. Pelican beaks."

Madelaine clucked her tongue, shook her head, and crossed her arms to make a shelf to rest her breasts on. "If we're going to have to live on the meat you shoot until my turnips come up, you're going to have to get spectacles."

Gabriel growled at her happily. Then he suddenly felt that queasy twinge he'd learned to recognize as the signal that the scar on his skull was about to revenge itself on him again. He stiffened every muscle in his body and pressed his back into the corner of the buggy seat—if he could stay propped up, it might come and go without alarming Madelaine. He could feel the eggshell body of the buggy angling sideways as the shift in weight unbalanced the springs. The black rump of the horse spread out to fill the corners of his eyes, and the gravitational pull of the earth shifted sideways. A big drum was booming. He saw the flash of the wheel rim spinning up through the darkness to meet him. It sawed across his right shoulder and bounced him into a delicious sensation of floating leisurely through the void—marred by a disturbing slow pinwheeling going on all around him. The anvil of the earth threw itself across his back. There was a taste of dust, and he was dragged across a grindstone until released by a lightning burst of splintering tree trunks and an earth-shivering crash. Funny, he thought to himself, didn't think they got real old-time prairie thunderstorms in the foothills country. And then he stopped thinking anything.

When he surfaced again, he thought he knew where he was and what had happened. But he gradually became aware of the fact that the grunts of the lung-shot buffalo lying on top of him and the thunderous drumming of the fleeing herd were the sounds of his own breathing and the blood pounding in his ears.

All right, so a buffalo hadn't fallen on him; it just felt like it. But there was no mistaking the sound of his buffalo runner's screaming or the feel of the spasmodic jerking of its head pulling his shoulder farther out of the socket by way of the reins wrapped around his hand.

The world swam back into focus, or at least a vertigo version. Gabriel struggled to his knees, peeled the straps off his hand, and went looking for Madelaine. He spotted a large calico lump in the ditch on the other side of the upturned buggy. She was lying doubled over with her plump valentine rump offered to the sun. He rolled her over. She moaned through her nose. A red dewdrop glistened at one corner of her mouth. Her chest grunted and rasped and heaved. Her eyes didn't open, but her tongue came out and licked at the blood, then her hand came up and wiped at it vaguely with one knuckle. "You're a dab hand at driving a wagon, old man."

He kissed her temple and started to press her torso against his, but her gasp of pain snapped the springs in his arms back open. He laid her back down gently, said: "I'll be just a moment," and stood up again. There was a gleam of polished brass in a patch of twitch grass by the side of the road. Gabriel three-footed it toward the gleam—the third foot being the knuckles of his right hand straight-arming down when the revolutions of the planet made themselves too apparent.

He picked up Le Petit, checked to see that it was still in one piece, and then moved toward the screaming ruin of a horse. One back leg was twisted sideways. The splintered end of a shattered harness shaft disappeared into the glossy black rib cage. Gabriel felt bad for the horse, and for Madelaine's brother, and glad that he'd made it a policy not to break Starface's spirit by hitching him to a wagon. He locked his hand into the cocking bracket, worked the lever back and forth, kissed the horse between the ear and the white-rimmed eye with the mouth of Le Petit, and pulled the trigger.

When he came back to Madelaine she hadn't moved one fraction of an inch, except for her eyelids. The black eyes speared his and tracked his approach. Her lips peeled themselves apart, and her tongue came out to moisten them. "Next?"

The doctor said she'd cracked a couple of ribs and wrapped her tits up tighter than a nun's. Gabriel fussed and fumbled and moped around their room in her brother's house, perching on the edge of the bed while she slurped up hot broth, until one day she hissed through her teeth: "You think this summer's going to last forever, old man? You go find us a place to put up a shanty and put in some potatoes, and by the time you get back I'll be ready to do all the heavy work for you."

By the time he got back she had gone from pallid to incandescent. He said: "How're you feeling?"

"Better."

"In that case—I got some moosehide for you to chew into moccasin leather, and these old clothes are falling off me, and there's some letters I want you to write. . . ."

She lowered one eyelid and snarled with her lips, but no sound came out. She found her breath again and spoke, but only the clicking, teeth-and-tongue sounds came out: "T . . . s . . . g . . . n . . ."

"Hey—you gotta speak slow and loud, old woman. My ears ain't what they was."

"Tell . . . tell me something . . . and I'll tell you something."

"If you think I haven't learned better'n to bargain with you after all these years . . . Well, all right. You first."

She shifted her eyes from side to side, perhaps believing that she was shaking her head. "You first, old man."

"Told you I ought've learned better by now. . . . All right, what's my ante?"

"Who's . . . who is . . . I've never asked you . . . Who's Annie's father?"

"What? No, I heard you. I don't . . . Look, Annie's mother was Marie Hélène Desjarlais—you remember Marie Hélène? Well, then you oughta know it ain't so easy to say. . . . Best I can figure, it was either Henri Boucher or Counts Horses Twice . . . or maybe one of the clerks at Fort Garry. That's the best I can guess."

"That's . . ." He watched her face contort into several lizardish gestures before he realized that she was trying to moisten her dry mouth with her dry tongue. He went and got a cup of water, dabbled his fingers in it, and patted the translucent skin across her lips. He set the cup aside and cupped both his hands around one of hers. Her skin felt hot enough to burn. She whispered: "That's your only guess?"

"I don't know much about it. Like I told you when I brought her home—I found Marie Hélène with her mouth froze to a bottle on the ice on the Assiniboine and this skinned little brown rabbit mewing against her breast. All I had was guesses, and there was Annie whether I guessed right or wrong. . . . Madelaine? It's your turn. Madelaine? . . . We had a deal, goddammit! Madelaine . . .''

Her hand was already growing cold.

Part Six

But when he speaks with animation, when he talks of his feats of arms, there emerges out of his mouth which opens with a strange contraction of the jaw a voice that echoes like a rolling barrel, a voice that would carry to thousands of men gathered on the plains as vast as his courage. Everything in this man is large, the sentiments and the heart as much as the physical solidity and the alert intelligence.

ANONYMOUS NEWSPAPER JOURNALIST,
"OLD GABRIEL DUMONT"

CHAPTER 57

᷍᷍᷍ "Ladies and Gentlemen! Buffalo Bill's Wild West is now proud to present to *you*, the great democratic republic of this the greatest city in the greatest country . . ."

As the introduction went on, a big man with a voluminous mustache excused his way toward his seat in the second tier of the canvas-roofed arena. The excessive breadth of his body made it a difficult squeeze for the other patrons along the row, but none of them complained aloud. Although he was dressed in a perfectly ordinary summer suit, with a gray topcoat draped casually over his right hand, the first question that anyone with any past connection to the military would have asked him was, "What's your regiment?"

". . . and the Hero of the Half-Breed Rebellion! The Only Genuine Political Exile on the North American Continent! The Prince of the Plains! Gabriel Doo-Mont!"

A white-stockinged bay horse charged into the arena from a vomitory under the vast-mustached man's tier of seats. He stiffened on his seat and shifted forward. On the horse's back was a bearded man with grizzled black hair streaming in the wind, slapping the bay rump with the barrel of a gleaming brass-worked Winchester carbine. As the horseman rounded the far end of the arena at full tilt, a young woman in a fanciful cowgirl outfit emerged from the vomitory he'd entered through. She threw three colored glass balls up in the air as the rider bearing down on her took the reins in his teeth and threw his rifle up to his shoulder. He fired three times from the saddle. All three glass balls shattered in midair. North America's Only Jen-You-Wine Poe-Litical Exile galloped past the cowgirl and was gone. The applause and cheering had an undercurrent of hesitancy—it had happened so fast, they weren't quite sure what had happened.

The Prince of the Plains appeared again in the finale, prancing his horse around the arena as part of the grand parade. As the last round of ovations died, the muftied military man heaved his rain-barrel torso upright and marched through the thinning crowd, out into the sunlight and around the back of the arena to the gaudy collection of awnings and pavilions that made up the performers' quarters. He put out his hand in front of a passing painted Sioux warrior in a tweed cap and asked him where he might find Gabriel Dumont. The Sioux didn't appear to understand English or French, so the big man asked the question again in sign talk, denoting the object of his hunt with the sign for "wagonman" and the spoken "Gabriel."

The tweed-capped red man pointed down a side alley of tent fronts. The white man wove his way along through knots of intermingled Wild Indians and Cow Boys and Sharpshooters and Trick Riders, most of them half out of their costumes and into their civvies, some of them scrubbing off war paint and making jokes about how much time they could have saved on the Little Bighorn if they'd known then about Leichner Grease Sticks. All of them were giving each other various high signs and cackling over how well they'd gone over in their first New York appearance.

He had just passed by a Coliseum-size dining tent with ranks of cooks basting spitted hogs and oxen when a voice behind him bellowed: "Crozier!" He stopped and turned. Down a side street of tents stood Gabriel Dumont with a revolver in his hand. The tweed-capped Sioux was skipping sideways away from him, and the laneful of show folk behind had all discovered a sudden urge to duck into their tents.

"How do, Gabriel."

"Show me what you got in your hand under the coat."

Crozier brought his left hand up slowly and folded back the coat to expose the half-evaporated bottle of J. Jameson & Sons' Finest Irish. "I know probably nobody gives a damn down here, but old habits die hard."

Gabriel laughed so hard, he had to sit down. "You keep up them habits, Superintendent, and you're going to get a bullet in the back of the neck one of these days," pointing with his pistol at the tweed-capped Wild Indian poking his head out of a tent. "He told me there was an English soldier, or maybe policeman, who was pretending not to be but was definitely looking for me, with something hidden in his right hand."

Crozier shifted the bottle to his left hand so he could reach down his right to shake Gabriel's and help him to his feet. Gabriel holstered his revolver and reached up. When he was on his feet, he poked Crozier in the belly and said: "Got too fat for your red coat?"

"Glass houses, Gabriel."

"Well, they feed us damned good, no question. You on a holiday?"

"Permanent, in terms of the Force, at least. After Macdonald appointed his next-door neighbor as commissioner, who took away my promotion to assistant commissioner to give it to his little brother . . ."

"Yeah, I guess they ain't ever going to forgive you for Duck Lake. Say—I could get somebody to write up a letter for me, to tell them if it'd been anybody but you leading the Police there, we would've killed them all."

Crozier laughed. "Somehow I doubt the Force would take a commendation from you as a recommendation for me. Anyway, it wasn't just Duck Lake. Most of the rest of the officers that came west with the first contingent are finding themselves in pretty much the same position."

"Huh. Got too close to the country, eh?"

"The country?"

"Yeah—Ottawa don't like its North West Mounted Police getting too close with the North West?"

"Something like that."

"I gotta admit, though, you did surprise me—marching out of Fort Carlton without waiting for your reinforcements. Not that it would've made any difference except more Police for us to kill. . . ."

"I didn't have much choice. Clarke said he was going to march out his volunteers whether we came along or not."

"Clarke?"

"Lawrence Clarke."

"Huh. He got around, didn't he? . . . Dry?" He elaborated on the last question by producing a shiny silver flask from a back pocket. Crozier unscrewed the stopper and took a taste, expecting to force down a polite sip of raw gin or American whiskey. What he got instead was a dash of warm liquid that exploded into cognac vapors at the back of his throat like the glass balls exploding in midair. He cocked the flask to his mouth again and cocked his eyebrows at Gabriel, who shrugged. "It's a hard life in the circus, no question."

"Gabe! There you are, ole hoss!" Crozier turned toward the

voice and was almost blinded by a glittering vision in beaded white buckskin and thigh-high riding boots, with the biggest brass-buckled cartridge belt this side of Blackbeard and more fringes than a shimmy dancer. "Wanted to have a word with you! Damn—where'd that interpreter go?"

"Colonel Cody? I'm Major Lief Crozier of the North West Mounted Police—retired."

"An honor and a privilege, Major! Say now, if you're retired from active duty—a genuine Mounted Police officer would be a fine touch in the show. Red tunic, white pith helmet, brass buttons, maybe a white horse . . . No, can't have more'n one white horse in the show. . . ."

"I do appreciate the offer, Colonel, but I doubt the Force would consent. But if you need someone to interpret to Gabriel for the moment . . ."

"That's mighty white of you, Major. Tell him I was just hankering to give him a bit of friendly advice, from one old plainsman to another. He's got a fine act, and the folks sure do admire him, but they'd admire him a lot more if he could throw in just a bit more . . . panache! Ee-spirit décor," gesturing grandly with his fringe-feathered arm by way of demonstration, sweeping off his yardwide Stetson to shake his bronze mane in the sun. "Give the folks a bit more of the noble savagery they expect." It took Crozier a moment to remember he had offered to act as interpreter, because he was mesmerised by Colonel Cody's hair. It wasn't exactly bronze—there were also tinges of gold and silver—but it was decidedly metallic and not like anything Crozier had seen on the head of man or beast.

Gabriel's response to Crozier's translation was: "You tell Buffalo Billy that this is the way a half-breed general moves his arm, this is the way the last Captain of the buffalo hunt takes off his hat, this is the way the Continent's Only Political Exile lifts his leg to fart. I can't pretend to be what I am."

Fortunately, Buffalo Bill didn't wait for Crozier to translate. Instead, he winked at Gabriel and patted his shoulder. "Knew I could count on you, ole hoss. Major—you could thrill the crowned heads of Europe with this picture of two strong mortal enemies united in friendship when the battle is o'er; the generosity of brave hearts . . . I feel a lump in my throat just thinking about it. Think it over." He flourished out a grand sign-talk farewell to Gabriel and was gone in a wave of white leather and bronze waves of hair.

Gabriel mimicked Buffalo Bill's sign-talk farewell and said: "Why would he ask if it was all right with me for his horse to copulate with my uncle's moccasins?"

"Now don't try to tell me you don't get some fun out of this."

"Who, me? Would I stand in front of my tent picking my teeth with my knife and making growly faces at the white city people come for a look? Come on over to the dinner tent—I'll tell 'em Buffalo Bill's trying to get you in the show. I'll lay you any odds the Police cooks didn't feed you like this."

Crozier was glad he hadn't taken the bet. Even though the Force's commissaries sometimes performed Christmas miracles, they certainly never dispensed endless relays of buckets of beer and jugs of wine and beakers of brandy. The dining tent was filled with a babble of languages and a riot of new acquaintances of Gabriel's who had to be introduced to his old friend and enemy, from Buck Taylor the Cowboy King to the Blood-thirsty Sioux War Chief American Horse. There turned out to be a few members of the corps of outriders that Crozier already knew, such as Michel Dumas.

Crozier and Gabriel and Michel Dumas rocked back in their chairs, patting their bellies and letting out sighs in between puffs on their Cuban cigars and sips of cognac-laced tea. Gabriel said: "So what are you going to do, now that you ain't a policeman no more?"

"I have a stateroom on a ship leaving New York for Ireland. I plan to suffer through a few months of being wined and dined through the home counties and setting aflutter the white breasts of the sea-green-eyed girls with tales of my adventures in the Wild West . . . told with manly modesty, of course."

Gabriel belched. "Of course. You going to stay on there, then?"

"Not a bit of it. I'm going back to school."

"To *what*?"

"I mean to study for the bar. I've never been fond of lawyers and politicians, but I've finally had to admit that it's better to be one than to be used by them."

"You going to take Macdonald's job away?"

"Given a choice, I would rather suck dead rats than set foot in the Dominion of Canada again. What are you planning on doing?"

Gabriel gave out a surprised grunt, as though he'd thought it was obvious. He gestured around the carnival tent and the bright-plumed live specimens whose raucousness was settling down to a satiated sunset murmur. "I ain't got much choice."

"What about the amnesty?"

Michel Dumas said: "The what?"

"Haven't you heard what's going on in Ottawa?"

Gabriel laughed. "Down here Ottawa's nothing but a funny-sounding Indian word."

"Parliament's considering an amnesty for all the exiles from the rebellion."

" 'Rebellion,' eh? Funny word to use on people who were there long before the government was. The last time I heard the word *amnesty* floating around was back in 'seventy, when Macdonald promised Riel an amnesty to get the Red River troubles over with, and then told him he imagined it. I'll believe it this time when Macdonald signs a piece of paper that he can't take back."

"I believe that's exactly what's about to happen. I don't have many friends in Ottawa—if I did, I'd be commissioner instead of retired—but the few I do have tell me all the signs point toward a formal amnesty."

Michel Dumas said: "Then we can go back, Gabriel."

"Back to what?"

EPILOGUE

Kitty was loitering on the boardwalk of Winnipeg's roistering Main Street while her mother and sisters ransacked the interior of a millinery store. She was a bit giddy with the family reunion. Her father had been re-posted to Fort Alexander on Lake Winnipeg immediately after the horrible hostage time—which seemed more and more like a grand adventure the more years went by—and Kitty had been boarded once again at The Red River Ladies' Academy with Elisabeth and Amelia to finish off the process of finishing school. Clan McLean had all come in from Fort Alexander for Kitty's graduation, but she wasn't quite sure what she had graduated to. The long winter nights in the dormitory had given her plenty of time to think of Stanley Simpson's gallantry while they were hostages together, but Stanley had drowned trying to save his chief factor from the white water of the Nelson River.

Kitty had stepped out onto the boardwalk to take a breather from matching the rest of the family's delirium about shopping in the big city. She had to be careful not to let her mother guess that she'd spent enough afternoons poking in and out of the shops along Saloon Row to grow blasé about the selection of buttons and bows.

Kitty had just marshalled the energy to march back to the millinery store when a strange phenomenon became apparent. There was a kind of wave of silence and stillness working its way along the street. Kitty stopped and looked back for the cause. On the other side of the street there was a squat man in a broad black hat that shadowed all his features except his grizzled beard, padding along the boardwalk in moccasins. He seemed to trail a wake of numb shock. The jaws of bustlers and loungers locked in midguffaw as he went by.

"Son of a bitch has got a lot of gall."

Kitty looked over her shoulder. Two rough-and-ready-looking

young men were standing with arms akimbo, glaring across the road. A balding, aproned shopkeeper leaned in the doorway behind them. The second young man said: "I got a good mind to go over there and teach him—"

He was cut off by the storekeeper's laughter. The brace of young men glared at him as he wheezed and choked and slapped his aproned belly. Finally he found enough breath to say: "If you boys want to try conclusions with Gabriel Dumont, you just go right ahead."

"Don't think we won't!"

"I just bet you will. Say, if you really want to bet, I'm the local agent for Lloyd's Life Insurance. . . ."

The storekeeper's cackles at his own joke faded into the background as Kitty's legs carried her of their own accord off the boardwalk, picking their way along the planks bridged across the street's spring gumbo. "Monsieur Dumont?"

The dark figure, no taller than she but three times as broad, stopped cold in midtrundle and turned on its heel. Up close, the hat-shaded features were no less indistinct, but she could see now two small black flames burning in the shadow. "Monsieur Dumont, my name is Kitty McLean. I was one of the—"

The rest of her speech choked off as a chesty voice rumbled out of the hat shadow: "You was one of the prisoners dragged back and forth all along the North Saskatchewan. My sister told me the only man she ever met braver'n me was Mademoiselle Kitty McLean."

She stammered and blushed and said: "Please give my respects to your wife."

"My wife?"

"Madame Madelaine. I'm sure she won't remember, but I met her once, in the spring before—"

"My wife is dead."

"Oh. I . . . I'm sorry. . . . She was . . . she was very kind to me."

"My Madelaine was very kind to everyone. Excuse me, I should've thought." One gnarled hand went up and swept his hat off. The face revealed to her was broad, heavy, and chopped over with scars, like an oak carving left out in the elements until all the softer pits between the grain have been eaten away. He laughed. "I used to be a lot prettier, but I fainted in a hardware store one day and went facedown in a keg of nails. Funny, ain't it—an old hard case like me fainting like some lady with them 'vapors'? But it don't happen no more. So, Mademoiselle Kitty McLean, now you're all growed up and lived to tell the tale. That's good.''

"And you?"

"Me? I'm just passing through here." He laughed again. "I been passing through everywhere—the American President's White House, Paris, Staten Island . . . A bunch of Quebec politicians even brought me in special to make speeches in Montreal, but they seemed to get real nervous when I started talking about how the priests betrayed us at Batoche. I'm just passing through the land office here to carve my name on some papers. Funny, ain't it? After all the dead and all the fighting, the government's come across with the land titles that were all we wanted in the first place."

She meant to say: "Monsieur Dumont," but all that came out was a squeak. She swallowed a couple of times, stiffened her spine, and tried again. Her voice sounded shrill, but she kept on going: "Monsieur Dumont—there are a great many things I don't understand, but I do know that I would feel privileged to shake you by the hand."

"Nope. From what my sister tells me, it'd be the other way around." As her hand slid into the pebble-palmed paw, he twisted his wrist to turn the handshake grip sideways and bowed forward to kiss the back of her hand, the wiry beard hairs tickling. He straightened his back without letting go of her hand and said: "You're too young to mourn for what's gone—leave that to old fellows like me. Your time is what's coming. Go on and make yourself another Madelaine for some lucky young fellow." He slipped his hand out of hers, covered his head with his hat again, and was gone.

Author's Note

The book you've just read (if you haven't, why the hell are you wasting your time reading this?) was never intended to be a history of the North West Rebellion but simply the story of Gabriel and Madelaine Dumont—with a side order of Kitty McLean. Countless fascinating incidents didn't fit into that story. Poundmaker's surrender to Middleton, for instance, remains one of the great tragicomedies to come out of the conquest of North America, or any other continent, for that matter. A number of interesting anecdotes directly involving Gabriel or Madelaine had to be left out as well—either because they didn't fit into this way of telling the overall story or because they didn't show us much we hadn't already learned from other incidents. There are a great many history books in existence that tell these other stories, and I would be pleased to think that this book had encouraged you to delve into a few of them—unless, of course, I find a way to squeeze a future book of my own out of the same material.

If I may, though, I would like to put in one note of caution before you go scuttling off to the history section. While history books should always be taken in moderate doses, they should never be taken singly. If one book on a given subject is your limit, Benjamin Disraeli had a prescription: "Read no history, nothing but biography, for that is life without theory."

The reason was best defined for me by a métis university student working the souvenir stand the first time I visited Batoche, back when I was young and limber. At that time, Batoche Historic Site consisted of the church and cemetery and a small museum with a souvenir-and-soda-pop shop attached. As I was poking about among the plastic Indian dolls, the woman behind the counter asked me if I'd been through the museum. I told her

I had and added: "They seem to've changed a few things in there."

"Oh, you've been here before?"

"No, I mean they've changed a few things from the way they happened."

Without blinking, she said: "Government version."

There are lots of different varieties of "government" or "official" versions. Central Canadian or Parisian historians continue to portray the North West Rebellion as an extension of the tensions along the Ontario-Quebec border—a struggle between "the two great races of European civilisation" (I wish that weren't a direct quote). The official version espoused by various historians of the Royal Canadian Mounted Police puts the events of 1885 through exquisite hoops to use them as an illustration of the effectiveness of the Force. The official reverse-racist version teaches that Riel was hung because the six-man jury was all white and therefore prejudiced, despite the fact that the only juror who ever broke the vow of silence said: "We were in a dilemma. We could not pass judgment on the Minister of the Interior, who was not on trial; and we had to give our finding on Riel according to the evidence. We refused to find him insane. The only thing we could do was to add the clause to our verdict recommending mercy. We knew it wasn't much, but it was not an empty formal expression, and it expressed the serious desire of every one of the six of us."

A history book has to have a thesis. Once a given official version has been squeezed dry, the budding historian has to come up with an antithesis and hope that it may become, in time, a full-fledged official version. A recent example is the theory that John A. Macdonald instigated the rebellion through his agent provocateur Lawrence Clarke. Another is that Gabriel Dumont was lying when he said he'd planned a campaign of guerrilla warfare, because the métis never fought except from defensive positions—which I'm sure is a great comfort to all those Sioux and Blackfoot killed in running skirmishes with métis buffalo hunters.

An interesting sidelight to the Macdonald/Clarke conspiracy theory is that the rebellion saved John A. Macdonald's career, his government, and his Canadian Pacific Railroad. William Van Horne, the American hired to build the railroad, vowed that he could have the troops in Montreal and Toronto mobilized and on the field in the Saskatchewan country within eleven days. It had taken two months to get troops to Winnipeg in 1870. After the railroad had thus saved the country from rebellion and Barbarous Acts Perpetrated Upon Defenseless White Women, no member of Parliament was suicidal enough to fight against another loan to the railroad, much less ask embarrassing questions about what had happened to the last one. The hanging of Riel, though, finished the federal Conservative party in Quebec for seventy years, until the advent of a prairie boy who liked to brag about the time he met Gabriel Dumont.

The most time-honored and pervasive of all official versions is the one that portrays Riel as the instigator and leader, with Dumont as a kind of sturdy strong-arm sidekick. One of the reasons it first came into being was plain political expediency for the government of the day—Riel had been executed and Dumont amnestied, ergo Riel had to have been the chief rebel. But the reason this official version remains entrenched long after John A. Macdonald and all his ministers have been laid amoldering in their graves is that history tends to be written by academics. With rare exceptions, people who have spent their lives in scholarly pursuits assume that an educated man like Riel—and like them—must have been the leader. An illiterate like Dumont couldn't possibly have served any purpose except to tag along faithfully and sweep the floors when things got too messy.

Even a cursory look into the firsthand accounts of the rebellion paints a far more complex picture of Dumont and his relations with Riel, but official versions are notoriously impervious. This particular official version has even been extended into a rather unpleasant sneering at Dumont for escaping to the States instead of sticking around to hang beside Riel—as though he'd got off easy by only losing his wife, his home, his brother, his father, many of his closest friends, and the material wealth he'd accumulated to make a comfortable old age.

One of the cornerstones of that official version was actually laid down by Dumont himself, namely the one-dimensional portraits of Riel as the humanitarian and Gabriel as the brutish primitive. During the time of Riel's trial and subsequent appeals, Dumont made a point of telling every journalist and government spy within earshot that he was utterly responsible for every act of violence perpetrated by the Army of the Exovedate, and that Riel had always advocated mercy and peace. While it's undeniable that Gabriel was always ruthless in a fight, and that Riel was never known to personally inflict physical harm on anyone, the official version plants those simplistic poles in every situation—asserting, for instance, that Riel stopped Dumont from murdering the hostages after Duck Lake. Peter Tompkins was one of the Indian Agency interpreters who got a close look down the barrel of Gabriel's revolver that night, so he'd be hardly likely to go out of his way to paint a rosy picture. His version is: "Gabriel Dumont . . . did not seem to act as a man as though he wanted to kill prisoners very bad. He just simply ordered them out, and then he seemed to quit there when he had ordered them out."

I have my own prejudices (strike that—other people have prejudices, I have opinions). I've never been able to understand the prevailing Canadian fascination with Riel—other than the fact that the people with a vested interest in the official version also happen to be the people teaching Canadian history. While there's no question that Riel had a profound effect on two pivotal moments in the formation of the country, not even his biographers suggest that he could pass the simple test that any central character should be put through before a writer inflicts him or her upon the reading public: "If this person dropped by unannounced for a cold beer and a conversation, would I want to answer the door?" But I must admit that the further I dug into Riel for the purposes of this story, the more my instinctive dog-to-a-cat reaction softened. I would still be inclined to hide in the bathroom and pretend I wasn't home, but in light of his personal history it would've been amazing if he *hadn't* started seeing fat, flowered serpents following Michel Dumas across the prairie.

But the major reason the official version factor means that history texts should never be taken singly is that historians have only a finite amount of time and energy, unlike the rest of us. When you have to concentrate your attention on proving a theory, little details tend to get lost. One history book informed me that the man who started the singing in Tourond's Coulee was Isidor Dumont, which was certainly a remarkable performance for a man who'd been shot to death a month earlier. Small wonder the Canadian soldiers were intimidated. Another book informed me that the song they sung was an old French ballad called "The Falcon's Song," which I would've taken as gospel if I hadn't read other books referring to the old métis songmaker Pierre Falcon.

At least two books authoritatively asterisk "Le Petit" as a "Henry .44-40." I accepted that as fact until I read Gabriel's reminiscences specifically referring to "my Winchester." By 1885, "Winchester" had become a generic term for any lever-action repeating rifle, but the apparent contradiction led me to discover that the notoriously fragile Henry rifle ceased being manufactured in 1866. The "Le Petit" that Gabriel is holding in the photographs taken at Fort Assiniboine bears a very strong resemblance to a Winchester carbine and very little resemblance to a Henry. While the picture isn't detailed enough to differentiate between several possible models of Winchester carbine, it does clearly show a wooden forestock, which was never incorporated into any version of the Henry rifle. But once several generations of historians have successively quoted each other in defining "Le Petit" as a "Henry .44-40" it becomes historical fact. Perhaps the original confusion arose from the fact that Winchester continued to mark its rim-fire cartridges with an "H" for Benjamin Henry, so the cartridges Dumont fired from his Winchester would have been Henry .44-40's, or more likely, Henry .44's.

Whether Le Petit was a Winchester or a Henry rifle makes little difference to a history book. But for a book like this one, which depends on placing you inside Gabriel in several battles, it's not unimportant to know whether he would have been reloading Le Petit through the side gate of a Winchester or through a tube opening under the muzzle of a Henry rifle. I just thought you were owed the assurance, having come this far through the loneliness of the long-distance reader, that this work of historical fiction is at least as accurate as any sober (as opposed to yours truly) history text on the market.

In defense of historians (this is what we call in the trade "pendulum writing" or "that old Liberal picket-poke"), writing a formal history book leaves far less room to maneuver than there is in a book like this. You can't write a history text without donning the mantle of Expert (described once as "a man with a briefcase fifty miles from home"). Once donned, you can't afford to let that mantle slip by salting in, "I ain't too sure about this," along the borders of your expertise.

There is also the fact that some facts can be very difficult to nail down. I have half a dozen different maps of the Battle of Batoche, all of them differing slightly in details of geography and troop movements. And the old adage of the witnesses to a car accident seems to multiply exponentially when it comes to events as tumultuous as the North West Rebellion. Taking only one for instance—the parley before the shooting started at Duck Lake. Depending on which eyewitness account you read, Isidor Dumont and Ahsiweyin may have been mounted or on foot, Crozier may have ridden out to meet them or walked, Gentleman Joe McKay may have accompanied Crozier as an interpreter or he may have come galloping out from the sleigh barricades to tell Crozier they were being surrounded, etcetera, etcetera, ad infinitum. I won't even get into the Police survivors who asserted such things as that the "rebel" parleyers were three Indians and Crozier wrestled one of them to the ground.

The version I chose to go with may or may not be correct, but it's based on four incontrovertible facts: 1) Isidor and Ahsiweyin were coming out to buy time, which suggests that they wouldn't be inclined to trot out smartly on horseback; 2) except for their advance scouts, the party from Fort Carlton was traveling in sleighs, so Crozier might not have had the option of climbing onto a saddle horse when he saw the white flag approaching; 3) Crozier spoke fluent French, so when he saw the very recognizable figure of Isidor Dumont approaching his first thought likely wasn't "I'd better bring along an interpreter"; and 4) Gentleman Joe McKay said he didn't fire a shot until he saw Isidor kneeling down to take aim at him. That last is undoubtedly a lie—Isidor was hardly likely to kneel down to take careful aim at a man less than ten feet away from him—but it's not the kind of lie anyone would make up about a man on horseback.

It was Gentleman Joe who also gave me the key out of the labyrinth of contradictory accounts of how the shooting started. His account is in a book by Trooper John Donkin, one of those arrogant one-termers whose perceptions were so different from Lief Crozier's and the other old hands in the Force. Donkin was a great admirer of Joe McKay's and delightedly concurred with McKay's descriptions of the rebels as "swarthy bandits" and "black devils." Donkin gleefully reports McKay bragging of how he'd "emptied his revolver into the Indian."

Out of all the varying versions of various events, I've tended to lean most on Gabriel's. He dictated two sets of memoirs. Some of the details obviously weren't transcribed correctly—I think he was probably aware that Tourond's Coulee is on the east side of the South Saskatchewan, not the west—but overall, the facts that can be checked against other sources (such as Canadian army records versus Gabriel's list of invading regiments) show that meticulous retention that the literate find so remarkable in those who have to depend entirely on their memories and oral traditions.

But the major reason I put so much credence in Gabriel's version of events is a character trait that rings unmistakably throughout. It could be described as honesty or a sense of humor or as a self-esteem so thoroughly grounded that it feels no need to justify itself to anybody. The best single example is the moment at Duck Lake when he loaned Le Petit to Baptiste Vandal—which no one would ever have known of if Gabriel hadn't chosen to include it in his reminiscences. A man with a selective memory geared toward representing himself heroically would have hardly gone out of his way to inform the world that the mix-up of cartridge belts made his pants fall down in the middle of the battle.

An obverse example of that trait is William Bleasdell Cameron, the lone white male survivor of the Frog Lake Massacre, who went on to a long career as a journalist. Although Cameron was an honest and accurate writer, in all his accounts of Frog Lake he somehow neglects to mention Pelagie Simpson putting one of her dresses on him and half carrying him to safety. Among his writings is one story that's very touching for oblique reasons. Cameron's best friend was Stanley Simpson, perhaps partly because they'd both lost an eye in childhood. Long after Stanley Simpson drowned trying to rescue his factor after their canoe overturned in white water, Cameron wrote a story about a fictional young Hudson's Bay Company clerk who loves the factor's daughter, and vice versa, but the factor won't entertain the notion of his daughter being courted by a lowly clerk. In the story, the factor and the clerk have their canoe overturned in white water, and the clerk tries to rescue him. But in this case the factor drowns, the clerk is saved, and he and the factor's daughter live happily ever after.

After all my caviling about historian's authoritative inaccuracies, it would be extremely remiss of me not to point out that I wouldn't have been able even to begin this book if it weren't for the legion of historians who'd spent long years ferreting information out of archives and turning it into books. Even while I was fumingly tracing down the original sources that some historian had offhandedly misquoted, I was aware that I wouldn't have known where to look for the original source if someone hadn't shown the way. In some cases, the historians whose theses I disagreed with the most were also the most helpful, since they forced me to examine things more closely. The full list of those who have gone on before would go on beyond the blue horizon, but I should make special mention of two Georges and a Joseph: Woodcock, Stanley, and Howard. In their own separate ways and times, those three pretty much invented the notion of seeing the North West Rebellion in terms of character—not only of the people who took part in the events, but of the country they lived in. I should also like to express my gratitude to Catherine Crozier, who supplied me with a great deal of information about her "uncle Lief" that doesn't figure in official histories.

As long as I'm in the thanking mode—I wouldn't have been able to get the information from Catherine Crozier if the Bruce County Museum hadn't put me in touch with her. And I would still be searching for a definitive answer to the Henry/Winchester question were it not for the help of Neil Smith, a self-confessed science fiction writer from Colorado. He also solved a quandary about the technically defined effective range of Le Petit and other rifles by mentioning that he'd seen "some of those old boys who lived with their rifles" do remarkable things with elevated arc shots. At the time that I was fortunate enough to be directed to Neil Smith, I was in the throes of tracing down a museum in Saskatchewan that was rumored to have "Gabriel Dumont's rifle" on display. I had a suspicion that it would prove to be the rifle he is holding in a turn-of-the-century photograph that is definitely not the Le Petit of 1885, but I was getting desperate for any concrete bit of information. The Museum of Natural History passed me on to someone at the R.C.M.P. museum, who said they'd had it but had passed it on to the Plains Museum. The people there informed me that it had been handed on to the Duck Lake Museum. The Duck Lake Museum was about to close for the season, but a person there promised to forward me a description and photograph. Two months passed with no information forthcoming, so I began to telephone the number I'd been given for the museum's chairman. After several fruitless attempts I tried the number of the closed-for-the-season museum. The *new* chairman answered. He was still familiarizing himself with the museum's artifacts, etc., but promised to look into it and get back to me. Two days later he phoned back and informed me that there was no record of the Duck Lake Museum ever having had Gabriel Dumont's rifle in its possession, "but we do have his pocketwatch."

A person at Environment Canada kindly provided me with a wealth of statistics that corroborated a notion that came out through happenstance. When I first started working on this story—originally as a musical for the theater (they can't all be gems)—I was in Winnipeg during a particularly brutal winter in the early 1980s. The weather reports kept saying that this was the coldest recorded December 14, or January 3, or whatever, since the winter of 1884–85. Since then, I've come across a few historians that made reference to the fact, but by and large history isn't affected by such mundane things as weather.

And now it appears I've run out of delaying mechanisms and have come to the point that became inevitable the moment I opened my trap about the shortcomings of historians. The fact is—O! gentle, patient, and forgiving reader—that this book contains a certain amount of fudging of its own. The dates of several peripheral events—such as the execution of Wandering Spirit—have been shifted slightly so that their effects on Madelaine and Gabriel could be brushed in without wrenching the whole canvas out of shape. The store and billiard table at Gabriel's Crossing were probably located in a side shed, although at least one source puts them in the twin addition to the main house. I simplified the answer to the question of whether they had secure title to their land at Gabriel's Crossing. The scenes that take place within meetings of the Exovedate aren't exactly as set down in Phillipe Garnot's minutes, but they do follow the general line of transcribed arguments and confrontations, and my own experience with minutes suggests that the notes taken aren't necessarily a perfect record of all that took place. Gabriel's title on the Exovedate was actually "Adjutant General," which would have been somewhat confusing to readers in those countries where the term means "Chief Military Lawyer."

Kitty Mclean has been altered somewhat. Her meetings with Gabriel and Madelaine are fabricated, although the documented movements and characters of all three puts the incidents within the realm of possibility. All the other events and the background of her childhood—the gift necklace from Sitting Bull and so forth—are documented. But in some cases I may or may not have combined her with her sister Elisabeth. The reason I say "may or may not" is because there is a certain amount of confusion about who did what. Elisabeth says it was she and Amelia who went out to the Cree camp to see if their father was safe. Duncan McLean—he of the "We mustn't let those darned In-

dians see us cry"—wrote: "It was Kitty who announced she
was going to see what had happened. Always impulsive, she
jumped over the barricade. Amelia said: 'I'm going with you.'
Nobody could have stopped them."

There is no evidence for Lief Crozier's visit to Gabriel's
Crossing, although if it had taken place, it would hardly have
figured in official reports. There is plenty of evidence that it
wouldn't have been out of character. Sir Cecil E. Denny, one of
Crozier's fellow Originals, wrote a book called *The Law
Marches West*. In it, he asserts that the only reason Crozier
wasn't killed at Duck Lake was because Gabriel Dumont had
given strict orders not to shoot at him. I think the story's probably spurious—Gabriel had other things on his mind at the
time—but the fact that Denny believed it says a good deal about
Crozier's relations with the people of the North West in general
and Dumont in particular.

I invented the romance between Annie and Michel Dumas.
Very little is known about Annie and not much more about
Michel Dumas. It grew out of the character that all the existing
evidence portrays Michel Dumas to have been: charming, handsome, physically brave, and maddeningly irresponsible. Many
of the minor characters—Moïse Ouellette, Phillipe Garnot, Jerome Henry, and others—had to be stitched together out of snip-
pets of information, snatches of conversation remembered
twenty years after the fact, and the occasional photograph. In
some cases, two equally reliable sources have labeled the same
group photograph with two different sets of names.

But the major work of invention in this book had to be Madelaine. There are no known photographs of her and very few
known facts. If that gives the disappointing notion that she was
invented out of whole cloth, a few of the proven facts I did have
to go on were that she was educated and took a strong hand in
Gabriel's business ventures, she had no children of her own but
played aunt to the whole territory, and that her relationship with
Gabriel contained a strong strain of bantering humor. The recorded anecdotes regarding her that I've managed to work into
the book include the incident at Fort Pitt when the Cree warrior
made a rude suggestion to her, her cooperative effort with Aicawpow to convince Gabriel to make the run for the medicine
line, and Gabriel telling her after the fall of Batoche: "If the
police catch you and try to blame you for what I did . . ."

The only outsider's description of Madelaine and her life with

Gabriel comes from John Andrew Kerr, who came west as a young volunteer with the Canadian troops sent to put down the Red River Rebellion and stayed on to ramble about the plains through the early 1870s. He attached himself for a time to Gabriel Dumont's group of buffalo hunters, and on one occasion they came across a young family of starving Cree:

> Gabriel told his wife, Madelaine, to get some meat from the storehouse. She was a fine comely woman, and people often wondered what she saw in such a homely chap as Gabriel— for he was homely. He looked older than his age, which had barely reached the middle thirties, and had rough-hewn features, an ungainly figure, and a scraggly beard. He has been described as gigantic, which was untrue, as he was of medium height only, but possessed of uncanny muscular strength. Both his father, Ai-caw-pow, and his uncle, Ska-kas-ta-ow, were much larger than he. In his own home Gabriel was never quarrelsome, and his wife and adopted daughter—he had no children of his own—never got an unkind word from him, so far as I ever knew or heard. Well, Madelaine grumbled, but she lugged in a leg of buffalo, weighing perhaps fifty pounds, and a half-sack of pemmican.

Kerr recorded a great many anecdotes about Dumont, but late in his life he wrote a short reflective overview that should be required reading for all those who still cling to the "official version" of Gabriel Dumont as nothing more than a kind of overamped Gabby Hayes. "Sometimes Dumont was intemperate, occasionally violent, but the genuine kindliness he showed me when I was a boy drew me to him. A quality hard to describe, fascinated me. He used a queer trick that has been traced back to older generations of buffalo hunters—he could call the buffalo in some mysterious manner. Possibly he used some mesmerism on me as well!"

Madelaine's attitudes toward the Riels are also necessarily invented. But the fact is that Gabriel was swayed by someone or something to abandon his subordinate role and burst out of Riel's control the day Middleton's column reached Clarke's Crossing. My portrayals of Louis and Marguerite Riel will no doubt cause offense to some people who prefer their icons without human faces, but out of all the characterizations in this book, those two had the most recorded evidence to build from—with the exception of Gabriel.

Before I drift off into the ether, you might be curious about what happened to a few people who passed in and out of the story. Marguerite Riel died of consumption within six months of her husband's execution. Marie Angelique died in childhood, and Jean Riel died in 1908, married but childless. So any claims of direct descent from Louis Riel are as spurious as those of a Manitoba woman who told me she was Gabriel Dumont's great-granddaughter. Perhaps Riel and Dumont both fathered illegitimate children who passed on their genes without their names, but that sort of thing is rather difficult to corroborate.

General Middleton's career in the Canadian military was ended by charges that he'd looted a fortune in furs from farms along the South Saskatchewan—not to mention Gabriel Dumont's billiard table. He retired to England, where he was elevated to Sir Frederick Middleton, Keeper of the Crown Jewels. Inspector Francis Dickens tried to mount a campaign to blame the surrender of Fort Pitt on Kitty's father, but it rebounded on him. Some wag resurrected the nickname that the inspector's revered father had conferred on him when he was a boy helping out with the grouse shooting on the Yorkshire moors: "Chickenstalker." Chickenstalker had never been much of a policeman to begin with. Internal reports throughout his earlier career show clearly that he was only kept on because none of his superiors wanted to sign their names to an order discharging the son of Charles Dickens. After the rebellion and his subsequent rechristening as "Chickenstalker," he applied himself seriously to the only task he'd ever applied himself seriously to—drinking himself to death—and succeeded within a year.

Lief Newry Fitzroy "Paddy" Crozier kept his vow to absent himself from the country that had treated him so shabbily. He completed his law studies and was licensed to practice in Oklahoma in 1891. He died unmarried, and his uniform tunic—one of the few NWMP commissioned officer's tunics still in existence—is on permanent display in the Bruce County Museum in Canada.

Both Poundmaker and Big Bear served only portions of their penitentiary sentences and died soon after their releases— Poundmaker in the camp of Crowfoot, his adoptive father and the head of the Blackfoot Confederacy that had stood aside in 1885 waiting to see which way the wind was going to blow. Fine

Day, Poundmaker's War Chief, lived out a peaceful life south of the Medicine Line and in his old age dictated a series of memoirs to the Museum of Natural History that gives us one of our clearest extant pictures of Plains tribe life in that brief period between the coming of the horse and the crushing victory of white civilization.

Annie married Will Hamilton and lived out her later life in Calgary. Moïse Ouellette, Phillipe Garnot, and the other Exovedes who'd survived the fighting served out their prison terms and returned to tend their own gardens on the South Saskatchewan. Some Saskatchewan métis pulled up stakes and drifted northwest. A number of them took up an offer to pool their land scrip in an area north of Edmonton. The priest who'd organized it eventually forced most of them off in favor of white Catholic immigrants from Quebec. Charles Nolin, after his brief incarceration at Prince Albert, was never charged. He became the prosecution's star witness in the trial of his cousin, Louis Riel. His wife lived to a hale and hearty old age and the statue of Our Lady of Lourdes that her husband had promised to the church if her novena worked still stands in the grotto at St. Laurent.

Joseph Honoré Jaxon, née William Henry Jackson, was committed to an asylum in Manitoba. One summer afternoon he simply walked away and made his way down to the States, living on nuts and berries. He spent the rest of his very long life touting various fringe labor movements, Populist causes, and the Bahai religion. In December of 1951, at the age of ninety, he was living in a basement apartment in New York City, employed as the building's caretaker. The owners decided he was too old to do the job anymore and evicted him, along with two tons of books and papers he'd collected over the years. Whether it was a collection of priceless information or just the nest lining of an obsessive packrat will never be known, because the whole mass was carted away off the sidewalks of New York and sold for scrap to cover the cost of removing it. He died a month later.

Gabriel's life in the years after Madelaine's death contained a number of details that didn't fit into this story. The amnesty ended his career as a headliner with Buffalo Bill's Wild West, since he was no longer North America's Only Genuine Political Exile. He did a few more stints as an anonymous extra—the show could always use a swarthy-looking fellow who could ride and shoot and be trusted to show up for the stagecoach scene on time. When the show toured Europe without him, it was discovered that there were still a lot of people there interested in Gabriel Dumont. Ambroise Lepine, Riel's old lieutenant from the Red River Rebellion, was presented to Queen Victoria as Gabriel Dumont. Michel Dumas impersonated him for a while until he was discharged for drunkenness.

For a few years, Gabriel tried to emulate Riel—advancing petitions to the White House and Ottawa for better treatment for the indigent métis in both countries. He gave a number of speeches to French-speaking enclaves on the American eastern seaboard but refused invitations from English groups where his words would have to be translated. He lived on Staten Island for a time, in a rooming house with a French-speaking landlord who wrote letters for him. After he returned to Canada to formalize the titles on his land, he went back south and spent a few years wandering the Dakotas and Montana. One night an unknown man snuck into his tent and tried to kill him. Gabriel got cut up pretty badly before he succeeded in taking the man's knife away. The rest of the camp was aroused by screams for help—not Gabriel's. Gabriel let him go and always believed that the man was an assassin hired by John A. Macdonald. It seems highly unlikely, but, if so, it was Macdonald's last gasp—the Prime Minister passed on a few weeks later.

Gabriel continued to wander a few years longer. He said in later years that his wanderings included crossing the ocean to France, but that's never been corroborated.

He eventually went back to the South Saskatchewan but he never lived again on the land he owned at Gabriel's Crossing. He built a little cabin on a corner of his "nephew" Alexis's farm and lived out the rest of his life as a self-contained old widower—wandering hundreds of miles on solitary hunting trips, playing checkers or cards with Father Moulin or the old Exovedes, telling stories to children and perching them on his knee so they could feel the puckered scar on the top of his head: "See? The English would've killed me if my skull wasn't so thick."

The one anecdote of his later years that seems to best illustrate "old Gabriel Dumont" concerns a piece of land he inherited from a female relative and sold off at considerably below market value. When Alexis's wife berated him for taking the first offer that came along, he said: "You're right. But would you have me make myself small by going from door to door for a few extra dollars?"

When he got too old and fat to ride long distances he would hunt on foot, walking the legs off the younger men trying to keep up with him. Twenty-one years to the day since he and Michel Dumas set off for the run to the Medicine Line, Gabriel came back from a walk across the prairie and stopped at Alexis's place for a bowl of soup. His chest had been annoying him lately, giving him pain whenever he walked more than five or six miles. Halfway through his bowl of soup, he said maybe he should lie down for a while on the cot in the corner. He was dead before he hit the bed.

There is one person whose story intersects with Gabriel Dumont's but didn't fit into the way this book chose to define itself. One of the children who sat on "Old Gabriel Dumont's" knee and ran his hand across the puckered scar was a paperboy from Prince Albert named Johnny Diefenbaker. Half a century later, John Diefenbaker and his "Prairie Cowboys" stormed into Ottawa with the largest parliamentary majority in Canadian history. To this date, John Diefenbaker remains the only Canadian Prime Minister who owed more to popular enthusiasm than party politics.

The story of his encounter with Dumont may or may not be true. Diefenbaker told it often, but no one ever accused him of a reluctance to fudge facts for the sake of theatrical effect. Whether factual or not, the telling fact—as with Sir Cecil E. Denny's story of Crozier at Duck Lake—is that the story was told, and who told it. Although Sir John A. was the Chief's major icon (in western Canada it is unnecessary to explain that "the Chief" rhymes with Dief, just as it's still unnecessary in the South Saskatchewan country to add a surname to "Gabriel"), John Diefenbaker had a notion that it would be to his advantage to link his name with Dumont's. Despite official versions, there is no name in Canadian history that is as likely to engender a smile and a nod anywhere from L'Anse aux Meadows to Vancouver Island as Gabriel Dumont's.

At Gabriel's Crossing there is now an iron bridge—painted bright blue. Duck Lake and Fish Creek (Tourond's Coulee) are national historic sites, each with a commemorative cairn that—on my last visit—had large blank spaces where the plaques had been removed. Perhaps the bronze wore out, or perhaps the official versions did. On the lip of Tourond's Coulee is a sign warning that, when the weather's wet, once you're in it can be tough to get back out again.

Batoche National Historic Site has changed a great deal since the first time I was there. The farmer's field on the flats has been expropriated for a display excavation of the few stone-foundationed buildings in the original village. I hope that's some consolation to the métis student who was working behind the souvenir counter on my first visit. She told me she'd earned the previous year's summer wages on the archaeological dig: "And come fall we filled it all back in again."

The old clapboard museum cum souvenir stand has been re-placed by a sprawling aluminum-and-glass complex housing displays of artifacts (such as Gabriel's revolver) and artful dioramas of métis men in rifle pits, métis women butchering buffalo, Canadian artillery emplacements, and the like. The once-popular government version of stalwart redcoats putting good British bayonets to wild-eyed swarthy rebels is now decidedly *de trop*. The new government version isn't much less simplistic, but perhaps that's inevitable when it comes to rendering life in display cards of twenty-five words or less. There is a certain amount of interdepartmental confusion—the colorful illustrations of the Battle of Batoche show the church with its current pointed spire, while the display at the church informs us that the original mushroom-capped bell tower wasn't replaced until years later.

But one thing at Batoche hasn't changed, and isn't likely to during my lifetime. When I first went there I forced myself to go through the museum, the souvenir shop, and the church before getting to what I really wanted to see—they were closer to the parking lot, and I've always eaten my pies crust-first. When I finally got past the gates of the cemetery, I worked my way through maniacally—noting in passing the gaudy new graves, the stone plinth inscribed with the names of Isidor Dumont, Ah-Si-We-Yin, and all the others, the fenced-in common grave of weather-silvered wooden crosses—saying to myself: "It's here somewhere, I know it's here. . . ." The cemetery ends where the prairie shears off to the river far below. I looked down at a white cloud of pelicans that wheeled and soared between the silver surface of the South Saskatchewan and the grave of Gabriel Dumont. There is no cross, no carved headstone. There is an upright slab of raw rock standing somewhat taller and broader than I am. It isn't particularly elegant or pretty, but it stands.

Nigh on a century of wind and weather have barely scratched its surface. Odds on, gentle reader, it will still be standing there long after thee and me have crumbled to dust.

About the Author

Alfred Silver has been a playwright, an actor, and a songwriter. In 1983–84 he was Playwright in Residence at the Manitoba Theatre Centre. He grew up in various locations across the Canadian prairies, including Winnipeg. He recently married and now lives in Nova Scotia. Although his novels are based on the lives of real people and are meticulously researched, Silver's primary goal is to tell a good story.